Songs
About
a Girl

Songs

About

a Girl

CHRIS RUSSELL

FLATIRON
BOOKS
NEW YORK

SONGS ABOUT A GIRL. Copyright © 2017 by Chris Russell. All rights reserved. Printed in the United States of America. For information, address Flatiron Books, 175 Fifth Avenue, New York, N.Y. 10010.

www.flatironbooks.com

The Library of Congress Cataloging-in-Publication Data is available upon request.

ISBN 978-1-250-09516-9 (trade paperback)
ISBN 978-1-250-09514-5 (e-book)

Our books may be purchased in bulk for promotional, educational, or business use. Please contact your local bookseller or the Macmillan Corporate and Premium Sales Department at 1-800-221-7945, extension 5442, or by e-mail at MacmillanSpecial Markets@macmillan.com.

First Edition: May 2017

10 9 8 7 6 5 4 3 2 1

For Pip, who can read me like a book

1

Olly Samson was a normal eighteen-year-old, in almost every way.

He used to live around the corner from me, on Marchwood Avenue, before he left school. He was easygoing, a nice guy, and always seemed to have plenty of friends. He was more into singing than football, which did make some of the boys wary of him, but other than that there was nothing that unusual about him. Just another face in the hall. The thing is, it didn't make sense that he would have noticed *me*, because he was two years above me and I tend to go out of my way not to be noticed.

Dear Charlie . . .

I stared again at his message on my screen, searching for signs it might be a prank. He didn't seem like the kind of person who would send this as a joke, but the things he'd written about me . . . I found them hard to believe.

Like I was saying, Olly was pretty much a normal eighteen-year-old. Nice to everyone, never caused any trouble, did his own thing.

He just also happened to be a member of the biggest boy band on the planet.

2

SO. EXCITED. Do you have tickets to the tour?? Comments below!! :) :) xxx

xox FIRE&LIGHTS FOREVER xox
The best Fire&Lights fan blog on the web!!

The usual crowd of Year Eight girls was huddled round their phones, squealing, their voices bouncing back and forth across the cafeteria. It was part of their daily ritual to read their favorite fan blog aloud over lunch, but today they were being particularly . . . well . . . squeally. I could hardly concentrate on my book.

"She wasn't good enough for Gabriel anyway."

"I heard all her pictures are Photoshopped."

"Gabriel's definitely better looking than her. He's way out of her league."

Thanks to Olly Samson, Fire&Lights fever had started early at our school. But even the fact that Olly had once worn a Caversham High tie wasn't enough to make him the most popular member of the band around here. Like it did everywhere else in the country, that honor went to unofficial front man Gabriel West.

"His hair is *amazing.*"

"I think it's his eyes. Amber eyes are, like, *super* rare."

"Imagine holding his hand."

More squealing. I fired off a message to Melissa.

Just finished lunch. Where are you?? xx

"Emmy has tickets to their concert on Saturday," another girl was saying. "She's made a banner just for Gabriel."

"God, he is *so* hot, it makes me want to die."

Sighing, I closed my book and packed it into my school bag.

I swear, some days it felt like I was the only girl in the world who wasn't in love with Gabriel West.

The little bird was hopping about on the edge of its nest, wings twitching. I adjusted the dial on my camera lens, shifting the focus, and zoomed in on its face. It was a sparrow, or a thrush, or something, and it came back to this spot every lunch break, around the same time. I could tell it was the same bird because it had a little orange spot on its back, just visible beneath the brown.

". . . I know, it's like Crouch actually thinks we care about some war from, like, a hundred years ago."

"I don't even listen, I just sit there."

"Yeah, me too."

The voices passed behind me, and I kept my gaze fixed on the viewfinder. The bird twitched its little head.

There was a sudden peal of sharp laughter.

"What's she doing?"

"I dunno."

"Same thing she always does."

The back of my neck bristled. I moved to squeeze the shutter, but the bird bolted.

"Anyone have any cigarettes?"

I lowered the camera and glanced over my shoulder. A group of girls was leaning against the railings outside the old science lab: Aimee Watts, Gemma Hockley, a few others. Aimce looked me up and down, and I tugged my hat over my ears.

"Hey, Charlie!" she called across the courtyard. "What are you doing?"

Aimee wore heavy eye makeup and had a habit of tying her hair back into a tight, angry bun, making her face look taut and severe.

I clicked on my lens cap.

"Nothing," I replied.

Aimee folded her arms across her crinkled school shirt. "Doesn't look like nothing."

One of the girls fished a cigarette from her bag and lit it. They began passing it around, blowing the smoke high into the air. I turned to walk away, and my phone beeped at me.

Aaaargh so sorry!! A message from Melissa. In art studio with miss woods

"Aw, she's leaving," said Gemma, as I made my way out of the courtyard. Aimee called after me.

"Hey, Charlie, where you going?" I sped up my walk. "Stay and have a smoke . . ."

Ducking down a narrow alleyway, I pressed my back against the wall and tapped out a reply to Melissa.

What are you doing with miss woods??

I could still hear the girls laughing round the corner.

Reorganizing art cupboard. Dull as. She was like "please, it won't take long" and I was all like "I DO HAVE A LIFE U KNOW"

I smiled.

Sucks to be you

Anyway, I MISS U she wrote back. Also, I have a fun plan for ur birthday. Tell u after school xxxxxxx

I frowned at the message. We had already made plans for my birthday.

Which meant Melissa was up to something.

★ ★ ★

"*Did you see the fan* blog, Charlie? Today's blog? Oh my *God*, Gabriel's single again . . . praise the Lord."

The main road through town was buzzing with traffic. Students flew across the street, ducking between cars and yelling at one another. Drivers honked as they passed.

"Just imagine," Melissa continued, "if he was your boyfriend. GOD."

Melissa Morris was a bony whirlwind of arms and legs who almost never stopped talking. We'd been neighbors and best friends for years, ever since Dad and I first moved to Reading, and for as long as I could remember we'd walked to and from school together.

She had a teeny, tiny obsession with Fire&Lights.

"I mean, think about it. You and gorgeous Gabriel . . . it could totally happen. He said in *Teen Hits* that he likes long dark hair—*check*—and big brown eyes—*check*—and you're easily pretty enough. Me, I'm a bit ginge, so I'd have to dye my hair . . ." She paused for breath. "Course, I'm saving myself for Aiden, as you know. Apparently he quite likes gingers."

We stopped at the traffic lights, and I thought of Olly's message sitting secretly on my computer. It felt wrong, keeping something so huge from Melissa, but I had to get my head around it first. I had to decide what to do.

Then I would tell her.

"Well," I said, poking at the crossing button, "Aiden would be lucky to have you. Ginger or otherwise."

Melissa grinned, exposing her newly straightened teeth.

"Ooh!" she said. "I almost forgot. Your birthday."

I eyed her from beneath the tattered edge of my hat.

"What about it?"

"I know exactly how we should celebrate."

The lights turned green, and we stepped together onto the road.

"But we already have plans. We're going for pizza."

Melissa squinted at this and raised a single finger.

"Or," she said, "*or* . . . we could get dressed up and hit the school dance."

I cocked my head at her.

"Erm . . . earth to Melissa?"

"Come on," she said, throwing her hands in the air. "You're sixteen in four days! That's a huge deal. You can't spend your biggest birthday yet just, like, sitting around with me eating endless garlic bread."

"Actually," I replied, "that sounds amazing." She stuck her tongue out at me. "Besides, you're the only person I really want to spend it with."

We reached the pavement, and Melissa stopped in front of me. She had a pained look on her face.

"I know, and normally I'd feel the same way, but . . ."

A smile tickled the side of my mouth. "What's this really about?"

Melissa chewed her lip. Her cheeks turned pink.

"OK, fine. There's a boy."

"A boy? Since when was there a boy?"

We started walking again.

"You see, *this* is why the school should never have separated us for double Geography: it's prime catching-up time. I miss you so much on Monday afternoons, Charlie, it's not even funny. Plus Miss Walker makes me sit next to Snotty Barwick, and he smells of cheese."

I poked the top of her head.

"Hello, Mel? Who's the boy?"

She fiddled with a clip on her backpack.

"Khaleed, from Computer Club."

I racked my brains. From what I could remember, Khaleed was a year below us and at least six inches shorter than Melissa.

"Do you even like Khaleed?"

Melissa started to say yes, then stopped herself.

"Well, sort of. Not really." She scrunched up her face. "He has nice ears."

"Ears?"

"Anyway, that's not the point," she continued huffily. "You'd feel the same way if you'd just had your braces taken off. I'm fifteen years and five months old, and I have never kissed a boy. It's beyond tragic."

Our road, Tower Close, was approaching up ahead. I took a deep breath and grabbed Melissa's hand.

"OK, then," I said. "We'll go to the dance. For you. But you'd better get that kiss."

"Yay! You're the best," she said, squeezing my fingers.

"Naah," I replied, squeezing hers back.

"And we are gonna have a LEGENDARY night," she said with a little skip. "I guarantee it."

"When have we ever had fun at a dance?" I asked. Melissa tapped a finger against her lips.

"Umm . . . how about two summers ago, when they had that epic sweet shop? That was fun."

I stared back at her.

"We spent half that night watching Becky Bates spewing pink gunk into a Dumpster."

Melissa looped her arm through mine.

"See what I mean? Fun times."

Arm in arm, we turned off the main road and onto Tower Close, the sound of traffic fading away behind us. Our street was, as always, still and serene. Mown lawns, silent houses.

"So, if you had to save any member of Fire&Lights from a burning building," said Melissa, "which one would you pick?"

Regardless of how many times I told her I wasn't into them, Melissa would still ask me these questions. Every single day.

"I really haven't given it much thought."

"Well, you should. You never know when you might unexpectedly bump into a pop star."

I raised an eyebrow at her.

"A pop star on fire, you mean?"

"Exactly."

She shrugged, matter-of-factly, and hummed a quick tune. We were nearly at our gates.

"You coming in for hot chocolate?"

"I can't. I've got that chemistry homework."

It was only a white lie, but I felt it in my chest.

"Oh God, yep. Fractional distillation." Melissa clicked her gate open. "Message me when you're done, OK?"

"You bet," I said, watching her peel off down the garden path, singing as she went.

Dad was frowning over a pile of papers when I walked past his study. He worked from home on Mondays.

"Oh, hello," he said as I drifted by his door. "Good day?"

"Mm-hmm," I replied, sweeping past him and disappearing up the stairs.

In the safety of my bedroom, I slid my laptop from its drawer and dumped my school bag under the desk. As the computer whirred to life, I tried to imagine what Melissa would do when she found out I'd been sent a private message by a member of Fire&Lights. She might actually explode.

Opening the browser, I went straight to Facebook, opened my inbox, clicked on Olly's message, and took a deep breath.

It was time I wrote my reply.

3

Dear Olly . . . many thanks for writing to me.

I sighed and deleted my opening sentence for the fourth time. What did I think this was, a job application?

Hey, Olly, cool to hear from you.

That was even worse. One thing school had taught me was that I, Charlie Bloom, was a very long way from cool.

I dropped backward onto my bed, arms folded. I had waited nearly two days to respond to Olly's message, and this already felt like two days too many. I scanned through his words again on the screen, trying to make sense of everything he'd said. There were two main things about his message that confused me:

First, why on earth would he even remember who I was?

Dear Charlie . . . you might not remember me, but . . .

(I might not remember *him*? Barely a day went by when I didn't see Olly's face smiling back at me from a backpack or a pencil case.)

. . . but i was a couple of years above you at Caversham High. Not sure if you follow Fire&Lights, but that's what i'm up to now, and i wanted to ask you something about your photography. I was looking through your gig pics, the ones you took of that school band, and they're amazing!! Thought you might be up for taking some backstage photos for us sometime . . . ??

Second, and more important, did he really want *me* to come and take photos for *his* band? The chart-topping Fire&Lights? I wasn't a real photographer, for a start, I was just a schoolkid with a secondhand camera. And the shots I took at the Diamond Storm gig were all right, I suppose, but they couldn't be good enough for a professional band . . . could they?

I clicked through to my photo archive and scrolled down to July. There were about forty photos from that night, the night near the end of term when Diamond Storm had played the school hall. Everyone knew Diamond Storm was The Best Band At Caversham High, but they'd decided you couldn't be a proper rock band unless you had a proper photographer.

As it turned out, I was their only option.

And although Diamond Storm posted the photos all over their blog, and some of them even got used in the school newspaper, I couldn't help but feel that I'd be out of my league shooting a world-famous band like Fire&Lights.

Way out of my league.

. . . Our management team has this new thing going on, read Olly's message. They have pro photographers taking all our concert pics, but they figure someone closer to our age would be better at the fun stuff backstage . . . you know, for the fan page of the website.

I didn't know much about Fire&Lights, but I did know that their fans were obsessive and fiercely loyal. If I agreed to this, what would happen if I did something wrong? What if they didn't like my pictures, or the fact that some random teenage girl—who wasn't even a fan—was getting to hang out with their idols? My name would be out there, on one of the biggest websites in the world, for anyone to see, and the idea of all those people knowing who I was . . . It closed up my throat just thinking about it.

. . . We're playing Reading Arena next Saturday, so i thought you might fancy coming along & giving it a go? P.S. Have sent you a friend request, hope that's cool.

One thing you could say about Olly was that he clearly hadn't let the fame thing go to his head. He was acting almost as if *I* was the famous one.

But I wasn't famous. And I wasn't really a photographer.

Which meant there was really only one thing I could say.

Hi, Olly, thanks for writing to me. Great to hear from you, and congratulations on the band. That's a really amazing offer, but . . .

I paused and looked out the window. Marchwood Avenue was only a stone's throw from my house. Olly would have taken pretty much the same route to school as me every day, dodging the crowds on the Peppard Road or taking a shortcut through the golf course.

Apart from that, we lived in completely different worlds.

. . . but I don't think I can do it. I've got loads of schoolwork on, and anyway I don't really think I'm good enough yet for something so big. It's nice of you to ask, though. Good luck with everything, Charlie.

My cursor hovered over the Send button. All I could do now was hope that I wasn't making a huge, huge mistake.

"You said yes. TELL ME YOU SAID YES."

I had told Melissa about the message. She was taking it . . . badly.

"Well, it's not quite as simple as that, M—"

"Not quite as simple? As what?! What?"

Melissa clenched her gloved hands, her frantic breath turning into steam in the frozen air. It was another chilly winter morning, very nearly November, and the trees on the roadside were tinged frosty white.

"I'm just . . . I'm not ready for something like this."

Melissa stepped in front of me.

"Yo, time out. Time. Out." She peered into my eyes. "This is, let's face it, the most exciting thing that has happened to any human being, ever. Agreed?"

"Well, I—"

"AND FURTHERMORE," she said, pressing a finger into my forehead, "it is happening to *my* best friend, which makes it my duty to ensure she doesn't mess it up."

I scratched the back of my head.

"I'm not sure it would have happened anyway, to be honest . . ."

"Hey, listen. When the second hottest member of the world's hottest band asks you to go on tour with them and hang out with them and stare at their lovely faces all day, you always say yes. No-brainer."

"He didn't ask me to go on tour with them, Mel. It was just one concert."

"Oh, just one concert? Just one concert with *Olly Samson from Fire&Lights*? Unless you message him back and say you've changed your mind, I will never, ever, ever talk to you again."

I sighed, pulling my coat tight around my body.

"And anyway," continued Melissa, "photography is totally your *thing*. It's your superpower. Aren't you bored of shooting flowers and insects all day?"

We stopped at the crossing, and I stared over the road at the school buildings, squat and gray in the frosty mist. Aimee Watts was leaning against the outside wall of the sports hall, her entourage buzzing around her.

"The truth is . . . I don't think I'm good enough."

"You what?"

"I'm not a good enough photographer. Not for this, anyway."

"That's crazy!" snapped Melissa. "You've got to stop putting yourself down all the time."

I itched at a freckle on the back of my hand, and the traffic lights beeped at us.

"Can we talk about something else now?"

"I mean, look at *me*," she continued, dragging me across the road by the coat sleeve. "I know what I'm good at."

"This is true."

"That computer programming thing we did yesterday afternoon was riDICulously easy. And everyone else was, like, erm, what the flip is HTML, and I was all like, hypertext markup language *thanks very much*."

"But you're an expert," I said as we passed through the school gates. "You spend every single evening on your computer, doing . . . well, whatever it is you do. Me, I'm not even a real photographer."

"You're going to fix this, Charlie. I know it. You know it."

"There's nothing to f—"

"Ah-ah-ah."

She stopped, turned to face me, and landed a hand on each of my shoulders.

"I'll only say this once, and then next time I see you we're going back to discussing who has the best hair out of Gabriel and Aiden. Even though it is obviously Aiden."

I stared at my feet.

"OK."

"You are my best friend, and you are always good enough."

A few seconds of silence passed between us, and then she smiled, curiously, and waved a purple glove at me.

"See you in assembly!"

"Simmer down, please," said Mr. Bennett from the stage, as students shuffled in their chairs, chatting with friends and scuffing their feet against the wooden floor. He waited, casting an eye across the hall, and row by row, silence fell.

He closed his file.

"Before we get started, as you are all aware, it's the Caversham High dance this Friday night."

The room filled with whoops and jeering, and Mr. Bennett waved a calming hand.

"Yes, good—we're all very excited, and the dance is always lots of fun. *But* . . . I would ask you to remember that, as the upper school, you are important role models for our younger students, and when it comes to your behavior on Friday evening, we expect you to set an example . . ."

Melissa leaned into my ear.

"I've worked out what I'm going to wear on Friday," she said in a harsh whisper. "My sparkly blue top."

I gave her a thumbs-up, and she squeezed her chest together.

"It makes the most of my frankly meager breasts," she added, and I had to cover my mouth so I wouldn't laugh out loud.

". . . Now," continued Mr. Bennett, "you may recall that during last term's event we had complaints from the local community over students drinking on the playing fields, and the police were nearly involved . . ."

Melissa leaned into me again.

"Do you think Khaleed will like it?"

"What?" I mouthed.

"My blue top."

I smiled back at her and whispered: "Definitely. You'll be the Kanye and Kim of Computer Club."

Melissa sniggered at this, and the sound vaulted high over our heads, stopping Mr. Bennett midsentence. He waited two seconds, then continued.

". . . So . . . let this be a reminder to you all of the school's zero-tolerance policy concerning drugs and alcohol. And this Friday night is no exception. I hope that's understood."

A commotion erupted a few rows behind us, and everyone turned round to find Aimee, Gemma, and a handful of Year Eleven boys sharing a joke. Mr. Bennett spoke above the noise.

"Do you have something to add, Miss Watts?"

The group went silent. Aimee shifted in her chair.

"Nah," she said with a sniff. "Just talking about how pumped we are for Friday, sir."

"I'm sure you were," said Mr. Bennett, watching her beneath lowered brow as he opened his file. And then again, almost inaudibly: "I'm sure you were."

The television murmured at us from the corner of the room. It was an advertisement for cat food, the kind where the cat is very glossy and gets its dinner on a little cushion. Dad was sitting in his armchair and I was sitting in mine, toying with my laptop. He was flicking through a pile of papers.

"Forty-four point . . . what? Well, that doesn't add up, clearly . . ." he muttered, irritably, over the festive jingle from the TV. A celebrity in a garish sweater was laughing at a Christmas tree.

In the kitchen, the oven dinged. I went to investigate.

"Dinner won't be long," I said moments later, walking back into the room with a tea towel. Dad looked up, distracted, and rubbed one eye behind his reading glasses.

"Thanks, kiddo."

I slumped back into my chair. I had been staring at the same history homework for nearly half an hour now, and had only added about nine words.

"How's that essay coming?" asked Dad.

I blinked in the glare from my laptop. "Um . . . not too bad."

He slid off his glasses and buffed the lenses with a shirt corner.

"I remember final-year history. Bits of it, anyway. Mainly dictators and genocide, isn't it?"

"Yeah," I said with a half smile. "It's pretty cheerful."

Dad replaced his glasses.

"This is why I prefer math. You know where you are with equations."

"That's kinda geeky, Dad."

"Well then, I must be a geek." He gave me a wonky smile and nudged his glasses up his nose. "You're doing all right in general, though . . . are you? At school?"

I frowned.

"What do you mean?"

"Well, just . . . Year Eleven. It can be pretty tough, from what I remember."

I fidgeted in my seat.

"I'm OK, Dad."

I returned to my essay, but I could sense him still watching me from his armchair. I read the title three or four times, pointlessly changed a couple of words, and then closed the file.

Opening my photography coursework folder, I scanned through some shots I'd taken the previous week, down by the canal. I'd been using some graphics software to intensify the colors, trying to inject some life into the concrete office blocks and the flat, featureless skyline, but I was fighting a losing battle. The canal was one of the nicer parts of town, but even so, Reading was not an exciting place to look at. It was all one shade. A grubby, brownish-gray, the gray of multistory parking garages.

"Looking forward to your birthday?" said Dad, setting down his papers. I shrugged with one shoulder.

"I guess. I don't know. I don't want to make a huge deal out of it."

"Sixteen . . . It's a big year. My girl's growing up." His eyes flickered, almost instinctively, toward a photo of me on the mantelpiece as a newborn baby. The old silver frame was tarnished and chipped. "You're sure you don't want a party?"

I didn't want a party. I wanted to go for pizza with Melissa and stay up all night watching bad movies and eating marshmallows.

"Thanks, Dad, but I'm fine." His eyes dropped to the floor, and I felt a twist of guilt. "We're going to the school dance."

"Oh, I see. Well, that'll be fun, right?"

Dad was waiting for a reply, but all I could think of was Becky Bates throwing up into a Dumpster.

"It wouldn't be Christmas without sausage rolls!" announced the TV over a plinky recording of "Winter Wonderland." *"And ours are half price until Ja—"*

Dad muted the sound.

"Perhaps we should bring back Birthday Cinema Club, eh?"

I glanced up at the small, two-person sofa on the far side of the room. When I was little, if my birthday fell on a weekday and Dad had to go to work, he would get up really early, make a big bowl of popcorn, and sneak up to my room to wake me. He'd carry me downstairs in the dark and then, with me yawning and still in my pajamas, we'd sit together on the sofa, eating hot, buttery popcorn and watching *Toy Story* while the sun came up. Usually I'd fall asleep and not wake again until the end credits, but it didn't matter. As the film played out, I would stir, drowsily, and Dad would be tapping his slippered foot on the carpet and singing along to "You've Got a Friend in Me."

We hadn't done it for years.

"I'm a bit old for that, aren't I?" I said, though I wasn't sure whether I meant it. Dad's eyes went wide for a moment, and then he picked up his papers and smoothed them down with one hand.

"Yes . . . yes, of course. Course."

He cleared his throat.

"We could do something on Saturday night, though? Get a meal in town?"

Something blinked at me from my laptop screen. It was a speech bubble in the top corner, telling me I had a new Facebook message.

Hey charlie

It was Olly Samson. *From Fire&Lights.*

"Charlie?"

Dad was leaning across the arm of his chair, trying to win my attention. My gaze stumbled from him to Olly's message and back again. My mouth was hanging open.

"Anywhere you like," Dad continued. "There's that new Mexican place on the high street. I do enjoy a burrito . . ."

I tried to keep my face blank, but my mind was a mess of questions. Why was Olly contacting me again? Hadn't he read my reply? What was I supposed to say to him now?

"Um, yeah. That'd be . . . great," I agreed, returning to my laptop. Straightaway, I noticed something I had missed before: there was a little green light next to Olly's name.

He was still online.

And while I was formulating an answer in my head—something that wouldn't make me sound like a dork or a groupie—a second, longer message joined the first.

And what it said didn't make any sense. At all.

4

I stared, baffled, at Olly's message.

Really glad you changed your mind about coming to the concert!! This is gonna be awesome . . .

I snapped my laptop shut and stood up from my chair. Dad was saying something to me as I walked from the room, but the words were lost as I headed up the stairs, taking two at a time, and slipped soundlessly into my bedroom.

You there . . . ? :) said the message on the screen.

"Charlie?" called Dad from the living room. "Everything OK?"

"Yep, sorry!" I shouted back down. I was sitting cross-legged on my bed, my fingers poised above the keys. "I just forgot something I need for . . . school . . ."

I had to reply to Olly. I had to say *something*.

Um, yeh, i'm here, I typed out hurriedly.

My heart was thudding in my chest.

Thirty seconds later, his response appeared.

Was just saying, great news that you changed your mind. You're gonna love it! I've told management you're coming, got your pass sorted, your name's on the VIP list . . . it's official! :) (I asked if you could bring a friend along, but we're already maxed out this weekend . . . really sorry about that!!)

I scrolled back through my messages. I had only contacted Olly that one time, the night before, but my inbox told a different story. Earlier that afternoon, I'd messaged him again:

Olly, i've changed my mind. Of course i'll come on saturday!! Please send me details, xoxo charlie :) :) P.S. can i bring a friend??

It was a message I hadn't written.

You don't need to worry you know

Olly again. I tapped out an answer.

Worry about what?

Everyone's really friendly, he wrote back, and you'll have loads of fun taking the pics. Plus, you know, Fire&Lights concerts are actually pretty cool :)

In the kitchen, the oven beeped three times. Our pizza was about to burn.

Of course, I typed, the smell of bubbling cheese wafting up the stairs. I bet it's amazing

Can't wait to see what you come up with, he replied, adding: I gotta go . . . will send details tomorrow—management have some kind of confidentiality thingy you have to sign. I'll be in touch xx

And then his little green light disappeared.

I tugged at the rim of my hat and glared at his final message. A confidentiality contract? That sounded serious. They would almost certainly want my father's signature, and I would almost certainly have to forge it.

For now, though, there was something far more pressing on my mind. Someone was pretending to be me.

And there was only one person that could be.

⋆ ⋆ ⋆

"I surely have no idea what you're talking about."

Melissa was hunched over the water fountain, jabbing at the tap. It dribbled feebly, and she bent down to catch the flow.

"I think you do, Mel," I replied, lowering my voice to a whisper. Behind us, people were jostling, shoving, and shouting on their way to second period. "You're the only person who knew about Olly messaging me. The only person in the world. And I can read you like a book."

Melissa stood up, sniffed, and wiped an arm across her mouth.

"So does this mean you're going to the concert, then?"

"Well, I don't really have a choice now, do I? He's told their management team I'm coming, he's organized a VIP pass . . . plus I can't exactly say I've changed my mind *again*, can I?"

Melissa shrugged.

"No, I s'pose not."

We joined the shuffling crowds, and the tide carried us along toward the science labs.

"I can't believe you hacked into my account!"

"Well, this I *will* say," replied Melissa smugly, hitching her schoolbag up her back. "If I *was* going to hack into your account, which obviously I didn't, it wouldn't be that difficult 'cause I've known your password for years."

I threw a sharp look at her.

"What?"

"KatherineCharlotte."

My stomach tightened. *Katherine Charlotte.* My mother's name. It had been years since I'd heard it spoken out loud.

"I'm right, aren't I?" asked Melissa, tutting as a lank-haired Year Seven bumped into her shoulder. I looked back at her through narrowed eyes.

"How did you know that?"

"Easy," she replied with a grin. "I can read you like a book."

She beamed at me, and the period bell rang for a second time.

"So listen," she continued, "I was watching *Pop Gossip* today and that presenter with the funny hair said that since F&L got back from America they've been on an epic exercise regime, and Olly's six-pack is looking *hot as*. Can you get me a photo?"

We slowed down as we arrived outside Chemistry One.

"I am not taking a photo of Olly Samson without his shirt on," I replied. Melissa puffed up her cheeks and stuck out her bottom lip.

"Spoilsport."

She peered through the window of the classroom, then checked the time on her phone.

"Man, I cannot believe that in three days' time you're going to see Olly's actual face," she said, shaking her head in disbelief. "His REAL-LIFE FACE."

"He's just a normal person like anyone else, Mel."

She gaped at me.

"Olly Samson is not a normal person, Charlie. Olly Samson is a god among men. And you're going to look at him with your real-life eyes, and he's going to fall in love with you, and then I shall be maid of honor at the wedding."

I folded my arms and bit back a smile.

"But anyway," she said, her hand on the doorknob, "I've got Computer Club after school, so you won't see me again for . . ." She checked her watch. "Seventeen hours and fifty-eight minutes. Will you miss me?"

It was impossible to stay mad at Melissa. "More than you could ever know," I said as she bounded off into the lab. A table of hard-looking girls in the corner jeered at her on the way in, but she didn't notice. She just weaved her way through the tables and crashed into an empty seat in the front row.

Outside the classroom, the corridor was still thrumming with people, and I blended back into the stream, lost in thought. *Olly Samson is not a normal person, Charlie. Olly Samson is a god among men.* Melissa was right, I guessed, but less than eighteen months ago, nobody outside Caversham High even knew who he was. He was just an average teenager in an average school, going to classes, worrying about grades, listening to music, and hanging out with his friends.

"Hi, I'm Olly."

Olly and I had talked just one time (at least, one time that I could remember), by the lockers, after assembly. I was packing my camera bag away, my cheeks still burning, my heart racing with adrenaline.

"Hi." He was holding tight to the straps of his backpack. "That was a really cool presentation."

The photography presentation hadn't been my idea. At the time, Mr. Bennett was encouraging students to "Leap into Our Future Careers," and if anyone showed even the slightest interest in something, they were asked to stand up in front of the whole school and talk about it.

I felt sick the entire time I was onstage.

"Um . . . thanks."

Olly sniffed and shoved his hands into his pockets. He was slight back then, with mousy hair and skinny legs and shirtsleeves that hung down below his wrists.

"Your photos are, like . . . awesome. Especially the live bands."

I wrinkled my nose at him. No one had seemed that interested in my presentation when I was giving it. "Really?"

"Yeah . . . you should do it professionally, or something. You're really good." He scratched the back of his neck and gave a small smile. "I'm actually thinking of going into music myself."

I shut my locker door and looked closer at him. "Oh? Like what?"

"I wanna be a singer. You know, in a band."

Olly twisted around and hissed "Shut up" at a group of passing friends who were laughing at him. They shouted something incoherent and shuffled away down the corridor.

"Not really sure if I'll make it, though," he said, turning back to me.

Half as a joke, I replied: "Maybe you should go on *Make or Break.*"

On Monday mornings, *Make or Break* was all anyone talked about at school. It was a Saturday-night talent show run by record-label boss Barry King, where budding pop stars would get up in front of a panel of judges, sing their hearts out, and, fairly often, make idiots of themselves. The few that didn't, though, got the chance to launch careers with the most powerful man in the music industry. I rarely watched it, unless I was with Melissa, but it was impossible to avoid online. Since it started, *Make or Break* had spawned some of the biggest pop groups in the country.

Six months later, it would create Fire&Lights.

"Yeah, maybe," said Olly, with a shrug. "I bet Barry King would tear me apart, though."

The bell rang above our heads, and Olly ran a hand through his short, neat hair.

"See you around, then?" he said, stepping away from the lockers.

"Maybe," I said, and within seconds he had slipped back into the stream, the sound of the bell mingling with the bustle and chatter of students.

Staring at my feet as I paced the tiled floor, I tried to picture myself on Saturday night, backstage with Olly and the rest of the band. An actual music photographer, in a professional venue, surrounded by pop stars.

My stomach flipped at the thought.

Nothing about it seemed real.

"You look starving, sweetheart. I'll rustle you up a sandwich."

Melissa's mum ran her hands under the tap, dried them on a dish-cloth, and flipped open the bread bin. I was perched on the edge of a kitchen chair, school bag between my legs, watching her move around the kitchen.

Melissa's cat, Megabyte, nuzzled my ankles with her little pink nose.

"Thanks, Rosie."

Rosie Morris was tall and soft-spoken and had curly red hair that hung down in ringlets on her shoulders. She was super-intelligent, like her daughter, and worked as a freelance writer for political magazines. I sometimes hung out next door after school when my dad was working late and, when Melissa and her dad were home too, I could pretend, for a while, that I had a normal family.

"I think Melissa might actually be running that Computer Club now," said Rosie, slapping two thick slices of bread onto a cutting board. "Honestly, obsessed with technology, that girl. I don't know what she does up there all night, tapping away on her laptop."

I smiled and took a sip of tea. Rosie knew exactly how to make it: nice and milky, with half a sugar.

"I think she's slowly taking over the world," I said, blowing on my drink. "She knows more about coding than most of the teachers."

Though she would never admit it, Melissa really just wanted to be like her big brother, Tom, who was studying computer science at Cambridge. That many smarts in one family might be annoying, if they weren't also the nicest people in England.

"And how about you, love?" said Rosie, spreading a thick wave of butter across the bread. "Everything going OK at school?"

"Mm-hmm."

She crossed to the fridge and lifted out a tower of Tupperware boxes.

"You sure?" she said, throwing me a sideways look. "Year Eleven can be a rough ride, you know."

"That's what my dad says," I replied, scratching Megabyte on the head. She purred contentedly. "But, honestly, I'm fine."

Rosie was back at the counter, layering slices of meat and cheese into my sandwich. I watched her working at the window, the curve of her back, the slow, steady movement of her hands. The tucking of a ringlet behind her ear.

"Your dad's just worried about you, Charlie. That's all."

She dropped the second slice of bread on top, pressed it with her palm, and sliced the sandwich in two.

"He shouldn't be," I replied.

"He's your father, of course he worries." Rosie rescued a cherry tomato that was rolling away toward the sink. "That's his job."

She popped the tomato into her mouth, slid my sandwich onto a plate, and crossed over to the table.

"Brian's the same, you know," she said, sitting down next to me. "Always fretting about Melissa. Dads and their little girls."

We used to be that way, too, but I wasn't a little girl anymore.

I picked at my food in silence.

"It's tough for you, too," continued Rosie. "I know that. You're growing up, all of you. Sixteen soon, goodness me." Megabyte hopped onto the table, and Rosie shooed her away. "But you have to understand, love, that you're everything he's got. It's not been easy for Ralph, since . . ."

She stopped herself. I took a bite of my sandwich, and we listened to the dripping of the tap for a while.

"You know, you're the spitting image of your mum these days."

I looked up from my food.

"Really?"

"Oh yes." She lifted her big mug of tea with both hands. "I saw the photos, years back. Like peas in a pod, you two."

I thought about the photos I had of my mother. Four dog-eared pictures that I kept tucked inside her old notebook, dates scrawled on the back in ballpoint pen.

Rosie smiled at me, and I sipped my tea.

It was easy being there, in Melissa's kitchen. It always was. The cat curling itself between my legs, steam rising lazily from our mugs. The washing machine humming in a nearby room.

Later that evening, I was sitting on my bed at home, music playing in the corner, photographs scattered in a circle around me.

In the first one, Mum sat on a tattered old sofa with me, just a baby, in her arms. A picture book lay open on her knee.

In another, she was standing on a low wall on a windswept beach, balancing on one leg. A wintry sun blazed in the background. The third was Mum and Dad sitting together in a pub making goofy faces at one another, and she was wearing her hat—my hat—the blue knitted beanie that I wore every day, at least in the winter. It was old and starting to fall apart now, threads dangling from the weave, but that didn't matter. It kept me warm, even with the holes.

The fourth was my favorite, because it had all three of us in it. We were in a park somewhere on a sunny day, and I was sitting on a picnic blanket while Mum and Dad fussed around me. I had my back to the camera, so you could see the distinctive birthmark on the back of my neck: white, about the size of an avocado stone, and shaped a bit like a flame. The doctors had never seen one like it, according to my dad. It made me special, Dad said, because that was the sort of thing adults said to children.

I wasn't sure who had taken the photo, perhaps a passerby, but it was the closest we had to a family portrait. My parents were young and scruffy, rosy-cheeked from the sun, their newborn baby wriggling in between them. Dad had a bit more hair back then, Mum was busy pouring the tea, and we looked like a real family.

We looked happy.

I had no memory of that time, so I only knew what my father had told me. It was before we moved to Reading, he said, when I was just a toddler, and he was studying in London. It was an exciting time, when Mum and Dad were newly married and they had their whole lives ahead of them.

Then, just before Christmas 2000, my mother was killed in a car crash.

Dad hadn't told me much about the accident. He didn't like to talk about it. "It wasn't her fault," he would say, when I was old enough to ask the question. "It was another driver, and he was going way too fast."

"Who was he?" I used to ask, because that seemed important to me at the time.

"He was just a stranger, Charlie. He made a mistake."

When I was younger, Dad used to talk about Mum all the time. He'd tell me how smart she was, how passionate, and how she would have told me every day to find something that I loved and chase after it. She'd be proud of me, he'd say; she'd tell me stories and sing me songs, and take me to the movies on rainy days.

I stared at my mother in the picture, then at myself in the mirror. I thought about what Rosie had said that afternoon, and realized she was right. In the last few months, something had changed.

I was beginning to look just like her.

I had her elfin build and her messy, milk-chocolate hair. I had her pale skin, too, with a handful of freckles on each cheek. And I had these big, chestnut-brown eyes that I'd always thought made me look childish, but on her they were bright, mesmerizing.

Reaching across the bed, I lifted Mum's notebook off the pillow and set it on my lap. Aside from the hat and the photographs, this notebook was my one memento of her life. It was a private journal, a thick, crinkled scrapbook filled with scribbled phrases and bits of poetry. I found it one day in the garage when I was about seven and, after some persuasion, Dad had let me keep it . . . though there'd been a pained look in his eyes at the time, which I'd never quite understood.

I lifted the cover, and the book fell open on one of my favorite pages.

Take me home
I've been dreaming of a girl I know
The sweetest thing, you know she makes me wanna sing
I still remember everything

On the opposite page, a second verse.

> *I call her name*
> *I keep her picture in a silver frame*
> *So she will know, just as soon as I come home*
> *That she will never be alone*

It was clear to me from the beginning: I was the girl in Mum's poem. I was the little girl she'd been dreaming of; I made her want to sing. She and Dad kept *my* picture in a silver frame. And the notebook, I had decided, was her gift to me, her legacy, and as long as I kept it safe, she'd never really be gone. For months, I pored over every page, every line, looking for clues and hidden meanings, trying to make connections with my own life.

One couplet appeared several times throughout the book.

> *She lives her life in pictures*
> *She keeps secrets in her heart*

Those lines were the reason I took up photography in the first place, those six words: *she lives her life in pictures*. I was so certain they were about me, or at least the person I might become. The person Mum wanted me to be. And this idea soothed me when I couldn't sleep at night, when my imagination just wanted to play car crashes and headlights and broken glass on the motorway.

As I read her words again, flipping through the pages, I remembered myself as a seven-year-old, hiding beneath the covers with a flashlight. Night after night, I would sit up in bed, whispering the words to myself, imagining that if I kept going long enough, one day she would come home.

". . . No, Jen, I'm talking about formatting here . . . Eh? Well, no, that's not really what I meant . . ."

Dad's voice carried upstairs from the hallway, and I could hear him throwing his keys on the front table and moving to the kitchen. I closed the notebook and slipped it under my bed.

". . . Yes, I know that," Dad was saying into his cell phone as I reached the bottom of the stairs, clutching one of Mum's photos. I drifted into the kitchen. "And that's fine for now, but if I come in tomorrow and find the report's not right, then—Jen . . . ? Jen? Damn signal."

Dad muttered something under his breath and walked to the dresser, where he started sifting through the mail.

"Hi," I said, from the doorway.

"Oh . . . hey there, Charlie," he said, putting the mail aside. "I didn't see you there. What are you up to?"

I shrugged. "Just . . . looking through some old stuff."

He nodded, clearly distracted, pulled a bottle of wine from the cupboard, and jabbed a corkscrew into it. I watched him twist it once, twice, a third time, and I glanced down at the photograph in my hand.

In the last couple of years, Dad had stopped talking about my mother. Not suddenly or all at once, but in fading fragments, like a radio losing power. The days fell away, and I awoke one morning to find she had slipped quietly from the room, in the middle of the night, like a forgotten houseguest. Now just mentioning her name felt awkward.

"What now . . . ?" mumbled Dad at the beeping of his phone on the kitchen counter. He squinted at the screen.

"Hey, Dad." I was still loitering in the doorway. "Melissa and I are going to hang out in town on Saturday evening, if that's cool with you."

I'd decided I needed an alibi for the Fire&Lights concert. Something told me that running around with a boy band wouldn't fit in with my dad's definition of Concentrating On Schoolwork, so I'd forged his signature on the confidentiality contract and agreed on a cover story with Melissa. I didn't exactly feel great about it, but it was only for one night.

"Oh." He slipped one hand into his pocket, jingled his change. "I thought we were going for a birthday dinner."

I touched my mouth. I had completely forgotten. "Sorry, Dad . . . it slipped my mind."

For a passing moment, our eyes locked across the room.

Then he waved a hand at me and, with the other, poured himself a large glass of wine.

"No, come on, that's fine. You don't need your dad following you around on your birthday."

He turned away, undoing the top button of his shirt.

"Don't be back late, though," he said with his back to me. "You've got a curfew, remember."

Dad took a sip of wine and loosened his tie. As I watched him pull it over his head and hang it on the back of a chair, I thought of his younger self in the photograph, kneeling on a picnic blanket, sleeves rolled up, squeezing my baby toes as I sat in the sun.

Before he could turn around again, I slid the photo into my back pocket and disappeared from the room.

5

"*Prepare yourself, oh bestest friend,* for the awesomest night of your life."

Melissa and I were standing by the climbing bars in the gym, watching sweaty boys fling themselves around the dance floor to something loud and thrashy. I shouted back at her over the noise.

"I think I'm prepared, Mel. When will it start being awesome?"

"What?"

I yelled into her ear. "WHEN WILL IT START BEING AWESOME?"

People were scattered in clumps around the room, mostly boy or girl clumps, while the music thrummed and boomed and bounced off the high concrete walls. Teachers sipped coffee from brown plastic cups, watching the mosh pit with expressions that were one part suspicion, two parts boredom.

Above our heads, sad paper streamers hung from exposed pipes, quivering to the beat.

"THE WORLD IS OUR OYSTER!" bellowed Melissa, swigging at her punch, leaving her top lip moist and orange. Across the hall, the thrashy song ended and a slushy R&B ballad started up.

"You've just turned sixteen," she continued. "Tomorrow you get to hang out with The Greatest Band In The History Of The World, and as for me . . . I'm about five minutes away from losing my kissing virginity to a gorgeous-eared boy with superior coding skills."

Sixteen. I stared into my drink.

"Do you think I'm supposed to feel any different?" I asked.

Melissa closed one eye. "Probably. Do you?"

I glanced around the sports hall. Drawn by the siren call of The Slow Dance, couples were shuffling awkwardly onto the dance floor, and the lights were beginning to dim.

"Not sure. Though according to BuzzFeed I can now legally pilot a glider, so that's good."

"There you go!" said Melissa, raising her drink. "You've always wanted to do that. You're a woman now, Charlie, and no mistake. You're basically Beyoncé."

I raised my cup to hers, and we pressed them together, releasing a plastic crunch. I took a sip of the tangy, sugary drink and winced as it coated my teeth.

"Oh my gosh," blurted Melissa, pointing ahead. "There's Khaleed!"

Khaleed was standing a few feet away from us in a pool of spinning white light. His shirt was tucked in, and he looked petrified.

"This is my moment," said Melissa, discarding her drink next to a giant bowl of potato chips. "Wish me luck."

"Go easy on him, Mel," I said, watching the light from a glitter ball rebound off Khaleed's hair-gelled head. "He's smaller than you are."

She didn't hear me, though, because she was already skipping over to Khaleed. She looped her arms around his back and, to the *thud-plick, thud-thud-plick* of the beat, the two of them began to rotate.

"D'you wanna, like, dance?" Suddenly, Tim Stallworthy was standing in front of me, unwrapping a miniature Snickers. He was bouncing slightly on the balls of his feet.

"What . . . now?" I said. Tim popped the chocolate into his mouth.

"Um, yeah," he said, chewing. "Sure."

I liked Tim. He was in my French class, and we were sometimes paired together for speaking exercises. He'd do funny voices for the characters in the textbooks, which always made me laugh.

"OK," I said, and, unsure whether to hold hands, we wandered together into the crowd.

Slow-dancing was weird. Nobody really knew how to do it right, and the whole time it was going on you were very, very aware that you were either kissing or not kissing. If you were kissing, that at least stopped you from thinking about the dancing, which was a good thing, but if you weren't kissing, you were mainly thinking about whether you were *about* to kiss, and that could be even more stressful than the kissing itself.

Tim was a nice guy, but I didn't want to kiss him. Which meant, just in case he wanted to kiss *me*, my safest bet was to rest my head on his shoulder, not say anything, and just ride it out until the song came to an end.

The music dragged on and we turned in our little circle, feet brushing, Tim's hands moving occasionally on my back. Now and again he would angle his head toward me, and I would close my eyes tight, hoping he wasn't about to make a move. His breath smelled of fruit punch and peanuts.

When I opened my eyes, I noticed a cluster of teachers in the far corner of the hall, watching the dancers and sharing a joke. They were supposed to be monitoring the proceedings, but as there hadn't been any puking, fights, or fallings-out yet, they seemed in a pretty relaxed mood. Gemma Hockley was standing with them, which seemed odd because by rights she should have been on the dance floor, fending off boys. Gemma was tall and gorgeous, all big eyes and cleavage, and had looked about twenty-one ever since the beginning of Year Ten. She was flirting with the younger teachers, Mr. Swift and Mr. Burnham, touching their arms and laughing into her drink.

Every so often, as Tim and I spun slowly round, she would glance in my direction.

At least, I had assumed it was my direction. Then I realized that Gemma was actually looking beyond me, toward the drinks table, which for the first time that evening was unattended. Everyone was coupled up, or bunched around the edges of the dance floor, and no one was watching the lone figure by the punch bowls, carrying two black plastic bags and exchanging furtive glances with Gemma. Blond hair tied back in a severe ponytail, eyes ringed thickly in blue eyeliner.

Unscrewing whatever was concealed in the first bag, Aimee poured the clear liquid generously into each bowl in turn, her face tight with concentration. She repeated this with the second bottle, and when the final few drops were gone, she looked over her shoulder to alert Gemma—and instead she found me.

Our eyes met, and her face froze.

Tim was still edging me around in circles, and within seconds my back was turned again. In the middle distance I could see Melissa kissing Khaleed, her hands clamped on his shoulders, his arms hanging dead straight by his sides.

Soon, a finger prodded me hard in the back.

"What the—?"

I broke apart from Tim. Aimee fixed me with a strange, hard smile.

"Hey, Charlie," she said, eyes bolted to mine. Tim stepped between us.

"We were dancing," he said, annoyed. Aimee looked at him like she'd just found him floating in her drink.

"And?"

Tim opened his mouth, but no sound came out. Aimee turned to me.

"Don't even think about it," she said. "OK?"

"I didn't see anything, Aimee. I don't care."

Calmly, she tilted her head to the side.

"Yeah? You'd better not."

Around us, the music began to change. The R&B was fading out, something ravey was pumping through the speakers, and Aimee was backing away from me, the lights dipping and diving around her. Just before she disappeared into the dark, she threw me a look that I felt beneath my fingernails.

"Stick a fork in me, I'm done."

Melissa was back by my side, breathless, her hair plastered across her forehead. Behind her I could see Khaleed, standing by himself in the middle of the room, wiping his mouth on his hand.

"Well, that . . ." she said thoughtfully, running her tongue around her mouth, ". . . was absolutely disgusting. But I *liked it.*"

I scanned the dance floor for Aimee, but she'd been swallowed by the crowd.

"I brought you some more punch."

Melissa was holding up two fresh cups, filled to the brim.

"Oh." I peered into the gloopy orangeness. "Thanks."

She took an enthusiastic gulp, and her eyebrows shot up her face.

"Whoa, did they bring out new punch?! This stuff is, like . . . *whoooa.*"

Over Melissa's shoulder, I could see students swarming around the drinks table, grabbing sweets and chips and refilling each other's drinks. Word was beginning to spread, and people were knocking back the spiked cocktails like water, their eyes widening, faces wincing, then diving back in for more.

As I watched it all unfold, punch bowls draining, oblivious teachers chatting across the hall, and Aimee sitting on a pile of crash mats with her friends, swinging her legs and seeing off drink after drink, I knew one thing for certain.

This wasn't going to end well.

"Man, I am glad that's over."

We had come home early from the dance. When Melissa had grown tired of hanging off Khaleed and the music went a bit clubby, we'd decided to go back to my house and mess around on YouTube for a while. This was fine by me, as I didn't particularly relish the idea of spending the rest of the evening trying to avoid Aimee, and besides, people were starting to get drunk from the vodka punch, and the atmosphere was beginning to sour.

"Come on," chirped Melissa. "It wasn't that bad."

Melissa and I were lying side by side on my bed, laptop playing music at our feet, a mound of multicolored jelly beans sitting in a bowl between us. Melissa was picking out all the yellow ones and lining them up along her tummy.

"I mean, you could have definitely got a cheeky kiss off Tim Stallworthy," she continued, adding another bean to her collection.

"I don't *want* a cheeky kiss off Tim Stallworthy."

"But he was watching you all night!"

I turned my head toward her. "I don't fancy him."

Melissa sat up a little, causing her jelly beans to quiver precariously.

"So what? Do you think I fancy Khaleed? Of course not!"

"You said he had nice ears."

"Of course I don't *fancy* him, doofus, but I did the right thing, didn't I? I *took things to the next level*. We're teenagers, Charlie. This is what we do."

I tossed a jelly bean into the air and caught it in my mouth.

"I think I'll just be kissing the boys I actually like, thanks very much."

"OK, fine, whatever," said Melissa, wobbling her head at me. "Just because you happen to be in possession of a deep and magnetic beauty . . ."

I dug an elbow into her side.

"Yeah, right."

"Ooh, wait!" Melissa gathered up her beans, shoveled them into her mouth, and grabbed my computer. "I just remembered what happened today," she said, chewing, and tapping furiously on the keys.

"What?" I replied, sitting up next to her.

"Fire&Lights posted tons of new photos on Instagram, from the tour. Look."

The band's Instagram page appeared on my laptop, and Melissa clicked on the first image. It showed the four boys lined up in a row, their arms draped along each other's shoulders, while above their heads, a banner read: "Fire&Lights are coming to YOUR town. On tour now!!"

I pretended not to be interested, but my eyes wouldn't shift from the screen.

"HOW. HOT. IS. THAT."

It was almost impossible, in my head, to connect the pop stars in the picture with the boys I would be meeting at Reading Arena the next day. They weren't real. Not even Olly, who just over a year ago was no different from any other teenager at my school.

"Ohmygosh . . . Aiden Roberts, you are the light of my life." Melissa was on the second photo now, a shot of Aiden onstage, strumming a guitar, a mile-wide grin on his face. "I would marry him so hard."

Click. The next shot was of Gabriel, also at a live concert, his hand punching the air. His bare forearm was dappled in purple light.

"Gabriel's been growing his hair out," said Melissa, considering the picture, "and I think that's a good thing. What do you think?"

I picked at my fingernails.

"I like the bald look, myself."

"Huh?" said Melissa, squinting at the screen.

"I said: I'd prefer it if he was bald."

Melissa turned to me, realized what I'd said, and stuck out her tongue. I swallowed a snort.

"Very funny," she said, a smile creeping onto her face. "You are *oh* so hilarious."

We sat there for a few minutes, music playing, while Melissa scrolled idly through the Fire&Lights picture feed. I had Facebook open on my phone but was keeping one eye on the laptop.

"So you really think someone spiked the punch tonight?" mused Melissa with a yawn.

"Yeah, definitely."

"How do you know?"

I'd considered telling Melissa about seeing Aimee with the vodka, but the way I saw it, the fewer people that knew about that, the better.

"I don't know, just a hunch."

Melissa grinned.

"A punch hunch."

"Exactly."

"Ohmygod! Check it out . . . he looks *soooo good* in this one." Melissa plucked another jelly bean from the bowl and, her eyes still glued to the computer, pushed it very slowly into her mouth. "Oliver . . . Alexander . . . Samson. *Hell* yes."

In the picture, Olly was kneeling at the corner of the stage, singing into a microphone, his free hand stretching out into the crowd. From below, fans reached up to touch him.

"Speaking of Olly, how psyched are you for tomorrow?"

I realized I was still staring at the photo, and broke away.

"Um . . . what?"

Melissa opened her arms wide, and I ducked out of the way.

"Super-psyched?" Then, even wider. "MEGA-PSYCHED?"

"I honestly don't know the difference between those two things."

"Right, well, either way"—Melissa reached out and slid our empty mugs off the windowsill—"I would like to propose a birthday toast."

She sniffed the mugs, passed one to me, then picked up the sweet bowl and filled them both with jelly beans. She puffed up her chest.

"To Charlie Bloom, my favorite person in the whole entire world, and her life-changing adventure with Fire&Lights."

We clinked our mugs together.

"This, my friend, could be the beginning of something *epic* . . ."

6

It was barely four o'clock, and already there were hundreds of girls gathered outside the arena. They were holding homemade banners and giggling at each other, huddled together for warmth. A few of them were watching me as I made my way along the line on the wrong side of the barrier.

I kept my eyes to the ground.

"Excuse me, miss."

The bouncer in front of me was huge and dressed in all black. He was holding up a thick palm to block my path.

"You can't come back here."

I tried to peer past him toward the main gate, but he took a side-step and blocked my view.

"I'm wi . . ."

I trailed off as I realized the girls at the front of the queue were all listening to me.

"I'm with the band," I tried again, this time with a lowered voice, feeling ridiculous just saying it. "I'm meeting Olly Samson."

The bouncer looked like he didn't believe me, but then I'm not sure I would have believed me either.

"What's your name?"

"Charlie Bloom."

Eyeing me the whole time, the man mumbled into a walkie-talkie on his shoulder and then stood with his legs wide apart, not saying anything. We both waited in the freezing cold for what felt like ages.

"So . . . should I—?"

A loud buzzer cut me off, and the gate creaked open. It was too dark to see what was beyond the door, but the bouncer indicated I should walk through, so I did. I could hear some of the queuing fans whispering about me as I disappeared.

". . . Oh my God, that is so *unfair*. Who is *she* anyway . . . ?"

The gate closed automatically behind me, an outside lamp flickered on, and there he was, lit by a single beam of light.

Olly Samson. Pop star.

A little gasp fell from my mouth.

"How's it going?" he asked, moving forward to hug me. I wasn't expecting this, so I froze, suddenly aware of his strong, warm hands against my back.

"I'm good," I said, as he pulled away again. Despite the cold, he was wearing only a tight V-neck T-shirt and dark slim-fit jeans. I thought about the boy I had met beside the lockers two years before, the slight, skinny sixteen-year-old with the dream of becoming a singer. Standing in front of me now he looked sort of like how I remembered him—handsome, with a kind face—but more polished, somehow, as if they had turned up the intensity in his colors, given his hair extra shine. Made his skin glow. And Melissa had been right about their exercise regime. I could see the fabric of Olly's T-shirt straining against his chest.

"Let's get inside; it's freezing out here."

·Olly led me round the back of the venue to the stage door as fireflies danced in my stomach. Another huge bouncer was standing guard, and inside I could hear microphones being tested and the sound of drums.

"Oh wait," said Olly, taking something from his pocket and nodding at the bouncer, who clicked open the door. "You'll need this."

Olly dangled a Fire&Lights wristband in front of me and, nudging back the cuff of my duffle coat, wrapped it around my wrist and secured it underneath. His fingers were warm against my cold skin.

"You're one of us now," he joked, showing me to the door.

And we walked inside.

A huge team of people was buzzing around inside the building, talking into headsets, folding clothes, unraveling cables. We passed through long, narrow corridors, up and down stairs, through countless doors, and finally out into a large backstage area with tables covered in chips, drinks, and colorful bowls of fruit.

"So this is it," said Olly, picking up two Cokes and offering one to me. I accepted, even though I wasn't sure I wanted it. "It gets pretty hectic round here before the show, but you'll be fine if you stick with me."

He smiled and gestured toward a nearby sofa. We both sat down, and he ran a hand through his short, sandy-brown hair.

"It's awesome that you came."

Olly had this striking, blue-eyed gaze that I'd never noticed at school. I shifted on the sofa.

"Thanks for asking me."

"Pleasure."

He popped open his drink, and my fireflies danced some more.

"I just hope I can do a good job."

"Are you kidding? Your photos are great."

"I don't know; my camera's not the best . . . it's secondhand."

Olly looked down at the camera case by my feet, and my face prickled with shame. Melissa told me once that, even though their album hadn't been released yet, the boys from Fire&Lights were probably already millionaires from their sponsorship deals and sold-out world tour. And here I was with a battered old camera my dad bought on eBay.

"Plus," I said, "I make most of it up as I go along, to be honest."

Olly leaned in toward me.

"You wanna know something?" he asked, glancing over his shoulder. I nodded, and his blue eyes sparkled at me. "So do I."

He sat back against the arm of the sofa.

"So how's the old school? Big-Ears Bennett still in charge?"

"Yep, he's still there. Ears still pretty huge."

Olly laughed.

"I shouldn't call him that, really, he was such a nice guy. They all were. Supporting me in the live finals. The whole school voted for us—it was mad."

Olly took a swig of his Coke, and I looked at my feet. Crossed them, uncrossed them.

"Everyone's obsessed with you guys at Caversham," I said.

"Hey, I'm just lucky. Anyone could be in my shoes."

But you're not just anyone, I thought. *You're Olly Samson, from Fire&Lights.*

"Yo, Olly. Got a question about your monitoring."

A short, stubbly man was standing above Olly, holding a metal box with an antenna sticking out of it. He was wearing black cargo shorts and a tour T-shirt for a band called Pulled Apart By Horses. His neck was plastered in tattoos.

"Sorry, Charlie . . . won't be a sec."

Olly started chatting with the man about something that sounded very technical, so I slipped my phone from my pocket and fired off a message to Melissa.

I'm sitting on a sofa with olly samson :) xx

Less than two seconds later, my phone pinged.

OH MY GOD I AM GOING TO PEE MYSELF

I stifled a laugh.

Please don't

I cannot believe I'm listening to old person music at my stupid cousin's wedding & ur chilling with celebs. PITY ME

:(:(:(

HAVE YOU TOLD HIM ABOUT ME YET

I glanced at Olly, who was turning a knob on the metal box and cracking a joke. The man with the neck tattoos was laughing and shaking his head.

It hasn't come up

Ping.

If he asks, make sure u tell him I've kissed tons of boys so I know what I'm doing

Ping.

But at the same time make it clear I am no hussy

I was halfway through writing back, when my screen lit up again.

OMG if u get to meet aiden I will literally die

Keep you posted x

Olly's conversation seemed to be wrapping up, and I was about to put my phone away when Melissa sent another message.

Oh btw, hot goss from y'day. After we left, 8 people were sick from the punch & 2 windows got smashed. Mr Bennett gonna go cray-craaaaay

From the sound of it, we'd left at the right time. The rumors were probably exaggerated, but even so, it would have taken some pretty oblivious teachers not to notice there was vodka in the punch.

Come Monday morning, Mr. Bennett would be on the warpath.

"Sorry about that," said Olly. "Boring stage stuff." He pointed to the table of food behind us. "Fancy a snack?"

"I'm good, thanks," I said, pocketing my phone. "I do have one question, though."

"Oh yeah?"

"While I'm here, what do you want me to, like . . . *do?*"

Olly smiled at this, as if he'd been waiting for me to ask. He moved closer again, and I got the faintest sense of his aftershave on the air, sweet and spicy, like cinnamon. Not like the boys at school, who smelled of cheap deodorant and soccer cleats.

"Truth is, it's up to you. We haven't done this before, so it's kind of an experiment. Our other photographers, they've all got tons of gear because they're shooting for magazines and stuff, but you . . . your pictures are for the fans. You should just hang out with us, get to know the guys, and if you see something cool, snap it. They won't let you shoot the concerts for some legal reason, but you can watch from backstage. Everything else is fair game."

I rubbed at a stain on the arm of the sofa.

"There is one other thing . . ."

Olly sat forward.

"What's that?"

"If my photos do get used on the fan page, which I guess they probably won't, but if they do . . . can you ask them not to use my name?" I tried my hardest not to blush. "It's just . . . the idea of all those people knowing who I am, it kind of freaks me out." I gave a nervous laugh. "That's not too weird, is it?"

Olly held up his hand. "Course not. I totally get it. You're not interested in the fame, right?" He gave me a grin, and then his face softened.
"Seriously, though, it's cool. Whatever you want. If you're happy, I'm
happy."

Suddenly, I felt a rush of excitement. This was actually happening.
"Amazing."

"Yo, Samson! Leave that poor girl alone."

A spiky-haired, half-Japanese boy I knew immediately as Yuki Harrison was approaching us from across the room, tossing an apple in
the air as he walked. Stopping by the sofa, he threw the apple upward,
nodded hello, and it dropped back perfectly into his hand. Then he took
a big, juicy bite.

"Photographer, right?"

I glanced at my camera.

"Sort of, yeah."

"This is Charlie Bloom," said Olly, sitting up. "Charlie, Yuki."

"Hi," I said with a small wave. Yuki swallowed his bite of apple.

"I'm glad you're here. That old dude we had last week kept catching me with my eyes closed. Plus he was kind of creepy."

Yuki was wearing a faded Muse T-shirt and charcoal-colored high-
top boots with the laces undone. He was angular and good-looking,
all cheekbones and dark lines, and his jet-black hair stuck up at the back
like a peacock's tail. At the front, it half covered his forehead in a just-
fell-out-of-bed fringe.

He hopped onto the edge of a large metal case beside us, munch-
ing, his legs dangling over the side.

"So where's Gabe?" asked Olly.

"Carla just showed," said Yuki, rolling his eyes. "I think he's off with
her somewhere."

Olly frowned. "I thought he wasn't into her?"

"He's not, but she's got a backstage pass, man, and she is HOT for him. Poor guy doesn't stand a chance."

"Who's Carla?" I asked, sipping at my drink.

"Martinez," said Yuki through the crunch of his apple.

"Who's that?"

Yuki raised his eyebrows and let out a long whistle.

"You don't know who Carla Martinez is?"

I looked from him to Olly and then back again. "Should I?"

"No way, man," laughed Yuki, leaning back on his elbows. "Don't sweat it."

"She's one of the leads on *Hampton Beach*," explained Olly, checking his watch.

"Oh . . . right." I thought about this. The odds were good that *Hampton Beach* was some kind of television show. "I guess I don't really watch that much TV."

Yuki studied my face for a moment in stunned silence. Just as this was starting to make me nervous, a huge grin spread across his face.

"I like you, Charlie Bloom," he announced, tossing his apple core into a nearby bin. "But yeah, she's, like, *GQ*'s Hottest Hottie of the Year or something dumb like that. In at number one."

After a quick glance around the room, Yuki hopped down off his box, perched on the arm of the sofa next to me, and said under his breath: "She's had her eye on Gabriel for weeks. I reckon she was waiting for him to break up with Ella, because—"

He stopped himself as the door opened and two people walked through. It was Gabriel West, in torn jeans and a baggy sweater, and a slim, elegant girl with shiny hair and catwalk looks. Dressed in a black leather jacket and swinging an expensive-looking handbag, Carla Martinez looked like she'd just walked off a film set, which in all probability, she had.

Gabriel and Carla were looking straight ahead as they drifted past the buffet tables, Gabriel grabbing a handful of snacks and a six-pack of Coke, Carla plucking a bottle of mineral water from the back and slipping it into her bag. She looked as if she didn't eat.

They were heading for the opposite door and clearly not stopping to say hello. In fact, it seemed as if they hadn't even noticed we were there. But just as Gabriel was leaving the room, he turned to look back in our direction and his amber eyes briefly met mine.

7

There was something not quite real about Gabriel West.

Tall, lean, and tanned, he had wavy black hair that broke out at the front in two or three cascading strands, and an intense, hypnotic gaze. A hint of stubble shadowed his jaw. All the boys were well known in the media, but for months now Gabriel had been the most photographed, the most interviewed, the most hounded member of the band. Even for someone like me, who didn't watch *Make or Break* or follow Fire&Lights, actually seeing his face in real life, staring back at me, it was strangely . . . unbelievable.

"She is going to eat him alive, bro." Yuki was watching Carla leave, one hand buried in Gabriel's choppy, chaotic hair.

Olly laughed. "She knows what she wants, I'll give her that."

I looked back toward the door, but by then Gabriel was gone, vanished into the dark with Carla. I had to admit, the girls in the cafeteria at school had been right about one thing: he did have amazing eyes. They were a brilliant, magnetic amber, and when our eyes met they'd flickered at me in the light . . . as if he was trying to tell me something.

And I could see how a certain type of girl might really fall for that.

"Come on," said Olly, standing up from the sofa. "Aiden's in the dressing room; he's really excited to meet you."

The Fire&Lights dressing room looked exactly the way I'd imagined it. There were lights around the mirrors, miniature fridges, and bowls full of M&M's. Aiden Roberts was sitting in the corner on his own, earphones in, nodding to the beat.

"Hey, Aid!"

Aiden, engrossed in his music, didn't respond, so Olly walked over and tapped him on the shoulder. Aiden spun round on his chair and, when he saw me, suddenly stood up, straightening his T-shirt. His earphones were tangled in his hands.

"Hey, er. Hi. You . . . are you Charlie?"

"That's me," I replied, slipping my camera bag off my shoulder. It seemed weird that they all knew who I was.

"Olly showed me the shots you took of that band," said Aiden, hands in his pockets. He had a strong, but soft, Irish accent. "They're, like . . . amazing."

"Really?" I said.

He nodded enthusiastically.

"Thanks."

Aiden was quite small, not much taller than me, and slim, with a mop of shaggy blond hair and very serious green eyes. According to Melissa, he came from this tiny fishing village near Galway, so the entire population of Ireland had voted for Fire&Lights in the big live final and they'd won by a landslide.

"You're doing some shots for us tonight, right?" he asked. Next to me, Yuki grabbed a fistful of M&M's and fed them into his mouth, one by one.

"Yeah," I said, fiddling with my sleeve. "At least, that's the plan."

"You'll be fine," Aiden replied, leaning back against the counter. A row of colored wristbands ran up his forearm. "In fact, I bet you'll be way better than that, um . . . that old guy last week, who was he? Clive something."

"EXACTLY," added Yuki with a mouthful of chocolate, pointing at me. "Exactly what I said. Creepy Clive."

I smiled at this, and Aiden smiled back.

Yuki threw an M&M at him and, when it missed, he lobbed two at Olly instead. Both hit Olly in the face, and they all fell about laughing.

"Hair and makeup, guys."

A woman had appeared in the open doorway. She was holding a clipboard and looked important.

"Thanks, Tara," said Olly. "We're coming."

The woman noticed me, and a disapproving glance flashed across her face. Then she disappeared.

"Charlie, you should come too," said Olly, as the boys all drifted toward the exit. "Maybe take a few snaps . . . ?"

"Yeah, watch us getting our faces put on," added Yuki. "Manly, right?"

On the way down the corridor I fell into step with Aiden, who was wrapping up his earphones, acoustic guitar strapped to his back. Up ahead, Yuki was ruffling Olly's hair and jabbing him in the ribs.

"So you and Olly went to the same school?" asked Aiden, shooting me a glance.

"Uh-huh. But we only met, like, once."

"Olly's the best. Incredible singer, too."

"Yeah . . . yeah, he is."

I stared at the floor as we walked.

"You'll like it here," said Aiden, zipping his earphones into their case. "I mean, it's crazy, but in a good way. Y'know?"

"Sure," I said, as we passed through a set of double doors into a brightly lit hallway. "I mean, normally on a Saturday night I'd be watching *The Breakfast Club* and eating Doritos straight from the bag, so I think I can handle crazy."

Aiden laughed, quietly at first, then a little louder. He cleared his throat.

"That's funny," he said, as much to himself as to me. "That's real funny."

In front of us, Yuki and Olly were rapping a nonsense song together, Yuki beatboxing and slapping a flat palm against the wall as he walked. Somewhere else in the building, someone was banging drums and tuning guitars.

"You wanna do this for a living then, like? When you leave school?"

I toyed with a loose thread on my camera case. "One day, maybe. I figured I'd do photography at college first, and see what happens. But now I'm here, shooting you guys . . . which is a bit scary."

We made fleeting eye contact. Aiden was one of those people who constantly looked like he was thinking deeply about something.

"I know how you feel," he said, turning away again. "One minute you're in school, normal like everyone else, then the next minute . . . you're here. And *nothing's* normal around here."

A man with a beard pushed by us, talking on his phone. "Yep—yep, Sian has the guest list. She'll be with you in ten . . ." He shot me a sideways look as he passed.

"Tell you one thing, though," continued Aiden, as we arrived in the main backstage area. A lady holding a pile of white towels took him by the hand, and as he walked away, he looked back over his shoulder and said: "Whatever happens . . . it's *mad*-exciting."

A team of makeup artists descended on the band, and I watched as the boys were shepherded to their chairs, Yuki and Olly still rapping, Aiden joining in over the top.

I was suddenly on my own.

"This your new direction then, boys?" said the towel lady, unscrewing the lid from a tin of hair wax. "Hip-hop?"

"All the money's in hip-hop," replied Yuki, picking up a copy of *Men's Health* and flicking casually through it. "All the green, an' all the *laydeez* . . ."

The towel lady tutted, a smile playing on her face, and began warming a ball of wax between her fingers.

As I looked down at my camera case, there was no escaping it. It was time to start doing my job. I pulled out my camera and, spinning the dial to portrait mode, crept into a corner and began to shoot. From where I was standing I was able to frame Olly, Yuki, and Aiden sitting in a perfect row, people buzzing around them, running product through their hair and dabbing on foundation.

At one point, one of the makeup artists turned around at the clicking of the shutter and frowned. I stopped for a moment, but then Yuki began flicking peanuts into his mouth and attacking Aiden with hair spray, and I started up again.

Screw her, I thought. *This is the reason I'm here.*

I had work to do.

Scrolling through the photos, I couldn't help but smile. The three of them were so laid-back, so carefree, laughing, telling jokes and flirting with the makeup girls. Fire&Lights was a manufactured group, everyone knew that, but I was starting to see that, over time, they'd become more than that. They'd become friends, brothers . . . a real band. Something nobody could fake.

And that, somehow, was what I had to capture on camera.

One thing, though, was nagging at me as I flicked through the gallery. An inescapable image, repeated in every photo. A single empty chair where Gabriel West should have been.

"Once more, please—and can we really *feel* it this time, boys?"

Yuki was standing on a chair in the middle of the green room, conducting his bandmates in a chaotic rendition of "God Save the Queen." The four of us were scattered around the large room: Aiden perched on a stool, strumming his guitar; Olly lying on a sofa with his feet up; and me in the corner, leaning against a wardrobe, camera focused on the action.

"It's no good," said Olly, shaking his head. "We are never going to make it in show business."

Aiden played a deliberately tuneless chord on his guitar.

"Hey, Charlie, whaddya think?" called Yuki, across the room. "That sound any good?"

I smiled at him from behind the camera.

"I'm a photographer," I said, twisting the focus. "I'm not officially here."

Yuki stuck his hands on his hips. "Wha'?"

"You're supposed to ignore me."

"Seems a bit rude," reflected Yuki, jumping down from the table. "Still, you're the boss. Consider yourself ignored."

He saluted me, then crossed to the sofa, where he lifted Olly's legs in the air and spun them round, making room for himself. He dropped down next to his bandmate and glanced at the clock. "D'you think we ought to rescue Gabe from Miss Martinez?"

"He's a big boy," said Olly. "He can take care of himself."

While they chatted, I scrolled through the pictures. There was a nice one of Yuki conducting, his arms held aloft, and a cute one of Aiden, concentrating on a guitar chord, tongue poking out of the corner of his mouth. Lowering the camera, I watched Aiden picking out a gentle tune on his guitar, singing to himself and flicking the hair out of his eyes. His gaze caught mine for a second, and he gave me a little smile.

"How they looking?" Olly was leaning against the wall next to me. I arched an eyebrow.

"I thought I told you I'm not officially here?"

"Good point," he said, bowing his head. "You did mention that."

He craned over my shoulder to peek at the photos. With a side smile, I pulled the camera away.

"It's time," said a voice from the hallway, and we all looked up. A stage manager was standing in the open door, a small, serious-looking man with spiky hair and thick-rimmed glasses. He clicked his fingers three times. "Boys?"

Yuki and Aiden stood up from their seats, and Olly pushed away from the wall.

"You coming?" he asked.

I looked around the room. "Coming where?"

He nodded at the door. "You'll see."

My pulse quickened as we were ushered from the room and herded down a tight corridor. The stage manager with the spiky hair was speaking into a walkie-talkie, which buzzed every few seconds with burps of static and fuzzy, urgent-sounding replies from the other end.

The corridor culminated in a short flight of stairs, leading upward to a black, windowless door reading "STAFF ONLY." The stage manager climbed the staircase and, pressing his ear against the door, pointed back in our direction.

"Everyone ready?"

I glanced at the band, wondering whether "everyone" included me. Yuki looked over his shoulder.

"What about Gabe?"

The man checked his watch and blew air through his lips. "Not ideal, but we're short of time. He's on his way. Let's just get this show on the road."

Around me, the boys all nodded, and the stage manager curled his hand around the doorknob. I gripped my camera tight, becoming aware of a distant thunder, a high-pitched roar, coming from somewhere beneath my feet.

"Now *this*," said Olly, as the handle slowly turned, "is really going to blow your mind."

8

The door creaked open, a wedge of sky appeared, and a noise like nothing I'd ever heard before tore through the walls of the building.

Impossible, unimaginable . . . *screaming*.

Yuki, Aiden, and Olly bounded up the stairs and out through the open doorway. As they emerged, the roar swelled and ruptured, and loud music blared through outdoor speakers. I was standing alone at the bottom of the staircase, unsure of whether I should follow, throwing furtive glances at the spiky-haired stage manager. Would I get in trouble if I joined them? Was that against the rules? Maybe it was, but the noise from outside was rising by the second, and I itched to be out there with them. When a crackling voice on the walkie-talkie distracted the man's attention, I stepped onto the stairs, flew up them two at a time, and dashed past him into the night.

Immediately outside was a small balcony, barely big enough for ten people, that looked out over a seething mass of fans. A crowd of thousands was yelling and screaming down below, while Olly, Yuki, and Aiden stood side by side on the balcony, grinning and waving, arms across each other's shoulders. On the ground, girls screeched and pleaded for a second of their attention, waving their banners, eyes brimming with tears.

Hidden behind a brick pillar, I crouched down and took a snap of the boys, their faces in profile against the purple sky, sculpted features picked out by a nearby floodlight. Next, I crept backward, careful to remain out of view, and captured the wider scene: the band's heads and shoulders from behind, and beyond, the howling, throbbing crowd.

As I flicked through the photos, my heart racing, I felt someone brush past my shoulder in the dark. I looked up, the racket vibrating in my ears, half expecting to find the stage manager standing in front of me, ordering me to leave . . . but he wasn't there. Someone else, tall and slim, in a fitted T-shirt and torn jeans, had joined us on the balcony and was clapping and waving to the fans.

It was Gabriel West.

The screaming suddenly doubled in volume.

"GabriEL! GabriEL!" chanted the crowd, rasping and shrieking, as Gabriel fell in with the rest of the band. He slipped an arm around Olly's shoulder and whispered something in his ear, and I ducked back to my original position behind the pillar to capture a shot of the four of them in profile.

As I zoomed in, I noticed something odd. Beside Gabriel, Olly's expression, though it hadn't exactly changed, went strangely tight, and his smile seemed to darken. It was too subtle for the fans below to notice, but I saw it. I saw . . . *something*. And my camera saw it too.

I squeezed the button and took the picture.

"OK, lads, that's enough, we're done!" said the stage manager, sweeping out onto the balcony. He spoke into the receiver on his shoulder, then repeated: "We're done! Let's go!"

The crowd wailed as the band was ushered from sight and back through the windowless door, and we all piled down the stairs, breathless, chattering, feet slapping against the wood.

When we reached the floor, I fell back against the wall, one hand to my chest, barely able to keep the smile off my face.

My heart was beating like a drum.

So what happened next??? Where are u now??

I was sitting alone in the dressing room. The boys were all waiting beside the stage, and the crew were scattered around the building, making the final preparations for the opening of the show. I could hear the muffled hysteria of the fans in the auditorium.

We went out on the balcony, I wrote back to Melissa. Looked out over thousands of people, all screaming, going nuts. It was unreal

Ping.

Oh. My. Actual. God. www.crazyjealous.com

It's so amazing here

Aiden's acoustic guitar lay on the counter in the corner of the room, and Olly's T-shirt was folded over the back of his chair, a pair of high-tops lined up neatly underneath. I thought about everything that had happened so far, the way it felt to crouch out of sight on that balcony, the freezing air chilling my fingertips, the skull-shaking noise from below. The first time I'd seen Olly standing in that spotlight. Staring at Melissa's name on my phone, I remembered how close I had come to missing out on it all.

Thank you for making me do this, mel xxxx

Ping.

No sweat, CB. That's what best friends are for :) xxxxx

I could see from the speech bubble that she was still typing.

Well that, and STEALING UNDERWEAR FROM THE DRESSING ROOM OF A CERTAIN IRISH POP STAR AND THEN DONATING SAID UNDERWEAR TO ONE'S AFOREMENTIONED BESTIE

I pulled a face at my phone.

What would you want with aiden's underwear? I wrote, then thought better of it. Actually, I don't wanna know

Melissa sent me a line of grinning emojis.

Gotta go, concert's starting. Through the walls, the crowd was reaching fever pitch. Message you later xx

Gathering up my bag, I caught a glimpse of myself in the mirror, tugged my hat down at the sides, and headed for the exit. One final message vibrated in my pocket.

Don't do anything i wouldn't do

And I stepped out the door.

I'd never been to a proper concert before. I'd seen live videos on You-Tube, of course, and festival footage from Glastonbury, but this was different. I'd never actually felt the heat from the crowd, inhaled the burned chemical smell of dry ice, or blinked in the glare from the spotlights. Never felt the bass moving in my bones.

Standing in the wings at the side of the stage, I peered out into the arena from behind a thick black pillar. Fire&Lights was due onstage at any moment, and the tension was building beneath pumping dance music and the hypnotic swirl of red lights. An ocean of fans, stretching up and out into the far reaches of the auditorium, churned and chanted, frantic with excitement, waving banners and screaming their lungs out, tiny white phone lights dancing in the dark.

In front of me, the stage was a playground of runways, balconies, and podiums, with a long, extended walkway that jutted out into the crowd. If you looked into the faces of the lucky few lining the walkway, you could see it in their eyes: *The boys will be close enough to touch.* One group of fans was holding a sign that said "GORGEOUS GABRIEL, WE WANT TO TAKE YOU HOME." It was huge, covered in glitter, and decorated with photos of Gabriel from magazines. One of the girls was laughing and crying at the same time.

A ripple of anticipation passed through the audience as the dance music died away and a group of shadowy figures, the band's musicians, swarmed onto the stage. One sat at the drums, others at keyboards, and others strapped on guitars, while on either side of them on the giant video screens, recorded footage of the band began to play. The drummer pounded his kit and the crowd clapped along in unison as, on film, the boys could be seen green-screened against various un- likely backgrounds: the Pyramids, the Taj Mahal, the Grand Canyon. Then, a clip of Yuki backflipping on a trampoline, Aiden waving as he walked up a metal staircase into an airplane, Olly singing into a microphone in a recording studio. And finally, a shot of Gabriel, step- ping out of a limo to the frenzied snapping of cameras, which sparked renewed shrieking from all corners of the arena.

Alone, beside the stage, my body pulsed and shuddered with every thump of the bass drum. The music was building, the guitars were be- ginning to howl, and soon, over the soundtrack, a booming voice-over could be heard.

"Reading Areeeeenaaaaaa . . . !"

An earsplitting answer from the crowd.

"Are you *ready* . . ."

Screaming, shouting, desperate cries.

". . . for FIRE . . ."

The whole building went dark.

"... AND ... LIGHTS?"

An almighty thunderclap shook the stage, and plumes of hot sparks erupted into the air, bright white light flooding every corner. High up above the musicians, four lithe figures could be seen lined up beneath an archway, steam billowing around them, their silhouettes unmistakable.

Spotlights hit the boys, and the crowd roared the roof off.

Fire&Lights had arrived.

Over a driving beat, Olly, Gabriel, Yuki, and Aiden split off between the runways and cascaded down toward their fans, high-fiving musicians as they passed, clapping their hands above their heads. The sight of them spilling out across the stage, lights flying, while thousands of people rose simultaneously from their seats was like something out of a movie. I hated to admit it, but it sent a shiver down my spine.

"People!" called Yuki, pointing into the auditorium.

"You guys ready to have some *fun*?" yelled Olly, throwing both arms up. At his command, the sea of heads became a sea of hands, grasping, waving, punching the air, and he led them in a steady clap with the drums, the growl of guitars building slowly underneath. The music swelled and grew, filling the space, until finally it dropped down to a single guitar, and Gabriel began to sing.

Straightaway, Gabriel's voice was joined by the voices of the fans, and they knew every single word. Mouths moved in unison, eyes shone like stars. Then Aiden took over, bouncing down toward the audience, pointing out into the arena as he sang. Yuki took the next verse, twirling his microphone between lines, one foot casually elevated on the rim of a low speaker. The slogan on his T-shirt read, "Almost Famous." Finally, Olly led everyone into the chorus, and the auditorium seemed to vibrate with the sound, thousands of people united in song, colored lights flashing, cymbals crashing, the boys jumping up and down with the beat.

I'd never seen anything like it in my life.

When the song ended, over throbbing applause, Olly wandered out onto the walkway and sat down on the side of the stage, swinging his legs. Girls immediately lunged forward to touch him, and he reached out, their fingers grasping for his.

"So how's everybody doing?" he said, as the camera zoomed in on his face. The giant screen showed off the whiteness of his teeth, the sparkle in his eyes. "You know this is my hometown, yeah?" The fans cheered back at him, and one group in particular, huddled together on the upper circle, clapped their hands and yelled for his attention, waving a banner that read "CAVERSHAM HIGH LOVES OLLY SAMSON!!!"

"I went to school here, back in the day."

The Caversham girls cried and hollered, furiously flapping their banner. Olly noticed, and pointed in their direction.

"That was me: Caversham High, class of 2012," he said with a dazzling smile, and the girls turned to each other and shrieked, leaping up and down.

"So we have an epic show lined up for you guys," he continued, standing up again. He strolled back toward the rest of the band. "A few songs you might have heard before." Rapturous cheers. "Aiden might even play some guitar."

Aiden smiled and took a little bow.

"Hey, Aiden," said Yuki, sauntering over to him. "You look good tonight, bud." He reached out and mussed up Aiden's hair. "I like your hair that way."

Aiden smoothed his fringe back down, laughing, and Yuki turned to the crowd.

"You guys are big Aiden fans, right?" They screamed back at him. "Thought so. Give it up for Aiden Roberts!!"

With the fans chanting Aiden's name, Yuki walked across the stage toward Gabriel. He leaned an elbow on his shoulder, and the two of them appeared on the big screens.

Yuki nodded sideways at his bandmate. "Hey . . . you guys wanna know a secret about Gabriel West?"

Everybody cheered and whistled and, for just a moment, the screens cut across to Olly. He bit his lip, and his eyes dropped to the ground.

The camera returned to the action.

"It takes Gabriel . . ." said Yuki, raising two fingers in the air, *"two hours . . .* to do his hair for the show." He nudged Gabriel in the ribs. "Ain't that right, G?"

Gabriel, unruffled, rubbed his jaw, then leaned into Yuki's microphone.

"Yuki," he said, his eyes trained on his bandmate, ". . . wears Ninja Turtles pajamas."

Cue ecstatic applause, laughter and whooping, and a modest bow from Yuki. The drummer piled into the next song and, to the stamping of feet, Gabriel planted his hands over Yuki's ears and kissed him hard on the forehead.

The concert passed by in a boisterous, intoxicating blur. Music soared, fireworks flew, blinding lights circled and swooped. All night my senses crackled, and everywhere I looked, something magical was happening: Olly sharing a private joke with Aiden, Gabriel winking at Yuki, Yuki stealing Olly's scarf and wrapping it around the drum kit. It was almost too much. It was a feast, a riot, and I didn't want it to end.

A few numbers from the end, during a guitar solo, Olly wandered over to my side of the stage. He was standing behind the guitarist, admiring his handiwork, the two of them head-banging in time with the rhythm. The guitarist wailed into his big finish and, on the big screen, Olly raised both his hands in triumph. The fans roared in response.

Then, just before he swept back into the action, Olly turned, lowered his microphone, and threw me a smile.

I felt as if my heart might burst from my chest.

A split second later, he was back with the group. I leaned against the pillar, my hands shaking, face hot, an involuntary laugh tumbling out of me. I turned my head to see the four band members bounding together down the walkway, stooping to touch the hands of girls in the front row, and I realized I'd been grinning from ear to ear since the concert began. I couldn't help it. Fire&Lights was infectious. Watching them perform filled me with this intense, electric joy that I could feel in my fingertips, and the crazy thing was, I hadn't seen it coming. I'd never followed the band, I didn't listen to their music or watch their videos, and the last thing I'd expected was to become a fan. But in that moment, standing beside that stage that was lit up like a neon sign, I finally got it. I understood the hype.

I was completely and utterly hooked.

9

The Fire&Lights after-party was in full swing. Hip-hop was booming through the sound system, Aiden was strumming along on his guitar, and Yuki was intermittently pressing a bottle of wine to Aiden's lips, tipping it upward, and more often than not, spilling it down his shirt. A group of VIP fans were gathered around them, talking over each other and giggling into their drinks. They laughed at everything Yuki said, whispering to each other in between, tugging subconsciously at the hems of their skirts. On the far side of the room, Carla was standing opposite Gabriel, leaning into him as she spoke. He was swigging from a bottle of beer.

It was nearly half past ten, and my dad's official curfew was eleven o'clock. I was still buzzing from the concert, but if I stayed any longer, I'd never get home on time.

"Hey, Charlie."

I was slipping my coat on when Olly appeared, hair still sweaty from the show, the bottle of water in his hand nearly drained.

"Hey."

"Everything OK?"

I thought of the look Olly had given me during the concert, while

I was standing backstage. That smile in front of thousands, meant only for me.

"The gig was awesome," I said, hitching my camera bag onto my shoulder. "Honestly, it blew me away."

"Hometown crowd," he said, with a shrug. "Can't fail. You not staying for the party?"

My eyes flickered toward the door. "I don't know if I should . . ."

"Come on, you're part of the team now," he replied, finishing his water.

Part of the team. I still couldn't get used to that.

"It's just . . . I should think about heading home . . ."

"You sure? This is the fun part."

I glanced around the room. Yuki was attempting to open two bottles of beer at once, while rapping. The girls were screaming with laughter.

"I suppose it might be good to get a few more pictures . . ."

"Exactly," agreed Olly. "In fact—"

"So *this* is the photographer."

The voice was coming from behind me, and I recognized it straightaway. Gabriel's voice was rich, deeper than his bandmates', strong and pure but with a catching, jagged edge, and it hit you somewhere unnerving, behind the chest. I turned to find him standing at my shoulder, his eyes glowing amber from behind those tumbling strands of hair.

"Gabe, this is Charlie Bloom," said Olly with the hint of a sigh.

"I'm Gabriel," he said, as if he wasn't near enough the most famous eighteen-year-old in the entire world.

"Hi," I replied, pulling my hat down over my ears.

"You're not leaving, are you?" he asked, nodding at my coat.

"I was thinking ab—"

"Hey, now listen," Gabriel said, addressing me but speaking loud enough for everyone to hear, "this is an *after-party*, right?"

Somebody in the room whooped.

"And from what I hear, you're a privileged guest."

His gaze was fixed on mine, and it was making me nervous. I couldn't tell whether he was being sincere.

"So stay," he added, sliding a can of Coke from a nearby table. "No one ever left a Fire&Lights party before closing time."

"I just—"

"Seriously. Have a drink, take some photos. We don't bite."

He passed me the Coke, and I gripped it unnecessarily hard. It had been an incredible night, and if I was being honest, I *wasn't* ready to go home. I thought about my curfew, and then my father, sitting in front of the TV. The flicker of adverts, falling asleep in his chair. I could be half an hour late. He wouldn't mind.

As I undid my coat, Gabriel's mouth curled up into a smile, and he pointed at me with both hands. "You made the right decision, Charlie Bloom," he said, backing away into the crowd.

"Coming through!"

Squealing and giggling erupted in the far corner as Yuki emerged from the doorway, riding a skateboard into the party. He zigzagged through the gaggle of fans. "Watch your back, kids!"

The crowd parted, and Yuki crashed into Gabriel from behind, spilling his beer. I slipped my camera from its case.

"What the—?" Gabriel turned around and, disentangling himself from his bandmate, shook the beer from his fingers. "You should be careful, Harrison. Riding that thing without a license."

Yuki stomped on the tip of his skateboard and caught it with one hand.

"OH, I HAVE A LICENSE," he said, forming his other hand into a pretend pistol, turning it sideways, and pointing it at Gabriel. *"License to be gnarly."*

Gabriel disguised a smile and addressed the room.

"OK, then," he said, sliding his drink onto a nearby shelf. "Who here thinks I have better board skills than Yuki 'look at my ridiculous hair' Harrison?" He winked at Yuki, who slowly shook his head.

I was standing by the drinks table, catching it all on camera.

"We do!" chorused some of the girls, and Gabriel clicked his fingers. "Challenge extended," he announced, gesturing for Yuki to pass him the skateboard. As he climbed on, the board wobbled beneath him, and he sniggered at himself.

"How do you do this again?!"

Yuki crossed his arms and tutted. "Dude, this is embarrassing."

"You just wait, my friend," said Gabriel, looking up. "You just wait. Any minute now you'll be staring at the greatest three-sixty flip you ever . . . whoooa!"

The skateboard flew out from underneath Gabriel's feet and skidded across the room. He tumbled to the ground, prompting a slow hand-clap from Yuki, and as Gabriel lay on the floor, short of breath and laughing, I zoomed in hard on his face, right into his eyes, and twisted the lens into focus.

As I pressed the shutter, I wondered where in the world he came from. His accent was English, but he looked almost South American.

"Well, I guess I was wrong," he said, extending a hand toward Yuki. "Help me up, brother."

Yuki pulled Gabriel from the floor and dusted him off. The girls in the corner applauded and shouted, "We love you!!"

"Yo, DJ, turn the music up!" called Yuki, pointing at the sound system. Nothing happened, and he cocked a single eyebrow. "Wait, there is no DJ. Who stole our DJ?!"

One of the pluckier fans reached over and boosted the volume on the speakers, and Yuki clambered onto a nearby table. One by one, the girls followed his lead, jumping onto the furniture, dancing and singing along. I studied the room for a while, then began to move around the space, capturing little moments. Everyone was playing up for the camera, and the mood was wild.

Snap—Yuki spinning a drumstick at a hundred miles an hour.

Snap—Aiden, laughing at Yuki, who was juggling fruit.

Snap—Olly and Gabriel, standing next to each other, but facing different ways.

Snap—the whole room, taken from the corner, with Gabriel in the middle. He was ballroom dancing with a VIP fan who looked like she was about to burst with joy.

Snap . . . snap . . . snap.

This, I dared myself to think, *might actually make a really great photo album.*

"Hey there." There was somebody standing directly in front of me. Through the lens I could see the angular face of Carla Martinez, and I slowly lowered my camera to meet her eyes.

"Um . . . hi," I said, trying to step backward. She had me cornered.

"Who are you?" She looked at me without blinking.

I clipped the cap back onto my camera lens. "I'm sort of a . . . photographer."

She let this hang in the air for a few moments.

"So are you, like, *friends* with Gabriel?"

I pointed at my chest. "What . . . me? No. God. We just met."

She considered this. "Just seemed like, maybe, you guys knew each other."

Carla was standing a little too close to me. I could see the smooth landscape of her foundation and the dark, precise curve of her eyebrows.

"No, really . . . we don't."

Suddenly, as if someone had turned on a switch in her brain, she smiled. "I'm Carla."

"Oh, er . . . Charlie."

"Nice to meet you."

A stiff silence settled between us.

"So . . . you're . . . here with Gabriel, then?" I said.

She glanced briefly over her shoulder. "Yeah," she said distantly. The smile was still on her face, but it had disappeared from her eyes. "I'm with Gabriel."

"Hey, guys." Olly appeared beside us, holding a cold beer and wiping the back of his neck with a towel. "What's happening?"

"I was just getting to know your photographer," said Carla, with her head cocked slightly to the side.

"Yeah," I agreed. "We were, um . . ." I trailed off.

"Do you guys want some food?" asked Olly. "They're bringing out pizzas in a sec."

"I don't know," I said. "Maybe I should go, actually."

Carla pressed a hand against her chest. "Of course, you probably have school tomorrow."

"I doubt it," said Olly, with a laugh. "Unless Caversham High turned into a convent after I left."

Carla's expression soured. "What?"

"It's Sunday tomor—" Olly held up a hand. "Never mind. But, Charlie, honestly. You're welcome to stick around."

"Um, yeah . . . th-thanks," I stammered back, shoving my camera into its case. "But I should really head home." I braved a glance at Carla. "It was nice meeting you, though."

"Sure," said Carla, touching Olly's arm. Then she turned and walked away, heels clicking across the floor.

"You don't have to leave on her account," said Olly, watching her go.

"No, it's fine," I said, pulling on my coat. "I have a curfew, anyway." I winced a little as I said it.

"Hey, don't be embarrassed. We have a curfew too. Bed by two a.m. or we get told off."

"Rock 'n' roll," I said, and we both smiled.

Olly took a sip of his beer. "You OK getting back? We've got drivers who can take you."

"Thanks, but my bus stop's just outside," I said, reading the clock on the wall. However I traveled, I'd be late getting home. "I'll send the photos through later in the week, if that's cool?"

"Sure," said Olly, flinging the towel over his shoulder. "And thanks again for tonight. Get home safe."

"I will."

As I was walking toward the door, the party bubbling noisily behind me, Olly spoke up again. "Charlie . . . ?"

"Uh-huh?"

I turned round, and he tipped his beer bottle at me. "You did great."

I smiled. Though I would never have believed it a week ago, it was just possible he was right.

Wrapping a scarf around my neck, I opened the main door, and it creaked loudly. Yuki spotted me from the drinks table and shouted good-bye, closely followed by Aiden, while Gabriel, obscured from view by Carla, raised a hand above his head.

"Later, Charlie Bloom," Gabriel said, as I slipped from the room.

Out in the corridor, the party muffled behind me, one sound soared out above everything else.

It was the smooth, measured arc of Carla's laughter.

A light rain was falling as the bus wound its way out of town and back up the hill toward home. I was sharing it with four strangers, who were drifting off, one by one, as we drove deeper into the suburbs. Faint music played behind me, trapped in headphones. Raindrops quivered on the windows.

I was sitting near the back, camera on, flicking through the photo roll.

The first batch was from the makeup session. I'd been far too timid with the framing, but still, there was a nice shot of Olly smiling at his makeup artist, and another good one of Yuki singing into a can of hair spray, Aiden behind him, his face creased up with laughter.

I decided to keep the photos of Gabriel's empty chair, more for my own curiosity than anything else. Why, before the concert, had he kept his distance from the rest of the band? Was he just busy with Carla, or did he consider himself above his bandmates somehow? Gabriel West, The Star. The Main Attraction.

My phone pinged.

Saturday night has been duuuuull without u

Make or break? :) I wrote back.

But of course, replied Melissa. There's some new girl with a shaved head who sang chasing cars. She sounded like a cat in a blender

I laughed, and a man in a black hoodie glanced up from his phone.

Gotta go, on a quiet bus . . . full lowdown tomorrow. Missed ya xx

Missed u too *dies of boredom* xxxx

I returned to the photo gallery. By the time we'd moved on to the dressing room, I was beginning to relax, and the boys were all playing up for the camera. One image showed Yuki playing conductor, his trousers pulled up high around his waist, with Olly and Aiden standing on either side, saluting him. Next came the balcony photos, various dramatic views of the boys from behind, with their devoted hordes far below, and two shots of their faces in profile. Then there was that odd moment—Gabriel and Olly standing side by side, arms draped across each other's shoulders. Gabriel's eyes were keen and focused as he waved at the fans, but Olly's smile was tight, his expression locked in place.

At the time, I thought I might have imagined it, but the evidence was right there in front of me. The second Gabriel arrived, Olly had tensed up. And that didn't seem like Olly at all.

Finally, the after-party. I'd managed to catch Gabriel midtumble on the skateboard, and a follow-up shot of Yuki helping him back up, their hands intertwined, muscles taut. Lots of pictures of Yuki juggling beer bottles, bananas, and shoes; Aiden singing to fans; and Olly passing out drinks, towel around his neck. Gabriel ballroom dancing with a fan, his hand pressed against her back, her face glowing as they spun.

There was one more photo left in the series, one I'd never intended to shoot in the first place. Carla Martinez at the after-party, super close-up, glaring into the lens.

I tapped a few buttons, and the picture was gone.

It was nearly eleven thirty by the time I got back to the house. Tower Close stood silent in the damp, misty air, cars glinting with condensation. A cat slunk behind a trash can.

I was hoping Dad would be in bed, but the second I opened the front door, I knew there'd be trouble.

"You're late." My father was standing in the hallway holding a work file. There were dark rings around his eyes.

"Sorry, I . . . we lost track of time."

He looked at me with his brow furrowed.

"Come on, Charlie. This isn't like you."

In the kitchen, the empty container from a microwave-ready meal lay discarded by the sink, fork handle sticking out. The only sound in the house was the fuzzy white drone from the television.

"I'm only twenty-five minutes late," I said, hanging my coat on the rack. "I sent you a text."

"That's not really the point."

I unraveled my scarf and draped it over my coat.

"I'm sorry, Dad. But I'm home now. I don't see what the big deal is."

"The *big deal*, Charlie, is that . . ." Dad stopped himself and swallowed. "It's just us, in this house, and . . . you're . . ."

My eyes dropped to the floor, and Rosie's words echoed in my mind. *You have to understand, love, that you're everything he's got.*

"Look," he continued, "I don't mind you seeing your friends, but you've got exams coming up. You're a smart kid. Don't throw that away."

"I'm not throwing anything away, Dad." I knew I wasn't being fair, but I was tired. "You're being dramatic."

Dad set down his file and, sighing, rubbed at his eyes with forefinger and thumb. "You know, sometimes, you're just like your mother."

I took a step backward and felt the door handle in the base of my spine. "What . . . ?"

My voice was breathy, barely there.

"Hang on," said Dad, both palms raised, "what I mean is, you're . . ." The house fell silent. "Sorry, that came out wrong."

"God, Dad . . . what does that even mean?"

He clamped his hands behind his head, elbows sticking out on either side. "I'm sorry, kiddo, I didn't mean to upset you. Really . . ."

My eyes were fixed on the space between us: the black of the hallway, the familiar line of the floorboards.

When Dad spoke, the words were brittle in his mouth. "I miss her too, you know."

I kept my eyes low. The curled wooden feet of the phone table. The corner of Dad's shirt, untucked at the front. His ring finger, empty.

"Let's talk about this, Charlie. I don't—"

"I have to go to bed now," I said, walking past him and climbing the staircase. He was still trying to find the words when I reached the landing, passed into my bedroom, and closed the door behind me.

Ten minutes later, his door closed too. A slow, cautious click.

Careful not to wake me.

Though it was late, I didn't feel like sleeping. With my bedside clock flashing 11:48, 11:57, 12:15, I sat curled up under the covers, legs to my chest, the photo of our family picnic balanced on my knees. As I gazed into this little piece of my past, Dad's words crept over me like a ghost . . . a whispering on my skin.

Sometimes you're just like your mother.

In the past ten years, I'd obsessed over every detail in this photo, trying to build a picture of her in my mind. There weren't many clues, so I clung to the only ones I had. Mum's T-shirt, for instance, had the phrase "Little Boy Blue" written across it, and years ago I'd asked Dad what it meant. He told me it came from the nursery rhyme, but that had never made much sense to me. Why would a woman in her mid-twenties have a nursery rhyme on her T-shirt?

I began to wonder whether it had something to do with this old folk song that was constantly stuck in my head, a Harry Chapin hit from the seventies called "Cat's in the Cradle." I would wake up sometimes with the song on a loop in my brain, and when we were tiny, Melissa and I used to march around the house singing it at the tops of our voices.

In the chorus, the singer lists all these random things from childhood, and "Little Boy Blue" is one of them. It had to mean something. But when I tried explaining the theory to Dad, he told me to stop imagining things and to go outside and play.

I hadn't thought seriously about the phrase "Little Boy Blue" or that song for years. Then, one day last summer, I was in a clothes shop with Melissa, rifling through racks of strappy tops, chatting about nothing, when "Cat's in the Cradle" came on the stereo. Instantly, a picture formed in my mind, like a cinema screen flickering on. I was in the back of the car and Mum was in the front passenger seat, Dad driving. We were on the motorway and it was dark and pouring with rain, and orange lights were dashing past outside the window. "Cat's in the Cradle" was playing on the radio, and I felt warm, and safe. Like I was coming home.

And that was all.

It felt like a memory, though it could just as easily have been a dream. I couldn't say for certain. Either way, all I had to do since was listen to that song, and the picture would come back to me. And sometimes, when I missed Mum the most, that was the closest thing to comfort I could find.

It was way past midnight when I reached under the bed, pulled out Mum's notebook, and began flicking through the pages, my eyelids growing heavy. The words swam and shivered in front of me, words that, over the years, had sunk into my memory like debris on the ocean floor.

. . . Take me home
I've been dreaming of a girl I know . . .
. . . With a shiver on my skin
I still remember everything . . .
. . . She lives her life in pictures
She keeps secrets in her heart . . .

I pushed on, looking for one particular page.

. . . One day she will run away
When she doesn't want to be found
I'd be the one to keep her safe
But there are too many ways to escape from this town . . .

Sometimes, when I was feeling down, I would turn to this page and run over the words in my head, imagining what it would be like to step onto a train and disappear. *This town*, I always thought . . . it could have been my town. Our town. Reading had a huge train station, one of the biggest outside London, and its railway lines crept out across the countryside in every direction, like veins under skin. You could get pretty much anywhere in the country from here. There really were a hundred ways to escape from this town.

I'd never actually do it, of course.

Exhaustion curling round me like a mist, I left the notebook open on the pillow and slid beneath the duvet, clutching my family photo. The three of us on our picnic, sprawled on a tartan blanket, Mum with her hair bunched on top of her head, Dad smiling at me in the sun. Young, bright-eyed, busy with his little family.

I fell asleep with the photo in my hand.

10

The atmosphere in the assembly hall was sullen.

Students were sitting with hunched shoulders, subdued, barely a whisper troubling the air. The room, as always, smelled faintly of French fries.

Everyone knew why we were there.

"You won't be surprised to hear," Mr. Bennett was saying, his foot tapping the lip of the stage, "that we're extremely disappointed by the events of Friday night. What could have been a wonderful evening was spoiled by two students who clearly have no respect for the well-being of their peers."

Melissa cupped her hand to my ear and whispered: "Like I said, LOTS of vomming."

I shifted in my seat. As I gazed across the sea of heads in front of me, it seemed absurd that just thirty-six hours earlier I'd been taking photographs for one of the biggest bands in the world. I looked up at the stage, imagining that instead of heavy red curtains and a stack of broken tables, it was filled with gleaming instruments, a thundering drum kit, and an army of guitarists, colored lights flashing, fireworks flying. Thousands of fans screaming for Fire&Lights.

"The good news," continued Mr. Bennett, "is that we've identified the culprits, and they're being punished as we speak. However, we're going to have to think seriously about future school events if this is the way"—a collective groan from the assembly hall—"I'm sorry, but if this is what's going to happen, we may have to rethink our upcoming events. And that includes the graduation ball."

Chatter broke loose among the whole of Year Eleven. Benches creaked, voices moaned and hissed, and teachers shushed from the sides. On the stage, Mr. Bennett waited patiently for silence. Turning around, I scanned the length of the back row, up and down the benches by the vending machines, and a small, hard knot formed in my stomach.

Aimee and Gemma weren't there.

"Today we'll be talking about *your futures,*" announced Mr. Crouch, shutting the classroom door behind him. Crossing to the whiteboard, he wiped it clean with three strokes and adjusted his glasses. From the back of the room, somebody threw a tiny projectile at him, and it dinged off his shoulder. He didn't notice.

"You might not realize it yet, but decisions you make now will affect the rest of your lives," he continued, turning to face us. "And while it doesn't seem like a big d—Jamie, put your phone *away*, please. Thank you. And while it doesn't seem like a big deal now, one day soon, *I promise it will.*"

Somebody made the sound of a small, sad trumpet being played, and a ripple of laughter passed through the room.

"Year Eleven, *please.*"

A sharp knock at the door silenced the class. Shadowy figures could be seen hovering behind the frosted glass.

"Come in . . . ?"

The door opened to reveal Aimee and Gemma, flanked by the school secretary. Mr. Crouch thanked her with a nod, and she left, closing the door behind her.

"Sit down, girls," said Mr. Crouch, as Aimee and Gemma slunk into the room, eyeing the rest of us with a combination of pride and hostility. Aimee weaved toward the back, passing my desk even though it wasn't on the way, and slumped down in her usual seat between Jamie Wheeler and Sam Croft, at least one of whom was her boyfriend.

"Now then, Miss Watts, we've just been talking about our futures. Perhaps you might care to share what you have in mind for yours?"

Aimee ran her tongue across her teeth. "Prime minister."

Mr. Crouch scratched the back of his balding head and exhaled wearily.

"Aimee, now is not the time. I can send you right back to Mr. Bennett if need be."

She glanced idly at the floor. "All right, then. What if I wanna be a techno DJ?"

Mr. Crouch nudged his spectacles up his nose, put his hands on his hips, and thought for a moment. "Well, do you?"

"I dunno, whatever."

I remembered the way Aimee had looked at me on Friday night, after our encounter by the drinks table. Panic began to crackle under my skin.

"Well, it's good to follow a dream, but you need decent grades under your belt first. This is precisely why you should be knuckling down this year, not horsing around, causing mayhem."

"I don't cause mayhem," said Aimee petulantly.

There was a scuffling at the back of the room, and a pencil clattered onto the floor. Mr. Crouch's face tightened.

"Anyway," she continued, "record labels don't care about exams, sir. They just care how much you know about fat beats."

Mr. Crouch puffed his cheeks out.

"And how much *do* you know about 'fat beats'?" He made quote signs with his fingers.

"Tons, obviously," said Aimee with a smirk.

"You see, in the entertainment business," said Mr. Crouch, pacing across the front of the class, "people are looking for tenacity, ambition . . . and talent. You have to be fearless if you want to make it." He clapped his hands together. "But anyway, who else? Do we have an aspiring restaurateur in the room, perhaps? Any budding neuroscientists?"

"I'm gonna work in McDonald's, sir."

That was Jamie Wheeler.

"Your mum works in McDonald's."

And that was Sam Croft.

"Come on now, Year Eleven, settle down. You really are too old to be making silly jokes about this. Let's have a sensible answer, please . . ."

"You should ask that Charlie Bloom."

The class went silent when Aimee said my name.

"Sorry, Aimee?"

"You should ask that Charlie Bloom what she wants to be when she grows up, 'cause she's *proper clever.*"

A prickly heat rose inside me as Mr. Crouch turned to look in my direction. "Um . . . well, why not. Charlie? Any career plans? What's your passion?"

I chewed on my thumbnail. "I don't know, sir."

"Yes, you do," answered Aimee from behind me. "You're always creeping around with that stupid camera, taking pictures of us."

This set free another ripple of laughter, which Mr. Crouch waved away. I sank down into my chair.

"Well, at least Charlie's doing something *constructive* with her time, Miss Watts. I daresay she has higher career expectations than you do."

There was an instant commotion in the room, a chorus of *oooohs* and hands drumming on tables, and a mild flash of panic passed across Mr. Crouch's face. He shouldn't have said that, and he knew it.

"A-anyway," he stuttered, running the back of his hand across his brow, "enough of that. Let's, um, let's move on to today's lesson, shall we? Where did we get to last week . . . ?"

Mumbling, Mr. Crouch turned to write some notes on the board.

A thick, heavy silence fell among my classmates, and I heard a chair scrape back across the tiles. Sensing movement behind my head, I kept my eyes to the front and tried to concentrate on my workbook, but the words were no more than blurry, meaningless scribbles on the page. Soon, I could feel the whole class watching me, and Aimee's breath on the back of my neck.

Then her voice, scratchy and low, too quiet for anyone but me to hear, whispered:

"I know it was you."

11

NEW FIRE&LIGHTS SINGLE OUT TODAY

F&L release "Dance with You,"
the new single from upcoming album

Songs About a Girl

AAArrrhggh! :) :) The new Fire&Lights song came out today and it's amaaaaaaazing!!! Have you got your copy yet? If not, WHY NOT??

We reckon it's EVEN BETTER than "Have You Seen My Girl" and "Hollywood Movie Star"—and we didn't think that was POSSIBLE!! :)

Also, who's heard the rumor about Yuki getting with Jenna Jackson in a minicab outside the Candy Club?? Anyone?? What's going on? Here at FLF we all think she's a bit boring. Not good enough for our Yuki, anyway!!!!

Not long now before the album comes out—we're counting the days. What about you guys? How excited are you about SONGS ABOUT A GIRL*?? Leave us a comment, people!! xxx*

xox FIRE&LIGHTS FOREVER xox
The best Fire&Lights fan blog on the web!!

It was pandemonium in the school cafeteria. One of the Year Eight girls was standing on a chair, playing Fire&Lights songs at full blast on her phone, while around her people were dancing between tables and singing at the tops of their voices.

"The new Fire&Lights single is a-may-ZING," Melissa was saying as she examined the contents of her sandwich. "Did they play it at the concert?"

I'd been watching the main entrance since we arrived, waiting for Aimee to appear. My food sat next to me, untouched.

"I don't remember," I replied distantly. Melissa bounced up and down in her seat.

"I can't believe you were actually backstage. It's *so* epic."

I touched a finger to my mouth.

"Sssh, Melissa . . . keep it down."

She glanced around the cafeteria, then leaned in toward me. "I still don't understand why you wouldn't want people to know. It's, like, the best gossip of all time ever."

I bunched up my shoulders to keep out the cold.

The best gossip of all time ever.

"Promise you haven't told anyone . . . ?" I said, and Melissa rolled her eyes.

"Obviously not. My lips are sealed."

Across the room, the Year Eight girls were clambering onto table-tops, shrieking with laughter as they helped each other up. A bored member of the kitchen staff watched them from behind the food counter.

"Holly, get up here!"

"I can't . . . ow! Quick, grab my hand . . ."

The girls stamped their feet, singing tunelessly at each other, and I peered past them into the corridor. I could see Mr. Swift approaching from the main building, appearing and disappearing as he strode past the windows.

"So, come on. What's up?"

Melissa was waving at me.

"Huh?"

"You've been miles away all day. What's going on?"

I tugged at the back of my hat.

"It's . . . I don't know." I threw her a nervous look. "It's Aimee Watts."

Melissa pulled a face and took a big bite from her sandwich. "Aimee Watts?" She chewed for a while. "What about her?"

"She thinks I ratted on her."

"Huh?"

"At the dance, I saw her spiking the punch. She thinks it was me who turned her in."

Melissa stopped chewing. "Oh." She put down her sandwich. "Oh."

The look on Melissa's face told me I was right to be worried. Aimee had been expelled from several schools before coming to Caversham High, and rumors about what she'd done often circulated the halls in gleeful whispers. Some had to have been made up, they were so ridiculous.

I turned away from Melissa, toward the window, and shielded my eyes against the blazing winter sun.

In the courtyard, a huddle of Year Elevens was chatting and laughing, rubbing their hands together for warmth, breath escaping their mouths in chilly white clouds. Jamie and Sam were punting a tattered soccer ball against the wall; it released a dull, flabby slap with every kick. Then, just outside the circle, being talked at by a friend, I saw Aimee. Her friend was standing right next to her, but Aimee wasn't listening. She wasn't even facing her.

She was staring into the building, eyes like glass, watching me.

"Down from there, immediately!" came a commanding voice from the main entrance. It was Mr. Swift, his face a little red, pointing at the dancing Year Eight girls and waving them down. The music stopped abruptly and, cowed into a nervous silence, the girls staggered down from their tables and fussed at each other on the ground. Mr. Swift paced over to them and, with his back turned to us, reproached them in a low, firm voice.

When Melissa spoke, her voice sounded thin and reedy. "Maybe she'll let it go . . ."

I wasn't looking out of the window anymore, but I could feel Aimee's eyes all over me. Crawling up my neck.

"I want this to be over. I think I should go talk to her."

Melissa nearly choked on her sandwich. "What? What do you mean?"

"I can't just ignore it, can I? I need to talk to her."

"Her dad's been in *prison*," said Melissa, trying to catch my eye. "You don't know what she might . . ."

Cafeteria noise clattered and clanged all around us. Plates being stacked, staff collapsing tables with sharp, metallic *thwacks*. The sickly gurgle of water heaters.

I looked out of the window again, but Aimee was gone.

"Let's have you all outside in five minutes, please," said Mr. Swift to the few remaining diners, as he exited the cafeteria with a smattering of sheepish Year Eights in tow. We sat in silence for a while, the room emptying around us.

Melissa grabbed my sleeve.

"Hey, why don't we listen to the new Fire&Lights song? Might cheer you up." She presented me with a rhubarb yogurt. "You can share my dessert?"

She pointed her spoon at me. When I failed to respond, she reached forward and hung it on the end of my nose.

I laughed, and the spoon dropped off with a clang.

"Sure," I said with a sigh.

Melissa rifled through her bag and pulled out a pair of earphones, knotted like spaghetti. Untangling them, she popped in an earpiece and passed the other end to me.

"Fire&Lights fix everything, as you well know."

I cast Melissa a skeptical look, but a smile crept onto my face. She wiggled a finger at my ear.

"Quick, it's starting!"

I slid the earpiece in, and the music began to build.

"Olly sings the first bit," Melissa explained, opening her yogurt. "Just you wait. His voice sounds *soooo* dreamy in this song . . ."

As the track unfolded—an echoey guitar part curling around a steady, thumping bass drum—I thought back to Saturday night. Had they played this song at the concert? I couldn't be sure. The show had been such a blur, and from the wings, you couldn't always hear the words above the pounding of drums.

Either way, Melissa was right: Olly's voice, pure and uplifting, sounded amazing as it soared above the track. But that wasn't what caught my attention.

There was something else.

Something *extraordinary*.

It passed in an instant, and I sat back in my chair, hairs raised on the back of my neck. I must have heard it wrong. That happened all the time, didn't it? People misheard lyrics all the time.

But . . . not like this.

> Take me home
> 'Cause I've been dreaming of a girl I know
> The night draws in, and with a shiver on my skin
> I still remember everything

What I'd heard—or, at least, what I thought I'd heard—was more than a little familiar. The opening lines of the song—they could almost have come from my mother's notebook. I remembered her exact words:

> Take me home
> I've been dreaming of a girl I know
> The sweetest thing, you know she makes me wanna sing
> I still remember everything

I shook my head, like I could shake off the entire idea.

The disaster with Aimee was clouding my brain, and I wasn't thinking straight. I was hearing things. Making connections that didn't exist.

But when the second verse hit, another stream of familiar words rang out through Melissa's earpiece.

> I call her name
> I keep her picture in a silver frame
> So she will know, that if I ever come home
> She will never be alone

That verse, those lyrics, they weren't just similar to Mum's poem, they were virtually identical. As if they'd been lifted straight from the pages of her notebook.

I felt a rising pressure inside me, like someone was inflating a balloon behind my rib cage. The music crashed over me like a flood, and I shut my eyes, my breathing unsteady, the driving drumbeat thudding in my chest.

> *I wanna dance with you, girl, till the sun goes down*
> *I wanna feel every rush that you feel*
> *I wanna hear every sound when your heart cries out*
> *So sing it with me tonight*

When the final chord had faded away, I sat rooted to my chair, pulse racing, eyes fixed on the floor. I thought about asking Melissa to replay the song, so I could listen harder, just to be sure. Just to be sure I wasn't losing my mind.

Because—and I knew this was impossible, and completely crazy—but somehow, *the song was about me.*

12

I couldn't concentrate on anything else for the rest of the day.

In class, on the sodden playing fields, on the walk home with Melissa, all I could hear were those words. Words that were supposed to be mine, and mine alone, hidden from the world in a cardboard box beneath my bed.

Take me home
'Cause I've been dreaming of a girl I know . . .
I call her name
I keep her picture in a silver frame . . .

As we wandered along the main road, questions circled my brain. Did anyone else know about this? Did it mean anything if they did? How could words written by my mother and kept locked up in our house since her death, turn up thirteen years later in a famous pop song?

It was almost like someone had stolen her thoughts.

". . . Some people think Aiden's a bit too quiet, but I *like* quiet boys, you know?" Melissa was chattering happily as she walked along next to me. "That's why I chose Khaleed for my first kiss. He doesn't really *talk* much. Actually, I don't know if I've ever heard him talk. Maybe he's on a silent protest . . ."

There'd be a rational explanation, of course. Everything had a rational explanation.

I was getting carried away.

". . . There was this kid once, d'you remember, at primary school? He didn't talk for, like, three whole years. We all figured he didn't have a tongue or something. Turned out he was just Portuguese . . ."

In any case, everyone knew boy bands didn't write their own music. So where had the lyrics come from? Some random songwriter?

". . . Can you imagine if I stopped talking for three years? That would be *so weird* . . ."

Plus there were only a limited number of words in the English language. Most likely, the whole thing was nothing more than a coincidence.

". . . I suppose if I stopped talking for a while then I *might* get other things done, like my German verb tables. But then, if I couldn't speak, how would I chat with the cat or order pizz—Are you all right?" Melissa had stopped right in front of me.

"What?"

She was eyeing me from beneath her hood, which was dotted with raindrops. On the road, cars hissed through shimmering puddles.

"Everything OK? You seem a bit . . . bleh."

Despite the cold, my cheeks were flushed.

"I'm . . . fine," I replied with a shake of my head.

Melissa considered me for a moment, like a curious doctor, then took me by the hand. "I know *exactly* what you need."

*   *   *

"*Hot chocolate coming up in* five!" called Melissa's mum from the kitchen, as the kettle began to boil. Melissa and I were sitting cross-legged on her bed, the door to her room ajar, twiddling on our phones.

"Yay!" chirped Melissa, sitting up straight. Then she shot off the bed, poked her head through the gap in the door, and shouted: "Can we have marshmallows?"

"You drive a hard bargain, young lady," Rosie called back, and there was a distant *clink* as she opened the cutlery drawer. "That bedroom better be tidy when I come up there . . ."

With a gasp, Melissa slammed the door, scanned the room, and started throwing clothes into drawers and kicking piles of notes under the desk. I watched her for a while, balling up her tops and stuffing them into the back of her wardrobe.

"D'you want a hand?"

"Nope," replied Melissa, her breath short, "I'm a master at this." She whipped a collection of colored pencils into her desk drawer, chucked a handful of dirty laundry into the basket and, just as she was hanging her dressing gown on its hook, there was a knock on the other side of the door.

Melissa leaped back onto the bed, smoothed down her manic hair, and affected a laid-back tone. "Come in."

The door creaked open and Melissa's mum appeared, carrying two big, steaming mugs of hot chocolate. Her bouncy red curls were stacked high on top of her head, one or two ringlets hanging loose at the sides.

"How's the homework going?" she asked, passing us the drinks.

"We're smashing it," lied Melissa.

"Hmm," replied Rosie, casting a suspicious eye over the closed textbooks piled on the bed. "I see you've tidied up in here, though."

She surveyed the room and, noticing a pink skirt peeking out of the wardrobe door, raised a skeptical eyebrow at Melissa.

"When Charlie's left, you'll do it properly, OK?"

Melissa nodded casually, the way she always did when Rosie nagged her, and suddenly, I wanted my mum. It hit me without warning, like a knife in the side.

Rosie turned to me. "How are things with you, love?"

"Um . . . fine," I replied, wrapping both hands around my mug. It said "WORLD'S GREATEST DAD" on it. Rosie tucked a curl behind her ear and looked at me as if she understood that things weren't really fine at all.

"Well, if you need me, I'll be downstairs, working on an article." She reached for the door handle and threw a sideways glance at her daughter. "More homework, less chatter, please."

Melissa plucked a dripping marshmallow from her drink and popped it in her mouth.

"You betcha, Ma."

When Rosie was gone, Melissa sat back against the headboard and swallowed the marshmallow. She gave me a concerned look.

"You sure you're all right?" she said, reminding me, fleetingly, of her mum. "You seem, I don't know, distracted."

Our eyes met, and my fingers twitched in my lap. I thought about my mother, the ink-spattered pages of her notebook, and the stolen words in the song. I longed to tell Melissa, but the more I thought about it . . . the crazier it sounded.

Even in my own head, it was embarrassing.

"Just . . . lots going on right now," I said, breaking eye contact. "Y'know—schoolwork. Aimee Watts."

"Oh, *boooo*. That waste of space." She put on a snooty accent. "I won't have her name spoken in my house."

I attempted a smile, and Melissa set down her mug.

"If you were ever really sad," she said, "d'you know what I'd do?"

I sipped my drink.

"Put on some Fire&Lights?"

She grinned. "Well yes, obviously. But I mean, like, *really* sad. Like, if something awful had just happened and you thought the world was going to end . . . know what I'd do?"

I shook my head.

"I'd fill your bedroom with marshmallows."

I squinted at her. "What?"

"Your entire room. I'd go out and spend all my money on marshmallows, and I'd fill up your bedroom from floor to ceiling, and then we'd just sit around for hours eating and laughing. It's impossible to be sad when you're eating marshmallows. That's a scientific fact."

I looked back at Melissa, whose palms were upturned as if to say, *No, really: that's a fact,* and a little light glowed inside me.

"Right then, come on," she said, drumming her hands on the bed. "You have to tell me the story of Saturday night again. What was Aiden wearing? Did you mention that before? You might have mentioned it." She squinted, thinking. "I don't care—tell me again."

I thought back to Saturday night, the noise and mayhem of the concert, the smoke and the fireworks, the wail of guitars and the deafening thrash of the drum kit. The girls in the crowd, reaching out to their idols.

"I can't remember."

"Useless, Charlie! You're my *insider*; I want juicy details. Secrets."

"I have a question for you, actually."

Surprised, Melissa raised her chin at me. Then she sighed, and pointed at our history notes.

"Is it about Hitler's rise to power? Because I am CRAZY-BORED of all that."

"No, actually. It's not."

"Then fire away."

I could feel myself frowning. "The new single . . . what do you think it's about?"

Melissa's whole face opened, very slowly.

"I knew it!" she said, pointing at me.

"What?"

She extended her pointing arm until she was bopping me on the nose. "YOU LOVE FIRE&LIGHTS."

I batted her away, but she kept bopping me and laughing.

"No . . . no." We were both laughing now. "I don't *necessarily* love Fire&Lights."

"You're totally into them."

"No, I . . ." I grabbed both of Melissa's hands. "I just wondered, that's all."

Melissa freed herself, leaned back against the wall, and scratched her head. "Um . . . well . . . I'm not really sure."

I crossed my arms.

"There's something *you* don't know about Fire&Lights?"

"I KNOW," she replied, eyes wide.

I cleared my throat and pressed a thumb into the duvet. "So, really. You don't have any ideas?"

I looked up. Melissa's brow was furrowed.

"I dunno, it's probably about . . . well, it's just about some girl, isn't it?" she said, picking up her phone.

As she scrolled the screen, singing to herself, I stared out of the window, over the skeletal, frosted trees, and into my own bedroom across the garden. Melissa's words throbbed insistently in my mind.

It's just about some girl.

Back at home that evening, I found myself sitting on my bed, the curtains drawn, doing something I never thought I'd do.

I was watching a Fire&Lights music video on repeat.

The video for "Dance with You" was shot on the lip of a cliff, somewhere warm, probably in the Mediterranean, while a blazing red sun sank over the ocean. The camera swooped and dived above the boys as they sang, cutting between the sun-drenched cliff side and a winding mountain road, the band flying past in a sleek, open-top sports car, Gabriel at the wheel.

The song already had millions of hits.

> *Take me home*
> *'Cause I've been dreaming of a girl I know*
> *The night draws in, and with a shiver on my skin*
> *I still remember everything*

There could be no mistaking it now. The official lyrics were posted in the blurb, and they were exactly as I'd heard them the first time. Something—*something*—was going on. And I had to find out what it was.

"'Dance with You' was the third single to be released from *Songs About a Girl*, the debut album by British all-male pop group Fire&Lights . . ."

The Wikipedia page for "Dance with You" told me that the track was written by a songwriting partnership called the Speedway Collective. Clicking through to their page, I found a short entry listing all the songwriters involved, copied and pasted the names, and then fed them, one by one, into Google. This dug up little of interest: a couple of LinkedIn accounts, which didn't tell me much, and an interview with one of the writers in a music magazine. I read the whole thing, but it was mostly about technology and music software. I gazed in silence at my computer screen. It felt like a dead end.

My phone chirped at me from my desk. A reply from Olly.

Yep, all's good thanks. Been a hectic week so far!! How are you? O xx

I looked up at the Fire&Lights video I'd been playing on a loop.

Busy :) I typed back. Think those pix are nearly ready . . . shall i send them over? xx

Yep, sounds great, just dropbox them to me xx P.S. Yuki says hi :)

After editing late into the night on Sunday, I had pulled together an album of twenty photos from Reading Arena. I was certain I could do better given another chance, but even so, I was pretty proud of the shots.

If Olly liked them, I knew exactly what I was going to do next.

Ok, great, will send them over in a s

I stopped typing as I noticed the comments section under "Dance with You" refreshing with new posts. Fire&Lights videos buzzed constantly with chatter, mostly girls bickering about who was the hottest member of the band, or the occasional troll writing "this group sux" or "ur all idiots." The comment at the top of the page was written by a user called gabrielsfuturewife.

omg this song is so about me

I stared at the comment, an itchy heat flushing my face. Was that what I had become? Some sad teenage girl sitting in her bedroom convinced her favorite pop stars were singing about her? Maybe I should change my name to gabrielsfuturewife, I thought.

Ping. A message from Melissa.

Still on the hitler chapter. This is so depressing

A short pause.

Also, I DO NOT LIKE HIS MUSTACHE

I don't think you're supposed to like his mustache .

There was a longer pause. My message seemed to have stumped her.

Not sure I'm cut out for year 11 history. It's too brutal

I sent her an emoji of a little mustachioed man, and she replied, randomly, with an octopus and a cheeseburger.

Upload complete, said my computer.

The pictures were ready to send.

On Saturday night, Fire&Lights was performing in Brighton. If the boys liked what I'd done with this batch of photos, I'd decided to invite myself back again. I would tell Dad I was off to a friend's birthday party in town that day, and since Brighton was just a couple of hours from Reading on the train, provided I left for home when the concert began, I'd make it back in time for curfew.

While I was there, I'd find some answers. Surely, if I asked enough people, something was bound to come up . . . ?

Returning to my laptop, I scrolled back up the YouTube page for "Dance with You" and, for the twentieth time that night, hit refresh on the player.

Two days passed, and I heard nothing from Olly.

Doubt crept into my thoughts. Sure, the band was busy, they always were, but why hadn't he messaged, even just to say he'd received the files? What if I was wrong about the pictures, and Olly hated them? What if I'd been right the first time? I wasn't a real photographer, I was just a kid with a secondhand camera, playing at being a grown-up. And now I'd been found out.

To make matters worse, Aimee was watching me at break times. She would brush past me in the hallway, linger by my desk in class. She'd walk home in the same direction as me, but on the other side of the road, never making eye contact. Just walking.

I couldn't avoid her forever. I had to talk to her, and I had to do it alone.

"Didn't your mum ever tell you it's rude to stare?"

Aimee was loitering behind the sports hall, chewing gum. Gemma was with her, along with Jamie Wheeler and Sam Croft, and two other girls I didn't know.

"Oh, wait," Aimee added, her head cocked. "I forgot."

Sam and Jamie both sniggered. I forced my mother from my mind.

"I want to talk about the dance," I said, my voice strong and steady. Aimee didn't reply; she just reached behind her head, casually, and fiddled with her headband.

I stepped forward, and her friends bristled.

"I know you think it was me, bu—"

"Actually," she said, leaning back against the wall, "I don't think it was you." She smiled: a flat, joyless smile. "I know it was you."

The sounds of the schoolyard played out all around us. Feet scuffling on tarmac, phone message tones. A soccer ball hitting a chain-link fence.

"It's got nothing to do with me. Why would I bother telling anyone?"

Calmly, with almost a yawn, Aimee said: "I don't care why you told them."

My chest thumped. I gritted my teeth.

"Here's the thing, Charlie," she continued in a chummy, oily tone. "Thanks to you, Bennett's got me on triple after-schools until Christmas." Her nostrils flared. "My dad went mental."

Jamie whispered something to Sam, who eyed me silently, head to toe, hands stuffed in his jacket pockets.

I folded my arms. "What do you want me to say?"

"Nothing," said Aimee, picking out dirt from beneath her fingernail. "One day, though, I'll pay you back."

She locked her gaze on mine. That same hard, glassy stare from the cafeteria.

"What's that supposed to mean?"

"Exactly what I said. I'll pay you back." She paused. "You just won't know when it's coming."

We watched each other for a while, my heartbeat stuttering in my chest, her mascaraed eyes unblinking. A plane passed overhead.

"This is useless," I said, shaking my head. "I don't know why I bothered . . ."

They're just words, I told myself. *They don't mean anything.* But as I turned to walk away, there was a dead weight in my stomach, gritty like wet sand.

"Charlie?"

I turned back round. Aimee was sniffing the end of an unlit cigarette and rummaging in her pocket for a lighter. She looked up, that same joyless smile on her face, and parked the cigarette in her mouth.

"See you around, yeah?"

Later that evening, I sat on my bed, surrounded by math textbooks and geometry equipment, drawing a series of halfhearted triangles in my workbook. I could hear Dad flicking between channels downstairs: "... *despite its modest size, the long-tailed field mouse will ... much stronger season for the lads, and training's been ... Scotland Yard confirmed that Mr. Mullins had been found guilty of tax fraud, seven years prior to the incident ...*"

I could picture the scene. A pile of work files on the arm of Dad's chair, his spectacles resting on top. Glass of red wine on the table.

We hadn't spoken much since the night of the concert.

Hey charlie!!

A Facebook notification hit my phone. When I saw the name, a rush of relief passed through me.

Hey olly ... you good? Did you get my photos?

Yep, got em, sorry i've been slow messaging u back. We just flew out to Dublin for a TV interview, it's been a bit crazy!

Downstairs, a studio audience applauded.

Anyway, we've all been checking out your pics today, and they look incredible!! I passed them on to our media team—they should be on the site by now

A smile spread across my face, and I closed my workbook.

Awesome, thanks. Just taking a look ...

I loaded up the Fire&Lights website, and as the home page appeared—a photo of the boys standing on a rooftop at night, city skyline blazing behind them—a cluster of hot nerves gathered in my belly. Clicking through to the fan page, I held my breath, unsure whether to feel excited or scared.

Found em yet? ;)

The banner at the top of the page read *FIRE&LIGHTS: FAN HQ*, and underneath were rows and rows of images of the boys, mostly backstage at gigs or on the tour bus. No photo shoots or staged pictures, just simple, candid shots of life on the road.

And there, about ten rows down, were the photos from Reading Arena.

My. Photos.

Oh my god . . . i see them

There was the picture of Yuki, launching peanuts into his mouth during makeup; Olly, lying on a sofa with his feet up, smiling at his bandmates; Gabriel, dancing with a fan at the after-party. And finally, perhaps my favorite image of the night: a simple shot of Aiden's guitar, propped up in the corner of the empty dressing room, a pile of his trademark wristbands nestled beside it.

Have you read the comments? wrote Olly. The fans are loving it!

He was right. Underneath each photo was a long stream of comments, every single one of them positive.

love love LOVE this shot!

sooooo cute <3 <3

mega cool photo woo-hooooooo

best pic EVER of gabriel!! xxxxx

I scrolled up and down the screen, my chest thumping. As promised, they hadn't published my name, but here was my work—*my photography*—being enjoyed by more people than I could ever, ever have imagined. I dropped back against the headboard, my cheeks tingling. It felt amazing.

I typed out a reply to Olly.

Wow . . . i can't believe my pix got used. Thank you so much

No need to thank me, charlie. You deserve it

I allowed myself a little squeak and sent a message to Melissa.

My shots got used on the F&L site

WHAT. THE. ACTUAL

I glanced out my window. Across the garden, I could see Melissa sitting at her computer, mug of hot chocolate steaming beside her.

On the fan page, about halfway down. Starts with a pic of yuki eating peanuts

Oh my gosh, I'm looking right now . . .

Melissa's head flitted from side to side as she took in the pictures, her finger trailing across the screen. She picked up her phone again, typing madly.

Charlie charlie charlie. So proud of u. SO PROUD. I may cry

A pause.

I am crying

Melissa turned, noticed me watching her, and padded over to the window. We grinned at each other across the divide, and then she wiped her eyes and gave me a big, goofy thumbs-up.

The phone rang in the hallway. I could hear Dad's chair creaking as he stood up, and the television being muted. I began another message to Olly.

Olly, i was thinking . . .

Beep-and-click: Dad picking up the receiver. His tone was hard, irritable. A cold caller.

. . . i'm free on saturday if you could use me at the brighton gig . . . ??

For thirty long seconds, I received no reply. I reread my message, finger tapping the screen. Was I asking too much? Was this only ever meant to be a onetime thing?

Definitely! came Olly's reply. We'd love that :)

A relieved laugh tumbled out of me, and my phone blipped again.

Maybe you could come down even earlier, get some pics of us with the fans, press, etc . . . ??

Great idea. :)

Tell you what, continued Olly, as I beamed at the screen, I'll get management to courier your wristband to you 2moro . . . that way you can arrive whenever you want, even if i'm busy. Sound good?

Sounds perfect. I'll aim for half past four. Can't wai

"Charlie?"

My father's voice, muffled by the bedroom door. Locking my phone, I hid it under the covers and leaned back against the end of the bed.

"Yep?"

The door opened and Dad tentatively set one foot inside the room.

"Can we talk a minute?"

I picked up a pencil and opened my math book.

"Sure."

Dad hovered. More muffled applause from the television.

"Homework going well?" he asked.

"Sort of. Pythagoras."

"Ah," he said, with a slow nod. "That old chestnut. The square of the hypotenuse is equal to the sum of the—"

"—squares of the other two sides," I said, tugging my sleeves down over my wrists. Dad smiled, frowned, then stared out the window.

In the distance, a dog barked.

"Charlie, I'm sorry about the other night." He rubbed the side of his neck. "I was annoyed about you missing curfew, but I shouldn't have . . . well. What I said, it was . . ."

"It's OK."

Dad cleared his throat.

"I hope I didn't upset you, talking about Katherine."

The word sounded stiff and formal in his mouth. She wasn't some woman named Katherine. She was my mum.

"I'm fine, Dad."

Dad's eyes made an awkward tour of my bedroom, as if something on the walls or the floor might help him understand me.

"Are you sure?"

"Yep."

He ventured across the room and sat down on the end of the bed. A protractor got caught under his leg. He plucked it out.

"D'you know, I was thinking today about that one Christmas—d'you remember, you were about seven—when Melissa brought that plastic microphone over and the two of you stomped around the house all day, singing at the tops of your voices." He smiled at the memory. "Singing your little hearts out."

I remembered every detail of that microphone set. The white, spongy head, the red plastic handle, the musical stickers on the side. We ran the batteries right down.

"Yeah . . . yeah, I do."

"It was 'Cat's in the Cradle,' wasn't it?"

I nodded.

"We used to listen to that song all the time when you were tiny, in the car and things. It was . . ." He hesitated, as if unsure whether to continue. "It was Katherine's favorite."

I stared at the floor, thoughts forming in my mind. Dad had never told me this before, but it made perfect sense. No wonder the song was always in my head. In fact, if "Cat's in the Cradle" really was Mum's favorite song, and we used to listen to it in the car when I was a kid, then maybe the memory I'd attached to it, the motorway and the radio and the orange lights dashing by . . . maybe that was real, too.

"Dad?"

He raised his head, drowsily.

"Uh-huh?"

"What was Mum like?"

A strange look drifted over Dad's face. He seemed almost panicked, like this was an exam question he hadn't revised for.

"What was she . . . ?" He searched for the words. "Well . . . she . . ."

I held my breath, willing him to finish the sentence. Dad spotted a crease in my duvet and tugged it flat.

"She was . . . smart. Especially with words. And funny, too."

I was sitting perfectly still, afraid to move, as if movement would break the spell, and Dad would close up again.

"She was fearless," he continued, half to himself. "She wasn't afraid of anything. And, boy, was she *stubborn* . . ."

The sound of a neighbor locking their car, *bip-crunch*, interrupted Dad's flow. Smart shoes paced up a gravel drive.

"Stubborn?" I repeated, prompting him. Dad looked up and allowed himself a smile.

"She hated being told what to do. I've always been a worrier, but your mum . . . she never worried. She lived her own way."

I thought back to our fight in the hallway, after the Fire&Lights concert. Dad stressing out because I'd missed curfew, me answering back. *Stop being dramatic*, I'd said. No wonder I'd reminded him of Mum.

"Anyway. That's all in the past now."

Dad was looking out into the garden, his eyes glazed. In the silence, I noticed one of his socks had a hole in the toe, and for some reason it made me feel very sad.

"We're all right, though, aren't we?" he said, turning back into the room. "You and me?"

There was so much more I wanted to know. But this was more than I'd got from Dad in years, and I didn't want to push it.

"Yeah, I guess."

"I know it's just you and me here, kiddo, but we're still a family."

Dad's gaze met mine, and I saw, for a vanishing moment, the young man on the picnic blanket. The bright eyes, that unshakable smile.

"I know, Dad."

"You're sixteen now, and I need to give you space. That's what Katherine would have told me. I just . . . I need you to promise you'll stick to my rules. OK?"

I thought of Olly's message, hidden beneath the duvet, and my half-written reply. I said, "OK," very quietly, and Dad passed me my protractor.

It would take me less than three days to break that promise.

13

An icy wind was blowing through the concourse at Reading station, and I wrapped my scarf tightly around my neck to keep out the chill. It was early afternoon on a Saturday and I was standing motionless in the middle of a busy crowd, hundreds of people milling and chatting and scurrying around me.

Dad thought I was going to a friend's party, but that had been a lie.

I was going to Brighton to hang out with a world-famous pop band.

As echoey announcements rang out around the building, I stared across the platforms and watched a cross-country service rumble in and slow to a stop, a sea of passengers surging toward it. People funneled into the carriages, herding small children and waving good-bye to friends, dragging their wheeled suitcases, and I wondered where they were headed. London, Cornwall, Birmingham, Manchester . . .

There are too many ways to escape from this town.

"This is a customer announcement: The two-ten to Gatwick Airport will now depart from platform five."

It was two o'clock, and that was my train. Weaving through the crowds, I made my way down a nearby escalator, gazing out across the concrete flats of the Reading skyline. As I reached the platform and the train pulled in, from the tinny speakers of someone's mobile phone came the sound of a familiar song.

> *. . . Take me home*
> *'Cause I've been dreaming of a girl I know . . .*

Everywhere I go, I thought, *Fire&Lights is there.*
And I stepped onto the train.

Brighton was nothing like Reading. It was colorful and pretty and smelled like the sea, and the sloping streets were lined with scruffy little shops and bustling pubs. There were musicians everywhere—buskers on street corners, kids carrying guitars, long-haired hippies chatting in café windows.

I was walking along the busy main road, weaving through crowds on the pavement, when the big, choppy ocean crept into view. The afternoon had been sunny, but now the air felt thick and heavy, like rain was coming, so I hurried down the street to the seafront. Seagull song mingled with the sound of passing cars.

Outside the concert venue, an excitable crowd of Fire&Lights fans had gathered, singing and shrieking at each other and playing "Dance with You" on their phones. One of them was holding a banner that said "HANDS OFF—OLLY'S MINE!!!" Underneath the words she'd glued a photo of herself next to Olly's face, with a big, red heart in between.

This time, I walked straight up to the nearest bouncer, told him I was one of the band's photographers, and showed him my VIP wristband. He let me through without question.

I could feel the eyes of every single girl in the queue boring into me from behind.

"Hey, it's Charlie!"

Around the back of the building, propped up beside the stage door reading a book, was Yuki. He had one booted foot pressed against the wall, tattered laces hanging down. A security guard stood a meter or so behind him, hands folded at his belt line.

"Hey," I replied, glancing up at the bruising sky. Rain was now definitely on the way. "What are you doing out here?"

"Enjoying some quiet time," he said, raising his book as evidence. "We've got a meet-and-greet with the fans in a sec. Tons of fun, man, but cah-ray-ZY."

I pointed at his book.

"What are you reading?"

He showed me the cover. It was called *The Human Genome*.

"Kinda nerdy for a rock star, isn't it?" I said.

Yuki held up his hands in surrender. "You got me. I'm a nerd."

I glanced at his spiky, anarchic hair and black sleeveless shirt, his skinny jeans torn at the knee.

"You hide it well."

He smiled.

"You should give it a read. Blow your mind."

I peered again at the cover.

"I don't know. Looks a bit too much like Mrs. Manning's physics class to me."

"Knowledge is power, Charlie Bloom," he said, snapping the book shut. "D'you know who said that?"

"Um . . . no?"

"Me neither. Jesus? Socrates? Who can say." He sucked in air through his nostrils. "Point is, one day, when I'm an eccentric billionaire with a string of supermodel wives and a helipad in my bedroom, I'm going to leave pop music behind and go into something else."

Yuki's eyes twinkled in the fading light. I leaned against the wall next to him.

"Like what?"

"Extreme sports. Aid work. Astrophysics."

"Astrophysics?"

"Or maybe stem cell research." He smirked. "My only worry is deciding which of my messed-up children gets to inherit the guitar-shaped swimming pool."

"It's a tough life," I agreed, and Yuki sighed theatrically. The security guard shuffled his feet.

"So how are you finding it?" asked Yuki.

I frowned at him. "Finding what?"

"This. Fire&Lights. Stepping behind the curtain."

A drop of rain landed on my nose. I blew it off.

"You lot are totally dysfunctional. I give you six months before you're all in rehab."

A smile broke onto my face and Yuki laughed, switching his feet against the wall. I straightened my hat.

"Can I ask you something?" he said.

I nodded.

"You're not really a *fan*, are you?"

I broke eye contact, suddenly very aware of the sound of girls singing and shrieking around the corner.

"Um . . . n-no, course I am. You guys are awesome."

"I mean, before Olly gave you The Opportunity Of A Lifetime and you started hanging out with pop stars . . . you weren't actually *into* the band, were you?"

I looked up. He was staring right at me.

"Well . . . look, no offense, but—"

"None taken, Charlie Bloom, none taken. I'm more into psychedelic rock myself." He poked his tongue into his cheek. "But honestly, that's fine by me. We meet girls every day, wherever we go, and some of them can be a bit . . . you know . . ."

He searched for the right words. I shoved my hands into my pockets.

"Intense and weepy?" I said, and Yuki sniggered. Then he grinned at me.

"Yeah. Yeah, exactly."

"Hey, Charlie!" Olly had appeared in the open doorway.

"Sorry I'm late," he said, pointing back inside the building with an outstretched thumb. "I was going through harmonies. You good?"

"I'm good."

The dying afternoon light fell across Olly's face as he leaned through the doorway. He was wearing a small silver pendant round his neck, and a tight-fitting, sky-blue T-shirt that matched his eyes.

"Yuki's not trying to make you read *The Human Genome*, is he?" Olly asked, glancing at his bandmate.

I wrinkled my nose. "A bit."

Olly jabbed him in the ribs.

"You're such a geek, Harrison."

"Better a geek than a freak."

"You wanna piece of me?" joked Olly, pulling him into a headlock, and the two boys tussled and tumbled through the door.

The guard nodded at me, and I followed them inside.

"Right, can we have those lighting cues locked down by five forty-five latest, DSM, stand by for props inventory, stage crew, report for drum soundcheck in five minutes *exactly*, please . . ."

Backstage, things were as hectic as last weekend, if not more so. There was the customary buffet table, piled high with sandwiches and fruit and potato chips, the legions of staff buzzing one way and the next, and the bearded men carrying cables and stands. Wherever I stood, it seemed I was in somebody's way.

"So how's school?" asked Olly, appearing by my side. I was leaning against the back of a sofa.

"School?" I puffed my cheeks out. "It's quite a bit less exciting than hanging out with you guys."

He laughed. "You'll be out soon."

It was easy to forget that just two years ago, Olly had been an ordinary Caversham High student. The idea of him queuing up outside classrooms, wearing our uniform, sitting through tedious assemblies . . . it was still so jarring.

"You make it sound like prison," I said.

"Nah," he replied with a wave of his hand. "The food is *way* better in prison."

We shared a smile, and Olly leaned against the sofa, next to me.

"So you guys have been busy?" I said.

"Always are."

"I heard the new single. It's great."

How much does he know? I wondered, thinking about "Dance with You" and the Speedway Collective. Olly was probably friends with the songwriters. They might even come to the concerts, now and again. Maybe I could meet them, talk to them . . . find out where their songs came from.

I opened my mouth to speak.

"Hey, listen," said Olly, before I could get the words out, "I've got something for you."

I looked at him, surprised.

"What do you mean?"

"D'you remember before the gig last week, when we were talking about your photography?"

"Yep . . ."

"You seemed a bit down about having a secondhand camera, so I gave it some thought, and . . ."

Olly bent down, past the arm of the sofa, and reappeared holding a soft black case with "CANON" written across it. He passed it to me.

"What's this?" I asked, although I knew exactly what it was.

"It's a camera," he said, nodding at it. I unclipped the lid and, inside, was a brand-new Canon EOS. My dream camera.

There was even a second lens, stowed in a side pocket.

"What . . . what's this for?"

He was staring straight at me.

"For you."

I tried to pass it back to him. "I can't take this, Olly."

"Yes, you can."

"I mean, it's really, *really* unbelievably kind of you, but . . . these things cost, like, six hundred pounds."

"Don't worry, honestly," he replied, pushing the case back toward me. "They pay us too much for this job anyway. All we do is run around and sing songs. It's people like you who do all the hard work."

He smiled at me, that perfect smile I'd seen a hundred times on the covers of magazines, and I fumbled for the right words.

"But . . . this is the camera I've always . . . God, how did you know?"

"It was written under one of your photos."

I frowned back at him. "What do you mean?"

"The Diamond Storm gig. In the comments."

Thinking back through the photo album I'd posted online, I realized what he meant. Beneath one of the pictures, I had written:

This photo's ok, but I couldn't get the light right. I definitely need a Canon EOS . . . #dreamcamera #iwish

I was astonished. This was pretty much the nicest thing anyone had ever done for me.

"Charlie!"

Aiden was hopping toward us with one shoe on.

"H-hi, Aiden," I said, still reeling.

Aiden beamed at me. "How's it going?"

"I'm . . . good, thanks."

I stared at the camera case in my hands, then over at Olly, then back at Aiden.

"I saw your photos from last week," said Aiden, slipping on his second shoe. "They're excellent."

"Really . . . ?"

He nodded, green eyes gleaming.

"Thanks. But I think I can do bette—"

"Boys," said a nearby woman with a headset, checking her watch. "Everyone's waiting in the enclosure. You guys ready?"

Yuki was standing behind the headset woman, unscrewing a bottle of water. He threw me a peace sign, and I smiled. Scanning the room, I spotted Gabriel in the far corner, by the exit, leaning against the wall. Dark loops of hair covered his face.

Olly stood up.

"Let's do this," he said.

The woman's eyes fell on me. "Who are you?"

"I'm Char—"

"She's with us," said Olly, stepping forward.

The woman's gaze lingered on mine. "Oh."

She blinked at me, silently, then clicked her fingers at the boys. "Come on then, guys, chop-chop . . ."

As the woman gathered Yuki, Aiden, and Olly into one group and guided them across the room toward Gabriel, I followed behind, blood rushing to my face. Why did the Fire&Lights management team always treat me like a hanger-on? It was their idea to bring me here in the first place.

"Wassup, Westie?" said Yuki, high-fiving Gabriel. "Where you been all my life?"

"Carla's here again," said Gabriel, peeling off the wall. As he joined the group, his eyes passed almost imperceptibly over mine. "And she brought her friends. I kind of had to say hello."

The group broke down into pairs as we passed into a narrow corridor, and I hung back, lifting the new camera from its case. I switched it on and the display screen lit up, a busy grid of numbers and symbols, blinding white in the dark. The machine felt clean and heavy in my hands.

"Boy, is that girl into you," said Yuki, patting Gabriel on the back, and I clicked the shutter to capture it.

Snap. *Dead on.*

"OK, so there's quite a few tabloids with us today," said the woman with the headset as we reached the end of the corridor. "Couple of music mags too, some bloggers. Give 'em some airtime, sign some autographs, then it's back inside in ten for makeup. Got it?"

With a loud clack, she pushed open the fire doors and the band strode out to the frantic clattering of cameras. I followed behind at a distance, my finger poised on the shutter release, eagerly snapping as I walked.

We were standing in a fenced-off enclosure, hidden away around the back of the building. Penned in behind a temporary barrier were, on one side, a screaming group of fans, and on the other, a jostling scrum of journalists. Bouncers stood guard at either end.

Olly, Gabriel, Yuki, and Aiden walked over to meet them, and the fans surged forward, holding out pens, scraps of paper, books, and posters for signing. The press barked questions over their heads.

"Hey, Gabriel. Gabriel!"

Gabriel was busy signing a girl's autograph book. When he'd finished, he leaned down and whispered something in her ear. Her eyes widened, her mouth fell open, and she bounced up and down with joy.

"Gabriel?"

Patiently, he returned the girl's autograph book.

"Yup?"

"Tell us about you and Carla," said a heavyset man with wiry, white-blond hair. "You guys together?"

"Yeah, Carla! Carla Martinez!"

"Are you an item?"

"Gabe!"

Gabriel raised both hands. "We're friends, and that's it. She's cool, but we're just . . . friends."

There was a brief pause, journalists glancing at each other, then back at Gabriel. The *clickety-clack* of photographs began to swell, and Gabriel returned to signing autographs.

Seconds later, the questions erupted again.

"Where's Barry King? Is he here?"

"Who's the girl in *Songs About a Girl*, lads? Give us a clue!"

"Gabe, is it Ella Mackenzie?"

For a moment, I was transported back to my bedroom and the lyrics in Mum's notebook. My face flushed red as I remembered how many times I'd watched the video for "Dance with You," and the You-Tube comment from gabrielsfuturewife. *This song is so about me . . .*

"Is it Ella, Gabe? Or Carla?"

"What about Tammie Austin?"

Tammie Austin was one of the biggest movie stars in Hollywood; Melissa and I had been to see her in a cheesy romantic comedy only a few weeks earlier. She was exactly the sort of girl a pop star actually *would* write an album about.

"Ella says she wants you back, Gabe!"

"Yeah, she definitely wants you back!"

The reporters weren't letting up. Gabriel smiled roguishly and signed a fan's poster with a flourish.

"We both know that's not true."

"Sure it is! Why did you guys break up?"

"Gabe! Gabe!"

I was in the middle of framing a shot of Gabriel posing for a selfie with a group of fans, when I noticed something over his shoulder. Pushing his way through the crowd was a tough, grizzled-looking man with patchy stubble and eyes like little black stones. He was shouting Gabriel's name and shouldering people out of his way. When he'd made it to the front, he waved a digital recorder in Gabriel's face.

"Tell us about your mum and dad."

Gabriel stopped in the middle of a signature. "What?"

"Go on," said the man, with a sniff. "Tell us about your parents."

Gabriel lowered his pen. "I don't talk about my family. You guys know that."

The man's nose twitched, like a rodent.

"Come on, mate. You said they're living in the South of France. They must be proud of you, yeah? Their pop-star son?"

Gabriel finished the autograph and passed it over the barrier to a girl in a Fire&Lights hoodie. As he did with every fan, he was careful to make eye contact with her before moving on. Her cheeks turned red, and her eyes welled up.

"Next question."

"Olly! Hey, Olly!" Attention swung across the yard, and the jungle of cameras and sound recorders pointed suddenly in Olly's direction. For a second I kept my lens fixed on Gabriel, which meant I was probably the only person to see the look he was giving the pushy journalist. His brow was lowered, jaw clenched. Eyes unblinking.

I caught it on camera.

"We talked to Jake last week," said a woman in a high-collared coat, thrusting a microphone toward Olly. "He's still pretty cut up—what d'you say about that?"

Olly exhaled and stepped backward from the crowd. Beside him, Yuki and Aiden were scribbling autographs and posing for selfies.

"Jake's a good friend of mine," he said, sticking his hands in his pockets. "He'll be OK. He'll bounce back."

"It's pretty bad, though, what happened. Don't you think?"

For the briefest split second, Olly's eyes flickered toward Gabriel.

"Jake's cool; he'll be fine."

I lowered my camera. Was I missing something here? Who was Jake?

"Sorry, everyone, that's time!" said the headset woman, herding up the boys with outstretched arms. They waved at the fans and walked backward toward the fire doors, girls screaming, journalists yelling questions, the man with the grizzled face eyeing Gabriel until the end.

"Charlie."

Back inside, I was sliding my camera into its case when Olly took me aside. "We're off to makeup in a bit," he said. "You OK to make your own way to the green room?"

Olly gave me directions and said he would meet me there when they were done. As he talked, I couldn't help but notice that while Yuki and Aiden were chatting behind him, Gabriel had, once again, disappeared.

"So how's the camera working out for you?"

I snapped back into the room. Olly was waiting for my reply.

"Oh my God . . . it's great, Olly. It's perfect."

He smiled.

"Good."

"I can't thank you enough."

"Hey," he said, as the woman in the headset took him by the arm. "You don't need to thank me. Honestly."

She began to lead him away.

"Just try not to get lost," he said, as I took in my surroundings. "This place is a labyrinth!"

Soon I was alone in the corridor, camera hanging off my shoulder, listening to the hum of the crowds outside. Slipping through a side door, I began to make my way through the maze of backstage passages, trying to remember Olly's directions. I messaged Melissa as I walked.

So brighton is waaaay nicer than reading

What's happening?? Any gossip?

I stopped and looked around. Predictably, I had already taken a wrong turn.

I pushed on.

Olly bought me a camera

WTF??!?!?

Yep, a canon EOS. Brand new

Hashtag dream camera!!

I know. I can't believe it

I came up against a door marked "NO EXIT." Turning around, I tried retracing my steps for a while, but it was no use. I was lost, and wandering the corridors virtually at random.

Wait . . . wait. Charlie. OLLY IS SO INTO U

Chill out, mel, he's just being nice

Classic Melissa, I thought, as I watched the last bar of signal disappear from my phone.

Always fantasizing.

Slipping my phone into my pocket, I tried a nearby door and, to my surprise, it opened. Behind it was a small, dusty room covered in fuse boxes and exposed wires. Walking through, I pulled aside a curtain and found myself standing in the wings at the side of the stage.

This was bad. I wasn't supposed to be here yet, especially not on my own. I searched around for another way out.

And that was when I heard his voice.

14

The voice was deep and a little husky, and he was singing very quietly, as if to himself.

I knew the voice instantly, and I knew the song too. I knew it very well indeed.

It was "Cat's in the Cradle."

"Gabriel?"

He turned round, slowly, as if he already knew it was me.

"Charlie Brown. What's happening?"

"My na . . . It's Bloom."

"I know," he said, "but I like Charlie Brown."

"Charlie Brown's a boy."

I blushed instantly. What kind of response was that? I waited for Gabriel to reply, but he said nothing. He just watched me, silently, from behind those dark, cascading locks of hair.

"I'm kinda lost," I said, the lyrics to "Cat's in the Cradle" now spinning through my brain. Gabriel smiled.

"You're not the only one."

"I mean . . . I shouldn't really be back here."

He shrugged.

"Neither should I. Wanna see the stage?"

Before I knew what was happening, Gabriel had taken me by the hand. I stammered out a halfhearted protest.

"I don't really think I'm supposed to . . ."

But my words trailed away as Gabriel dragged me from the dark, through thick black curtains, and out onto the stage. Immediately my world lit up, a burst of blinding lights flooding my vision, bleaching everything white, and I lifted an arm to shield my eyes. When the glare had faded, I found myself standing in the center of an impossible scene, hand in hand with a pop star, like two tiny figurines in a snow globe. I gazed up at the high ceiling, and then over my shoulder, struggling to take everything in: the network of runways; the giant Fire&Lights banner hanging on the back wall; the gleaming bank of guitars, keyboards, drum kits, and microphones surrounding us on all sides. Finally, beyond the stage loomed the auditorium, vast and empty, ready to be filled by the crowds I'd seen queuing outside. Everything was pin-drop silent, awaiting the rush of thousands.

As we stood there alone, still connected at the fingers, I felt dizzy with awe.

It was breathtaking.

"Pretty special, huh?"

Rows and rows of empty seating fanned away from the stage, lighting rigs hung like scaffolding above our heads, instruments glistened, and the air tingled with anticipation. This, it dawned on me, was the view Gabriel had almost every night. This, but with thousands of girls screaming his name.

This was *normal* for him.

"How do you . . . I mean . . ." My mouth felt dry, the words stumbling out. "This is unbelievable."

Gabriel let go of my hand, and his fingertips brushed against mine. "We should take some photos."

I laughed.

"Wh—what do you mean, take photos?"

His eyes were locked on me.

"You're a photographer, aren't you?"

"Well, yes, but—"

"So don't you think you should be doing your job?"

I tried to smile, but my muscles wouldn't move. Was he serious, or just toying with me?

"I don't think so," I replied, hitching the camera bag up my shoulder. I gave him a look that I hoped conveyed disapproval, but in truth I was still thinking about his hand wrapped around mine.

"I'm your boss, technically, so really it's my decision." He clicked his fingers. "Pass the camera."

I lifted the camera off my shoulder and passed it to him. He unzipped the case, pulled out the Canon, and scratched his head.

"Fancy machine."

"It was a present," I replied. "From Olly."

A shadow passed over his eyes.

"What?"

"I know—crazy, right? He just gave it to me, out of the blue."

Gabriel stared at the camera. He seemed to be thinking, very carefully, about something. Then, switching it on, he closed the gap between us, held the camera out at arm's length with the lens pointing back in our direction and began rapidly clicking the shutter release.

His palm was pressing against the small of my back. I wondered if I should step away, but for some reason, I didn't.

"This is you," he was saying, snapping and pointing at seemingly random angles. "This is you, onstage with a celebrity, and on Monday you can show this to all your friends at school, and—"

"I don't have that many friends."

"Nice, Charlie Brown. Nice."

"But—"

"You can go into school next week, you can show these pics to all your friends, and everyone will think *you*"—he aimed one final shot at us, more carefully this time, and clicked the release—"are the coolest damn human being on the planet."

I grabbed for the camera, but he held it out of my reach. He was studying the image on the screen.

"That's not bad," he said. "Take a look."

Slipping the strap around my neck, I stared down at the screen and saw myself—Charlie Bloom of 33 Tower Close, Reading—standing next to Gabriel West from Fire&Lights, alone onstage in an empty venue.

"So what d'you wanna do now?" he asked, as if we were the only two people alive on earth.

"Well . . . shouldn't you be in makeup?"

"Makeup? Like they could improve on this?"

He made a circular gesture round his face with one finger. I crossed my arms.

"What, I'm kidding," he said, running a hand through his wavy hair, sending the dark locks tumbling. I didn't answer. "You know the whole arrogant-pop-star thing is an act, right?"

I shrugged.

"Unless . . . don't tell me you believe everything you read on the Internet?"

"If you mean gossip sites," I said smugly, "I don't read them."

"Yeah, well. That's good. You shouldn't."

Talking about gossip seemed to rile him. I decided to change the subject.

"That song," I said, nodding back toward the wings. "The one you were singing when I found you . . ."

Gabriel said nothing. He just watched, and waited.

"Why were you singing it?"

He stuck his hands in his pockets.

"It's kind of a warm-up."

"Right, but . . . why that song?"

"Why any song?"

I bit my tongue. It was maddening, the way he kept dodging me.

"Shouldn't you be warming up with the others, though?"

"Well, I don't . . . I mean . . . it works better on my own."

Unusually for Gabriel, he seemed flustered by this. Was he embarrassed that I'd busted him? The great Gabriel West, too important to warm up with his bandmates?

"I used to listen to 'Cat's in the Cradle' when I was a kid," I said, casually. "It's a great song."

Gabriel nodded, and I tried to read his strangely blank expression. He was either disinterested in my questions or spooked. And what exactly was I planning to say to him, anyway? *Hey, Gabriel, it turns out you like a song that my dead mother also liked, once.* It would have sounded pretty random to anyone else, but in my head . . . in my head it felt like a piece in a puzzle that I hadn't realized I was trying to solve.

"Follow me."

Suddenly, Gabriel was striding up a nearby runway toward a square, railed platform, high up above the main stage. I trailed him along the steep ramp, peering down at the instruments below me: the glistening cymbals, the rows of guitars.

Gabriel reached the platform and sat down on the edge. He raised his chin at me.

"You joining?"

Hanging my camera on the metal railing, I lowered myself down and threaded my feet through the rails. We sat there in silence for a moment, our legs dangling over the side, the great empty space staring back at us. Dust motes floated in the black.

"Best seat in the house, huh?"

Gabriel's voice floated out into the yawning silence.

"It's all right," I said, with a smile.

"Well, I like it." He looked at his feet. "Calms me down."

I leaned my elbows on the railing.

"So come on, seriously . . . what were you doing back there on your own?"

He sniffed.

"Stalking victims, mainly. Did I mention I'm a vampire?"

"Was that supposed to be a joke?" I said dryly.

"I don't tell jokes, Charlie Brown."

"Just as well."

I adjusted my hat.

"It's a bit weird, though, don't you think? Hanging out here on your ow—"

I cut myself off, as Gabriel didn't seem to be listening. He was lowering himself, backward, to the ground. Soon he was lying completely flat against the platform.

"What are you doing?"

He looked up at me.

"Lie down."

"Excuse me?"

He made a flattening gesture with his hand.

"Lie down."

I obliged guardedly, watching him from the corner of my eye.

"Now look up."

He pointed upward, to the ceiling, and I followed the line of his finger into the vaulting recesses of the building. Above our heads was a complex network of metal poles, on which hung a dazzling array of stage lights in a rainbow of colors, dotting the black expanse like stars in the night sky.

My lungs filled with air.

"Pretty cool, right?"

"Right," I said breathily, blinking in the glare. It was stunning.

Gabriel pointed over to the right, where three yellow lights hung in a curved row.

"That, Charlie Brown . . . is Orion's Belt."

I smiled, and he moved his pointing finger back over to the left.

"That big guy on the end, that's, like, Jupiter or whatever . . . and *that*"—he indicated a tight cluster of lights, some red, some blue—"that is, um . . . Ursa Major."

I laughed.

"You are so full of it."

He tilted his head toward me.

"Do you want to learn or not?"

I turned my face to his. In the distance, very faintly, I could hear the screaming of fans.

"What's your deal, Charlie Brown?"

I drew my head back slightly.

"My deal?"

"You know . . . your deal. Who are you?" A lock of hair fell down in front of his eyes, and he brushed it away. "Got any secrets?"

"What?"

"I'd like to hear a secret, please."

"What . . . kind of secret?"

"Anything. But if it isn't really a secret, I'll know."

It was hard to think with his eyes fixed on me.

"I . . . can't think of anything."

"Then try harder," he teased.

"Fine. But you have to tell me one in return."

Gabriel smiled, a smile that threatened to envelop the world.

"You haggling with me?"

"No," I said, faking a sulk. "But fine, you win." I thought for a moment. "When I was nine, I stole a mechanical pencil from the school cupboard. Never took it back."

"Wow," mocked Gabriel. "I didn't have you pegged as a rebel."

I glowered at him.

"Charlie Brown, pencil thief."

"My turn," I said. "And no dodging this time."

He looked up at the ceiling again.

"Fair enough."

"Who are the Speedway Collective?"

He eyed me sideways.

"You've got a lot of questions for a photographer, y'know."

"Hey," I said, kicking my feet against the wall. "I gave you one of my best secrets."

"That is true," he conceded.

"So who are they?"

He paused, and sat up.

"Have you been Googling Fire&Lights?"

"*No*," I said, sitting up next to him, my elbows on the railings. "Wikipedia, actually."

Gabriel leaned back on his palms.

"Speedway writes our songs. Hitmakers, Barry calls them."

"Do you guys know them? The writers, I mean?"

"We meet up pretty regularly. They bring the music to us, Barry picks the best stuff, words get added on top."

I narrowed my gaze.

"What do you mean, the words get added? They don't write the lyrics?"

Gabriel shook his head.

"Who does, then?"

There was a wall of spotlights at the far end of the stage, behind Gabriel's head. As I looked at him, he was half silhouetted against the bright, burning lamps, tousled hair framed in white.

His eyes gleamed at me as he replied.

"I do."

15

"You write the words?"

My voice was forceful, a little on edge.

Gabriel laughed to himself. "I'm not as simple as I look, you know."

I stared out into the empty auditorium, my mind beginning to race.

Take me home . . . 'cause I've been dreaming of a girl I know . . .

"But it didn't mention that online . . ."

"It's kind of a new thing. Barry's been trying me out, for the album."
He tipped his head to one side. "You OK?"

I stalled, for slightly too long, before replying.

"Yep. No, yep, I'm fine. It's just . . . some of your lyrics, they—"

"Um, hello, *Gabriel?*"

A hint of irritation twitched across Gabriel's face at the sound of
the voice from behind. He looked over my shoulder and gave a small,
weak-armed wave.

"Oh . . . hey, Carla . . ."

High heels clopped toward us across the stage, and we pulled ourselves up by the railings. Carla's hair was swooshing as she walked,
glowing with an impossible, shampoo-advertisement shine.

"Yuki said I might find you up here," she said playfully. Her eyes made a fleeting glance in my direction before returning to Gabriel. "What are you doing?"

Gabriel drew in a breath, his hands wedged in his back pockets.

"Just . . . hanging out."

Carla considered me for a moment, mouth slightly open.

"Have we met?"

I picked up my camera bag and slid it onto my shoulder.

"Last week, in Reading . . . at the after-party?"

She shook her head, lips pressed together.

"I'm Charlie."

"Oh, *Charlie*. Right. My bad. You must just have . . . one of those faces." She turned back to Gabriel. "They're looking for you downstairs, you know. You're so silly, hiding away on your own."

Gabriel stepped off the platform and back onto the runway. I wasn't sure if I should follow him, so I stayed where I was, gripping the metal rail.

"Fine, you got me," he said. "Busted."

Gabriel walked down to meet Carla, and she touched his arm, her eyes fixed on me.

"You OK making your way back to the green room?" said Gabriel.

I screwed my mouth up and looked around. "I'm kinda . . . lost."

He pointed past my shoulder.

"Out of that door, end of the hallway, there's a long staircase that takes you right to the door. If we haven't heard from you in forty-eight hours, I'll send a search party."

I smiled at this. Carla did not.

"Catch you later," said Gabriel.

"Sure," I replied, watching as he led Carla away across the stage. I could hear her talking about me, in hushed tones, as they walked.

". . . Who is she, anyway? Some random groupie?"

"She's Charlie," said Gabriel, and I drew a sudden breath. Something about the way he said my name sent a thrill pulsing through me.

"It's so *weird*," replied Carla. "She's, like, not even famous . . ."

I made my way toward the exit Gabriel had shown me, weaving past instrument cases and over curled cables. Carla's voice reverberated around the stage.

". . . Anyway, have you heard what Brooke DeLacy has been saying about me? She was like, Carla Martinez is way jealous of my modeling career, and I was like, whatever, Brooke, in your *actual dreams* . . ."

Just before they vanished into the wings, Gabriel looked over his shoulder, caught my eye and mouthed, *HELP ME*.

I put my hand to my mouth to cover the smile.

Aiden was sitting on a tabletop, strumming his guitar and singing "Viva la Vida." He always looked great on camera, gazing out from behind his shaggy blond hair, thoughtful expression on his face.

I fired off a round of shots and flicked through them on the screen.

"These look cool," I said, stopping on a close-up of his face. His cheeks were dotted with freckles.

"Really?" He brushed the hair away from his eyes. "I think I need a haircut."

I shook my head.

"Nah, you're good. It's the natural look."

Aiden smiled at me and went back to strumming his guitar. When I returned to the viewfinder, I found Yuki creeping up behind him wearing a cardboard Gabriel West mask, the kind you see outside tacky souvenir shops. He glanced at me and touched a finger to his (well, Gabriel's) lips.

"Surrender, Irish pig-dog!" he yelled, and Aiden jumped several inches into the air, releasing a metallic twang from the guitar. Yuki hooked an arm around Aiden's neck and, leaning over his shoulder, affected a deep, swaggering voice.

"Greetings, I am *Gabriel West*. I am mysterious and brooding, and women fall to pieces in my presence."

Laughing, Aiden tried to free himself, but his bandmate was too strong. Yuki looked up at me, straight into the camera, and I flicked off a round of pictures. It was eerie, capturing Gabriel's face, but with Yuki staring from the eye holes.

"I have astonishing hair," continued Yuki, spinning Aiden round, "and I write songs of heartbreaking genius! Kiss me, you fool!"

Aiden folded into a shaking ball of laughter as Yuki mauled his neck. Eventually, with Aiden gasping for breath, Yuki released him, turned to face me, and stuck his fists on his hips.

"How do I look, Charlie B? Handsome? Devastating?" He cocked his masked head. "Devastatingly handsome?"

I squinted at him.

"You look kinda dorky," I said, and Yuki pulled the mask off, revealing his mouth wide open in a mock-offended O.

"Gabriel West will not be pleased to hear *that*," he said, lobbing the mask over his shoulder. It spun like a Frisbee and crash-landed in a box full of clothes.

"Hey, guys." I was switching lenses on the camera. I kept my eyes down, my tone indifferent. "Can I ask you something about Gabriel?"

Olly and Gabriel were in some distant room on the other side of the building, being interviewed for *Pop Mania*. They weren't due back for at least ten minutes.

Yuki slumped down in a chair and unscrewed a bottle of water.

"You want his phone number, don't you?"

I cast him a withering look. He grinned.

"No, *actually* . . . it's about his lyrics."

Aiden looked up from his guitar.

"What about them?" he asked, stowing his pick between the strings. I slipped the original lens back into its case and rotated the second one onto the body of the camera. It fixed in with a click.

"It's nothing, really . . . I was just wondering . . . where they came from."

Yuki wrinkled his nose.

"I don't know. He just makes them up, I guess."

I twisted the focus on the new lens, peering through the viewfinder at the floor.

"He's never, like . . . talked to you about his songs?"

"He's pretty private about it," said Yuki. "Mind you, he's private about most things."

I thought back to the band's run-in with the paparazzi earlier that afternoon.

"Like his family?"

"*Especially* his family."

"So you really don't know, then?" I asked, setting the camera down on a table. I looked up, and Yuki was staring at me blankly.

"Absolutely no idea."

The countryside flew past, black and shapeless, as my train made its way toward Reading. My reflection peered back at me from the window.

This time, I wouldn't miss curfew.

But I had missed most of the concert.

"Make some noiiise, Brighton!" Olly had yelled, as Fire&Lights spilled onto the stage amid a glittering cascade of fireworks. Yuki went straight to the drummer, pumping his fist with every stamp of the bass drum, and Gabriel and Aiden led the fans in a fast hand-clap, jumping up and down on either side of the stage. I stood in the wings, half hidden behind a curtain, the noise pounding in my skull, the screaming and the crying, the earsplitting roar, the razor-edged wail of the guitars.

Just hours before, I'd been standing on that stage with Gabriel, the building empty and serene around us.

"Tickets, please. Tickets from Brighton . . ."

I'd been sad not to stay beyond the first song, but as luck would have it, Fire&Lights had opened with "Dance with You." Over thumping drums and shimmering keyboards, scenes from the music video played on the big screens: the sun-drenched cliff side, the gleaming, azure-blue ocean, the band in their open-top sports car. Guiltily, I realized I knew almost every frame.

The four bandmates ventured onto the audience walkway, two on each side, hands stretched out as they filed past the crowd. Though it was nearly impossible to make out the lyrics above the booming of the band and the screaming of the fans, I knew exactly what I was waiting for. The words were seared into my brain.

> *. . . Take me home*
> *'Cause I've been dreaming of a girl I know . . .*
> *. . . I call her name*
> *I keep her picture in a silver frame . . .*

The boys were reaching out into the auditorium, singing those words, *Mum's words*, to thousands of adoring fans, and I tried telling myself that it meant nothing. Somewhere, there was an explanation for all of this that would make my growing obsession seem ridiculous. There had to be.

"Excuse me, miss?"

I looked up. A kind-faced inspector was holding out his hand.

"Oh. Sorry . . . yes. One sec."

I reached into the camera case for my ticket. As I pulled it out, I spotted a folded piece of paper, nestled in the lens pocket, with something handwritten on the inside.

The inspector clicked a little hole in my ticket, and I opened the note.

Send me that pic? I'll look you up on FB. Gabriel

I thought back to our impromptu photo shoot on the stage. The picture Gabriel had shown me was kind of cool, I suppose, as a keepsake for me . . . but why would a famous pop star want a photo of us together?

"There you go," said the inspector, handing my ticket back.

"Thanks."

As I sat there with my train ticket in one hand, Gabriel's note in the other, I watched the inspector wander off down the train, *tickets please*, swaying slightly as the carriage curved around a corner. The train thrummed rhythmically beneath my feet and, looking down at the note, I found a second message at the bottom.

You're all right, Charlie Brown. You should come again. Xx

16

Sunday, late morning, and Melissa and I were sitting opposite each other on my bed, cups of tea steaming on the desk, a mess of French textbooks lying open between us. Melissa was chewing the end of a pencil.

"So, hang on," she said, her voice muffled by the pencil, "the imperfect tense is for talking about what something *was* like, and the pluperfect tense is for . . . what?! What does that even mean?"

"I'm confused," I said, reading the same dull sentence for the seventh time.

"I don't even *want* to go to France again," complained Melissa. "I've been tons of times. I'd much rather learn Swahili."

I threw an eraser at her, and it bounced off her knee.

"Because you hang out in Africa all the time, right?"

"All the time."

I put my head in my hands and groaned.

"I am so bored."

"Right, that's it!" proclaimed Melissa, sliding off the bed. "I'm staging an intervention. Where's your laptop?"

I gestured beneath the bed, and Melissa leaned over the side, hanging upside down, her hair coiling on the carpet. A moment later she emerged with my computer and clicked the lid open.

"Jack Callaghan's interview with Fire&Lights goes online today, and I'd say we've earned ourselves a break."

I checked the time.

"Mel, we've done eight minutes of French homework."

"Minutes schminutes," she replied, loading up YouTube. "I need my fix of Fire&Lights. Just because you get to hang out with them *every Saturday night* now . . ."

I made a face at her.

"Actually," continued Melissa, typing words into the search box, "since we're on the subject . . . when do I get to meet the band?"

"What?"

She looked up from my laptop.

"You've been to two concerts now—you must be able to sneak me into the next one."

"That's not really how it works, Mel."

"Please, Charlie. *Pleeease.*"

"I barely know them. I can't just start bringing my friends along."

"Not all your friends, doofus. One friend. Me. The Morris."

I scratched my head through my hat.

"I don't know, they're pretty tight on security at the con—"

Melissa grabbed me by the shoulders, and shook me.

"GIVE ME SOMETHING TO LIVE FOR."

"OK, fine," I said, peeling her hands off me and cradling them in mine. "How's this? If an opportunity comes up—*if* it does—I promise: I will take you to meet Fire&Lights."

Melissa's whole face lit up.

"I love you so much, Charlie Bloom, sometimes I think I might pop."

I smiled, shaking my head, and Melissa turned back to the computer screen, where a list of videos had appeared. She pointed at the top one and clapped.

"Ah! Here it is. I am proper excited. Jack Callaghan is the FUNNI-EST . . ."

Jack Callaghan was an Irish TV presenter whose Saturday night chat show, *Jack's Night In*, was the natural opening act for *Make or Break*. He interviewed all the hottest bands, movie stars, and celebrities, interspersed with stand-up comedy and live performances. The show got massive ratings every week.

". . . I'm sure you all know what's coming next," Jack was saying as the video began. Lights swirled around the studio, and the audience began to applaud. "Ladies and gentlemen, the HOTTEST pop act on planet Earth right now . . . Fire&Lights!"

The house band launched into an instrumental version of "Dance with You," and Gabriel, Olly, Yuki, and Aiden emerged from backstage, waving at the crowd, their eyes bright, skin glowing.

They were dressed in immaculate tailored suits.

"Oh my," said Melissa. "They. Are. Looking. Sharp."

"Calm down, everyone," said Jack, once the band had settled on the sofa. Yells and catcalls spilled down from the audience. "I know, I know . . . how long have I wanted these boys on my show? How long?"

Whooping and cheers, a flourish from the drummer.

The band were all smiles.

"OK lads, first off. What . . . a . . . *year*, eh?" Clapping and whistles from the studio. "I mean, what, just last summer you were ordinary guys, living your lives, and now . . . now you can't walk down the street without being mobbed. Is it just . . . It's got to be *crazy*, hasn't it?"

The boys all looked at each other.

Olly cleared his throat. "We love it," he said, "it's a dream come true. But it's all down to the fans, really. They made it happen."

The audience cheered, and Jack nodded sagely. Yuki stretched his arm out along the back of the sofa and poked Olly in the ear.

"But . . . yeah," continued Olly, batting Yuki away. "It's pretty crazy. It's changed everything."

"We get to stay up past eleven every night," said Yuki. "It's off the hook."

"'Cause there you were," continued Jack, throwing a smile at Yuki, "you won *Make or Break*, and one year later, your first album isn't even out yet and you're already international superstars. You're here, you're everywhere, you're on the telly, you're hanging out with Kaitlyn Jones . . ."

The camera cut to the feed from the green room. Kaitlyn Jones, America's hottest and blondest pop starlet, waved and blew a kiss.

"Love you guys!" she said, sweetly.

"Aiden's got a crush on Kaitlyn," said Yuki, as the boys appeared on-screen again. "He's got it bad."

"I think we've all got a crush on Kaitlyn," said Jack, from the corner of his mouth. Yuki stood up on the sofa, spilling the cushions, and cupped his hands around his mouth.

"Hey, Kaitlyn!" The camera cut to the green room again. "Kaitlyn, WILL YOU GO STEADY WITH AIDEN? HE'S VERY RELIABLE AND HAS HIS OWN CAR—"

"Stop it, you," said Jack, as the feed returned to the studio, the audience howling with laughter. Jack tugged Yuki back down into his seat and rapped him on the knee. "You're disrupting things."

Yuki made a guilty face.

"So, moving on. Moving on. The new album. This'll be news to all you guys at home, but a little birdie tells me that you, Gabriel West, wrote most of the lyrics on *Songs About a Girl* . . . is that right?"

Gabriel nodded slowly, and I felt a little thrill as it dawned on me that, up until now, this had been a secret.

"Oh my God, no way!" said Melissa, clapping her hands.

"With this in mind, Gabe," continued Jack, "I'm sure we'd all like to know . . . who's the girl in the title?"

The audience *oohed* and wolf-whistled. Gabriel coughed into his fist.

"I couldn't possibly tell you that, Jack."

Jack looked at the audience and made his mouth into a little circle.

"He's coy, isn't he?"

More cheering spilled down from the crowd, and someone shouted, "We love you, Gabriel!"

Under his breath, Jack said: "Get in line, lady." Cue raucous laughter.

"But come on, let's be honest: you've been linked to all *kinds* of famous ladies in the past year. The always glamorous Tammie Austin, for instance. A bona fide movie star."

"Tammie's just a friend," said Gabriel, leaning back into the sofa. "Cross my heart."

"Fine, but you just came out of that tempestuous relationship with Ella Mackenzie, and we all know Miss Martinez from *Hampton Beach* is after you . . . so what's the deal? *Who's your muse*, Gabriel Horatio West?"

"Horatio?" echoed Yuki.

"Where did that come from?" asked Olly.

Jack leaned his elbow on the desk, his chin on his fist. "I've no idea, I just made it up. But he looks like he could be a Horatio, don'tcha think? That strong jawline . . . he's like a Roman soldier."

Aiden reached over and stroked Gabriel's jaw. Gabriel grabbed his hand and gave it a little kiss.

"This wasn't in the script," said Olly.

"I know, I know," said Jack, spinning around on his chair, "I'm getting off topic. But heck, it's my show."

Peals of laughter.

"So where were we? Oh yes. Your *muuuse*."

He pointed his cards at Gabriel. Gabriel smiled.

"I don't kiss and tell."

"Is that so, Mr. West? A gentleman, no less."

Jack held his hands in the air.

"But no, come on, this isn't *The Gabriel West Show*, children. Let's chat with you other fellas for a bit. Aiden . . . *Aiden* . . ." He touched a hand to his heart and docked his head to the side. "Our Irish prince."

Boisterous applause.

"You know over here in Dublin we all think you're the best one, don't you?"

Aiden released a little smile.

"Oh lordy," said Melissa, grabbing the laptop screen. "He is so cute I just wanna roll him in a pancake."

"Are you happy, Aiden? Do they treat you well, the other lads?"

Aiden stuck out his bottom lip.

"They're all right."

"Hey," said Yuki, sitting forward, "I iron your boxer briefs every morning, bro. Where's your gratitude?"

"He's lying," said Gabriel, with a sly smile. "Aiden doesn't wear underwear."

"Is that right?" asked Jack.

"None of us do," said Olly.

"Crikey . . ." Jack laughed and fanned himself with a cue card. "I'm losing my train of thought. Ooh, yes: here's something I've been wondering about." He pointed to each member of the band in turn. "Why aren't there five of you?"

A strange, icy silence fell over the band. Hurriedly, Aiden broke it.

"Why aren't there five of *you*, Jack?"

"Trust me, kid, the world ain't ready." More cheers. "But seriously. Boy bands do normally have five members, no?"

"Hanson didn't," said Olly. "Or Boyz II Men."

"Or the Jonas Brothers," added Aiden.

"What about the Beatles?" said Yuki, clicking his fingers. "They were the original boy band."

Jack thought about this and clacked his cards against the table.

"Touché, Mr. Harrison. Touché."

"Plus," said Olly, "one guy always leaves, right? And then you're left with four anyway, like Take That. Or Boyzone."

"That's the beginning of the end, man," said Yuki. "Once the first guy quits, you're all toast."

Jack smoothed down his tie.

"But . . . *but* . . . my point is, it so easily *could* have been five, couldn't it? There was—and forgive me if I'm scratching old wounds here—an obvious fifth member . . . ?"

The boys exchanged uneasy glances.

"I don't want to stir any bad blood, chaps, but . . . Jake Woodrow?"

"Ohmygosh I can't believe he brought up Jake!" blurted Melissa, sitting up straight on my bed. "That is so *awk*ward . . . !"

I thought back to the previous afternoon, outside the venue in Brighton, and the reporters questioning Olly. *He's still pretty cut up . . . what d'you say about that?*

"Can we get a picture of Jake on-screen, please?"

A photograph of a good-looking teenage boy, around sixteen years old, with cornrows and a diamond stud earring appeared in the bottom corner of the screen. He was onstage on *Make or Break*, standing next to Olly, holding a microphone.

"For those of you who don't watch *Make or Break* . . . all three of you"—laughter and whooping—"Jake Woodrow was, well, how do I put this? The Pete Best of Fire&Lights."

"Wasn't he a footballer?" said Aiden. Yuki thwacked him on the back of the head.

"That's *George* Best, you twit."

"Fine, fine. For anyone under thirty-five," explained Jack, "Pete Best was the original drummer in the Beatles, but he got booted out for Ringo Starr. Controversial, of course, and speaking of which . . ." He leaned his elbows on the desk. "What *happened* there? Olly?"

Olly didn't reply right away. He gathered himself and glanced briefly up at the audience.

"There's no big secret, Jack. You all saw it on TV. The band was the four of us—me, Yuki, Aiden, and Jake—but when the show went into the finals, Barry just didn't think it was working."

"A chemistry thing, right?"

Olly made an indeterminate sound. Gabriel stared at the floor.

"Yeah . . . yeah, I guess. A chemistry thing. Gabe was doing really well in the solo category, and Barry had been watching him for years, from his previous auditions . . . and he just saw a match."

Jack leaned back in his chair.

"But if I'd been Barry King, I dunno, maybe I'd have kept poor ol' Jake in the lineup. Seems a bit cruel, no?"

"Barry knows what he's doing," said Yuki. "You might s—"

"Don't say it," hissed Aiden, clamping his hand over Yuki's mouth. Yuki pulled it off and yelled over Aiden's fingers.

"YOU MIGHT SAY HE'S THE KING."

Jack sniggered at this and gave Yuki a mini round of applause.

"So in other words," he continued, "you've got a one-in-one-out policy, have you? Sorta like a nightclub?"

He winked at the audience, and they rewarded him with laughter. Olly tried hard to smile.

"Nah, I'm putting you on. I'm awful. Now listen . . ." Jack swung side to side on his chair, moving papers around his desk. "Do we have the audience questions here? Somewhere?" He touched a finger to his ear and listened. "Oh, right . . . yep. I'm being told, yes, here we go . . . *Honestly,*" he said, through his teeth, "someone should fire the host . . ." Whooping from the crowd. "Got 'em."

He picked up a stray cue card and squinted at it.

"We're going to finish up here with a couple of *fan questions,* plucked from our lovely studio audience. And the first one, here, is from . . . oh, I can't read this. Emily? Looks like Emily. Emily wants to know: 'What does the band name mean?'"

The boys looked at each other blankly.

"Most band names don't mean anything, do they?" pondered Aiden.

"Some do," replied Olly.

"I wanted to call the band Yuki & the Hotrods," said Yuki, leaning back into the sofa, "but Barry was all, 'You're not the lead singer, dude. Get over it.'"

Jack patted him on the shoulder.

"It's tough not being loved, eh, kid?"

Yuki shook his head, sadly, and an almighty, *"Awww"* emanated from the back of the studio, peppered with laughter and applause. Then, underneath the noise, so quiet it was barely audible, Gabriel said:

"I'm the fire, he's the light."

But the audience missed it.

"You don't ever worry that people might mistake y'all for an emergency service, perhaps? Or a fireworks shop?"

Yuki pointed directly into the camera and raised one eyebrow.

"Kids, Fire&Lights do not endorse the sale of fireworks to minors."

"*Oooookay*, very good, Mr. Harrison, very good." Jack ran his finger down the cue card. "We have time for one more question, and this one comes from, let me see, someone who calls themselves 'Oggy.' What kind of a name is Oggy?" Sniggers from the crowd. "Oggy would like to know . . . 'Who will have the most successful solo career?' "

The audience *oohed* gleefully, and Jack covered his mouth with his hand. Olly shuffled in his seat.

"Con . . . tro . . . VERsial," said Jack, leaning back in his chair. "Oggy, I don't think we're letting *you* back in the studio, you little scamp."

"Who said we're ever splitting up?" said Yuki, lifting his arm and dropping it around Aiden's neck.

"Yeah, what if we wanna grow old together?" added Aiden.

"We're not thinking about that sort of thing yet," said Olly, diplomatically. "Maybe get the album out first, eh?"

Jack cast aside his cards and drummed his hands on the table.

Gabriel stayed silent.

"Well, gentlemen, it's been a pleasure. You're performing for us later, aren't you, with Kaitlyn?" They all nodded, and the crowd stamped and hollered. "Thanks for chatting with us; you've been a riot. Ladies and gentlemen, Fire . . . & . . . Lights!"

Jack stood up, crossed over to the sofa, and shook the hands of each band member in turn, ruffling Aiden's hair as he passed. The house band crashed back into their instrumental version of "Dance with You."

"SO much fun," said Melissa, as the video faded away. "Oh, the banter. Mind you, I can't *believe* he asked them about Jake."

I remembered how, the previous day, when the topic of Jake came up, the focus had all been on Olly. Just like on the show.

"Were Olly and Jake . . . close?" I said.

Melissa sipped her tea.

"Oh yeah. *Really* close. It was kinda sad when they got split apart. But hey-ho, in Jake's place, the Lord hath delivered GABRIEL WEST."

She clutched a hand to her heart.

"Speaking of which, I can't believe he wrote the lyrics on the new album! Beauty *and* brains. Yes please."

"Actually, about that . . ." I closed my laptop and slid it out of the way. "If I show you something, Mel, will you promise to keep it a secret?"

On the train home from Brighton, I had made a decision: I had to tell Melissa about Gabriel's lyrics. Even if I felt stupid doing it, I couldn't keep it to myself any longer. And if there was one person in the world I didn't mind feeling stupid in front of, it was Melissa.

"Well, duh," she said, squeezing my hand. "Always."

I reached under the bed for Mum's book.

"Hey, isn't that . . . ?"

"My mum's notebook."

I passed it to Melissa, and she ran a finger down the spine.

"I haven't seen this in years. That's cute that you still have it."

I lifted the cover and opened it to a page in the middle, the one with the lyrics from "Dance with You" scattered across it. The corner was well thumbed, the page faintly yellowed.

"What am I looking at here?" asked Melissa. I pointed at the first verse, near the top of the page, and her face opened like a parachute.

"Whoa. *Whoa*." She looked up. "Wait . . . did you just write this?"

"No, Melissa . . . my mum did." I swallowed, and tucked my hair behind my ears. "Fifteen years ago."

Melissa exhaled very slowly.

"That is so weird." She chewed the end of her pencil. "What a weird coincidence."

My shoulders dropped. *A coincidence.*

"Unless . . ."

Melissa turned the page and ran her finger down it. Then she flipped another page, scanning the words, and soon she was zipping through the book furiously, her eyes flitting from side to side.

She lowered the book into her lap.

"What?" I said. Melissa's face was barely moving.

"Gabriel's songs . . . they're on almost every page."

17

I wasn't supposed to be in Dad's study.

The dark, cluttered room was served by only one window, and even that was half obscured behind a tottering pile of files and folders, slips of paper poking out the sides. Dad was extremely private about his workspace. I'd always suspected this was because he kept secret memories of Mum in there, and though I was curious to find out, even as a child I somehow knew the room was out of bounds. In all the years we'd lived in the house, I'd barely set foot in the place.

Until now.

"Here, let me show you. You're not going to believe this . . ."

Ten minutes earlier, Melissa and I had sat huddled together on the edge of my bed, studying the pages of Mum's notebook. Melissa's foot was tapping with excitement.

"Here," she said, her finger pressed into the page. A silent charge passed through me. She was pointing to one of my favorite lines.

"*She lives her life in pictures . . . she keeps secrets in her heart,*" she read. "That's from 'Hollywood Movie Star.' Their last single."

She flicked on a few pages.

"And there, look. These are weirdly similar to 'Have You Seen My Girl . . .'"

> *When you see my girl*
> *You will know that you've found her*
> *When you look in those big brown eyes*
> *When you see my girl*
> *Wait until she smiles*
> *And she'll bring you right back to life*

"This is too much, Charlie. This is huge."

My heart was thudding. I closed the notebook.

"What does it mean?"

"I . . . don't know," said Melissa, rubbing her eyes. "It makes no sense. Maybe . . ."

She glanced at the clock.

"Dammit, I have to go. Tennis with Mum." She grabbed both my hands. "You're going back again, aren't you? To see the band?"

"I don't know. They have a video shoot in London next weekend, but—"

"You have to go, Charlie. You have to figure this out."

She squeezed my fingers.

"I'll message you later," she said, sliding off the bed and slinging her bag over her shoulder. "This . . ." She was standing in the open doorway. "This is . . . *huge.*"

She raced from the room, flew down the stairs, and pulled the front door shut behind her. For several minutes I sat on my bed alone, staring at the wall, quietly stunned.

Melissa might have been overexcited, she might have been blinded by fandom, but I knew she was right. I had to go back.

Downstairs, I scanned the drawers, cupboards, and filing cabinets in Dad's study, trying to decide where to start. There must be clues in this room, I thought, memories, keepsakes from the past, some fragment from my mother's life that would explain all this.

I opened the top drawer of Dad's desk and sifted through the papers inside. Finding only spreadsheets, pay slips, and office paperwork, I moved on to the next drawer down. The story was the same with each new drawer I tried, until I reached the bottom, when my hand brushed against a stack of old, crusty papers tied together with string. I pulled the papers out, spread them on the desk, and picked one at random. It was an academic certificate, worn at the edges, gold leaf peeling off the border.

UNIVERSITY COLLEGE LONDON
DEPARTMENT OF MATHEMATICS
Outstanding Undergraduate Student of the Year, 1994

Ralph Charles Bloom

And that wasn't the only one. There was a whole stack of certificates, academic awards, and university press clippings: "UCL Graduate Delivers Hallmark Speech at Mathematics Conference," "Ralph Bloom Published in Leading Academic Journal," "Gifted PhD Student Begins Groundbreaking Research Program."

They were all about my father . . . but this wasn't the Ralph Bloom I knew. It was the person he used to be. Before my mother died.

I pushed on, sifting through the certificates and newspaper cuttings, trying to ignore the sinking feeling in my chest. Was I wasting my time?

Was there *any* trace of my mother in this room? But then, hidden amid the stack, I found an unsealed envelope, addressed in Dad's handwriting to a motel in North America. There was a letter inside.

I slid it out, and began to read.

Katherine

We can't go on like this anymore. I've hardly heard from you in weeks, just a few late-night phone calls, and barely a single e-mail. No letters. I'm only trying this address because when I called the number you gave me, they said this was the last place you stayed. I have no idea if this will ever reach you.

I want to know you're OK. I want to know you're safe, and that you're coming home, because we need you here. Charlie needs a mother. I can't do this on my own.

Things are getting bad, and I don't see any way out. Between extra shifts, paying the rent, and taking care of Charlie, I've run out of time for studying. The university say they've been patient, but I've fallen behind on my research and, if things don't change, they're going to cancel my PhD. I'll have to take some lousy job somewhere, we'll have to move out of London. I'm scared, K, but we have to put Charlie first. We have to give her the life she deserves.

And that's the main thing. You're missing her childhood, and she gets more beautiful every day. You'd be so proud of her.

I know I am.

Please come home.

Ralph

I reread the closing paragraph, a pressure building behind my eyes. *You'd be so proud of her . . . I know I am.* I ran a thumb along the words, the ink faded with age, the paper discolored. Did my father still feel that way about me? If he did, he certainly never said it.

Replacing the letter, I examined the front of the envelope. Though the address had been filled out—Wildwood Motel, Atlantic Avenue, Blueville, NJ—it had no postmark. What's more, the date inside read *25 November 2000* . . . just days before my mother died.

In all likelihood, she never even saw this.

My head was buzzing with questions. Did the crash happen in America? Why was Mum even out there when I was just a baby? And why had Dad never told me any of this?

I was sitting there, staring at the ceiling, my dad's private papers scattered far and wide across his desk, when something snapped me from my reverie.

The sound of his key turning in the lock.

The front door opened and I glanced around, panicked, at the mess of papers on Dad's desk.

I didn't have time to fix this.

"Charlie . . . ?"

The *scritch-scratch* of Dad wiping his feet on the mat. Folding the letter, I slipped it into my back pocket and began desperately gathering up the rest of the documents.

I froze when I heard Dad breathing behind me.

"What's going on?"

He was standing in the doorway, his eyes tracing a ring around the devastation.

"I was . . ." I lifted up a folder and pretended to search underneath it. "The school needs my birth certificate."

Dad lowered his shopping bags to the floor. His cheeks were flushed, and he kept blinking.

"This is my study, Charlie. There are . . . work documents in here. You can't just barge in without asking me."

Work documents, I thought. *Work documents.*

"If you needed something, you should have waited."

Dad raked a hand through his hair, and his gaze fell on the university award on the desk. His eyes glazed over.

"Dad . . . ?"

There was something he wasn't telling me. I was sure of it.

But I couldn't find the words.

"Please, Charlie, just put everything back where you found it."

"But—"

"*Charlie,*" he snapped, his eyes trained on the floor. "I'm tired."

I could make him tell me the truth, I thought. About the crash, about the letter to my mum and what happened to her in America. I could ask him if he was still proud of his daughter.

But instead, as a single tree branch tapped insistently against the small study window, I watched as my father picked up his sagging shopping bags and walked slowly from the room.

"Come on, girls, hurry up! This race won't run itself."

My breath was sticking in my throat as I laced up my trainers and listened to the rain pounding on the roof of the changing rooms. I hated PE, partly because I wasn't very good at it, but mainly because it was the hardest lesson to be invisible in.

"Apparently the boys have been ready for five whole minutes . . ."

Miss Blake checked her watch again and continued patrolling the room. Lots of the girls were still only half dressed, laughing and chatting and rifling through washbags. I swear some of them put makeup on *before* going for a run.

"They'll be starting the cross-country without you if you don't get a move on."

I was struggling to concentrate at school. Thoughts battled for attention inside my head: lines from Gabriel's songs, the argument I'd had with my father, the letter he'd never sent. I didn't like the way Dad had reacted to finding me in his study, how he'd snapped at me, the fact that all the while he could barely look me in the eye.

We'd hardly spoken since.

"Keep the noise down, Year Eleven," crowed Miss Blake, whistle in hand, as we all stood shivering on the starting line. I glanced up the row, assessing my classmates, remembering from last year's cross-country who was fast and who was slow. My tactic was to drop back early on so as not to end up near the front, but to stay ahead of the stragglers so that I'd finish somewhere in the middle.

"Ready, set . . . go!"

The rain lashed at our faces and bare legs as we trudged round the sodden, muddy sports field. The usual people were out in front, the unfit ones were at the back, and everyone else—including me—was bunched in the middle. I was surrounded on all sides, which was making it all the more obvious that people were talking about me.

It started small, with just one or two girls. This happened a lot at school, and so at first I ignored it, but then they began to pass the secret around. It was like a giant, mobile game of Chinese whispers, and whatever they were sharing soon made its way around the entire year group. In all directions were whispering mouths, nudging fingers, and astonished eyes.

An hour later, I had finished the race. I showered and got dressed as quickly as I could, left the changing rooms without talking to anyone, and found an empty table in the cafeteria. Melissa took violin lessons on Thursday lunchtimes, so I'd been sitting alone for nearly twenty minutes when I heard the voices behind me.

"We should talk to her . . ."

"You do it."

Scattered giggles.

"I'm scared."

"I'm not. Hey, Charlie. Charlie!"

I swiveled round on my chair. A group of Year Eight girls were huddled together by the adjacent table, beaming from ear to ear. I recognized them straightaway: they were the ones who read the Fire&Lights fan blog aloud every day over lunch.

"We all saw it," said the girl at the front, the tallest in the group. Her friends jiggled behind her. They looked like they were about to burst.

I put down my sandwich.

"Saw what?"

Their little faces dropped.

"The fan blog," said the tall girl. She glanced at her friends. "Y'know . . . today's blog?"

I started to turn back round when she whipped out her phone.

"Wait, Charlie! Look."

She walked over to me and held her iPhone in front of my face. It was dotted with chip salt.

The web browser was open on a Fire&Lights fan site.

PHOTO EXCLUSIVE!! GABRIEL WEST DATING MYSTERY GIRL??

*Secret leaked photo of Gabriel onstage
with female fan*

*Listen up, guys, because today's entry is a JUICY one!! This
photo—sent to us by an anonymous source—shows our beautiful
Gabriel West with his arm round a fan, on an empty stage . . .
and our source says they might even be TOGETHER?!*

*WHAT DOES THIS MEAN, GUYS??? Is she just a random
groupie, or Gabriel's new GF??! Comments below people!! :) :) :)
xxx*

P.S. Remember, you heard it here first!! :-)

*xox FIRE&LIGHTS FOREVER xox
The best Fire&Lights fan blog on the web!!*

Underneath the article was a blurred photograph. The photograph of
me and Gabriel, onstage in Brighton, that he'd taken with my camera.
The picture I had sent to him, only hours afterward, with a little note
that read: "Thanks for modeling for me. Charlie x."

I felt sick.

"Ohmygod it's so amazing!" blurted all the Year Eights at once.

The tall girl clapped her hands together. "I can't believe you've met him, it's just the coolest. What's he like? I bet he's the BEST in person . . ."

How had this happened? What was one of my photos doing on a fan blog? And who started the rumor that we "might be together"?

I scrolled down the page, the chatter and the giggles fading away beneath the rising thud of my heartbeat, pounding in my ears. The post already had nearly two hundred likes, and a smattering of comments.

she is SOOOOO not hot enough for him

um, yeah, like Gabriel would date some random groupie?? as if

ugh what a wannabe

At the bottom of the page, buried among the likes and the reblogs, a user called crazyfaker55 had left a longer comment. As I read it, the words sank into me slowly, like I was ingesting a poison.

i know this girl, she goes to my school. totally up herself. no way gabriel's into her, unless he likes boring skanks LMFAO. she's mymusicpix on instagram. we should troll the bitch

I stumbled down into my chair, my stomach churning.

"Charlie . . . ?"

The tall girl was standing above me, the room swimming around her. I lifted up her phone, and she took it back.

"Are you OK?"

In a trance, I slid my own phone, still switched off from PE, out of my bag. It loaded sluggishly, ponderously, the little white circle spinning and twinkling on the screen.

I could sense the Year Eights drifting away from me, blurred shapes, muffled voices, the clink of plates and the scraping of metal chair legs. I felt light-headed, ghostly, like a superimposed image, disconnected

from the world. When my home screen finally appeared, I opened the
Instagram app, thumb trembling, and the orange notification bar
popped up in the corner. Over fifty new comments.

None of them good.

haha nice pix, boy band slut

gabriel don't sleep with skanks like u

BACK OFF BITCH!!!! GABRIEL'S MINE

ur face sux & so do ur pix

hurry up & die wannabe slut

A hot pain, barbed like thistles, was swelling behind my eyes. The
phone was heavy in my hand, buzzing with vibrations, and I dropped
it onto the table, one hand clutched to my stomach.

"She doesn't look happy, Gem."

"Is she gonna vom?"

I looked up, a flood of tears building, and through my shimmering
gaze, I saw Aimee Watts. I knew, straightaway, that I was staring into
the eyes of crazyfaker55.

"You all right?" she said, parking herself on the edge of the table.

I couldn't speak.

Aimee glanced at my phone, and winced.

"Ouch," she said, with a shake of her head. Her hair was still greasy
from PE. "That is nasty, Charlie Bloom."

I glared back at her, my cheeks burning. Her smile was long and
thin, like a blade.

You won't know when it's coming.

Throwing my book, my phone, and my lunch into my bag, I scraped
back the chair, pushed past Aimee and Gemma, and headed for the corridor. Weaving through pockets of people staring at me, whispering
to each other, I ran to the toilets, locked myself in a cubicle, and let the
tears fall.

* * *

A familiar pair of shoes appeared underneath the cubicle door. Outside in the hallway, feet squeaked against the linoleum, and I could hear Miss Woods ushering students into the courtyard. Pipes moaned and creaked behind the tiled walls.

"Charlie, is that you?"

I wiped my eyes with the back of my hand, a wet slash of tears smearing my cheek.

"Melissa . . . ?"

"Yes, oh my gosh, Charlie . . . let me in."

I pressed my ear to the door, listening for other people in the room.

"It's just me," said Melissa, as if she'd heard what I was thinking. I opened the door and she bundled in, locking it behind her.

"Oh my God, Charlie . . ."

She opened her arms, and I fell into them. For a while, I sobbed, quietly, into her shoulder.

"Are you OK?"

I stepped backward, sniffling, and shook my head.

"Look, I know you're upset," she said, a hand on my arm, "but when you think about it, it's kind of cool, isn't it? Most people think you're the biggest legend at Caversham High since Olly Samson."

I plucked a strip of toilet paper from the roll.

"I don't care," I said, dabbing at my eyes. "I don't want people talking about me. I don't want them staring at me."

Melissa took my hand, and I stuffed the tissue paper into my pocket.

"Besides, did you see what happened? Someone left a comment with my Instagram handle in it. It was Aimee, I know it was. People are saying horrible things . . ."

"They'll delete the comment, Charlie. They probably already have."

"But that's not the point. It's out there now." I stared at my hand, cradled in Melissa's. "Maybe I should close my accou—"

I stopped abruptly at the sound of the main door swinging hard against the tiles, metal handle cracking into the wall. Our hands broke apart, and I touched a finger to my lips. Melissa held her breath.

"Oh my God, I'm *desperate* for a wee," said one girl, rushing into the adjacent cubicle. Through the narrow slit in the door, I could see a second girl standing in front of the mirror, fiddling with her hair.

"Can you believe that photo of Charlie Bloom with Gabriel West?" said the girl at the mirror, shaking her hair out behind her.

"I *know*, right?" said the voice from the cubicle. "It's got to be a hoax."

My eyes met Melissa's.

"Yeah," said the girl at the sink. "I mean . . . Charlie Bloom?"

"I know. Why would he be into her? She's so . . . quiet."

Melissa grabbed my hand again.

"He's hot, though, right?"

"Gabriel? *Crazy* hot."

The girl at the mirror twirled her hair three times and flicked on a hairband. She spun round suddenly, and I shrank backward, afraid she might see me through the slit.

"You done yet?"

"Yep!" said the second girl, flushing the toilet and opening the cubicle. They walked past us and out through the door, and I sat down on the closed toilet, my head in my hands.

"Don't listen to *them*," said Melissa, dismissively. "That was Vicky Mathers—she can barely tie her own shoelaces."

I managed a weak smile. Melissa's face creased with concern.

"Where do you think those bloggers got the photo?" she said. I shrugged.

"I don't know, but . . . it had to be Gabriel. Nothing else makes sense. *God*, I feel so stupid for trusting him."

I wouldn't make that mistake again. That was for sure.

"Shall we go outside? I'll be with you the whole time. I promise . . ."

I couldn't stand to stay in school for the afternoon. I decided to sneak out before lunch break ended, and although Melissa said she'd come with me, I quickly convinced her to stay. I didn't want her getting in trouble, and in any case, I needed some time on my own. So, once everyone was outside on the playing fields and the corridors were empty, I snuck through the main gates, unnoticed, and walked out of school without looking back.

I spent the afternoon wandering along the canal. Aside from the occasional dog walker, there was no one around to bother me, and as I walked up and down the gravel paths, deep in thought, the sun lost its hold on the day, and the hours fell quietly away.

It was something I'd worried about a lot: what might happen if my secret got out. How it might change things at school. And now, in one morning, my disguise had been taken from me. I couldn't blend into the crowd anymore or keep my head down in class. I was a story. I was public property.

My one comfort was that I'd kept my Instagram handle anonymous. Outside of Caversham High, no one knew who I was, so in a way, I was lucky . . . but I didn't feel it. The words in my comment feed had lodged in my skin like splinters. *Slut. Skank. Bitch.* What right did they have to call me those things? What made people so spiteful toward a total stranger?

My phone burned in my pocket, begging me to unlock it, to get online and see what the world was saying about me. I had locked my Instagram account and blocked the trolls, but I still felt exposed. They were all out there, somewhere. Hating me.

And as for Gabriel, why would he have bothered leaking the photo in the first place? Was he trying to make a point? Was he trying to show me that I didn't belong in his world? He'd been so keen that I send the picture to him—maybe this was his plan all along. To teach me a lesson.

If that was true, it had certainly worked.

Later that evening, as I turned the corner into Tower Close, I was gripped by a sudden fear. What if the school had noticed I was gone and phoned my father? Since we'd argued the other night there'd been a weird tension in the house, a silent wall between us, and skipping school would only make things worse.

When I stepped into the hallway, he was waiting for me.

"Charlie, what's going on?"

I needed an excuse, and fast.

"Dad, I can explain, it w—"

"Look at this."

He was holding a sheet of paper at arm's length. I peered at it in the low light: a blurred image in the center, and a message at the bottom.

"Do you know who did this?"

I took a step closer and, as the image shifted into focus, a sticky heat spread through me. Down my arms, and into my fingertips.

"Where did you get that?"

"Someone posted it through our letter box," said Dad, "which worries me in itself." He shook the paper in my direction. "Charlie, this is you."

The image on the page was a poor-quality enlarged printout of the photograph from the fan blog, my infamous Gabriel West selfie. Our names were scrawled above us in black marker: "Charlie+Gabriel <3 <3 <3." I read the message underneath, heart juddering, and goose bumps prickled my arm. *She used to be such a good girl.*

"What is this?" Dad croaked, the paper trembling a little in his hand. "Who's Gabriel?"

It sounded dry and bitter in his mouth, the word "Gabriel," like he'd accidentally swallowed gunpowder. The name seemed to upset him.

"He's just a kid in my year, Dad. I barely even know him."

"The school needs to know about this." He scraped his hair back from his forehead. "I'm calling the principal in the morning."

"N-no, please don't," I stammered, tears rising in my throat. "It won't happen again, Dad, it's just idiots joking around. *Please* don't tell the school."

The last thing I needed at Caversham High was more attention.

"Dad . . . ?"

There was the slightest tremor in my voice, and Dad heard it too. His face changed, softened, and he faltered forward, arms rising, as if to embrace me. His hand brushed my shoulder and I flinched, stepping away.

"Kiddo, come on. I didn't mean to upset you. This is . . ." He looked down at the poster. "This is horrible. Are you all right?"

I dumped my bag by the wall.

"I don't care, Dad. It's just idiots at school."

He touched a cautious hand to my shoulder. This time, I let him.

"Is there something you're not telling me?"

Dad waited for me to speak, and I had to bite my tongue to keep my thoughts inside. *Is there something* you're *not telling* me? I wanted to say. *Do you want to explain what that letter means, why you don't talk about*

Mum anymore, or what the hell actually happened in America? Do you want to explain that?

A light rain pattered on the windows.

"No," I replied, and my voice sounded tiny in the dark.

We stood opposite each other for a moment, listening to the rain. Dad dropped the folded poster on the phone table.

"Fine. That's . . . fine."

Rubbing his temples, he walked down the hallway and mounted the stairs. I could hear his socked feet padding against the wood.

When he reached the landing, I picked up the sheet of paper, unfolded it, and stared at the patchy photo of me and Gabriel. A quiet dread trickled down my spine.

Someone had scratched out our eyes.

18

The next day at school, it barely let up for a minute.

Wherever I went—in the hallways, the playing fields, or the class-rooms—I was followed by a constant, buzzing chatter like a swarm of blackflies. Melissa was right: most people were excited, even impressed, but that made no difference to me. I was supposed to walk these halls unnoticed, not talked about at every turn.

"That's her . . . Charlie Bloom . . ."

"What . . . you mean *Gabriel West* from Fire&Lights? No way . . ."

"I'm so jealous. Do you think she had sex with him?"

"Is she famous now . . . ?"

"I bet she's done it with Olly too . . ."

"It's so weird, I never imagined she'd be such a sl—"

"Hey," said Melissa, sitting down next to me. She spread her science books out across the table. "How you doing?"

Mrs. Manning had been delayed by a staff meeting, and we'd been waiting in the physics lab, unattended, for nearly fifteen minutes. People were mucking around with test tubes and gossiping across tables. Behind my head, I could hear a row of boys talking about me. "I'd sleep with her, easy."

"I've been better."

One of the boys called my name. Melissa twisted round on her chair.

"Shut up, Matt."

I closed my eyes, willing it all away. Maybe this was just a bad dream, and any second now, I would wake up.

"I wasn't talking to you, virgin."

"So what if I *am* a virgin?" said Melissa. Matt's friends sniggered.

"Tell Charlie she can have my phone number if she wants."

"Yeah, if she's looking for someone to take the trash out, I'll tell her to give you a call."

Melissa turned back round and unzipped her pencil case.

"What a douche."

I could feel the boys staring at me. I could feel it on my skin.

"You don't have to do that, you know."

"No, I do. They can't talk about you that way. It's not right."

I glanced up at Melissa and managed half a smile. She bumped her chair closer to mine.

"So anyway," she said, in a low voice. "I've been thinking."

"About what?"

"About your mum's notebook. And Gabriel's songs."

I picked at the corner of my textbook. Despite what had happened, I'd been thinking about them too.

"You're still going to the video shoot tomorrow, right?"

"I don't know," I said, scribbling a curly doodle in my workbook. "What if I end up on some fan blog again? I just want this whole thing to go away."

"It will. I know it will." She tugged at my sleeve. "But don't you think you should talk to Gabriel?"

"As far as I know, he's the whole reason this is happening to me."

"That doesn't change what's in your mum's book, though. Don't you want to know what it means?"

I looked at her, a tangled knot in my belly. She was right, I did want to know. I *had* to know.

I just wasn't sure I was ready to face Gabriel.

Are you ok, charlie?

That night, at around eight thirty, I heard from Olly. I was sitting at my desk, frowning at a half-written French essay, when his Facebook message hit my screen.

I'm ok, I wrote back. Why do you ask?

I heard about what happened

I felt queasy, embarrassed, knowing that Olly had seen the photo. It had been shared on various sites, but I somehow doubted pop stars read their own gossip columns. He must have been looking out for me.

Pretty lame, huh

Not at all. Celeb pics get leaked all the time

I suddenly remembered the confidentiality agreement I had signed. "All images will remain property of Kingdom Records. Unauthorized publication in any form is strictly prohibited."

Will i get in trouble for this?

Of course not, it wasn't your fault. A pause. In fact, i feel kind of responsible

What? That's crazy

I got you involved with the band, i should have protected you from this stuff

Don't feel guilty, olly . . . please

Hidden beneath my desk, nestled in its case, was the Canon EOS. I had to keep it out of my father's sight—how would I explain a brand-new, six-hundred-pound camera?—but looking at it now, I was reminded of how sweet Olly had been the past few weeks. How much he'd done for me since I started hanging out with the band. The way that, when I was around him, I almost forgot he was a celebrity.

Hey, if it makes you feel any better, your new photos are up on our fan page

Really? No way . . .

Check em out :)

Pushing my essay aside, I loaded up the Fire&Lights website and headed straight for Fan HQ. Several rows of photos from my Brighton reel had been published on the page, and they'd already amassed thousands of views. Aiden with his guitar, singing "Viva la Vida," Yuki horsing around in his Gabriel West mask, the band lined up in the VIP enclosure signing autographs.

Underneath the photos were strings of glowing comments from excited fans. No hate, no insults, just compliments.

D'you know what? I wrote back to Olly. That does make me feel better :)

I know this fan blog stuff really sucks, but if you're still up for coming to the shoot tomorrow, we'd love to have you . . . xx

I missed Olly. I'd barely seen him at the Brighton gig, and I still hadn't thanked him properly for the camera. Apart from anything else, I knew that seeing the boys again and throwing myself into photography was guaranteed to lift my spirits. I could avoid Gabriel if I needed to. He seemed to avoid everyone else most of the time anyway.

I took a deep breath and typed my reply.

Thanks, olly. You're the best. I'll see you there

* * *

I was standing outside a noisy train station, on a busy London street, opposite a large redbrick building called the Clapham Grand. To my left, a man in a yellow waterproof was thrusting a free newspaper at me. Ahead, a lady with a sagging money belt was selling flowers, shaking a bucket of roses at passing pedestrians. Buses and taxis creaked and honked on the road.

None of these people knew it, but across the street, Fire&Lights were filming their latest music video.

"Yo yo yo, Charlie B."

Once I'd passed security, Yuki and Aiden were the first to greet me. They were flicking a rolled-up ball of foil at each other across a large metal case.

"Hey, guys."

I set my camera down on the floor, and Yuki interrupted their game to play-punch me on the shoulder.

"So whaddya think?" he asked, arms spread wide. "Excited to be on a real-life video shoot?"

"Sure am," I said, looking round the building. The Clapham Grand had very high, ornate ceilings, a purple-lit bar, and a large, multicolored dance floor. It looked like someone had built a nightclub in an old theater. Temporary walls were being erected around the dance floor, and a team of engineers dressed in black were tinkering with lights and taping down cables.

Aiden was rolling the tinfoil ball beneath his finger, taking aim at Yuki.

"Good week?" he asked, looking up at me. As the words left his mouth, a deleted Instagram comment flashed up, uninvited, in my mind.

stay away from gabriel u dumb bitch

"Oh . . . you know. The usual crushing boredom. How about you?"
Aiden smiled.

"Yeah, same. Flew to Italy on a private jet, did some live TV. Flew back again." He flicked the ball across the table. "Yawn."

"It's a hard life. Where are the others?"

Yuki looked around the building.

"Olly's doing a phone interview for Radio One, and Gabriel's . . . uh . . . Gabriel's off somewhere."

I sat down on the arm of a chair and picked at the fabric. The boys batted their miniature soccer ball back and forth.

"Seems like Gabriel's always . . . off somewhere."

"Huh?" said Yuki, without looking up.

"I mean, it's just . . . I don't know, at the concerts I've been to, he never hangs out with you guys before the show."

Yuki and Aiden halted their game and exchanged silent glances.

"What?" I asked. Aiden tugged his jumper down over his waist.

"Look, don't tell anyone this, but—"

"Whoa, Aid . . . Aid. Chill out, bro," interrupted Yuki, with a forced laugh. "Charlie doesn't care about all that."

"About what?" I asked. Yuki waved the conversation away.

"Nothing. Enough about Gabe. Who wants a snack?"

He grabbed a banana from a nearby fruit bowl and pointed it at me.

"I'm fine . . . thanks," I said, confused. Why were they being so secretive?

"Are you sure?" Yuki peeled the sides of his banana, one by one. "Long day ahead of us, Charlie B."

"Oh?"

"Yep. Video shoots are basically four hours of hanging around, nine minutes of prancing about, and then another million bajillion hours of sitting on your bum."

He chewed his banana and grinned.

"It's *so dull*," clarified Aiden, his arms hanging loose by his sides. "People think our lives are, like, twenty-four-hour partying, but they are *so not*."

"Oh no, my friend," corrected Yuki, wagging the banana at his bandmate. "My life is totally a twenty-four-hour party. I'm partying right now. Check me out."

Yuki leaped onto the corner of the multicolored dance floor and, banana poking from his mouth, proceeded to moonwalk into the center, weaving around kneeling engineers.

Aiden and I applauded and whooped, and Yuki started to body-pop.

"Can you move out of the way?" came a voice to my right. A stage tech was waiting to get by, holding a stack of lighting gels. "Trying to do my job here."

I mumbled apologies and shuffled from his path.

"Is your stage team always this moody?" I asked Aiden, when the tech was out of earshot.

"What do you mean?"

"I don't know . . ." I looked back over my shoulder at the man with the lighting gels as he disappeared into a store cupboard. "Maybe I'm being paranoid, but it kind of feels like everyone who works for you guys . . . hates me."

Aiden peered back at me.

"What are you talking about?"

Yuki rejoined us, launching the tinfoil ball at his bandmate. It pinged off Aiden's head.

"I don't know," I said, folding my arms. "I just feel like I'm in the way all the time. Which is weird, because your management are the ones who wanted me here in the first place."

"Come again?" said Yuki.

"You know, the whole thing about wanting young photographers to do your backstage pics, and . . . uh . . . why are you looking at me like that?"

Yuki's face had creased up.

"What are you talking about?"

"Olly said that—"

"You think Barry King would want *more* young people hanging around here? That guy?" Yuki was pointing backward at the stage. "Teenagers irritate him."

"Keep your voice down," hissed Aiden, glancing around the room.

"Naaah, I don't care," scoffed Yuki. "I've made that man more money than Richard Branson. He can kiss my Japanese ass."

Aiden swallowed uncomfortably.

"Anyway," continued Yuki, "point is, more kids bombing about is the last thing Barry wants. If he had his way we wouldn't let any groupies in here at all." He stopped himself and smirked. "Not that you're a groupie, obviously."

My cheeks blushed crimson. Did he know about the fan blog?

"But if the management team don't want me involved," I asked, "then why am I here?"

Yuki and Aiden shared a puzzled look. Just as they were about to speak, we were interrupted.

"Hi, guys."

It was Olly.

All three of us went quiet.

"What's wrong with you two? Hi, Charlie."

I waved a little hello. Yuki stumbled on his words, then cleared his throat.

"Erm . . . Aid, don't we have to go and . . . do that . . . thing?"

Aiden wasn't listening. Yuki kicked him on the shin.

"Oh. Yeah!" exclaimed Aiden, awakening. "That . . . thing. We're off to do a thing."

"What's up with them?" asked Olly, with a laugh, as his bandmates walked away across the venue, nattering at each other. I told him I didn't know, but the thought nagged at me. If this whole thing wasn't part of some Fire&Lights scheme, then why *had* Olly invited me here?

He touched a hand to my shoulder.

"You feeling better?"

I took a deep breath.

"Honestly?" I asked.

"Honestly."

"Then no."

Despite my answer, we both laughed.

"I think I know how to cheer you up," he said, tapping a finger against his lips. "D'you wanna see something really cool?"

He extended an arm toward me, and I felt my fingers tingle.

"Sure," I said, and he wrapped his hand around mine.

"Not a bad view, right?" Olly said, as he led me out onto the Clapham Grand's upper circle. Like the ground floor, it was decorative and lavish, with gold-rimmed windows and luxurious red wallpaper. We had the whole level to ourselves.

"Amazing," I said in a half whisper, sitting down next to him on the front row. You could see everything from up here: the set, the lighting rig, the auditorium, engineers banging about on the dance floor.

"Most people don't get to see this place when it's empty," said Olly, leaning his elbows on the banister. "Thought you might get a kick out of it."

Olly was right—the building looked stunning—but as I surveyed the view, I couldn't help thinking of Gabriel. The way he'd swept me out onto that stage in Brighton, the glare from the lights, the pin-drop silence. The feeling that we were the only two people in the world.

"Charlie?"

Olly tilted his head at me.

"Huh?"

"Everything all right?" he asked.

I shook off the memory, and smiled.

"Sure, course."

"You seemed miles away, that's all."

"No, sorry. Was just . . . distracted. This is awesome."

"Wait," said Olly, slipping his phone from his pocket. "I'm not done yet."

Olly speed-dialed a number and waited for an answer. After a couple of rings, the call connected.

"Yo, Danny. It's Olly." A voice from the other end. "No, I know, I'm upstairs. I'm calling for a favor."

On the ground floor, someone knocked a piece of equipment over and cursed loudly.

"You're standing at the desk, right?" asked Olly, peering over the balcony. "Yep. I see you. Listen, I want to show Charlie something. Can you run the live intro for me?"

The voice on the other end sounded angry. Olly held a hand in the air.

"No . . . yep, I know, I know . . . Danny, you won't get in trouble, I promise." More grumbling from the end of the line. "Charlie . . . *Charlie Bloom*. She's our backstage photographer." My face flushed when he said this. "No, seriously, it's fine . . . you can tell them I talked you into it."

The disembodied voice moaned down the receiver. Whatever Olly was trying to do, it wasn't working.

"OK," he said, sitting back in his seat. "I tell you what. You do this for me, and I'll make you my plus one at the FHM Awards next week. Sound good?" Olly waited and, slowly nodding, directed a thumbs-up at me. "Yeah, *there you go*. I love ya, Danny. Catch you later."

Olly hung up the call and directed my attention to the stage. Nothing was happening.

"What am I supposed to . . . ?"

"Just one second," said Olly, gesturing for me to lean on the banister next to him. "Now watch this."

In front of my eyes, the set began to change. The house lights dropped and the stage filled with dry ice, billowing smoke, and white, searching spotlights. A booming soundtrack was building through the speakers.

"This is how the video's going to start," Olly explained, over the music. "We'll get lowered down on a moving platform, and then the voice-over kicks in. It's going to be epic."

"*Aiden Roberts . . . Yuki Harrison . . . Olly Samson . . . Gabriel West . . .*"

I could feel Olly's leg brushing against mine and the bass pulsing inside my chest. It felt like the whole building was coming alive.

"*. . . Ladies and gentlemen, Fire . . . & . . . LIGHTS!*"

Then, in one spectacular flash, the lights burst open and the song kicked in, and the bass drum was pounding, and Olly's foot was tapping next to mine, and everything was smoke and noise and color and madness.

"Hey, hey! What the hell's going on?!"

Downstairs, one of the engineers was shouting over the soundtrack. "Who's mucking about with the rig?"

Olly ducked down behind the barrier, pulling me with him, and pressed a finger to his lips. The engineer sounded annoyed, but Olly was enjoying himself. As we crouched there, he touched a hand to my forearm, and my skin instantly warmed.

"Danny!" the man called across the dance floor. "What on earth are you doing?"

"Sorry, Steve," replied a sullen voice from below. The music was fading away. "It was a test. I'm done now."

"You're a bloody liability, mate," said the man, and Olly made a guilty face at me, as if to say "oops."

When the music had stopped, we both stood up again and dropped into adjacent seats. A few little wisps of dry-ice vapor were winding their way toward the ceiling.

"Thanks," I said, smiling at Olly. "That was super-cool."

"My pleasure," he replied. Then his mouth twisted up at the side. "Though this does mean I have to take Danny to the FHM Awards next Thursday, and that guy is a giant pervert."

I laughed, and Olly's eyes sparkled.

"So listen," he said, sitting up straight. "About this fan blog fiasco . . ."

"It's fine," I said, playing it down. "It's just some dumb photo."

"Actually, I know about the trolling. I know people have been harassing you online. It's awful."

I pulled at a strand of hair that had escaped from my hat. "Oh . . . right." I tucked it behind my ear. "I guess I just didn't expect you guys would read your own fan blogs."

"We don't, normally. But I wanted to keep an eye on things."

So my instinct had been right. Olly *was* looking out for me.

"I'm kind of embarrassed you know about it, to be honest," I said, but he held up one hand to stop me.

"You shouldn't be. You've done nothing wrong. Plus . . . I sort of understand what you're going through."

I fiddled with the strap of my camera bag.

"You do?"

"In a way. I mean, just over a year ago, I was a totally normal teenager, right? Then all this happened, and boom . . . I'm famous. I love it, don't get me wrong, but it changes your life. And you can't undo that."

An image of Olly, pre-Fire&Lights, flashed up in my mind. His hair fluffy, shirtsleeves hanging past his wrists.

"Having everyone talk about you all the time *sounds* fun, but it can be pretty exhausting. And I know exactly what that's like." He rubbed the back of his neck. "You and I, we're not that different, really."

"I don't know about that," I said, with a laugh. "Half the world knows who you are."

Olly shrugged.

"Still, if something like this happens again, you can always call me. Any time. We're friends now, right?"

I smiled at him. I felt lighter than I had in days.

"Right."

He extended his hand, formally, and I shook it, both of us nodding solemnly, like businessmen. He held on to my hand for just a microsecond afterward, before letting go.

"So," I said, shifting in my seat, "I was chatting with Yuki and Aiden downstairs, and—"

"Oh, I wouldn't recommend that."

"Me neither," I said, and Olly laughed. "But the thing is . . . they said that what you told me about management wanting young people on the team . . . they said it's not really true."

"Ah. Right." Olly paused, and touched his palms together. "I figured that would come out eventually."

I cocked my head at him. He thought for a second and brushed some dust off his jeans.

"A few months back, the head of music at Caversham asked our management company if there was anything I could do to help that school band, Diamond Storm. I wasn't sure at first, because the industry doesn't really work like that, but everyone at school was so supportive of me in the early days, I wanted to give something back. So I said I'd take a look at their website, and that's when I found your photos."

He was looking straight at me now.

"They were *amazing*, Charlie. Like, easily as good as some of the photographers we've worked with, and those guys are pretty much the best in the business. I remembered you from that presentation in assembly, how you wanted to make a career from it . . . and it's so hard to get ahead in this industry . . . So I figured, I can't really help Diamond Storm, but I *can* help you. And I didn't know whether you'd take me seriously, so I made up that story, and maybe I shouldn't have done that, but—"

"I'm glad you did," I interrupted, and Olly smiled, suddenly relieved.

"Yeah. Me too."

"Only . . ." I dropped my head, hands balanced on my knees.

"What?"

"Well . . . if it was *your* idea to bring me here," I continued, tentatively, "then I was right about your management team, and your stage crew. They must just think I'm some random groupie with a camera."

I almost laughed at myself. *Random groupie.* Even I was saying it now.

"No, they don't," said Olly, firmly. "Honestly. I explained to them why I wanted you here, and they were cool with it. If they're giving you the cold shoulder, it's nothing to worry about. They're just looking out for us. Truth is, most girls who manage to get backstage, they're only really interested in one thing. But you . . . you're different."

He paused to look at me. I tightened my grip on the camera bag strap.

"Besides, as soon as they start taking notice of how popular your shots are with the fans, they'll change their tune. They'll see . . . they'll see what I see."

We shared a few seconds of silent eye contact, and I thought about the strange sequence of events that had led us here, to the empty balcony of an old London theater. The photos of Diamond Storm, the presentation I'd never wanted to give.

The local boy in a famous pop band.

"Thank you," I said.

"Don't mention it."

"No, I mean . . . thank you for everything. For helping me out, for the backstage passes, the new camera. It's just so nice of you." His perfect blue eyes met mine. "You didn't need to do all this."

Olly thought about this for a moment, and the building seemed to fall silent.

"Actually, I did."

"Here you are, Olly! We've been looking for you everywhere."

A woman in a pink tracksuit was standing in the entrance to the upper circle.

"We need you for warm-ups."

"Yep, I'm there," replied Olly, gathering his things.

"Where's Gabe?" asked the pink woman. Olly craned his head over the balcony.

"Still in the piano studio, I think."

"Great. We'll grab him in twenty. Let's do this."

As she led him away, Olly pointed back at me.

"We'll do some pictures before the shoot starts, OK . . . ?"

"OK," I said, watching him go, the woman touching a manicured hand to his back. They disappeared through the doorway, and I could hear Olly talking as they walked down the stairs, his voice soft, his laughter warm, uplifting.

Alone again, I clutched my camera case and looked out through the exit. Peering into the dark, I could just about make out a sign across the corridor that read: "REHEARSAL STUDIOS: AUTHORIZED ACCESS ONLY."

I stood up.

If I was going to confront Gabriel, now was the time to do it.

19

At the top of the first flight of stairs, a sign read "PIANO STUDIO: SECOND FLOOR," so I kept climbing. Soon I could hear music and the sound of Gabriel's voice.

When I reached the door, I peered through the grubby glass panel into the room. It was small, with dark purple walls and a leopard-print sofa, and in the far corner, Gabriel was sitting at a battered upright piano, playing a song. A large, round mirror hung on the wall above him.

Cautiously, I turned the handle and stepped inside. He stopped singing and glanced into the mirror.

"Charlie Brown."

I stood there, listening to the sound of my own breathing. Eventually, Gabriel spun round on the piano stool.

"I didn't know you played the piano," I said, lowering my camera bag to the floor.

"Most people don't."

I stuck close to the wall, my fingers fidgeting in my sleeves. Did he have any idea what had happened to me online? Had it even registered in his world?

"So apparently I'm supposed to get some pictures of you," I said, opening my case. We both listened to the angry tear of the Velcro.

"What if I'm not in the mood?" said Gabriel, provocatively.

"Where do you want to be?" I replied, ignoring him. "In here?"

He tinkled a couple of notes on the piano.

"I'm shy, Charlie Brown. Plus my hair . . . it's just not working today. Shouldn't have slept in my rollers. Maybe we—"

"Why did you do it?" I burst out, staying tight to the wall. Gabriel frowned.

"What?"

Everything was twisting in on itself inside my head, like tangled tree roots: the humiliation at school, Gabriel's lyrics, the way he was acting like nothing had happened. I closed my eyes, wishing I was still on the upper circle with Olly, hiding from the grown-ups.

"That photo of us, from Brighton. It's been posted online. I'm being trolled, people won't leave me alone, and I don't—"

"Charlie, slow down for a second." He closed the lid of the piano and stood up. "What are you talking about?"

He walked toward me, and I fought the threat of tears.

"Someone leaked the photo on a fan blog."

"What photo?"

I glanced up. He looked genuinely confused.

"The photo of us, onstage, in Brighton. The one I sent to you. No one knew about it apart from us, but some fan blog has posted it online, and . . ."

Gabriel closed his eyes and let out a long, slow breath.

"Wait. I think I know what happened."

He stepped back from me, hands interlocked on the back of his head.

"Carla came round to my hotel suite last Sunday, asked me out for coffee, and I . . . I don't know, I'd sort of had enough, so I told her I wasn't interested. I guess she's not used to hearing that, 'cause she went off the rails a bit. Kept going on about how we were the perfect celebrity couple." He ran both hands through his hair. "Anyway, she talked about you *a lot*. Asking why you were always around, why I was hanging out with someone who wasn't even famous, stuff like that. Then I get a call from Barry. I was in the bedroom for ages, talking to him, and when I came back, she was gone. My laptop was open on your e-mail."

His eyes glazed over.

"She must have found your message, stolen the photo . . . and leaked it."

I chewed my fingernail.

"But . . . that doesn't make sense. Why would Carla want everyone to think we were . . ."

I didn't say *together*. It felt too ridiculous.

"Because . . . I don't know, because she figured it would make your life hell. Carla knows how the press works. If you're getting trolled, you can bet she knew that would happen. She probably started it herself."

I dropped down on the arm of the leopard-print sofa.

Of course it was Carla.

The way she'd sized me up at the after-party. The way she'd looked at me when she found me with Gabriel, calling me a "random groupie," just like in the article.

"But why would anyone do that? It's just so . . . mean."

Gabriel ran a hand down one side of his face.

"Carla's a bit like that. You've read *Teen Hits*, right?"

"No."

He lifted his chin and half smiled.

"Oh yeah, I forgot. You don't read gossip."

I crossed my arms.

"Anyway," he continued, "it was a stupid mistake, and you shouldn't have been dragged into it. But don't listen to what idiots say about you on the Internet. I never do."

Gabriel came closer again. I glanced up at him.

"You really think she would do that to me?"

"She's done worse to other people, believe me."

"But . . . I don't understand," I said, shaking my head. "Carla's famous. She's on TV. Me, I'm just . . ."

Gabriel looked at me, amber light shining in his eyes.

"Charlie, trust me. You're not just *anything*."

The only sound in the room was the careful swell of my breathing, falling in step with his.

"Hey, wanna hear a song?"

"Huh?"

He gestured at the piano.

"A song. Something from the new album."

"Um . . . sure," I said, with a sniff.

Gabriel walked back to the piano, lifted the lid, and sat down. He placed his strong, tanned hands on the keys, but just as he was about to play the first chord, I stopped him.

"You have to tell me something first, though."

He twisted round on the stool.

"What are your songs about?"

Gabriel stared directly at me, right down inside me, until I felt a murmur in my bones.

"Just things around me," he replied, and began to play.

Gilded by the light from the tiny window, Gabriel's hands moved deftly across the keys, and the big, echoey sound wrapped itself around me. Deep, thunderous notes and high, fragile chimes. He started to sing, and his voice hung magically in the air, strong and pure yet dark and hard at the same time. When he reached the chorus, my pulse began to beat double-time.

> *One day she will run away*
> *When she doesn't want to be found*
> *I'd be the one to keep her safe*
> *But there are too many ways to escape from this town*
> *There are too many ways to escape from this town*

All the breath was rushing from my lungs.

His lyrics were ringing in my ears, filling my mind, and he was inside my head again, singing about my thoughts, my fears. My life. It was impossible, but it sent a buzzing heat right through me.

The song ended, and for a very long time, I didn't say anything.

"You're a tough crowd, Charlie Brown."

I shook my head and put a hand to my mouth.

"No, God . . . no. I loved it. I loved it. It's just . . . did you . . ."

Gabriel smiled oddly and leaned back against the piano.

"Did I what?"

I couldn't say it. I didn't know how to. It would sound crazy.

It *was* crazy.

"Nothing," I said, pushing the thought from my mind. "It's . . . nothing."

There had to be a simple explanation for all this. There had to be.

"So, do you play?"

Gabriel tapped a fist against the scratched wooden panels of the piano.

"Me?" I laughed. "No, no way."

He patted the space at the end of the piano stool.

"Come here. I'll teach you something."

Watching him, doubtfully, I crossed the room and slid onto the piano stool. Our legs pressed together, and he touched his fingers to the keys.

"How about a chord? Reckon you can handle one chord?"

I raised an unimpressed eyebrow.

"OK, so this is how it goes . . ."

He curled his hand over mine and lifted them both to the keyboard. I stared at my fingers, white and small, hidden beneath his.

"Your thumb, here, that goes on middle *C* . . ." He was carefully positioning each of my fingers against the stained ivory. "And then, every finger has its own key . . . no, like this."

He smirked at me.

"You have to relax, Charlie Brown. You're all tense." He leaned an elbow on the upturned piano lid. "You know, playing the piano is a lot like making love to a beautiful woman."

I glared back at him. His face, at first perfectly serious, soon broke out into laughter.

"I can't believe you just said that."

"Concentrate," he said, "or you'll never make it as a concert pianist. Now, you want to play these three keys here . . . yep, those three. At the same time."

Timidly, I pressed down the keys, but the notes all rang out at different times. The chord sounded fragile and thin.

"Was that good?"

Gabriel rocked his hand from side to side.

"I've seen better." He smiled. "You're not Rachmaninov yet, but it's early days."

I placed my fingers back on the keys and tried the chord for a second time. Once again, it came out weak, uneven.

"Hey, what's that?"

I stopped playing. Gabriel was staring at my neck.

"What's what?"

"That mark."

I brushed a lock of hair across it.

"It's just a birthmark," I said.

"It's amazing," said Gabriel, fixated. "I've never seen anything like it. It kind of looks like a . . . *flame*."

"I've always hated it."

"Oh." Gabriel thought about this. "You shouldn't."

He leaned backward a little and looked at me like he was searching my face for something. Studying me.

"Don't you ever let your hair down?"

I folded my arms.

"Yeah, course . . . I've been to loads of parties."

This was a lie.

"No," he replied, laughing at me. "I mean literally. Let your hair down."

He was staring at my hat with lowered brow, like he was trying to see through it. I couldn't speak, I just sat there rooted to the stool as he lifted a hand toward the top of my head.

Gently, he removed my hat, unleashing a few random strands of hair. They were messed up and matted from being shoved inside the hat, and I pawed at them self-consciously to flatten out the kinks.

"I knew it," he said.

"Knew . . . what?"

I was so uncomfortable without my hat, I could barely look at him.

"You are, far and away, the most beautiful girl I have ever seen."

It felt like my heart had stopped. The silence in the room seemed to grow, to swell up and envelop me, and all I could hear was my own breathing, rushing through my skull. When I thought about it—really, honestly thought about it—there was a 99.9 percent chance that Gabriel was lying.

But that 0.1 percent was killing me.

"You shouldn't tease people like that."

His eyes narrowed at this, like he was offended, and he tilted his head to the side, still watching. Always watching. Then, he seemed to lean forward, imperceptibly, into the space between us, and suddenly I knew.

I knew, with a certainty that shook me inside, that Gabriel West was going to kiss me.

20

"Hey, Gabriel! You still up here?"

A voice from the corridor. Olly's voice.

"Gabe?"

Gabriel and I shared a guilty look. I stood up and stepped away from him, but Olly was already standing in the doorway.

"Oh . . . Charlie?"

Olly was holding two bottles of water. He looked at Gabriel, then at me.

"What's going on?"

The short silence felt hot, and heavy.

"We were just . . . doing some photos," I said. We all looked at my camera, which I'd discarded on the sofa. It was still in its case.

Olly grabbed the door handle.

"We need you downstairs."

Gabriel closed one eye.

"Really? Charlie was about to nail 'Flight of the Bumblebee.'"

Olly didn't laugh.

"Jesus, Gabe, it's not up to me." He stepped back out into the corridor. "Stay up here if you want—I'm not your minder."

"OK, chill, I'm coming," said Gabriel, standing up from the piano. He grabbed his bag from the corner of the room, but Olly had already disappeared.

"Olly, dude, slow down . . ."

Gabriel hurried out into the hallway, then stopped, spun on his heel, and leaned back into the room.

"I forgot: here's your hat." He tossed it through the air, and I caught it. "But, Charlie . . ."

"Uh-huh?"

"Your hair . . . I like it that way."

I touched a hand to my head, my hair still matted, and a wavy lock tumbled down into my face.

When I looked up, Gabriel was gone.

"Aiden Roberts . . . Yuki Harrison . . . Olly Samson . . . Gabriel West . . ."

The booming voice-over filled the entire building, dry-ice vapor billowing across the stage, spotlights breaking through like car headlights in the mist. The moving platform was descending steadily toward the stage, and the four members of Fire&Lights were lined up across it, lit dramatically from behind. Watching from the floor, I could feel the bass drum pumping in the soles of my feet.

". . . Ladies and gentlemen, Fire . . . & . . . LI—"

"Stop, whoa! Stop. Kill it." A woman in a blue fleece walked out from the wings, batting the smoke away with her hands. She looked out across the venue, shielding her eyes, and the soundtrack disappeared. "Thanks, Danny. Now why does this keep happening . : . are the cues off or something . . . ?"

This, I was fast learning, was the reality of a pop music video shoot.

Just as the band were getting into full flow, something would go wrong and the stage manager would stride out onto the stage, brow creased, complaining about some problem to do with timing, framing, or the position of the lights. The boys' faces would drop, and they'd spend the next twenty-five minutes sitting on the edge of the stage, kicking their legs and throwing peanuts at each other.

This may not have been great for the shoot schedule, but it worked out perfectly for me. Some of my best photos came from moments like this.

"Hey, guys," said Yuki, grabbing a fistful of nuts from the bowl. "You know, um . . . you know SpongeBob SquarePants?"

Aiden was flicking at his phone. He didn't look up.

"Yeah?"

Yuki leaned forward and, in a hushed tone, said: "His pants, man . . . *they're not square.*"

Gabriel sneered at this.

"Shut up, they are."

"I'm telling you, bro," said Yuki, tossing nuts into his mouth, "his pants aren't square. They're rectangular. They're freaking *cuboid.*"

Gabriel stole a nut from Yuki's hand and flashed him a smile. I hit the shutter release, capturing it perfectly.

"So what if they are?" said Gabriel.

"I'm just saying," said Yuki, through the crunching of nuts, "that's his defining feature, and it's *based on a lie*. Dude's a fraud. They should call him SpongeBob RectangularPants."

Behind the camera, I let out a little laugh. Yuki pointed at me.

"Yeeeah. Charlie knows."

"One of you guys is standing a little out of place up there."

I peered over the viewfinder. The stage manager in the blue fleece was addressing the boys.

"Olly," she said, "I think it's you."

Olly was standing at the buffet table, with his back to us.

"I doubt it. I was really careful in that last take." He picked up a sandwich, inspected it, and put it down again. "It's probably Gabe."

The stage manager turned to Gabriel, who exhaled loudly.

"I'm on the end, Olly. It's not gonna be me."

Olly stood completely still.

"That's right, 'cause it couldn't possibly be Gabriel, could it?"

Gabriel's eyebrows shot upward. Yuki and Aiden looked up from their phones.

"What did you just say?" replied Gabriel, dropping off the stage and walking toward the buffet table.

Unaware of his approach, Olly picked up a bottle of water, unscrewed the lid, and took a swig.

"Olly." Gabe was standing right behind him now. "I'm talking to you."

Olly turned round, finding himself face-to-face with his bandmate. He straightened to meet Gabriel's gaze and ran a forearm across his mouth.

"Look, I don't really care what we do. Let's just get this right."

The stage manager checked her watch.

"Yes, please." Then, under her breath: "Or we'll never get out of here."

As Olly pushed past him, Gabriel threw me a glance, his face dark with irritation, and I couldn't resist. I hit the button and caught it on camera.

TROUBLE IN PARADISE??

Is this Gabriel West and Olly Samson FIGHTING at a live concert . . . ?!

Can it really be true?? Does this fan video show Gabriel & Olly getting into a scrap at the Fire&Lights concert in Bournemouth on Sunday . . . ?? It can't be!!!

No one else managed to film it, so this ten-second video is all we have . . . and it's pretty blurred . . . but it looks like Gabriel steps in front of Olly in the middle of a song, and Olly shoves him out of the way!! WTF?

If it's true, what were they fighting over? Chances are it's probably a girl, right?? :) :) Who would you choose, F&L fans? Olly or Gabriel . . . ?? COMMENTS BELOW!!!!!! :) :) xxx

xox FIRE&LIGHTS FOREVER xox
The best Fire&Lights fan blog on the web!!

"This is unbelievable. Do you know what they were fighting about?"

Melissa and I were sitting together in art class, working on charcoal drawings. The room was busy with gentle scribbling.

"No idea."

"It's not . . . they weren't fighting over *you*, were they?"

I picked up a fresh stick of charcoal.

"Good one, Melissa."

"What? It could happen . . ."

The video of Olly and Gabriel was pretty poor quality, but it definitely showed some kind of scuffle. There was something brewing between them, and the longer I spent with the band, the more obvious it became.

"Seriously, though. Think about it. Olly's buying you all this stuff, Gabriel's writing songs about you—"

"Olly bought me one thing, Mel. And as for Gabe . . . we still don't know what any of that means."

Secretly, though, Gabriel's song from Saturday was circling in my head. Those familiar words, the soothing sound of the piano. His rich, husky voice. *One day, she will run away . . .*

"So ask him, then."

"What am I supposed to say?" I put down my charcoal stick. "Hey, Gabe, I know you're the world's biggest pop star and everything, but did you steal all your lyrics off my mum?"

Melissa sucked the end of her pencil.

"That could work."

Somebody tapped me on the back. I sat up, swiveled round, and a small folded note was dropped into my hand. Miss Woods glanced up from her marking.

"Tracy, sit down, please."

A nearby table of girls whispered to each other, giggling, and at the edge of my vision I saw Tracy Sales slipping back into her chair.

Calm returned to the classroom. I unfolded the note.

is it true? about you and gabriel? we can't believe it, he is crazy hot!!!! are you still hanging out with him?? we're having a party on saturday, u should come. free house. RSVP . . . tracy/mia/holly/erica xoxoxo

I screwed up the note and dropped it on the table. Even if I *was* interested in using my newfound notoriety to become popular at school, which I wasn't, all this did was remind me of the things people had said on my Instagram feed the week before. People I had never met, who didn't know a single thing about me.

stop tryin to get famous, slut
ur desperate & ugly
gabriel doesn't want u skank
why don't u shut up & die

"I'm popping down to the design suite for some pens, Year Eleven," said Miss Woods, rising from her chair. "I'll be five minutes—please try to behave while I'm gone."

As soon as she was out of earshot, chatter bubbled up in the room.

"You coming for drinks on Friday?"

"I'm thinking of getting highlights, whaddya reckon?"

"I heard she slept with both of them."

"What, you mean Charlie Bloom?"

"Nah, I reckon she made it up."

"She's got, like, four million haters now."

And then, from Aimee Watts: "The bitch had it coming."

I stood up. Melissa grabbed my hand and whispered something urgently to me, but I tugged myself free. Aimee was sitting a few rows behind us in between Gemma, Jamie, and Sam. My hands balled into fists.

"If you have something to say, Aimee, say it to my face."

Her nose twitched.

"All right then. *You had it coming.*"

I stepped forward, through the desks. Students scraped their chairs out of the way, as if to clear a battleground.

"I know you posted that picture through my door."

"What picture?"

The whole class was watching us.

"Don't bother, Aimee."

"What? Give it a rest—I don't even know where you live."

I prickled with anger.

"All you ever do is lie."

"Who are you, the police?"

I didn't move. Melissa said my name quietly behind me.

"Come on then, Charlie," goaded Aimee. "What are you gonna do?"

It was a good question. What *was* I going to do?

"You're not worth it," I said, stepping back toward my desk. But as I did, she whispered three words into the air.

"Thirty-three Tower Close."

A fuse went in my brain. I turned on Aimee, my vision clouded with anger, tables jabbing into my thighs, but before I knew what was happening, I was being dragged backward by Melissa through a tangled mess of furniture. Miss Woods was standing in the doorway, a box of marker pens in hand, watching us, agog.

"Charlie? Melissa . . . ?" She wandered into the classroom. "This isn't like you two. What's happening?"

I looked at Aimee. She tipped her head back and stared at the ceiling, mouth hanging open.

"Nothing," I said, straightening my crumpled shirt.

"Well . . . good. Good." She inspected the scattered furniture. "Tables and chairs back to where they belong, please. Dear me, Year Eleven."

In subdued silence, people began rearranging their tables and sliding back into their seats. Miss Woods crossed over to the white-board, pulling open her box of pens and muttering under her breath.

As I sat down, I couldn't stop myself looking back in Aimee's direction one more time. She returned my gaze and pulled her lips back into a smile.

The nights were drawing in. We were deep into winter now, and it was dark by the time I arrived home from school. My father and I were keeping our distance: we ate meals together, we made small talk, but we didn't discuss Aimee's poster, or Dad's study, or my mother. We kept to ourselves, mostly, and my evenings were spent chatting with Melissa online and wading through homework.

One night, I was sitting at my desk, science homework open on my laptop, when my phone beeped with a message.

I've had an idea

It was Gabriel.

Is that so? I replied.

His speech bubble flickered at me, and while I sat there, waiting for his response, a Facebook notification popped up on my computer.

Hey charlie

It was Olly.

My gaze hopped from my computer, to my phone, and back again.

How are things?

Not bad, I started to write, if you happen to be a fan of ionic compou

Ping. Another message from Gabriel.

Come away with me

I stared at the words. What did he mean? Away . . . where?

What are you talking about?

When my message had sent, I finished writing back to Olly. Gabriel's reply hit my phone.

We're down in the southwest this weekend, couple of shows in devon, bristol. You should come

I can't

Olly, on my computer screen:

I've been thinking . . . we're playing some shows on the coast this weekend—be great if you could join us?

I pressed my fingers to my temples. The light from my laptop was pulsing in my eyes.

I'll get you a hotel room, **said Gabriel,** you can ride on the tour bus. Proper rock 'n' roll

I returned to my computer.

I'd love to come, olly . . . i just don't know if i can

Ping. Gabriel.

I want to spend some proper time with you

Blip. Olly.

Sure, i understand. But if it helps, we'll organize your hotel, you can travel on the bus. It'll be fun, i promise :)

My breathing quickened. I didn't know who to reply to first.

It'd give us a chance to hang out properly, added Olly.

I know you're there, charlie brown. **Gabriel.**

Up to you, obviously . . .

I won't take no for an answer

I slammed my laptop shut and tossed my phone onto the bed.

My room was suddenly quiet.

A whole weekend away from home? Breaking curfew by an hour was one thing, but this was in a different league.

I looked out of the window. Naked trees shivered in the inky, black air, and across the garden, Melissa's bedroom window shone yellow in the darkness. Olly and Gabriel stared at me from a poster on her wall.

I wanted to go. I wanted to get away from home, from Caversham High, and lose myself for two days. I wanted to see Olly and Gabriel, and Yuki and Aiden, and soak up the noise of the concerts, hide behind my camera and forget about the mess at school.

But that would mean lying to my father again.

And this lie would have to be big.

21

I *knocked on the door* three times. Tower Close was frosty and silent all around me, curtains half closed, light from televisions spilling through the gaps. The air had that distinctive wintry scent, smoky and clean, like bonfires in the distance.

The hallway light clicked on.

"Oh, hey there, Charlie," said Rosie, standing in the doorway in slippered feet. "Let's get you in from the cold."

Melissa's house was warm, and the oven glowed in the kitchen. The television mumbled through the living room wall.

"Hi, Charlie!" called Melissa's father from the sofa.

"Hey, Brian . . ."

"Excuse us," said Rosie, with a guilty smile. "We're just watching our favorite Scandinavian drama. Bit gruesome, they just found some poor soul at the bottom of a ravine." She tightened the cord on her dressing gown. "Oh, and Melissa's upstairs."

"Thanks, Rosie."

Melissa was on her bed, lying flat on her stomach, headphones on, scrolling through Facebook.

"Mel. Mel."

I tapped her on the head. She jumped, then grinned, tugging off her headphones.

"Yay, Charlie! What are you doing here?"

I sat down on the end of the bed.

"I need your help."

I told her about the boys' messages and the band's trip to the coast. She sat and listened to me, her mouth wide open.

"Whoa," she said, eyes glazed, when I had finished. "That sounds *epic*."

We looked at each other.

"You have to go, Charlie."

"I know," I said, pressing my eyes with the heels of my palms. "But it's a whole weekend away. And things are really weird between me and Dad right now."

Melissa sat up abruptly.

"You could take your mum's notebook," she said, staring into space. "You could show Gabriel everything, and then—"

"I can't just run away, Mel. And I've already used all the cover stories I can think of."

Melissa considered me silently, then turned to her laptop and started tapping away. I watched as she opened up some kind of graphics program and loaded an old file.

"You came to the right place," she said, intense concentration on her face. "I have so got this covered."

Dad was in his study, elbow on the desk, head in his hand. He was muttering figures to himself.

"Dad."

He didn't hear me.

"*Dad.*"

He spun round on his chair. His face was twitchy, his eyes circled with gray.

"Oh. Charlie. Sorry, I'm a bit . . ." He sighed. "Everything all right?"

My eyes danced around the room. It was all in here, somewhere: Dad's university papers, his letters to Mum. Remnants of a past life.

"Yeah, I'm fine."

I looked at my father, and a strange heat, something like shame, spread to my fingertips.

"I shouldn't have come in here last week without asking you first. I'm sorry."

Dad looked surprised. He removed his glasses.

"Well . . . I suppose, but . . ." He rubbed his eyes, and sat back in his chair. "Not to worry."

I fingered the letter in my back pocket.

"You're sure there's nothing bothering you?" he said, and a sadness rose up inside my chest. I swallowed it back down.

"Yep, I just came in because . . ." I took out the letter and unfolded it. "I'm going on a writers' weekend on Friday, with the school. I thought I should remind you."

He knitted his brow.

"A writers' weekend?"

"To Devon, you know. For English."

I passed him the forgery, and he slid his glasses back on.

"Devon?"

"I told you about it months ago—the school does it every year. Look."

He scanned the letter, up and down. Melissa had done an amazing job.

"Well, I suppose I do sometimes . . . forget . . ." He wiped a hand down his face. "And this is part of your coursework?"

I nodded and passed him a pen from the pot.

"I just need a signature."

I watched him scribble his name across the dotted line. The plan had worked, but I didn't feel triumphant or relieved. I felt hollow and sick.

"There you go," said Dad, folding the letter and passing it back. "Have I paid for this yet?"

"Yep, ages ago."

"Oh, right. Good."

For a while, we said nothing. The tree tapped feebly against the window.

"That'll be fun, then?" said Dad, rubbing the arm of his chair. "Weekend in Devon."

My grip tightened around the letter.

"I guess."

"We had a great holiday in Devon once, when you were little. Ninety-nine, it must have been . . ."

I nearly turned to leave, but something was stopping me. Dad rarely brought these things up on his own, and part of me wanted to stay longer, to ask him questions. Where had we stayed? Did we go to the beach? Were there pictures somewhere, photographs I'd never seen? But this new lie, the biggest I'd told yet, was burning bright under my skin, and I needed to get out of that room. I took a small backward step toward the door.

"Not long until Christmas now," said Dad suddenly, glancing at the calendar on his wall. "Is there anything you want?"

I bit the side of my tongue. Something Dad had said to me the week before, sitting on the edge of my bed, was running through my mind. *I know it's just you and me here, kiddo, but we're still a family.*

"I don't know . . . I'll have a think."

"Good. Good." Dad blinked at me. "What's for dinner?"

"Baked potatoes," I said, clicking open the door. I slipped from the room, and the sight that greeted me in the hallway left a twist of guilt in my stomach.

It was my coat, hanging next to his, on the rack.

The inside of the Fire&Lights tour bus was, far and away, the coolest thing I had ever seen.

It was pretty much a hotel on wheels, a double-decker behemoth complete with pool and foosball tables, arcade machines, a jukebox, and plasma TVs. There were bunks for all four band members, fridges stuffed full of food and drink, and, scattered across the ceiling in a majestic wave, a miniature universe of glow-in-the-dark stars.

Whenever the bus drove through towns, people would run out of shops and houses to wave and yell as we passed. Some girls even seemed to know the route in advance, camping out in little groups with banners and picnics. Now and again, the boys would open the windows and wave back, causing total pandemonium.

"So what d'you think of our bus?"

Aiden and I were sitting together on one of the curved leather sofas. I was drinking a Dr Pepper, fresh from the fridge.

"How do I put this?" I drew a line down the condensation on the can with my thumb. "It's basically the most incredible thing I've ever seen with my own eyes."

Aiden laughed.

"The first time I saw this thing, I thought I was dreaming." He leaned back and gazed at the star-spotted ceiling. "Mind you, half the things that happen to me, I'm, like . . . this *has* to be a dream."

I had thought the same thing, more than once, though not always in a good way. When you get messages from strangers on the Internet telling you to kill yourself, part of you wishes you could just wake up.

"Like, last week, y'know, we had this mad-busy day, and right in the middle we had to go and record a live session for MTV . . ."

I found myself smiling. It was nice, hearing Aiden talk. He was normally so quiet.

". . . and this big group of lasses were waiting for us out front, and I don't think security saw it coming, because they broke through our bodyguards and they were snatching at us, and screaming, and it was actually pretty scary. And I'm there, thinking: how did this happen? Like, I used to be just some kid, a nobody, and now . . ."

He trailed off, staring at the floor.

"I can't imagine," I said, even though, in a very small way, I could. I used to be a nobody, but now—

"Do you mind if I tell you something?"

Aiden was looking at me thoughtfully, from beneath his shaggy blond fringe. I flicked at the ring pull on my Dr Pepper.

"Um . . . no, of course."

He looked guilty, suddenly, like a child.

"I didn't really want any of this."

I sat back, surprised.

"What?"

He opened his mouth, then scratched his head, flustered.

"I mean . . . that came out wrong. I did, obviously. It's been my dream since I was five. Playing music, being in a band—I love it. But everyone knowing who I am, that takes some getting used to, y'know?"

He glanced over his shoulder, then turned back to me.

"Some days, I don't know . . . I wonder what . . . what it would be like to be invisible again." He sniffed. "Does that sound crazy?"

I couldn't help smiling again. It was comforting to hear someone else say it.

"No, it doesn't," I said. "Not one bit."

Aiden nodded happily, as if that was exactly what he wanted to hear.

"So how are you finding it?" he asked, after a pause.

"Finding . . . what?"

"Being with the band."

"Oh. Well, it's . . . exciting," I said, wondering how truthful I should be, "and scary. And totally not real."

"You're doing a great job, though. With the photos."

"Really? I think the fancy camera helps."

Aiden shook his head.

"Having the gear's one thing, but there's more to it than that." He brushed the hair from his eyes. "You have to understand people. You have to . . . *get* them."

I looked around the room.

"It helps when you like the people you're shooting."

"Yeah, that helps," agreed Aiden, with a smile. He glanced over at Olly, who was sitting on a nearby stool reading a magazine. "Sorry if we get a bit much sometimes, though. It's not really normal, spending so much time with the same people."

"You guys get on pretty well, don't you?"

"We do, yeah." He gnawed at his thumbnail. "Most of the time."

Aiden's nail clicked as he bit it off. Keeping an eye on his bandmates, he lowered his voice.

"I mean, Yuki's cool and everything, but Olly and Gabe . . . I dunno. They're always *competing* over something, and sometimes I worry about—"

"Worry about what?"

Gabriel was standing above us, pulling a thick, red licorice lace from a dispenser on the wall. He clipped it off, and Aiden stammered a reply.

"J-just that . . . um . . ."

"Come on, Aid, you can say it." Gabriel waggled the licorice lace at him. "You're worried about whether you can hold hands on the first date, right?"

He pinched Aiden's cheek.

"Everything will be fine, as long as you treat her with respect." He took a big bite of the licorice. "And buy her a strawberry milk-shake."

Aiden jabbed him in the stomach, and Gabriel slumped down on to the sofa next to him. The leather moaned beneath his weight.

"I'm gonna go say hi to the driver," said Aiden, standing up. "I'll catch you guys later."

"Later," said Gabriel, as Aiden passed through the curtain that led to the front of the bus. It flapped lazily behind him.

"Say hi to the driver?" I repeated, puzzled. Gabriel chewed on his licorice.

"He does it all the time, the softie. He's worried the driver gets lonely up there on his own."

I took a sip of my drink and smiled at the thought of Aiden, perched on the front seat of the bus, chatting with the driver about roadworks and the price of petrol.

"I could get used to this touring business, y'know," I said.

"Yeah?"

"Let's just say your bus is *slightly* nicer than the one we use for school trips."

Gabriel leaned back into the leather.

"I asked for a hot tub, but Barry vetoed it . . ."

The bus slowed down as we joined a roundabout, and I peered through the tinted windows at the approaching road signs—"Bristol 49 miles."

We still had an hour or so left on the road.

The Killers were playing on the jukebox, and arcade machines twinkled and blipped in the corner. Farther down the bus, through the curtains, I could hear the roadies sharing a joke, chatting in beefy voices.

Olly turned a page in his magazine.

"Did you and Olly really have a fight last weekend?" I asked Gabriel, in a hushed voice. He turned to face me and trained his amber eyes on mine, and I felt like I'd burst into flames.

"What do you think, Charlie Brown?"

A drop of moisture trickled off my Dr Pepper and onto my jeans.

"I don't know. I just saw it on a blog."

"I thought you didn't read that stuff?" he teased, throwing the last chunk of licorice into his mouth.

"I don't, but . . . people were talking about it at school."

Gabriel thought about this for a few seconds, then reached into the fridge and pulled out a Coke.

"I mean, for a start," he said, popping the can, "if I really did start a fight with Olly, don't you think I would win?"

He said the last three words loud enough for everyone to hear, even above the jukebox, and Olly turned round from his perch on a nearby stool. Yuki was tapping at a handheld computer and, after looking up momentarily, returned to his game with a shake of his head. Aiden poked his head through the curtain.

"Hey, guys, Bob says we're stopping in twenty mi—"

"What was that, Gabe?" asked Olly, lowering his magazine. Gabriel pretended to read the back of his Coke, his feet crossed on the coffee table.

"I was just telling Charlie that I'd beat you in a fight."

Olly's face folded in confusion.

"What? Why are you even talking about that?"

Gabriel's mouth fell open for a moment, and he locked eyes with Olly. Then he waved him away.

"Nah, never mind."

An uncomfortable silence spread through the bus. Olly almost went back to his magazine, but as he reached for it, his face tightened, and he turned back to Gabriel.

"If you're talking about the other night, then—"

"I was just saying," interrupted Gabriel, raising his eyebrows at me, "I'm stronger than you are, and I'd win in a fight. That's all."

Olly shook his head and flicked over a page in his magazine.

"This is pathetic, Gabe."

Gabriel raised a single palm.

"Look, if it bothers you that much, we could . . . I don't know . . . arm wrestle for it?"

Olly looked up and scoffed. He was the musclier of the two by far, and while Gabriel was lean and fit, his arms were small and skinny by comparison.

"You're serious?" said Olly, pushing his magazine away.

"Sure," replied Gabriel, with a shrug. "Three hundred to the winner?"

I almost choked on my drink. *Three hundred pounds?*

"You guys are tools," commented Yuki, still glued to his game. His bandmates ignored him.

"Fine," agreed Olly, sliding off his stool and moving to a nearby counter. "You're on."

As I watched Olly rolling up his sleeves, I wondered whether I should stop them, but within seconds Gabriel had crossed over to join him.

"Guys . . . don't," I pleaded weakly.

"Yeah, come on, lads," said Aiden, pushing through the curtain. "This is stupid."

Olly and Gabriel weren't listening. They were facing off across the table, Gabriel smiling, Olly looking steely and determined. Behind them, the never-ending gray motorway raced by at high speed.

They locked into each other, and Gabriel's forearm looked slight, almost delicate, against Olly's.

"You sure you want to do this?" said Olly.

"Don't worry about me, Samson." Their eyes met, and a knot formed in my stomach. "Do the honors?"

Olly sucked in a breath.

"Three . . . two . . . one . . . *go.*"

At first, nothing happened. Their arms were tensed, but there was very little movement in either direction. I'd assumed Gabriel didn't stand a chance, but he looked calm, amused even, while Olly seemed to be straining, faint pearls of sweat forming at his hairline.

Time ticked by, and neither arm budged.

"OK," said Gabriel, eventually, with a glance out the window. "I'm done with this."

In an instant, he slammed Olly's arm down onto the tabletop and their hands snapped apart. Gabriel stepped backward and, across the counter, Olly stared in disbelief at his now-empty fingers. They were striped red from Gabriel's grip.

"Olly, are you OK?" I said uselessly, but he wouldn't return my eye contact. He just rose back up again, rubbing his wrist, eyes wide and fixed on Gabriel. He was out of breath, his cheeks flushed.

"Happy now?" he said his voice a little ragged. Gabriel was leaning against the jukebox, unruffled, the lights from the machine flashing all around him.

"Doesn't make any difference to me, mate."

"Nothing does, does it?"

"What's that supposed to mean?"

Olly exhaled, slowly, as if trying to calm himself down. "Just forget it."

Gabriel tapped his tongue against his teeth.

"If you've got something to say, Olly, just say it."

"Leave it. Seriously."

Gabriel narrowed his eyes and lowered his voice.

"This is about Jake, isn't it?"

Olly took several deep breaths, staring at the floor. Then he clapped his hands together.

"Yeah. D'you know what . . . ? Yes. It *is* about Jake. It's about you pushing him out of the band."

Gabriel's eyebrows jumped upward.

"Me? Wh—? Get over yourself, Samson. It was Barry who chucked Jake out of the band, not me."

Olly leaned both hands on the counter.

"And you just happened to be there to fill his shoes, right?"

"Oh, you have got to be kidding me—"

"We *had* something before you came along, Gabe—it was coming together. It would have worked out."

"And we don't have something now?" said Gabriel, gesturing at our surroundings. "Luxury tour bus not enough for you, is that it? Huh? Besides, I *earned* my place in this band. You're singing *my* songs, for a start." He looked around the space, at each of us, then back at Olly. "How many hits have you written this year?"

Olly's top lip curled into a sneer.

"You really think you're better than the rest of us, don't you?" he spat across the bus.

Gabriel raised both hands and shook his head. "Your words, Olly. Not mine."

Olly sprang toward him and grabbed him by the collar, causing the jukebox to rock on its base and sending nearby cutlery and bowls scattering to the floor. Aiden leaped in between them, pulling them apart, and Olly relented, his chest swiftly rising and falling, his T-shirt tangled. He stumbled back against the toilet door.

Gabriel still hadn't broken a sweat.

"There's your money," said Olly, slipping his wallet from his back pocket and pulling out a wad of cash. He tossed the notes at Gabriel, and they fluttered and flapped to the floor. I watched them in amazement.

"Keep it, bro," said Gabriel, stepping over the money on his way back to the sofa. As the final few twenties came to rest on the ground, Olly ran a hand down his face, took one final look at Gabriel, and vanished through the curtains.

Silence fell. Aiden sat on his bunk and plucked some awkward chords; Gabriel passed a hand through his tousled hair. Yuki cursed at his computer game.

How long, I wondered, could a group of people spend every waking minute together, with tensions riding high, before it all came crashing down around them?

Something, eventually, would have to give.

22

We arrived at the hotel late, around two thirty in the morning. It had been an exhausting day for the band: hours of traveling, a lengthy television interview, and a two-hour concert in Bristol. For the final hour of the journey, everyone on the tour bus, driver aside, had been fast asleep.

The bus meandered up the long hotel driveway, its headlights illuminating snatches of mown lawns and manicured hedges, and pulled up outside the building's grand façade. Pistons sounded as the suspension lowered.

We were stepping off the bus when a figure approached us from the dark.

"Gabriel . . . hey, Gabe!"

Gabriel stepped down onto the tarmac, and his bodyguards closed in around him. A wash of light from the hotel lobby passed over the figure's face, and I felt a dart of recognition.

I'd seen him somewhere before.

"Gabe, mate, Paul Morgan from *The Record*. Listen, I—"

"No press," said one of the bodyguards, warding the man away with an outstretched hand. I studied his face—the scruffy stubble, the small, beady eyes—and it came back to me. He'd been in the huddle of reporters outside the venue in Brighton, pushing Gabriel about his parents.

"Come on, mate, I've been waiting for hours."

"Mr. Morgan, it's two o'clock in the morning."

Gabriel kept his head down and, flanked by the rest of the band, pushed on toward the hotel entrance. I followed a few paces behind.

"Gabe, come on!" called Paul, across the driveway. "Tell us about your family. The people want the full story, just give me ten mi—"

"*Back off.*"

Three bodyguards had broken away from the band and formed a triangular barricade around the journalist. Trapped behind them, he looked small, vulnerable, like a rat in a cage.

"Don't make us call the police," said one of the guards sternly.

Paul threw his hands up in surrender. "Jesus Christ, fine, keep your wig on." As he backed away, he cupped his hands over his mouth and shouted in our direction. "Sleep well, boys . . ."

The bodyguards stood their ground until Paul had retreated all the way back to his car. As we crossed the threshold into the lobby, he clicked open the car door, dropped inside, and drove off into the night.

The hotel lobby was spectacular. It had a high, arched ceiling and a sweeping staircase, all cream-colored marble and polished brass, complete with ornate mirrors and glittering chandeliers. A bustling band of hotel staff arrived to show people to their rooms, and before I knew it, my luggage had been loaded onto a posh-looking trolley, and a man in a smartly pressed uniform was holding the lift door open. I said good night to the boys and was shown to my room, high up on the fifth floor.

Five minutes later, I was standing barefoot at the window of my hotel room, bathed in a deep, rich silence, the golden eye of a lighthouse pulsating in the distance. Flashes of that night's concert came back to me: the roar of the crowd, the thundering of drums, the sound of the boys' voices united in harmony. I'd spent the whole show waiting for someone to break, for Gabriel or Olly to turn on one another, but it hadn't happened.

Perhaps they'd got it out of their systems.

Perhaps this was just what tour life was like.

You awake?

I looked down at Gabriel's message, and my mouth curled up into a smile.

Nope, I replied. Fast asleep

In my head, this made him laugh. I waited for the reply.

Soooo . . . I'm looking at my schedule

Sounds riveting, I wrote back.

And tomorrow afternoon is wide open

I left him hanging. After a few seconds, my phone pinged again.

You + me, chilling out . . . whaddya say?

What did you have in mind?

Dunno yet. I'll think of something

I glanced up from my phone, through the window, at a cluster of stars twinkling in the dark. Perhaps if we spent some proper time together, I could finally confront Gabriel about his lyrics, away from the others. Somewhere private. Just like Melissa said.

I'm in, I replied.

3 p.m.?

3 it is

Night, charlie brown xx

Night x

I wriggled my toes into the deep, luxurious carpet. Dad and I had occasionally stayed in hotels on holiday, but I'd never been in one this expensive, and certainly not on my own. I had a stunning sea view, an en suite bathroom with dark slate tiles, a fluffy bathrobe, and a huge double bed. Holding up my phone, I stood back against the window to take a photo and then sent it to Melissa.

Oh SHUT UP

I know

Melissa had stayed up late, sending me message after message. I imagined her curled up in bed at home, the house cloaked in darkness, the bluish glimmer from her iPhone lighting up her face.

I cannot believe your life right now

It was true. I couldn't believe my life right now either. Back at home, there were things waiting for me that twisted my stomach: Aimee Watts, the lies I'd told my father, the whispering in every corner of the school.

But out here, for the next two days, I was free from all that. I could forget it all, if only for forty-eight hours.

A tide of relief washed over me.

I fell backward on to the bed and spread out like a starfish.

When I awoke, a crisp, wintry sun was slicing across the center of my room. I had slept late, past one o'clock, unable to budge from the impossibly comfortable bed, and my limbs felt satisfyingly fuzzy. I rolled out of bed and crossed over to the glass table in the corner, where a huge bowl of fruit and a glinting coffee machine sat next to a basket of cookies, muffins, and fancy chocolates. Sliding one of the muffins from its plastic packaging, I plucked out a soft, gooey chunk, popped it in my mouth, and padded to the window.

Our hotel was perched on the edge of a cliff, overlooking a bay. Small waves crested in the choppy, turquoise sea, and in the distance, birds hovered above the water, feathers flapping against the wind.

The hotel to your tastes, ma'am?

A message from Olly. I sat down in the large bay window and typed my reply.

It'll do. Though i don't appear to have a butler

How awful. My people will fix ASAP

A pause. His speech bubble was pulsating.

Wanna hang out?

I checked the time. If I got moving, I could spend at least an hour with Olly before meeting Gabriel.

I smiled and took a big bite from the muffin.

Hell yeah. Gimme 20, I wrote, before bounding off into the shower.

When I opened the door, Olly was looking sheepish, and a little tired.

"Hey. You all right?"

He cleared his throat.

"I feel kind of bad about yesterday."

He had a guitar strapped to his back, which seemed unusual. I had no idea he could play.

"Why?"

"That dumb standoff I had with Gabriel. It was childish. I owe you an apology."

"You don't—it's fine."

"No, I do. I was acting like a jerk. I shouldn't have let him suck me in. It's just . . . God, he really winds me up sometimes."

Tell me about it, I thought.

"Last weekend, too, in the piano studio. I think I was a bit . . . off with you." He squinted one eye. "Forgive me?"

"That's sweet, but you haven't done anything wrong." I nodded at his instrument. "Why the guitar?"

"You'll see," he said, with a crooked smile. He glanced over my shoulder at the panoramic sea view. "Fancy a walk on the beach?"

Our hotel had its own private stretch of sand—a picturesque, semicircular cove nestled at the foot of the cliffs. Unsurprisingly, on a chilly day in November, it was entirely deserted.

"Have you thought about what you'll do when you finish school?" Olly was saying as we wandered along the shoreline. Our feet were leaving shallow imprints in the damp sand, and they disappeared as we walked.

"A bit," I said, tightening my scarf. It was cold down by the water. "My dad asks about it sometimes. He'll say things like, 'This is an important year for you, Charlie,' and I know he's right, but . . . y'know."

"Yep," agreed Olly, "parents can be a pain. My mum and dad were cool about me auditioning, but they never expected it to go anywhere. Dad wanted me to be an architect."

We both laughed at this: Olly Samson, the architect. Though, when I thought about it, it was easy to imagine Olly living a normal life, with a house, a dog, and a family. He was much better than Gabriel at forgetting to be a pop star.

"Are your parents musical?" I asked.

"My mum used to be an actor, but she never got anywhere. Actually, I think that's why Dad wanted me to get a sensible job. They know how hard it can be."

I kicked apart a pile of sandy pebbles.

"It's a good thing you didn't listen to him, right?"

Olly shrugged.

"He was just trying to protect me, that's all."

I thought about my father, the secrets in his study, and the distance that he kept between me and my mother. Maybe he was only trying to protect me, too.

I just wished I knew what he was protecting me from.

"So anyway," said Olly, veering away from the sea. We were heading in the direction of some sand dunes at the base of the cliffs. "I have a favor to ask you."

"Oh?"

"There's this new song I'm working on, and . . . well . . . I wanted to play it to you first."

"Me?"

We arrived at the dunes and, lifting the guitar off his back, Olly sat down on a little tuft of grass.

"Sure." He smiled. "You can help me figure out whether it's any good."

"But I don't know anything about songwriting."

I joined Olly on the ground, dropping my camera bag beside me. Olly unzipped his guitar case.

"That doesn't matter. I just need someone I can trust."

We barely know each other, I wanted to say, but then I realized that wasn't what he'd said. He'd said "trust." And it felt like we did trust each other, even though we'd been friends for less than three weeks.

"I didn't know you played an instrument," I said, as Olly tweaked the silver knobs on the head of the guitar, tuning the strings. In the distance, the sea washed up and down on the shoreline. Gulls barked overhead.

"I'm not that good yet," he replied, laughing at himself. "So go easy on me."

Stumbling a little at first, Olly started to play. He was concentrating hard, forming the chord shapes very deliberately and wincing at small mistakes, but though his fingers sometimes slipped, and though he clearly hadn't been learning for long, the sound lifted me up; it spread out inside me like wings.

As Olly's hands danced around the strings, the chords singing out in the cold, salty air, I thought about everything he'd done for me this past month. The new camera, the VIP passes, making up a story to get me here in the first place. He'd broken the rules for me. He'd taken me away from home, from school, from everything ordinary, and brought me here, to an amazing place at the edge of the world where I never imagined I'd be.

And that was when he started to sing.

Olly's voice was different from Gabriel's—cleaner, with softer edges—and it melted into the music, curling around the chords. It sounded even better up close than on the records, or even live onstage. Unamplified, untouched, it sank into me like sunshine.

I tried not to read too much into the lyrics he was singing: I'd made that mistake before. But the song was sweet and moving, and I could imagine the band performing it; I could hear it on the radio. As the final guitar note faded away, I searched my head for a response, but could only think of clichés.

"That was . . . incredible," I said inadequately.

"God, thank you," he replied, relieved, tapping a foot on the sand. "You really think so?"

"Definitely."

"Thanks. That means everything, it really does."

"Like I said, I don't know anything about music . . . but I thought it was beautiful."

"Sometimes you just need something to write about."

I was sitting there, heart beating in my throat, wondering if he was talking about me, when Olly laid down his guitar, shifted across the sand, and settled next to me on the crest of the dune. His eyes were the same color as the sky.

"I like you, Charlie," he said, with the ocean behind him. "I really, really like you."

The sound of his song was still in my ears as my gaze fell into his. Gabriel had eyes you could get lost in, but, somehow, Olly had eyes that always found you.

"*Aaannd* once again Harrison beats Roberts to the finish!" came a dramatic cry from overhead as, amid an arc of spraying sand, Yuki and Aiden crashed into our peaceful little scene, tumbling and laughing and gasping for breath.

Olly and I were left staring at one another, baffled, his bandmates writhing in a pile between us.

"Um . . . hi, boys," said Olly, rescuing his guitar from the scrum. Yuki sat bolt upright, his sand-covered hair sticking out at fifteen angles.

"Well, look who it is! My favorite photographer and, erm . . ." He arched an eyebrow at Olly. "One of her stalkers?"

Olly flicked sand at him, and Yuki toppled backward.

"We were racing," explained Aiden breathlessly, retrieving one of his shoes from a nearby shrub. "I nearly beat him this time."

"The thing our little Irish friend here fails to acknowledge," explained Yuki, "is that I have the willowy limbs of a gazelle, whereas he . . ." He considered Aiden for a moment. "He has the athletic prowess of a slightly asthmatic dachshund."

Aiden scoffed at this and kicked Yuki in the shin.

"That's mean!"

"Cool your boots, Roberts. It's your brain I'm attracted to."

Yuki slung an arm around Aiden's neck and ruffled his hair. Aiden laughed cheerfully, and turned to us, brushing sand from his jeans.

"So what are you guys up to?"

Olly and I looked at each other but said nothing.

"*Wwwait* a minute," said Yuki, wagging a finger at us. "Did we gatecrash some kind of romantic scenario here?"

My mobile buzzed in my pocket.

"Very funny," countered Olly, and I rolled my eyes, pulling out my phone.

"We were just hanging out," Olly added, "playing some guitar . . ."

I glanced at the screen, and five little words stole my heart.

Meet me downstairs, charlie brown

"Weren't we, Charlie?"

I realized all three boys were looking at me.

"Huh?"

"Everything all right?" asked Olly, after a pause.

"Um . . . yep, yeah. Fine."

I attempted a casual smile, but Olly looked unconvinced. He turned to the others.

"I was just playing Charlie my new song, actually."

"Nice," said Yuki, picking the guitar up off the sand. "Though I doubt it compares to my latest masterpiece, which I like to call 'Yuke-mian Rhapsody.' "

He strummed a clumsy chord on the guitar and sang his name in a high voice.

My phone vibrated again.

Stop raiding the minibar and get down here

"So what do you think, Charlie B?" asked Yuki, arms crossed on top of the guitar. "Is Olly the next Chris Martin?"

And again:

I promise it'll be worth it

"Charlie?"

I looked up. I had lost track of the conversation.

"I just . . . I think I . . ." Staring at Gabriel's message, I stumbled on my words. "Olly, can I talk to you for a sec?"

Olly nodded and, retrieving his guitar from Yuki, slid it into its case. I stood up, flicking the sand from my clothes.

"You're not off, are you?" asked Aiden, looking crestfallen. Behind him, Yuki slid on a huge pair of sunglasses. I lifted my bag onto my shoulder.

"Y-yeah, I think so. I'll catch you guys on the bus later."

The boys waved good-bye, and Olly and I began walking back to the cliffs. After a few steps, I stopped in front of him.

"Listen," I said, above the sound of the ocean, "I'm sorry I have to go, but I kind of have plans . . . with Gabriel."

"Yeah," he said, his hair lifting slightly in the breeze. "I figured that."

"What you said, just now . . ." I touched a hand to his arm. "I like you too, Olly. I think you're amazing. And I know I'm being unfair to you, I just . . . I promised Gabe I'd spend some time with him this week-end, and I don't . . ."

My words were swallowed by the bubbling wash of the sea. Olly nearly reached out to me but clenched his fists instead.

"The thing is, he's not . . . I mean, Gabriel's not . . ." He ran both hands through his hair. "You don't know him like I do, OK?"

I frowned.

"What are you talking about?"

"He's angry, Charlie. I see it sometimes, in his eyes. He's angry about something. And, you . . . you deserve the best, all right?" He sighed and shook his head. "That's all."

His eyes dropped to the sand. A small flock of birds rose up into the air above us, scattering as they flew.

"If you have to go," he said finally, lifting his head, "just promise me something."

I pulled my coat tight around me.

"What?"

"Be careful around him, will you?"

It seemed a strange thing to say. What did he think was going to happen?

"I . . . promise," I said, and, with heavy shoulders, Olly turned and walked away. When he reached the dunes, Yuki and Aiden mobbed him like excitable puppies, laughing and tugging at his clothes. I watched them for a while, play-fighting on the sand, then climbed the winding steps back up to the hotel, a growing weight in my heart.

In the building's sweeping driveway, Gabriel was sitting in the driver's seat of a stunning open-top sports car, wearing aviator shades and a Jim Morrison T-shirt with the sleeves rolled up.

I pointed at the gleaming bodywork.

"Whose car is th—"

"Been for a walk?" he interrupted, looking back toward the ocean.

"Um . . . yeah. Sort of."

He went quiet for a second, and I wondered if he knew who I'd been with. Then, suddenly, he drummed the steering wheel.

"You coming, then?" he said.

I peered into the car and laughed at him.

"Coming where?"

"You'll see."

I glanced back inside the hotel.

"But we can't just . . . leave . . . can we?"

"Course we can—get in."

I faltered, but he opened the passenger door and held out his hand.

"I'm not going without you," he said, and as I walked tentatively toward the car, he took my hand and guided me inside.

"We need to move quick," he said, yanking the car into gear and reversing round the driveway's mini roundabout, one arm stretched out behind my seat. His skin was brushing the back of my neck. "Because when my security guards realize I've gone out without them, they . . . are . . . gonna . . . go . . . *ballistic*."

And with the engine purring in the crisp November air, we sped away from the hotel and onto the open road.

It was the first sunny day I could remember since Brighton, but it was nervous sunlight, the kind that can turn to rain in seconds. The sky stretched out above a rolling gray ocean, and in the distance a handful of tiny houses dotted the cliff side. Salt air clung to my skin.

"So, come on," I said, as the craggy coast flew by, "where are we going?"

Gabriel had one hand on the wheel, the other in his hair.

"You know your problem, Charlie Brown?" he said from behind his shades. He was looking at me instead of the road. "You don't trust me."

No, I thought. *I don't.* And I remembered Olly, sitting on the beach, carefully tuning his guitar. The sound of his song above the crashing waves.

"You're a rock star. Why would anyone trust you?"

Gabriel laughed at this but didn't answer. I stole a look at my camera bag, nestled at my feet. Mum's notebook was in there, hidden in the inside pocket. I still wasn't sure if I'd have the guts to show it to him.

"If you won't tell me where we're going," I said after a while, "at least tell me where you got the car."

The car we were traveling in was a bloodred, bullet-shaped convertible with a winged Aston Martin logo on the steering wheel. I didn't know much about cars, but it had to be worth more than my dad earned in a year.

Gabriel was gazing into the rearview mirror, curling a strand of hair round his finger.

"I bought it."

"You *what*?"

"I bought it. Where else do you get a car from?"

"Well, anywhere," I spluttered back, astonished. "You could have hired it, or borrowed it. I mean . . . Jesus, how much did it cost?"

"I dunno, a hundred . . . and something. I can't remember."

"A hundred *grand*?"

It was at times like these when I remembered that Gabriel and I lived in completely different worlds.

"That's crazy," I said, shaking my head, but Gabriel's lack of response suggested he wasn't interested in talking about money. I sat back in my seat.

"Can I ask you something?"

"Can I dodge the question?" replied Gabriel with a smirk, and I gave him a look. He shifted up a gear.

"Why don't you hang out with the others on show days?"

Gabriel's smirk vanished, and he took a small, sharp breath. For several moments, he said nothing.

"You wouldn't believe me, even if I told you," he said finally.

I kept my eyes on the road. "Try me."

A bright blue camper van whizzed by us. Gabriel let out a long sigh.

"Stage fright."

I laughed, involuntarily.

"You're not serious?" I said, my voice climbing several pitches. Gabriel cleared his throat and picked at the steering wheel.

"Yep."

"You . . . get *stage fright*?"

No wonder Yuki and Aiden were so secretive when I asked them about it. They were protecting him.

"Uh-huh."

I thought back to our time on the empty stage in Brighton, and something Gabriel had said that day suddenly made so much more sense.

What are you doing up here on your own?

I like it . . . calms me down.

"But . . . you're—"

"Gabriel West from Fire&Lights? Yeah, that's what everyone thinks." His eyes dropped. "I'm not indestructible, you know."

I scanned the dashboard, trying to square this new information

with the way the world saw him. The flawless teen idol, super-real, un-
touchable.

"I just never would have guessed."

"People have no idea what it's like. They look at us performing and
they think it's easy, they think we just roll out of bed and onto the
stage. But sometimes . . . it's terrifying up there."

All this time, the way he'd kept to himself, hiding backstage, it
wasn't arrogance at all. It was fear.

"Embarrassing, right?" he said.

"No, not at all. It's just—"

We were interrupted by the ringing of Gabriel's phone. He pulled
it from his pocket and cursed.

"Who is it?"

"My bodyguards."

"Shouldn't you answer?"

He looked at the screen, clicked his tongue, and then, without warning, lobbed the phone from the car. It spun into the undergrowth at
the side of the road and vanished behind us.

"Oh my God, Gabe . . . !"

He turned to me.

"Now we'll have peace."

"But . . . won't you get in trouble for driving off like this?"

"Oh, definitely. My security team think if I spend more than five
minutes in the daylight I'll burst into flames."

"So you *are* a vampire . . ." I whispered, and Gabriel smiled, apparently pleased that I'd remembered his joke.

"Anyway, turns out I'm supposed to be doing some crappy magazine interview this afternoon, but why would I do that when I can run
away with you? Plus, everyone knows you can't do press interviews
when you're traveling at ninety miles an hour."

I clocked the speedometer.

"We're not traveling at ninety miles an hour."

"Not yet," he said, flooring the accelerator.

My stomach leaped into my mouth as the car sped up dramatically, growling like a tiger. We were approaching the crest of a hill, and our speed was climbing, and climbing fast. My hat threatened to blow off into the road, and I had to pull it down hard to keep it in place.

"What are you doing?" I said, checking my seat belt. It was at this point I noticed Gabriel wasn't wearing one.

"Taking a ride," he replied, both hands on the wheel. The quivering dial on the speedometer crept up toward ninety, and then past ninety, to ninety-five, ninety-six, ninety-seven.

If this was how he planned to distract me from the stage fright conversation, it was definitely working.

"This is too fast," I said, above the throaty snarl of the engine. Gabriel slid his glasses back into his hair.

"Trust me."

There it was again. *That word.*

We powered over the lip of the hill, our tires almost leaving the tarmac, and emerged onto an open stretch of road. The dial told me we were traveling at over a hundred miles an hour.

I pulled my hat off and shoved it into my lap.

"Gabe . . . ?"

The road was thundering underneath us like a turbo-charged conveyor belt, trees and rocks and road signs hurtling past on either side. I had my hands clamped tight to the seat edge, knuckles turning white, when beneath the roaring engine, I heard Gabriel say something that sounded like: "I've got you."

I shut my eyes tight, and his hand closed over mine.

As his touch warmed my skin, I relaxed my grip, and a strange calm sank into me. I felt like I was watching us from above, as if in a music video, the camera swooping, an epic soundtrack booming in my ears. I opened my eyes again, the wind lashing at my face, hair whipping in every direction, and the world in front of me was beautiful, frightening, and moving at breakneck speed. Gabriel was there, and everything was connected; everything was shadows. Everything was alive.

I knew it was reckless, and my dad would have had a heart attack, but I didn't care. I sank back in my seat, elated, blood pulsing through my body, ocean spray coating my bare arms. Above us, the sky rolled out for miles.

Eventually, as we approached a shallow bend in the road, Gabriel eased off the pedal. The speedometer dial sighed its way back down to forty, and we passed a few seconds in silence, dots of cold rain landing on our cheeks. Gabriel's fingers rose gently off mine.

"Nice one, boy racer," I said, my heart still thumping. Gabriel dropped down a gear, and the car's husky groan slowed to a comforting purr.

"That was fun though, right?"

I swallowed a smile.

"No comment."

Gabriel glanced in the rearview mirror and turned the steering wheel.

"We're here."

He pulled into a small parking area on the cliff side and rolled to a stop opposite a weather-beaten picnic bench. The car drifted to sleep, engine ticking as it cooled.

"Where's here?" I asked, sliding my hat on again over my tangled hair. Gabriel tipped his glasses back in front of his eyes and smiled.

"Paradise."

* * *

Gabriel was leading me along a short, narrow path that snaked from the car park down to the cliff edge. The weather was beginning to turn, and the sun had retreated behind a bank of angry clouds. There were maybe twenty minutes of decent light left in the day.

Ahead of us, stretching out toward the horizon, was mile after mile of open ocean, impossibly endless, a churning black landscape. We were just a couple of meters from the precipice, and all that stood between us and the sheer drop was an old wooden sign that read, "Beware, Danger of Death."

"Come on," said Gabriel, steering me past the sign. My feet started to protest.

"But we might fall—"

"We won't," interrupted Gabriel, taking my hand. His was warm, and strong, and enveloped my small, freezing fingers. As he guided me to the edge of the cliff, I braved a downward glance and my head swam at the sight. A hundred meters below, maybe more, the sea thundered and smashed against the rocks.

"It's almost like you're *trying* to freak me out," I said, peering over the verge.

"As if I would do something like that," said Gabriel, with a smile.

"So what *are* we doing all the way out here, then?"

He looked out to sea, hair whipping against his forehead.

"Do we really need a reason?"

"No, it's beautiful . . . it is. But . . ."

He turned to face me.

"Truth is, I wanted to spend some time with you that wouldn't be interrupted by journalists or security guards. Or fans. And I don't get to do that without running away."

Running away, I thought. It was almost funny. Gabriel was rich, famous, and adored, but he couldn't leave his hotel without asking someone's permission. It was as if he'd never left school.

"You live a strange life," I said with a smile.

"Yeah. We do."

I took in the view again, sucking in the sea air. A long, industrial tanker came into sight on the horizon, then disappeared again.

"Actually . . . I'm kind of worried about you guys," I said. Gabriel smirked at me.

"Fire&Lights?"

"Uh-huh."

"Why?"

Olly's song from the beach was still reverberating in my mind. The ringing of guitar strings, his voice, strong and pure, soaring out over the waves.

"You and Olly, the fights. The arguments. It's getting worse."

Gabriel buried his hands in his pockets.

"He doesn't trust me, that's what it is. He blames me for Jake."

"That wasn't your fault, though."

"Maybe not, but Olly doesn't see it that way, and I can't talk him round. They were really close friends." He picked at a fingernail. "Still are."

"What you boys have, though, it's really special. And I don't mean the fans and the money. I mean the four of you, together. It's magical. I see it every weekend."

Gabriel considered me for a while, through the gentle curve of his sunglasses. I couldn't see his eyes, only my own reflection, distorted in the lens.

"You're like no one else I've ever met, Charlie Brown. You know that?"

"Is that a good thing?"

Gabriel removed his glasses and hung them on the neck of his T-shirt. Over his shoulder, birds wheeled above the trees, calling to each other across the sky.

"Course it is."

I took several deep breaths. We were alone out here, miles from anywhere. I had Mum's notebook in my bag. If I didn't tell him now, I never would.

"If I tell you something, and it sounds crazy . . . will you promise not to laugh at me?"

"You can tell me anything."

The wind picked up around us, whistling in our ears. I tugged at the edge of my hat.

"My mum died when I was three."

Sadness softened Gabriel's face. He started to reply.

"It was a car accident," I continued, cutting him off. "I was too young to remember anything, really. My dad brought me up on his own."

I avoided Gabriel's gaze. I could hear him breathing beneath the restless churn of the ocean.

"God, Charlie . . . that's awful. But why would I lau—"

"That's not it," I said, rubbing my eyes. "There's something else."

I unclipped the lid of my camera bag and slid out the notebook. When I passed it to Gabriel, his brow furrowed.

"What's this?"

"Take it," I said, guiding it into his hand. He took it, mystified.

"Before she died, Mum kept this book. It's a scrapbook, I guess, for writing down all her ideas—bits of poetry and stuff. I keep it under my bed."

Gabriel glanced at me fleetingly, then returned to the notebook. He ran a single finger along the outside edge of the old, crinkled pages.

"I've turned a page down. Look."

I pointed to the folded page, and Gabriel slid in his thumb. The moment he lifted the cover, I saw the words. *She lives her life in pictures . . . she keeps secrets in her heart.* For a few seconds, Gabriel just read, in silence, but when he reached those familiar lines, his face shifted, then hardened, like it was turning to stone. He looked surprised, almost afraid.

"Aren't you going to say something?"

For a long time, he didn't reply. I could see his mind turning over, thoughts racing.

"Gabriel, those are lyrics from your . . ."

The sentence died in my mouth as Gabriel closed the notebook and fixed his eyes on mine. The air was cold now, bitter on our skin.

"Can you keep a secret?" he said.

"A secret?"

"If I tell you something no one else knows . . . can I trust you?"

I tugged a damp strand of hair from my face.

"Of course . . . but what's this got to do with—"

"Just give me a chance to explain, OK?" he said, gritting his teeth. "I'm not really sure how to say this."

23

The wind whipped at our faces, cold and sharp. Gabriel's eyes were focused on a point somewhere in the distance.

"I've been lying, Charlie. To everyone. The press, our fans. The rest of the band. You."

I tipped my head to the side.

"Wh . . . Gabe, what are you talking about?"

He tapped a fist against his lips.

"My parents."

I thought back to the paparazzi enclosure in Brighton. The clacking of cameras, the chattering of fans, the barking voices. Gabriel's refusal to talk about his family.

"They're living in the South of France . . . right?" I said. Gabriel shook his head.

"I made that up. It isn't true."

He paused, breathing slowly. I hugged myself against the cold and waited.

"When I was a kid," he continued, finally, "my dad was hardly ever around. We lived in this miserable London flat, just me and Mum, most of the time. She didn't speak English—she's from Brazil—and I think she was pretty lonely. She was on all these depression meds. I used to help her count out her pills for the week.

"Anyway . . . I never really knew what Dad did for cash. Looking back, it was probably drugs. Sometimes, when he was away, people would knock on our door in the middle of the night, saying he owed them money, yelling at Mum when she didn't understand. I remember Dad coming home once with a plastic bag full of banknotes and chucking them across the bed, but most of the time, we were broke. We ate noodles and watched TV until the meter ran out." He ran a hand round the back of his neck. "One day, I woke up and found Mum in the bathroom. She'd taken an overdose."

His eyes dropped to the ground.

"I'm sure she didn't mean to do it. I mean . . . she couldn't . . . Maybe she didn't understand the instructions on the bottle."

There was the slightest quiver on his cheekbone.

"So that just left my dad, looking after me on his own. But he couldn't do it." He blinked several times. "He didn't want to be a father."

I curled both my hands around his.

"I ended up in foster care, and after that, Dad left London. Went away for months. One night, my carers told me he wasn't coming home. They said he'd killed himself."

Gabriel's mouth kept moving after he spoke, almost as if he were admitting it to himself for the first time. There was an exposed look in his eyes too, a look I hadn't seen before, and I wondered how often he'd said this out loud, if ever. He looked strangely afraid, stripped of his pop-star bravado, no longer the invincible Gabriel West.

"Gabe . . . I'm so sorry. I can't even imagine . . ."

"Don't be. We were never a real family, even before Mum was gone. And you can't miss what you never had."

"Why did you tell everyone they were living in France, though?"

Gabriel stared out across the ocean, waves cresting in the sprawling gray mass.

"Keeps the press off my back. Only Barry knows the truth." He raised a hand. "Well, Barry . . . and now you."

"But . . . what does this have to do with Mum's notebook?"

Gabriel swallowed, hard.

"There's something else I need to tell you. Something not even Barry knows."

I dropped his hand. My brain was spinning, a mass of tangled threads, knotted like vines, and nothing made sense yet. I needed answers, and all I had were more questions.

"My parents," continued Gabriel, "they didn't leave me much. They didn't have much. But Dad left me this one thing, after he was gone, a CD for some band he was in. It was him and three other guys, though we'd never met them or seen them play. I only know their names because they're written in the album sleeve: Harry, Owen, Kit, Jermaine. Under that, it says, 'All songs by Harry West' . . . and the rest of it's blank.

"When I was a bit older, I started listening to the album . . . and I liked it. I hated him for what he'd done, but something about his music, it spoke to me. I listened to it every night."

Gabriel bent down and picked up a stone from the dirt. He rubbed at it with his finger.

"I was a quiet kid, but I was angry. When I was old enough, I started hanging out in town, mostly with the other foster kids, and getting into trouble. Just roaming around, shoplifting, smashing things up.

"Then, when I turned thirteen, this old lady started coming round the care home every Wednesday night. She used to read stories to the kids, and play piano on this knackered upright they had"—for a brief moment, he smiled—"and when I heard the sound, it reminded me of my dad's album. I asked her to teach me, and she did, every week, just a few chords here and there. After that, I sat in every night, writing.

"I'd sit at the piano, writing music, and sometimes I'd mix a few of Dad's lyrics in with my own. It was childish, but I thought . . . I thought if I used his words in my songs, then—"

"He'd never really be gone."

Gabriel tossed the stone over the cliff edge.

"Dumb, really."

I watched the stone plummet, in a curved arc, toward the water.

"That doesn't sound dumb to me," I said.

"I suppose some people might say I was stealing, but those words were the only thing my dad ever gave me. He *owed* them to me."

Gabriel's jaw shifted slowly from side to side.

He turned back to me and shrugged.

"So . . . point is, the words in my songs, some of them aren't mine." He looked at the notebook, still clutched in his hand, and passed it back to me. "The lyrics in that book, they all come from this obscure nineties band called Little Boy Blue."

As I was slipping the book back into my bag, the name suddenly sank in. My eyes widened.

"What did you say?"

"Little Boy Blue. That's what they were called."

I put my hands on top of my head. I almost felt like laughing.

"Little . . . Boy Blue . . ."

Gabriel tried to catch my attention.

"What? What is it?"

"My mum . . . She was a *groupie?*"

I knew exactly what Aimee would say, if she were here.

Like mother, like daughter.

"What are you talking about?"

I looked out toward the horizon, shaking my head.

"I am such an idiot."

A confused smile played on Gabriel's face.

"What do you mean?"

"I have this photo of Mum at home, from like, 1998, wearing a Little Boy Blue T-shirt. *That's* why she filled her book with those lyrics. She was just a really huge fan."

Was this why Dad had fobbed me off with the story about the nursery rhyme? Because admitting his wife was obsessed with some rock band was just too . . . embarrassing?

"Hey," said Gabriel with a laugh, "at least they had some fans." Then his smile faded. "At least my dad did something right."

A light rain was beginning to fall. I peered at my feet, remembering why I'd started this conversation in the first place, and decided I might as well come clean.

"When I heard your lyrics, and they matched the ones in Mum's book . . . I thought . . . God, I can't believe I'm telling you this. It's stupid." I closed my eyes. "I thought you were writings songs about me."

For a while, Gabriel said nothing. I began to blush.

"That's not stupid."

"Yeah, right."

I kicked at the grass.

"It's not," he insisted, taking my hand again. "It's kind of beautiful."

"Gabe, seriously."

"I mean it."

We gazed at each other, fingers entwined. Gabriel's hair twinkled with dots of rain.

"I have one last question, then."

Gabriel cocked his head at me. I waited a moment, picturing him beside that stage in Brighton, with his back to me, singing to himself. Singing my song.

"That song you were singing, backstage in Brighton. Your warm-up song."

"'Cat's in the Cradle'?"

"That's where the band name comes from, isn't it? It's in the lyrics."

Gabriel nodded.

"I think so. It would make a lot of sense."

Something else was starting to make sense, too. Me, sitting in the back of the car, fading in and out of sleep, with Mum in the passenger seat and Dad driving. "Cat's in the Cradle" playing on the stereo.

No wonder she was obsessed with that song.

"D'you know that feeling," said Gabriel suddenly, "when you hear a song from your childhood, and it kind of . . . haunts you?"

I felt a murmur under my skin. I knew the feeling exactly.

"Yeah. Yeah, I do."

"And it stirs all these memories inside you, like . . . *deep inside you.* Memories that normally stay buried, and only come out when you hear this one particular song . . . ?"

The motorway, the falling rain. Orange lights on the window.

"And straightaway you get a picture in your mind. Like, for me, when I hear 'Cat's in the Cradle,' I'm with my dad, and we're running around on an empty beach, kicking a ball to each other. My dad's so tall he blocks out the sun, and I don't even know if it's a real memory or not, but when I hear that song, I feel . . . safe."

Out at sea, waves broke on icy waters.

". . . Does that make sense?"

I couldn't speak. I just nodded, lost in his eyes.

"That feeling, Charlie Brown . . . that's what I feel when I'm with you. That's what I feel. In my gut."

A burning heat was filling me up inside. I wanted to fall into his arms so intensely, my bones ached.

"Gabe . . ."

I shivered as the rain picked up, and Gabriel pulled me into him, shielding me from the cold. He looked deep into my eyes, and my limbs felt weak, like disappearing sand.

"How are you doing this?" I said.

Gabriel searched my face, those dark locks of hair quivering in the wind.

"Doing what?" he asked, passing a hand along my cheek and round to the back of my head, his fingers sliding into my hair. My whole body prickled in response.

"It feels like you're looking inside me."

Though the air had turned bitter, I could feel his warmth, and his weight, against me, and it felt like my nerve endings were on fire. The sound of our breathing became the sound of crashing waves, and the rain lashed harder, and his lips drifted toward mine.

"Hey, Gabriel."

We broke apart at the intrusion of a gruff, boozy voice. A silhouetted man was standing a few meters away from us, dressed in one of those big parka jackets with the hood up. Behind him, a second car was parked next to Gabriel's, headlights on, indicator ticking.

"How's it going, pal?"

Gabriel's arm moved instinctively in front of me, grazing my stomach.

"Look, if you want an autograph or anything, this is my afternoon off, so . . ."

The man stepped forward into the glow from his headlights. The yellowish light washed over him, revealing pinhole eyes and a mean, stubble-flecked face.

It was Paul Morgan. From *The Record*.

"I was hoping we could have a little chat," he said, nudging a cigarette from a crumpled packet.

"Who are you?" demanded Gabriel, straining to see the man's face in the dying light. The sun had disappeared, and we had barely noticed. "Are you press?"

"You should pay more attention, Gabriel. I've been trying to talk to you all week, but your people never cut me a break."

He slipped a lighter from his pocket.

"Did you follow us here?" said Gabriel assertively, but I could hear an unusual tone in his voice. It sounded like fear.

"It's a free country, mate," said Paul, lighting his cigarette. He sucked a long, indulgent draw, and the tip danced orange in the darkness. "But since we're here, I've got a few questions." He looked straight at Gabriel. "About your parents, actually."

Gabriel stepped forward.

"Leave us alone."

"I've been trying to pin you down for a while," Paul continued, flicking ash on to the ground. "I've been looking into your history, kid, and something doesn't add up."

He paused for a few seconds, his voice replaced by the rhythmic wash of the sea and the steady *tick-tick* of his car indicator.

"Fancy telling me about it?"

"I'm not talking to you about anyth—"

"Your dad," said Paul, calmly. "Tell me about your dad."

Gabriel opened his arms.

"What about him?"

"He's dead, isn't he?"

"You don't know what you're talking about, and if you don't leave us alo—"

"You'll do what, exactly?" interrupted Paul. "Call the police? This is public property."

He blew out a plume of smoke, and it corkscrewed into the air.

"Not easy to get an appointment with you, West, I'll tell you that," he continued casually. "You haven't been outside without security in, oh, I dunno. Weeks."

Gabriel straightened, his hands forming into fists.

"How long have you been following me?"

"Bottom line is, I've got a juicy lead on the world's hottest pop star, and you don't want me poking around your closet looking for God-knows-what. I mean, think of your little fans." He looked at me when he said this. "The groupies."

"This is ridiculous," scoffed Gabriel, taking my hand and leading us back toward the car. "You should get a proper job."

Flicking his half-finished cigarette to the ground, Paul stepped directly into our path, forcing us to stop. He was close enough now that I could smell the smoke on his breath.

"Don't mess me around," he said in a low voice. "I know you're hiding something, and I'll find out sooner or later so you might as well talk."

Gabriel took a step toward him until they were almost face-to-face.

"I'm not scared of you."

"Maybe not," Paul replied, with a shrug. "But she is."

A dart of fear pierced my chest. Paul was looking at me now, over Gabriel's shoulder. He smiled, parked another cigarette in his mouth, and flicked repeatedly at his lighter, which kept snuffing out in the wind.

As he was looking down, Gabriel charged at him.

Taken by surprise, Paul called out in shock and stumbled back onto the hood of his car. Gabriel clamped an arm across his neck and pinned him.

"If you touch her, I'll kill you. Don't think I won't."

Paul, though he was clearly losing the fight, seemed to be laughing.

"Calm down, West! You're not bloody Spider-Man."

Gabriel drew back his fist to hit him, and Paul held both hands up in surrender.

"OK, OK, let's just chill out here for a minute . . ."

Hesitantly, Gabriel dropped his fist and stepped back from the car. Paul stood up again, straightening his crumpled clothes.

"This is my number," he said, placing a business card on top of a nearby fence post. "When you decide to talk, gimme a ring. We can go for a nice beer, just us boys. Bear in mind, though"—he spotted his lit cigarette in the grass and stubbed it out with a tattered boot—"if you don't talk, I'll publish it anyway. Your call."

He leered at me.

"Catch you later, precious."

Then he walked backward onto the gravel, opened his car door, dropped inside, and skidded in reverse out of the car park.

"What the hell, Gabe?"

We were back on the open road, wipers swooshing, fat black

raindrops slapping against the windshield. Gabriel hadn't spoken since leaving the cliff side.

"Why is that guy following you around? Do you think he heard our conversation?"

"I don't know, and I don't care."

The outline of his face was just visible in the light from the dashboard, a silvery-white glow kissing the contours of his cheekbones. His eyes were dark spaces.

"Talk to me. Please." I was still clutching the edge of my seat. "And slow down."

Gabriel exhaled and switched down a gear.

"People like that, they spend their entire lives digging up dirt. They're pathetic."

I felt the urge to touch him, to lay a hand on his. His fingers twitched on his thigh, as if he knew what I was thinking.

"Maybe . . . maybe it wouldn't be such a big deal if everyone found out. About your parents, I mean?"

We passed through a silent cliff-side hamlet. A cluster of tiny houses were huddled together for warmth, yellow lamps glowing in their windows. Gabriel was looking straight ahead, one finger tapping the steering wheel.

"I just want one little piece of me to stay private, y'know? People expect you to give up everything just because you're famous, but I won't give them this." He stared out of the window. "You probably wouldn't understand that."

I studied the back of Gabriel's head as he gazed out the window. The light was almost gone now, the ocean vast and unforgiving in the distance.

"Actually, these days . . . I kind of do."

This drew Gabriel's gaze back inside the car, and the whites of his eyes flashed like diamonds in the dark. I folded my bare arms across my chest, my skin still cool from the cliff side.

"Sorry, Charlie . . . I should have thought . . ."

We sat in silence as the winding coastal road took us ever nearer the town. I thought about Paul Morgan, watching us on the cliff edge. The smoke in his clothes; the strange, moist click in his voice.

"Gabriel."

"Uh-huh."

"What are you going to do about that journalist?"

"I don't need to do anything. He's bluffing."

I chewed on my thumbnail.

"Maybe you should just talk to him, like he said. Then he'll go away."

"That's not the point." We passed back into town, the hotel rising up above the rooftops, grand and solemn on the cliff edge. "I don't want the whole world perving over my life story, and I won't be bullied by scum like that."

Gabriel meant what he said, I was sure of that. But as I watched him navigate the empty streets, the beams from our headlamps spotlighting the tarmac, I couldn't help but wonder: did he really have a choice?

"We need to get inside, before they find us."

Gabriel had parked outside the hotel and was leading me by the hand through the lobby.

"Evening, Mr. West," said the girl behind reception. Gabriel nodded back and, as he guided me toward the lift, I watched her pick up the phone with one eye trained on us.

The lift door pinged, and we stepped inside.

"I think that girl was phoning someone about you, Ga—"

"I know. They'll be waiting for me. Listen . . ." He hit the button for the third floor and turned to face me. "You mean a lot to me, Charlie Brown."

His eyes were fixed on mine, almost glowing in the dim light.

"Me too," I said, as the gears of the lift clunked into motion.

"You're the only person I've met since joining this band who really sees me . . ."

He moved closer, placing one hand in the small of my back, and pulled me toward him. Our chests met, and I fell into him, holding his arms tight to keep my balance. The lift reached the third floor, and there was a loud knock on the door.

"Damn, that's my security."

"Gabriel, you in there?" came a voice from the corridor. Gabriel didn't answer, and there was the sound of a muffled conversation, then another hard knock.

"Gabe, buddy, seriously. Open the door."

Gabriel slammed on the door-hold button, and didn't let go.

"I can't put it into words, Charlie, but . . . we're connected. I knew it the first moment I saw you."

I didn't need to say anything back. I didn't need to speak a single word. Because I knew, with all of my heart, that he was right.

And then he pressed me up against the wall of the lift, his hand on the side of my face, fingers in my hair, and kissed me.

And I lost all sense of where I was, and where I'd been, and what any of this meant, and I was weightless and terrified and broken all at once, and I wanted him like a fever, like a sickness, all things rushing, all things bright.

Suddenly, Gabriel pulled away from me, leaving me gripping the handrail, my heart thumping wildly. The lift doors had opened to reveal two massive security guards on the other side.

"You're in trouble, man," one said, as Gabriel staggered out into the corridor. "Barry wants your head on a plate."

24

The following morning, Fire&Lights' manager Barry King paid Gabriel a private visit. Unsurprisingly, he didn't take any prisoners.

"Are you *trying* to push my buttons, Gabe?" came the gravelly voice from inside Gabriel's hotel room. Standing in the corridor, I waited for Gabriel to respond, but all I could hear through the closed door was his television, yapping away in the corner.

"Because trust me," continued Barry, "you really don't want to go there."

I rarely watched *Make or Break*, but even I knew that Barry King was blunt and short-tempered and had no time for people who didn't do exactly what he asked, whenever he asked it. He had a reputation on the show for making contestants cry and even sacked another judge once during a live broadcast. Melissa told me there were rumors he had connections to organized crime, though they were probably started by one of the many wannabe pop stars he'd trashed on his program.

Either way, he was a frightening man.

"I gave you everything you've got. Don't think I've forgotten that before you met me you were just some scruffy little runt with an attitude."

"*You . . . gave me . . . everything?* That's a laugh," scoffed Gabriel, and I could just imagine him standing there, chin held high, arms crossed in defiance. "Where would you be without my songs? Still trying to break that crap string quartet—what were they called?"

"You can leave Paradiso out of this, son," replied Barry, his patience clearly thinning. I remembered Paradiso. They were supposed to make classical music sexy, but in the end they just made it annoying. "Listen, I'm first to admit you're good at what you do, but that doesn't give you the right to act like the bloody king of the world. You're not Axl Rose, for Christ's sake."

"Who's Axl Rose?"

"Good one, mate. Hilarious."

A member of the hotel staff passed by and nodded me a "good morning."

"Point is, I own you. You know that; I know that. When I tell you to do an interview, you do an interview. When I tell you to sing, you sing. When I tell you to put on a leotard and dance the Macarena, *you bloody do it.*"

I leaned back against the wall, flicking through last night's photos on my phone. Even on the small screen, they were looking fantastic, and I couldn't wait to see how the fans would react to them. My favorites were of Yuki and Aiden singing together backstage, Aiden on the guitar, Yuki spinning a drumstick and tapping it on the tabletop. I'd even managed to capture one of Gabriel and Olly together, and getting that picture was never easy.

I had come downstairs to see Gabriel, but it sounded like Barry wasn't planning on letting him go any time soon.

"I was great onstage last night though, right?" Gabriel was saying when I tuned back in. I smiled. He was right—last night had been the best I'd ever seen him perform. His energy was insatiable as he swept from one side of the stage to the other, his face lit up, his voice soaring.

I dared to think, just quietly, to myself, that our kiss might have been responsible . . .

"People, let's hear ya!" Gabriel had called out to the vast, rippling crowd, who roared in response. "This next song, we think you *just* might recognize it. Number one last week, and hopefully staying there tomorrow . . ."

The fans whooped and cheered. Yuki sauntered up behind Gabriel and draped an arm around his shoulder.

"You wanna tell 'em what it's called, Yuki?"

Yuki leaned toward the crowd and said, very slowly, into his microphone: " 'Dance . . . with . . . You.' "

The audience erupted, and the guitarist began playing the insistent, echoey riff that opened the song. I stood backstage, a tingle on my spine, waiting for those lines. *Take me home, 'cause I've been dreaming of a girl I know.* The truth about Mum's notebook might not have been quite what I expected, but it didn't matter. The words still lit me up inside. They still made my heart ache and shudder and sing.

When the song ended, a triumphant Yuki lifted his hand for Gabriel to high-five and, when their palms met, for a fraction of a second, Gabriel's eyes locked onto mine.

Behind him, thousands screamed his name.

"That's not the point," Barry was arguing irritably, as I drifted out of my daydream. "I set you up with one of the top music magazines in the country yesterday, and you don't even bother turning up! You're off gallivanting with that, who is she, that amateur photographer you boys have all got the horn for all of a sudden. She's not even famous."

"Not even famous" was becoming my tagline. Perhaps I should put it on a business card.

"Don't talk about Charlie like that," said Gabriel sternly. I pressed my ear to the wall, imagining him on the other side, defending me in front of Barry King, the most powerful man in the music industry.

It gave me chills.

"I'll talk about Charlie Bucket, and you, and every last one of you whining little divas however I want. And I don't want to be in here again, having this conversation. You understand?"

No response from Gabriel. I glanced up and down the hotel corridor, wondering how long I'd have to stand out here. Maybe I should take a walk on the bea—

Ping. A message on my phone. Melissa, no doubt, pressing for an update. I hadn't told her about the kiss yet: I was waiting to see her in person. I was worried she might spontaneously combust.

I looked at the screen. An unknown number.

Screw u bitch

For a moment, I stared at the message, unable to process the words. Then another arrived.

Hands off gabriel

And another.

Lying slut

Ur pathetic

Ur not good enough for gabriel

And another, and another, and another. Different numbers, every time.

With trembling fingers, I opened my web browser and tried a few search terms.

Fire&Lights

Fire&Lights news
Fire&Lights groupie

The third attempt brought up a string of fan sites and gossip pages, all queuing up to shout different versions of the same thing.

GABRIEL TAKES MYSTERY GROUPIE ON ROAD TRIP
SECRET PHOTO OF GABRIEL WITH RANDOM FAN
IS SHE GROUPIE OR GIRLFRIEND, GABRIEL WEST??

Hurriedly, I clicked the images tab. The top hit was a horrible, grainy photo of me, rain-soaked and white-skinned, stepping out of Gabriel's car outside the hotel.

Someone had been watching us. Paul Morgan, perhaps? Or some other reporter? Whoever it was, they—

My phone buzzed in my hand. A new message lit up the screen.

I know who you are

It was another unknown number, a string of unfamiliar digits. And moments later, from the same sender, a follow-up message arrived.

Charlie bloom

I blinked, horrified, at the screen. *They knew my name.*

Panicked, I opened the Internet again, scrolled down the search results, and at the bottom of page two, found a familiar site: FIRE&LIGHTS FOREVER. I stared in disbelief at the headline.

REVEALED: THE IDENTITY
OF GABRIEL'S MYSTERY GIRL

You don't wanna miss this one,
readers!!!!

This is a big one, guys . . . we've found out who the mystery girl
is. Aaaaaagggghhh!!!!

Her name is Charlie Bloom, and she goes to Caversham High in
Reading—which is where Olly went to school (gold star if you
knew that!! ;) ;))

Also, she's not just some random fan, she's actually the band's
new backstage photographer . . . which is pretty amazing!!! We
know that some F&L fans have been trolling her, but that is
NOT COOL, people. :(:(PLEASE stop and think before you post
mean things about someone. It's so not worth it!

Sooooo . . . what's going to happen with Gabriel & Charlie??
What does the pic of them outside his hotel MEAN?!?! Leave a
comment below, and tell us what you think!!! :) :) :)

xox FIRE&LIGHTS FOREVER xox
The best Fire&Lights fan blog on the web!!

As the words throbbed and shivered in front of me, I felt the walls
closing in.

Three more messages hit my phone.

U make me sick, charlie bloom

Stupid bitch

Haha I'm comin to ur house charlie

This couldn't be happening. This couldn't be real.

But it was. Because underneath the blog was a comment, posted within the last five minutes, by a user called Wattsgoingon.

The name sent a shiver through my blood.

It had to be Aimee.

charlie bloom is asking for it. i go to her school and she's telling everyone she slept with gabriel, it's BS

And then, five words that made my insides crawl.

this is her phone number

My mind went dark, a pulsating, black space, a scream of nothing. A single sob burst out of me and I clamped a hand to my mouth, forcing it back down.

Gabriel's door swung open.

". . . So just, you know, *think* in the future, will you?" Barry was saying as he left the room. "You might be Gabriel West, but you're not above the law."

He noticed me.

"Oh. Hello." I quickly wiped my eyes, and Barry considered me in silence. He nodded back in Gabriel's direction. "Sort him out, would you? Apparently he listens to you."

Barry's phone started to ring and, as he walked down the corridor, he whipped it to his ear.

"King?"

Gabriel was leaning against the door frame, watching him go.

"Charlie Brown, what's new?" He saw me, and his face fell. "Oh my God, Charlie . . . ?"

He ducked out of his room.

"What's going on?" he said, glancing up and down the hallway.

"Nothing."

"Come inside . . ."

Gabriel backed into his room, and I followed him in reluctantly. The door clicked shut behind us.

"You should sit down."

"I'm OK," I said, hovering by the door. Gabriel reached out to touch me, then thought better of it.

"Tell me what's going on."

I avoided his gaze, my eyes brimming with tears.

"Charlie, talk to m—"

"I can't, it's too . . . it's just . . ."

Gabriel switched off the television and tossed the remote onto the bed. I took a deep breath, and the words stumbled thickly out of me.

"There's another photo of us online. They know my name. And my phone number's been published."

I pulled out my mobile, opened the message inbox, and passed it to Gabriel. He scrolled the screen, eyes widening as he read.

"Jesus, Charlie . . . this is horrible." He set the phone down on the desk and dropped back against the wall. "Where did the new photo come from?"

I looked up. An angry heat was growing inside me.

"You're the celebrity—you tell me."

His face crumpled in confusion, and I felt guilty, instantly, for taking it out on him.

"Sorry, I—"

"You don't still think I had something to do with all this, do you?"

"No . . . no, I don't. It's just . . ."

"What?"

I dared to look at him, properly, for the first time.

"All I know is that when I'm around you . . . bad things happen."

Gabriel's jaw twitched. I closed my eyes, and two hot tears dropped down my cheeks.

"You know I'd never do anything to hurt you, don't you?" he said after a pause, but I didn't reply. I just wiped away the tears and stared at the carpet. Gabriel paced to the window and leaned on the ledge, thinking, his fist pressed to his mouth.

"I can't change what Carla did, starting all this," he said, patiently. "Believe me, I would if I could. But I can't. We just have to get past it."

"Get past it? Gabe, this is my life."

A second wave of tears was building in my throat. I caught a glimpse of myself in the mirror: a mess of matted hair, big red eyes.

"What's in the photo? The new one, I mean."

"It's us, getting out of your car. On the driveway, outside."

Gabriel's head lolled backward, like it was suddenly heavy, and he let out a deep sigh.

"That guy from the cliffs followed us home."

"So *he* did all this, then? Is that what you're saying?"

"I don't know, Charlie, but this is exactly what losers like that are paid to do. Make people feel crap about themselves. Because *that sells*."

The idea of that creepy reporter following us in the dark, watching us from his car, twisted me up inside. I fought off a shiver.

We both fell silent for a while, listening to the sound of the churning sea. I stared out the window and felt homesick.

"I can't take this," I said finally, in a very small voice. "I'm not strong enough."

Gabriel walked back toward me.

"Yes, you are. I'm not letting you go."

I hung my head. A numbness was spreading through my body.

"You don't need me. You're Gabriel West. You could have any girl on the planet."

"Maybe I could," he said. He touched one finger to my chin and lifted my gaze to meet his. "But the only one I want is you."

His amber eyes sank into mine, and my feet curled with desire.

"Every single person I meet treats me like Gabriel West, pop star. But the way you look at me, it's as if . . . as if I'm just like you."

He tucked a strand of hair behind my ear.

"You make me feel normal again."

I gazed up at him, eyes stinging with tears. Everyone I knew wanted to be a celebrity, and yet the world-famous Gabriel West missed being normal.

But he could never be normal.

"I have to go. I'm sorry . . . I can't do this."

"Charlie, come on, this is crazy, stay h—"

"I just want to go home. I can't be here anymore."

Pulling away from him, I stood up and walked to the door. He was saying my name as I left, but I ignored him, swinging the door shut behind me. I only made it a few steps down the hall before stumbling to the wall, covering my eyes, and sliding down to my knees, sobbing.

I was in a strange place, with people I barely knew, while the world gossiped about me over the Internet.

I felt, suddenly, very alone.

25

Aiden sat down next to me on the leather sofa and pulled his knees up against his chest.

"You OK, Charlie?" he said in his soft, lilting accent.

"Uh-huh."

He gave this some thought. In front of us, through the windows of the tour bus, the trees and fields flew by under a gray sheet of rain.

"You're kinda quiet. I'm worried."

I shook my head and tried to smile. Aiden's eyebrows were raised in concern, his lips thin.

"Don't worry," I said. "I'm fine."

The long journey back to London was passing painfully slowly. Yuki was lying along one of the other sofas, reading a book, his legs crossed over the edge of the flickering pinball machine. Olly was sitting in the corner, scribbling in a notebook, and Gabriel, who had shunned the tour bus, was driving his new car back to London, accompanied by a bodyguard. It seemed quiet without him.

"I heard about what happened."

I kept my eyes on my lap. I'd been hoping the rest of the band wouldn't find out.

"It's nothing, really."

Aiden bit one of his nails.

"Right . . ."

There was a long silence. He cleared his throat.

"I don't like getting papped either."

I blinked at him.

"What?"

"It makes me sad."

"Yeah," I said, taking my hat off. "Me too."

We both looked out the window, and a service station drifted by. Concrete towers, queuing cars.

"Two weeks after we won *Make or Break*," Aiden began, turning back to me, "the papers printed this photo of me, my sister, and my ma, out for a fish supper. It was dumb, really, it wasn't even a posh place, just this little café in Galway, but they still papped us. And I wasn't ready for it. I didn't like it. My baby sister, she's only seven. She's a kid."

He paused.

"It was like they owned me, or something."

There was the screech of bus brakes as we slowed for a traffic jam.

"I guess what I'm saying is . . . I know how you feel."

I tugged at my sleeve.

"Thanks, Aiden."

"S-sure," he said hesitantly, standing up from the sofa. He hovered for a moment, unsure of what to do.

"If you want to talk or anything, you just shout, OK?"

I looked up at him.

"I will."

He nodded thoughtfully, then walked over to the drinks machine, looked it up and down, and settled on the top button. A can of Pepsi clattered out the bottom.

About an hour later, as the rain finally cleared, Olly appeared above me, holding his notebook.

"This seat taken?" he asked, pointing a pen at the empty space next to me. I shifted uncomfortably.

"Um, not exa—"

"You don't have to talk to me," he said, with a calming hand. "I just thought you might like some company."

I shuffled up against the window.

Olly sat down next to me and opened his book.

"Olly, I—"

"Hey," he said, a smile playing on his lips. "I thought I told you not to talk."

"I just . . . about yesterday, on the beach—"

"I get it," he said, setting his pen down between the pages. "You and Gabriel have . . . something going on. And whatever that is, it's none of my business." He shrugged. "I just wanted you to know, that's all."

I stared at my hands.

"I'm not sure what to s—"

"Pipe down, you," said Olly, returning to his book, a twinkle in his eye. "I'm trying to work."

He smiled again, and for the first time in hours, I almost did too.

We sat there for a few minutes, the engine whirring beneath us, while outside the window, moody blue skies began to break through the clouds. Olly was scanning the text in his notebook, twirling his pen between thumb and forefinger and reading very faintly to himself. I lifted up my feet to sit cross-legged, caught a glimpse of the page, and realized it was his song.

Drowsily, I read the lines in the chorus, remembering his voice

from yesterday, the sand between my fingers, and the hypnotic sound
of the sea.

> *She is the fire in my fingertips*
> *The warm rain that tells me where the thunder is*
> *And I know that somebody has found her heart*
> *But that won't keep us apart*
>
> *She keeps a piece of herself inside*
> *But she speaks, and every single star collides*
> *And I know that somebody has found her heart*
> *But that won't keep us apart*

Then, as a shaft of late-afternoon sun settled across us both, I laid
my head on Olly's shoulder and drifted to sleep.

That evening, I was walking down the garden path with earphones in,
ready to go straight to bed and shut out the world, when I noticed my
dad standing in the living room window. The TV glowed behind him.

"Where were you this weekend?" he said when I walked in through
the door. I slipped the bag off my back and dumped it on the floor.

"Um . . . the *writers' retreat*, Dad?"

"Funny, because I was chatting with Melissa's mum earlier today,
and she didn't know anything about any writers' retreat."

A nervous heat was rising inside me.

"Melissa didn't come. She's into computers—she doesn't go on English trips."

I made a move for the stairs, but Dad was standing in the way.

"That would be convincing if it wasn't for the fact that I contacted the head about it, and he said the school has never run a writers' retreat in Devon. Not this year . . . not ever."

I had no answer to this. I tried not to breathe, and Dad finally broke.

"Where the hell have you been all this time?"

"I . . . Dad . . ."

There wasn't time to make anything up. Perhaps, though, I could get away with telling him the truth . . . just not the *whole* truth.

"I was with a band."

Dad stared back at me. He looked confused at first, and then the confusion turned to anger.

"A band? What band?"

"Just a band who used to go to Caversham High. They asked me to go on tour with them and take photos. It's no big deal."

He grabbed me by the wrist, and it stung.

"Believe me, this is a *very* big deal. It's inappropriate for a girl your age, and it's dangerous, and I won't allow it. Do you understand?"

I didn't reply.

"Where were you?"

"I already told you. Devon."

"Jesus, Charlie. Anything could have happened."

Dad's shirt quivered with his uneasy breathing.

"First the curfew, then the message through the door, now this. What's happened to you? We can't go on this way."

I was losing the fight, and it was fraying my temper. I knew I'd regret whatever came out of my mouth next.

"What are you going to do then, Dad? Ground me?"

"That's exactly what I'm going to do."

I glared back at him. He'd never disciplined me before. Not like this. "What?"

"Go to your room. This conversation is over."

"Fine. I couldn't care less anyway," I said, snatching my bag from the floor, shoving past him, and walking up the stairs.

"If you want to be treated like an adult," he called after me, "you'll need to start behaving like one."

I called back over my shoulder.

"Well done, Dad, that one was right out of *The Idiot's Guide to Parenting*."

"What did you say?"

"Nothing," I yelled back, slamming the bedroom door behind me.

Downstairs, a kitchen drawer clinked angrily, and I heard the cork popping from a wine bottle. I crossed over to my drawer, took out the photograph of my parents, and stared into it as if trying to peer backward through time. My head was filled with noise: the hateful messages on my phone, lines from Gabriel's songs, the letter to my mother, my father's secrets, the roaring of an engine, the man in the dark on the rain-ruined cliff side. The noise filled my ears until my brain began to scream, my eyes wet with tears, a hammering pain in my rib cage.

I lay down and pulled the sheets around me, fists clutched to my chest, tears coating my cheeks. I ached for someone to hold me, to tell me everything would be all right, to dry my eyes and stroke my hair and say "sweet dreams" and sing me to sleep. I missed her.

I missed her more than I ever had before.

26

The next morning, before I had even made it to my first lesson, I was called into the head teacher's office.

"Charlie, we're all a little . . . worried about you."

I had barely slept the night before, and it was written all over my face. My eyes throbbed in their sockets, my vision was speckled, my shoulders were heavy from exhaustion.

"I'm OK."

Mr. Bennett was doing that thing he always did, his curved fingers spread out with the tips touching, like he was gripping an invisible crystal ball.

"You'll be aware that your father called me over the weekend, presumably? And while it's not really my business what our students do on their own time, it is rather worrying that you would use a fake school trip as cover for . . . well, for whatever."

"Sorry," I said, although I wasn't really sure what I was apologizing for.

"Well, like I say, it's not my business exactly, but your father is extremely concerned. And, look . . ." He cleared his throat. "We know you're being targeted at school."

I was still receiving the messages. Not nearly as often now, but even so, every few hours a new one would arrive. Aimee's comment had long been deleted from the blog, but my number was out there now. It could be on any one of the fan forums.

Get lost, charlie bloom

Leave gabriel alone

I seen u on the internet. Lookin at ur pics rite now

"It's nothing," I said, folding my arms.

"Actually," replied Mr. Bennett, crossing his legs and pursing his lips, "I'm not sure that it is."

Mr. Bennett was right. Before Fire&Lights, I'd been ignored at school. A ghost in the hall. But now, people I didn't know, people who were hardly even acquaintances, let alone friends, were going out of their way to talk to me.

"Yo, Charlie."

Just ten minutes earlier, on my way to Mr. Bennett's office, I'd been approached at the lockers by Nathan Gaines. Nathan and I sat opposite each other in Geography. We were in the same group once on a field trip, but other than that we'd barely had a single conversation in four years.

"What?" I replied.

"Is it true?" said Nathan, chewing gum. He was standing a little too close to me.

"Is what true?"

"People are saying you slept with Gabriel West."

People are saying, I thought. *People.*

"I'm not talking to you about that."

He leaned an arm against the lockers.

"Come on, seriously. Just tell me." He smiled, baring teeth. "It's kinda hot."

I slammed my locker closed.

"If this is the kind of thing that turns you on, there's something seriously wrong with you."

Nathan spluttered out an embarrassed laugh, and behind him, his friends sniggered and whooped, fist-bumping each other.

"Whoa, *ice* queen!"

"Dude, she took you *down*."

I turned to them.

"What's wrong with you?" They looked confused. "Don't you have anything better to do?"

Their grins wilted. No one said anything.

I threw my bag onto my shoulder and walked off . . .

"As your head teacher," continued Mr. Bennett, pressing his fingers into the desk, "I am responsible not just for your academic life but also, partly, for your welfare." He glanced at a pile of papers. "Your father informed me about the threatening note passed through your door."

My heart sank.

"Really, it's no big dea—"

"On the contrary," he interrupted, "we take matters of this sort very seriously. In fact, I've been made aware that Aimee Watts has been responsible for similar behavior in the past, at previous schools."

"You don't know it was her."

Mr. Bennett shifted in his seat, and I could tell, though I was avoiding eye contact, that he was looking right at me. He lowered his voice a little.

"Actually, we do. We had a pretty strong hunch about it, so I challenged her this morning and more or less squeezed out a confession. We may even take the matter to the police."

"Please, don't do that—"

"You have nothing to worry about, Charlie," he said, leaning forward on the desk. "You concern yourself with your upcoming exams, and we'll deal with Miss Watts. OK?"

They always said things like that, teachers. *You have nothing to worry about . . . we'll deal with it.* Maybe they'd forgotten what tended to happen the second they turned their backs.

I'm done, **said Melissa's message.** See you in 5. And we are spending all lunchtime talking about the kiss. ALL LUNCHTIME. Xx

I was in the back courtyard with my camera, photographing the bird with the orange mark on its back. We had passed half an hour together, uninterrupted, the only sound the rhythmic clicking of the camera, when I heard the scuffle of feet on the paving stones behind me.

The voice told me it wasn't Melissa.

"Hello, Charlotte."

The bird twitched its little head and listened. I didn't look up from my camera.

"Oi, *Charlie.*"

I turned round. Aimee had six girls with her.

"What do you want?" I said decisively, but there was the faintest tremor in my voice.

"You know what I want."

The girls began to close in on both sides, and my chest tightened.

"I want an apology."

"What for?"

Aimee walked toward me, frowning. To our right, the bird had gone, and the nest was empty.

"Here's something funny. I come into school today, and Bennett pulls me into his office to say a 'threatening note' has been posted though Charlie Bloom's door and did I have anything to do with it?" One of the other girls whispered something to a friend, her eyes on me, and they both laughed. "And because I got kicked out of Woodtree for the same thing, he reckons he's got me pinned."

She closed the gap between us to just a few centimeters.

"I'm not apologizing for something you did," I said. Aimee glared at me.

"I think you are."

Before I could stop her, Aimee pulled the hat off my head and hid it behind her back.

"Give that back." Aimee slipped the hat to Gemma. Gemma looked at it, gave it a little stretch, and stuck it on her head. *"Give it back."*

"Actually, I don't think we will."

"It was my mum's," I said, my voice catching. Aimee pouted at me.

"Aw, really? Mum's hat?" She took another step toward me. "Apologize."

I shook my head, breathing through my nose.

"All right, then. Maybe there's something else you can give me."

"I don't have any money."

"Maybe not," she said, her eyes dropping downward. "But you do have that camera."

I retreated against the wall, the camera behind my back. The idea of her taking Olly's gift from me made me feel sick to my stomach.

"You're not taking this."

"Watch me," she said, reaching for it. I held her off at first, but the other girls closed in and all six of them worked together to pin back my arms. Their fingers were all over me, digging and groping, and as I struggled to break free, I felt nails scrape along my collarbone, draw-

ing blood. I squeezed my eyes shut, swallowing the pain, and one of the girls prized the camera from my weakened grip. When I opened my eyes again, Aimee had wrapped the strap around her fist so that the camera dangled downward, and she was swinging it back and forth, gently, just above the ground. Like a medieval weapon.

The look on her face was one of pure scorn.

"They've got me on a disciplinary warning now," she said, her voice suddenly hoarse. "Any idea what that means, Charlie? It means if I do one thing wrong, they'll—"

"Hey! Hey, let go of her!"

Melissa was running toward us from the far corner of the courtyard. I struggled, but the girls held me fast.

"What are you doing?" she shouted. "Let go. Aimee, stop it!"

Aimee wheeled round and sighed melodramatically.

"Piss off, Melissa."

"You piss off."

Aimee lowered my camera onto the ground, dangerously close to a puddle. The strap slipped off her hand and wilted around the puddle.

"What did you say?"

"Let go of Charlie—she never did anything to you."

"Melissa, don't—" I began to say, but it was too late. Aimee grabbed a fistful of Melissa's coat and shunted her across the courtyard. Melissa was lashing out desperately, but she didn't have half Aimee's strength. With both hands, Aimee slammed her into the chain-link fence.

She held Melissa's face to the rusting metal.

"What did you say?"

Melissa's voice was muffled as she tried to get words out.

"Let her go," she said, reaching out awkwardly behind her back. "She's my best friend . . ."

Aimee twisted Melissa round to face me and, with her gaze fixed on mine, leaned in toward her and whispered something in her ear. Melissa nodded, her eyes glistening.

Then Aimee let go, shoving Melissa away, and started walking back toward me.

"Anyway, Bloom, like I was saying . . ."

Melissa stepped away from the fence. I urged her back with a careful shake of my head.

". . . Bennett's really got it in for me now," continued Aimee, plucking my camera from the wet concrete. "One strike and I'm out, he says. So don't tell anyone about this, yeah?"

I kept my eyes open, unblinking. She was in my face now.

"About what?"

Chewing her tongue, Aimee pulled the camera strap tight across her fist. A little blob of spit had appeared in the corner of her mouth. Then, stepping backward until she was level with a small wall, she dangled the camera behind her back, sucked in a lungful of air, and swung it over her head into the brickwork. With a metallic splinter, it collided hard with the wall, and the lens smashed instantly, showering small, fragile pieces of glass across the paving stones.

Aimee waited a few seconds, breathing in and out, staring at me. Then she braced herself, held the camera at a distance, and swung it once more into the wall. More broken glass, and the sound of cracked plastic.

Then she swung it again. And again. And again.

Each time, the camera broke down still further, until it was misshapen and bent, barely hanging together. I was watching her, helpless, anger burning in my throat, thinking about how Olly would feel if he ever found out, when I noticed someone approaching across the courtyard.

"Aimee, I—"

But she ignored me, her hair falling free in front of her face, and launched the camera into the wall one last time. It broke open on impact, destroyed, irretrievable, little silver parts scuttling away across the paving stones like tiny fleeing beetles.

I held my breath, and Aimee's eyes met mine.

"What a shame," she said. "No more pop-star selfies."

A hand came down on her shoulder.

"Inside, Miss Watts."

Confusion spread across Aimee's face.

"Wh—?"

"Inside, now."

Aimee turned around and, when she saw Mr. Crouch, tried to pull away. He had a tight hold on her arm, though, and began dragging her toward the school.

"Let go of me, you pervert!" she screeched.

"No chance, young lady. You've had it. Game over. You're going to Mr. Bennett, and this time *you will be expelled*."

Around me, the other girls scattered, and I watched Gemma disappear down an alleyway, Mum's hat askew on her head. Melissa was running toward me, her cheeks flushed, on the verge of tears.

"You'd better hope you don't see me outside school, Bloom!" Aimee was yelling as Mr. Crouch escorted her inside. "This isn't over . . ."

Her words echoed and died away somewhere inside the long, empty corridors as I slumped against the wall, scratch marks stinging in the winter air, the broken shards of my camera lying silent all around me.

I hadn't said a word to my father in days. I would come home from school, go straight to my room, and stay there all evening, half working, half gazing at the walls. I avoided him in the hallway; I let him cook his own meals. I barely ate myself.

Several times a day, I'd hear from Gabriel.

Thinking about you, charlie brown xxx

I stared at the message, like I stared at all of them, with my chest tight, my teeth on edge. I could tell him the truth. I could tell him I was thinking about him too, but what good would that do?

Flicking my phone to silent, I slid it under the covers, out of sight, and opened my laptop. We'd been studying *Romeo and Juliet* in English, and I'd planned to spend the evening watching movie clips online and kidding myself it was research. I entered the search term, scanned the list of videos, then heard a shrinking knock at my door.

"Charlie?"

The floorboards creaked as my father hovered.

"What?"

The door opened slowly, and he stepped half inside the room. You could almost taste the air between us, bitter and flat, like stagnant water.

"Is everything . . . uh . . ."

"Yep," I said, the word clipped and cold, like the locking of a door. Dad pressed his lips together, nodding into the silence. The only sound around us was the creaking of dry, dead branches outside my window.

"That graze on your neck still looks bad."

The wound on my collarbone had scabbed over into two distinct claw lines. I covered it with a strand of hair.

"It's nothing."

"This Aimee Watts is going to pay for a new camera, Charlie. Take it from me."

"I told you, Dad, don't bother. I can save up for a new one. Just leave it."

"Well . . . anyway. We can talk about that another time." He cleared his throat. "Now listen, I've, um . . . I've been called away on business this week."

"OK."

I returned to my computer screen.

"Tomorrow and Friday I'll be up in Birmingham, back on Saturday morning. Around eleven-ish. You'll be OK on your own?"

"Mm-hmm."

He took a small step forward, his fingers slipping off the doorknob.

"I know it's the anniversary tomorrow, Charlie." He wrung his hands. "I'm sorry I won't be here. We can lay flowers next week, if you like?"

Dad usually took me to London on 28 November to visit Mum's grave. In the car, on the way, he would talk to me about school, or about so-and-so's house being on the market. Anything but her.

"Don't worry."

He straightened up.

"This doesn't change anything, mind you. You're still grounded."

"I know."

I had no camera (at least not a decent one), no invitation, and no reason to go back. My father had nothing to worry about.

"I'll leave some money on the kitchen table. You can always call me, you know."

My phone vibrated again, under the covers. We both heard it.

"Sure. Good night."

He lingered for a moment, scratched the top of his head, then left the room. I reached for my phone and opened the message.

We're doing a shoot with an "award-winning" photographer from vogue magazine today. Everyone prefers you. G x

I clenched my jaw. Surely the teenage girl was supposed to stalk the pop star, not the other way round?

Still holding my phone in one hand, I began scrolling through *Romeo and Juliet* videos on my computer, skimming the descriptions, trying to ignore the voice in the back of my head. Did Gabriel really mean that, or was he just appealing to my ego? Was he hoping to trick me into replying? Shaking the thought away, I tossed my phone across the bed.

My laptop flickered, and I realized that while lost in thought, I had clicked on a random video and it was about to play. An advert was loading and, when it began, four faces I knew very well appeared on the screen.

"Hey guys!"

My shoulders slumped. They really were impossible to avoid.

"We're Fire&Lights," continued Olly breezily, "and we're here to tell you about a very special single we've just released."

Olly was sitting with the rest of his bandmates on a leather sofa in what looked like a recording studio, and a song I didn't recognize was playing in the background. In the bottom right-hand corner, a little black box read *Skip Ad*. All I had to do was click it.

All I had to do was click it, and get on with my life.

"It wasn't planned," added Aiden, "but we've been trying to finish this track for months, and Gabriel finally found the right lyrics."

Gabriel was sitting at the end of the row. He smiled distractedly.

Yuki took over. "The song's called '2 a.m. (The Sound of Your Heart Breaking),' which I think is a pretty cool title. I like songs that tell you what time it is."

"*Anyway*," said Olly, as Aiden play-punched Yuki on the arm, "we decided to release it this week as an unexpected treat for you guys before our debut album, *Songs About a Girl,* comes out next month. We even shot a video, which you can watch at the link below."

"So click the link," said Gabriel mechanically, "and check it out. Let us know what you think."

There was something not quite right about Gabriel's expression. It would've been lost on most people, but if you'd ever spent any time with him, you'd know. Something was wrong.

"Enjoy," said all four boys in unison, and the advert faded away. As I sat there, motionless, Mercutio's death scene began to run on the video player, and I hit the space bar to pause it.

One listen wouldn't hurt, would it?

An old version of Charlie, pre-Gabriel, would have laughed at this: me sitting in my room, alone, unable to concentrate on school-work because Fire&Lights had released a new single. But things had changed, and I wasn't the same person anymore. They had infected me. And so, plugging my earphones into my computer, I typed *fire&lights 2 a.m.* into the search bar, clicked the top hit, and turned up the volume.

The video began to play. Gabriel, his face half in shadow, was sitting on the edge of a bed in a dark, anonymous-looking hotel room. The colors were nocturnal, grays and blues, and a passing siren could be heard in the distance. Slowly, a lightly picked guitar part faded in, and in his rich, jagged voice, Gabriel began to sing.

The opening lines stole the breath from my lungs.

> *Charlie, I know how your heart beats*
> *Quietly, with secrets that you can't keep*

I'd been here before. I'd sat in my room, convincing myself that one of the world's biggest pop stars was singing about me, and I'd got it wrong.

But this was different.

He was singing my name.

> *Charlie, I know how your heart beats*
> *Quietly, with secrets that you can't keep*

> *Believe me, I know that I did you wrong*
> *But lately, I feel as if I can't go on*

I screwed my eyes shut, but there was no getting away from it. These weren't scraps of poetry from an old notebook, lifted from some forgotten indie band. These were Gabriel's thoughts, his fears, laid bare for everyone to see.

The song was about me.

It was about us.

Gabriel was alone in the video. This was unusual, but then he *was* singing the lead vocal entirely on his own, and they clearly hadn't had long to put this together. So there was only him, the boy who had consumed me, singing my song into the darkness. Desolate, defeated. Heartbroken.

As the chorus began to swell, I felt the walls fall away around me.

> *It's 2 a.m. and I am here alone*
> *Empty bottle and a silent phone*
> *I can feel you, when I'm without you*
> *Even now*

And I don't wanna fall asleep tonight
Unless I can have you by my side
'Cause when I'm sleeping, it keeps repeating
Round and round

The sound of your heart breaking
The sound of your heart breaking
I don't think that I can take it
The sound of your heart breaking

The words echoed through my brain.

I can feel you, when I'm without you . . . even now.

I thought about the things Gabriel had said to me, trapped inside that lift, before we kissed. *I can't put it into words, Charlie, but . . . we're connected. I knew it the first moment I saw you.* And he was right. There *was* something between us. Something indescribable. Maybe it was losing our parents as kids, maybe we were just reaching out to someone who understood what that meant, but whatever it was, it was there, and I felt it too. In my gut.

That feeling, Charlie Brown . . . that's what I feel when I'm with you.

As the video played out on my computer, and Gabriel spoke to me, so clearly, through his music, I knew that I had to see him. I had to touch him, talk to him; I had to hold him close to me and hear his heart-beat and warm his skin and smell his scent, and fall into his arms. I didn't care what had happened.

I didn't care if I got hurt.

Because the truth was, I was falling for him, irretrievably, and there could be no turning back.

27

"You OK?"

I peered across the lunch table at Melissa. She was poking at her sandwich with a stick of carrot, her eyes misted over.

Since the incident with Aimee, she'd been quieter than usual.

"Huh?"

"Everything all right?"

We were sitting alone at a table in the most remote corner of the cafeteria, while around us the room clattered with cutlery and gossip. The school felt like a different place without Aimee, but hardly a safer one. Her friends blamed me for what happened, and they were making no secret of it.

"It's her fault Aimee was expelled . . ."

"She always goes crying to Mr. Bennett . . ."

"Has Gabriel dumped her yet . . . ?"

"People are saying it's her in that song . . ."

"No way, it's that dancer, Charlotte Stevens . . ."

I rolled a tomato across the table toward Melissa.

"Hey, Chuckles."

The tomato came to rest next to Melissa's lunchbox, and she eyed it, confused. I clicked my fingers at her.

"Talk to me."

"Um . . . yeah, sorry. I'm fine."

My phone went off in my bag, and I felt a familiar twinge. It was still there, every time: the fear of an unknown number.

"I'm worried. I've never seen you like this."

Melissa gave me a weak smile.

"Just school . . . it's getting me down. Big-time."

I know the feeling, I thought. I opened up my phone and, to my relief, found a message from Gabriel.

What's new, charlie brown?

I looked up from my phone. Across the cafeteria, a table of Year Sevens were throwing fries at each other.

Nothing much. Just hanging around the cafeteria, like a loser :)

Life in the fast lane, wrote Gabriel, and I smiled.

After hearing his new song, I had broken my silence with Gabriel. Just a single message, at first, to say I was thinking about him. To ask him about his day. Soon, though, it escalated, and by Wednesday lunchtime we were messaging feverishly: I would tell him about my lessons, my teachers, and my mock exam papers, and he would tell me about the band's radio interviews, the midweek charts (it looked like "Dance with You" was staying at number one) and Yuki's fling with Jenna Jackson. We hadn't talked about "2 a.m." yet, but it was always there, in the back of my mind. In the hours after the release, I had a few phone calls from withheld numbers—reporters, I imagined, connecting me to the song—but I ignored them all, and they soon dried up completely. I was surprised at first, but then I heard an interview Gabriel had given on the radio, just after the single went live. They asked him about that line, and he hinted that he'd written it about a backing dancer called Charlotte Stevens who he'd supposedly had a fling with during *Make or Break*.

It could be true, I told myself. It could be true . . . but somehow I knew that it wasn't.

Life in the fast lane? **I repeated.** You've clearly never been to my school

Sounds like you need some drama in your life, **replied Gabriel.**

I'm not cut out for drama. It doesn't suit me

Course it does, charlie brown. You're wild, inside

Those last three words sounded like a song lyric, I thought. Perhaps, in a month's time, I'd hear them on the radio.

Come to the gig tomorrow. Last show of the tour, london complex. I want you there with me

I drafted several replies, declining his invite, but deleted them all. A plan was already forming in my mind. It was only London, less than half an hour on the train. And Dad would be away the whole time. I could get there and back without him ever knowing.

My good camera's broken

As I wrote the words, I thought, guiltily, of Olly. I still hadn't told him about the camera. I wasn't sure how to.

I'm inviting you as a guest, **replied Gabriel,** not a photographer. Bring a friend if you want, make a night of it

I knew it was possible. I knew, technically, the chances of my father finding out were very small. And I knew, most of all, that I burned to see him.

In case you'd forgotten, I'm grounded. For which I blame you entirely

Charm your way out of it

We can't all sail through life on charm, gabe

I imagined him smiling at this and bit my lip.

I have to see you, came the reply, and I sent mine straight back.

Me too

There was a long pause.

I know you've had a rough time, came Gabriel's message eventually, but I never meant for those things to happen. I never meant for you to get hurt

I wrote two words, then deleted them . . . then wrote them again.

I know

Plus . . . I could do with a friend. This time of year's kinda crappy for me

I hesitated over the keypad. I was still never sure how much to push him on these things.

Really? Why?

Another pause.

Hard to explain. I'd just be happier if you were there

I took a long, slow breath, remembering the mechanical tone of his voice in the "2 a.m." promo video, and his weak, distracted smile. My instinct had been right. Something was weighing him down.

Another message lit up my screen.

So come. There'll be a big party afterward . . . bring your coolest friend, management's doubling our guest list

I glanced up. Melissa was rolling the tomato around the table with one finger. She saw me looking at her and narrowed her eyes.

"What?"

"I think I have something that'll cheer you up."

I walked round to her side of the table, sat down next to her, and handed her my phone.

"Read this," I said.

Gingerly, she took my phone and began scrolling through the messages. My gaze wandered the cafeteria, and I caught Gemma's eye, at a distant table, for just a second. Her face darkened, and I broke away.

"Um . . . what? Ohmygosh . . ."

Melissa was glued to my phone, lips moving as she read.

"Ohmygosh . . . Gabriel . . . A message from Ga—a massive p— sounds like he's inviting you to the . . . party . . ." She sprang up from her chair. "Ohmygodcharlie, I'm your coolest friend!"

"Yes. Yes, you are." I quickly scanned the nearby tables. "But keep it down, will you?"

"We HAVE to go!"

Grabbing her by the arm, I yanked her down on to the bench and clamped my hand across her mouth.

"If I take my hand away, do you promise not to say anything?"

Melissa nodded from behind my hand, her eyes bulging.

"Promise?"

"Mm-hmm."

I let go, and she fell about in a dramatic fit of gasping.

"Ohmygod ohmygod ohmygod . . . I'm going to meet . . . Fire& Lights . . ."

I leaned in front of her, waving a hand directly in her face.

"Mel, Mel. Just listen to me for a second."

"Yip."

"If we do this, then—"

"HOLY HECK WE'RE ACTUALLY GOING."

I grabbed her by the cheeks and squeezed.

"Wait, wait. Just . . . shut up. Shut up a sec. If we do this—*if we do this*—I need you to promise you'll act like . . ." She gulped at me through her squidged mouth. "Like a normal human being."

Hesitantly, I let go of her face. Sporting a grin so huge that it joined one ear to the other, she stood up and saluted me.

"Orders received loud and clear, Cap'n Bloom."

"Yep. It's stuff like that. That's exactly what I'm talking about."

Melissa pulled a bright-red lipstick from her bag and, while she waved it around and blathered about how short her skirt was going to be at the concert, I plucked my phone from her hand, wrote Gabriel another message, and clicked Send.

A thrill powered through me, and I closed my eyes.

At least this time I'd have my best friend at my side.

28

By the time we reached the stage door, Melissa was at boiling point.

"Charlie, Charlie. Charlie. Charlie."

I placed a hand on each of her shoulders and tried to establish eye contact.

"Mel, you have to calm down. This is not cool."

"I know, I know, but every time I think about meeting the band I'm scared I'm going to pee my pants. Is that bad?"

Melissa had agonized for hours over her look for the evening. In the end she had gone for sequins, high heels, and a pink miniskirt. Her makeup had been painstakingly applied, with smoky eye shadow and little glittery sparkles twinkling under her lower lashes.

I stared into her manic eyes.

"Is it bad if you pee your pants?" I repeated.

"Uh-huh."

"Yes, Melissa, that would be bad."

"OK, noted. No pants-peeing."

"Hey, Yuki . . . !"

Yuki was standing in the stage door. When he turned around he beamed at us and threw me a high five. The security guards flanking the doorway gave me a nod.

"Charlie! The Bloomster." Yuki pointed at my head. "Hey, where's your hat?"

Aimee's face flashed up in my mind. I flattened my hair at the back.

"I'm . . . trying a new look."

"Nice! I like it." His eyes fell on Melissa. "And who's your friend?"

We both waited for Melissa to reply. She appeared to be holding her breath.

"Mel?" I said, tugging on her sleeve. She swallowed.

"M . . . Melissa," she said, looking up at him, her eyes unblinking. "You're Yuki Benjamin Harrison."

Yuki smiled.

"I sure am," he said, stretching out his arm. "Come on in."

Melissa stepped through the doorway hesitantly, like a kitten exploring its new home, and I followed her inside. The guards closed the door behind us.

The London Complex show had been billed as the band's homecoming concert, and Gabriel said it had sold out in under thirty seconds. The queue outside the lobby was the biggest I'd seen so far, and inside, even in the bowels of the building, you could still hear the cheering.

Yuki was leading us through winding back corridors toward the dressing room, with Melissa hiccupping—as she often did when she was overexcited—and whispering, "This is the coolest," to herself.

When we arrived, Aiden and Olly were lying on sofas, listening to music. Olly immediately sat up when he saw me.

"Charlie!" he said, his smile, as always, all teeth. Perfect white teeth. "You brought company."

"This is Melissa," I said, and everybody waved hello. Melissa waved back.

"This your first Fire&Lights concert, Melissa?" asked Aiden, plucking a bottle of water from the fridge. Melissa stared back at him. Her eyes had gone wide and bright, like little moons.

"First time," I confirmed, taking her hand. "She's a huge fan."

"Hey, you girls fancy seeing the stage before they let anyone in?"

Olly was gesturing toward the doorway. Melissa's mouth dropped open, and her eyes began to flit from side to side. She didn't know whether to gawp at Aiden or Olly.

"I'd love to, Olly," I said, "but I promised I'd . . . I mean, I said to Gabriel that—"

"It's cool," said Olly, our eyes locking for the briefest split second. An energy passed between us, and it felt like he was trying to tell me something.

I turned to Melissa.

"You wanna stay here?" I said, feeling a bit like a parent at a theme park. "Hang out with the guys, maybe see the stage?"

Melissa was dumbstruck. This was probably the longest she'd gone without speaking in her entire life.

"Melissa? That sound good?"

She nodded at me, very slowly.

"Right, then," I said, reaching for the door handle. "I'll see you in a bit. Stay out of trouble, Mel."

Avoiding Olly's stare, I slipped from the dressing room and closed the door behind me. Gabriel's last message had told me he was, for some reason, up on the roof of the building . . . but how did I get up there? There were no maps on the wall, no signs to guide my way. Standing in the dark, I looked both ways for an exit, while through the walls I could hear Aiden strumming quiet chords on his guitar. This would surely be too much for Melissa. If he actually started singing to her, there was every chance she might drop dead on the spot.

"Wait, Charlie."

I swiveled round to find Olly standing behind me, lit by a single spotlight.

"He's not in a good place tonight."

"Gabriel? What do you mean?"

I might have sounded surprised to Olly, but I wasn't. After Gabriel's cryptic messages the day before, I'd half expected something like this.

Olly glanced over his shoulder.

"I don't know what it is, but I've never seen him like this. Just . . . I don't want you to get hurt, Charlie. Watch your back. Please."

A silence lingered in the air between us. Weirdly, I felt kind of ashamed.

"Do you know how I get onto the roof?"

"The *roof* . . . ? Seriously?"

"It's fine, Olly. I'll be fine."

He sighed and threaded a hand through his hair.

"Yeah, sure. There's a little staircase at the end of the hallway. Follow it all the way up."

As I climbed the metal stairs to the top floor, I chewed over Olly's words in my head. He seemed genuinely worried about me, and I'd always trusted his intentions, but what had Aiden said to me last weekend, on the tour bus? *Olly and Gabe . . . they're always competing over something.* I could believe that, I thought, I just never imagined that something would be me.

At the top of the stairs, I pushed open a small door and found myself in a musty boiler room that was dark and smelled of wet metal.

After fumbling for the light switch for a while, I noticed an exterior door, nudged it open, and stepped out into the cold. The wind clung instantly to my cheeks.

Directly in front of me was a wrought-iron ladder, so I clambered up it and emerged onto the main section of the roof. Stretching out in every direction were the rooftops of London, the skyscrapers and chimney stacks, the church spires and construction cranes. And standing right in the middle of it all, his tall, lithe figure framed against the burning city lights, was Gabriel.

"Gabe . . . Gabe! Christ, what are you doing?"

He spun round when he heard my voice, and I saw that his face was ravaged with cold tears. There was a half-finished bottle of Jack Daniel's in his hand.

"What's going on? Why are you up here?"

I took hold of his arm, and he stared back at me. His eyes were ringed with dark circles.

"Charlie Brown."

"Are you OK? What's happened?"

Gabriel shook his head, confused, and took a swig from the bottle. He stumbled, and I grabbed him by the wrists.

"It's not safe up here," I said, trying not to think about how high up we were. "Come inside—you need to sober up."

"This wasn't supposed to happen," he said in a low voice, more at the rest of the world than at me. *This wasn't . . . supposed . . . to happen.*

"Gabe, please. Talk to me."

I pulled him toward me to block out the wind. Even though he was only in a T-shirt up here, his skin felt warm and soft.

"They were supposed to stay buried."

"Tell me what's going on," I said gently. "Please."

Beneath us, huge crowds of people were waiting to be let into the building. Lights flashed and cars honked, and music blared from inside the main entrance. I recognized the song immediately: it was "2 a.m."

"All these people," he said, huskily, his voice barely there, "they've got me wrong. They think I'm worth something. They should go home . . . get out of the cold . . ."

As Gabriel spoke, familiar lyrics floated up to me through the night air. *It's 2 a.m. and I am here alone . . . empty bottle and a silent phone . . . I can feel you, when I'm without you, even now . . .*

"You're not making sense," I said. He took a long, slow breath.

"It's today."

"What is?"

"The twenty-ninth. My dad killed himself on the twenty-ninth of November."

The coincidence stung. The anniversaries of my mom's death and Gabriel's dad's were one day apart.

I shook it off.

"Gabe, maybe you sh—"

"How do you do it?" he said, looking down at me. His eyes were skittish, unable to focus.

"Do what?"

"Get on with life . . . without her."

I pictured my mother in the beach photograph, standing on a low wall, smile lighting up her face. Hair tumbling from her hat.

"I don't, Gabe." I took his hand. "I don't."

He stared out over the rooftops.

"That reporter, Charlie . . . he's on to me. And when he figures out the whole story, he'll print it. He'll tell everyone that Harry West killed himself because . . ." The words stuck in his throat, and his eyes glistened in the dark. "Because he couldn't face being my father."

He clenched his jaw against the tears.

"I know this doesn't make it any easier," I said, "but he must have had a reason."

"I was five," Gabriel choked, wiping his eyes with the back of his arm. "I didn't have *anyone*. Who leaves a kid on his own like that? Who . . ."

His voice stumbled and died, replaced by blaring music from the streets below. The final words of his song soared out over the rooftops.

I don't know if I can take it . . . the sound of your heart breaking . . .

"You don't know why he did it," I said, and Gabriel blinked at me, looking lost, his face strangely blank. I thought about his stage fright, the way he hid himself from the world before going onstage. The fact that people thought he was this indestructible force, but really, underneath the pop-star armor, he was as scared as anyone else.

"Maybe your dad was just afraid."

Gabriel searched my face, his eyes red and stinging. Sirens blasted somewhere in the city.

"You always see the best in people, Charlie Brown."

My hands closed tight around Gabriel's bare arms, and I looked up at him underneath the vast black expanse of the sky. Pulling me in, he ran his thumb around my chin and down the contours of my neck, sending little rivers of warmth right down to my feet. I longed for him, but something didn't feel right. The freezing wind, the half-finished whiskey.

I pulled away.

"Don't you think . . . I mean, the whiskey?"

He lifted the drink to his mouth again.

"I need this."

"You don't," I said, reaching for the bottle. He dodged me, so I grabbed for it again, batting it away from his lips, and a few black drops spattered across the rooftop. Gabriel half hid the bottle behind his back, and something changed in his face; a darkness closed over him, like a blind being drawn.

"I'm not worth it, Charlie. You shouldn't waste your time."

"You're wrong," I protested, squaring up to him. "You can't do this on your own."

"But what if I'm no different than him?"

"That's your choice, not his."

"I'm turning into him, Charlie. I can feel it."

I thought about my mother, how I'd stared at her photograph and seen myself, and I knew there was a chance that Gabriel was right. But he was stepping backward now, nudging ever closer to the edge of the roof.

"Don't think like that, Gabriel. Don't ever think like that."

"He's part of me," he said, his voice hoarse, brittle. *"He's in my blood."*

I thought suddenly that he might jump, and so I ran for him, pulling him back toward me. He dropped the bottle, and as it clattered to the floor, I closed my arms around him, holding him tight. He fought me at first but then surrendered, burying his face in my neck, his hands clamped to my back. Together, we listened to the crowds on the street below, shrieking and laughing, singing their hearts out to Gabriel's songs.

For a long time, his body shook, silently, against mine.

29

"This is the greatest day of my life, EVER. Please, God, let me die tomorrow so I never have to live another day not hanging out with Fire&Lights."

Melissa and I were watching the concert from the side of the stage, and she'd been in a constant state of jiggle since the music began. I was still shaken from my encounter with Gabriel.

"Mel . . . *Mel.*"

I poked her four or five times on the shoulder. Eventually she turned round.

"Yip?"

"Will you be doing that all night?"

Her jiggling sped up as the boys leaped on to a moving platform, and red lights flashed all around them.

"Yes. Yes I will."

"Good to know."

I'd seen the moving platform trick several times by now. In fact, I pretty much knew the show inside out, which was why it was all the more obvious to me that Gabriel was missing his cues.

Before the concert began, there'd been a collective effort to sober him up. Pepsi and black coffee, ice-cold washcloths on the face, people fussing in every direction. Gabriel insisted he was fine, but even so, the stage crew were keeping him as far away as possible from Barry King. Mr. King had no idea his star performer was intoxicated and, after last weekend, the crew was determined to keep it that way.

Later, onstage, though the thousands of screaming Fire&Lights fans were blissfully unaware of it, Gabriel was not himself. The person I'd found on the roof of the building, that wasn't the Gabriel I knew. There was a new monster in him tonight, and it was pulling his strings. Singing his songs.

And that was the thing. It wasn't just his lazy choreography, or the artificial smile that painted his face throughout the show. It was the way he sang certain lines, lines I'd heard before but that tonight sounded, somehow, darker. He was missing out words, fluffing lines, and standing motionless for entire songs. In between numbers, he barely spoke.

One of Gabriel's talents, I knew only too well, was convincing girls in the crowd he was singing directly to them. He would move to the edge of the stage and perform a whole verse to a single fan in the front row, one hand outstretched toward her, her fingers grasping for his, her eyes filled with longing. Tonight, though, he shied away from this, and sang the lines inwardly, with a quiet malice, as if the music was consuming him, controlling him.

On the big screen, his eyes had lost their shine.

An hour and a half later, to the flashing of lights and thundering of drums, the four members of Fire&Lights were soaking up the final, deafening applause of the tour. Yuki was walking backward, pointing both hands at the vibrating upper levels. Aiden was holding an acoustic guitar, which he always played in the last song of the set, and when he threw his plectrum into the crowd, a scrum of girls collapsed in on themselves, scrambling for the prize. Gabriel waved halfheartedly to the fans, lost in his own head, and I wondered, as I so often did, what he was thinking. What was it like to feel isolated, to feel alone, while being adored by twenty thousand people . . . ?

Finally, behind Gabriel, walked Olly; and it was Olly who drew my attention. He wasn't looking at the crowd, he wasn't applauding the backing band as he normally did at the end of a show, and he wasn't staring straight ahead, into the wings.

He was watching Gabriel like a hawk.

"Gather round, troops. Who here reckons I can sink this beer pong backward? Huh?"

The Fire&Lights end-of-tour after-party was a raucous affair. Crates of alcohol were stacked high against the walls, and champagne bottles were popping in every corner. Yuki was standing on a table in the middle of the room, surrounded by a rapt audience of VIP fans and Fire&Lights musicians, while noisy pop songs played on the sound system.

Aiden threw a muffin at him, but it missed.

"You're all talk, Harrison."

"Oh yeah? *Oh yeah?*"

"I bet you can do it!" called Melissa, who had finally come out of her shell. "I bet you can do *anything.*"

"Well, Melissa," replied Yuki, juggling briefly with his Ping-Pong balls, "you are one *special lady,* I'll tell you that."

Melissa spun round to look at me when he said this and opened her mouth very, very wide.

". . . But there are some things I can't do, if I'm honest. Nuclear fission, basket weaving. Beer pong, though?" He held aloft one of the balls. "I will RUIN you people."

He turned round and threw the ball backward over his head, and it landed in one of the assembled cups. Everyone went crazy. Melissa looked like she was, as threatened, about to pee her pants.

"Game on, Roberts," laughed Yuki, as he and Aiden squared off at either end of the table. Meanwhile, I was perched on a desk in the corner of the room, nursing a lemonade, chasing ice cubes round the glass with a straw.

"Hey, Charlie Brown."

Gabriel was walking over to my little corner, hidden behind his aviators. He seemed perkier than when he'd left the stage, although that might have had something to do with the bottle of red wine swinging in his hand.

"Hey."

He hopped onto the desk next to me and slid along until our legs were touching. I edged away.

"You're drunk."

"That is a scandalous accusation," he replied, but when he saw the expression on my face, he hung his head.

"Listen . . ." He slid his glasses back into his hair, his eyes a beautiful mess. "I'm sorry about earlier. I shouldn't load all that stuff onto you."

He fixed me with that deep, hypnotic stare, the one that, right now, girls all over the world were gazing at on their bedroom walls. Even after all our time together, it still had the power to make my pulse race.

"You don't have to become your dad, you know."

Gabriel picked at the label of his wine bottle.

"I hope you're right."

"No, come on. Our parents don't get to decide what kind of people we are. That's up to us."

I knew this was what Gabriel needed to hear, but I wasn't quite sure I believed it. Weren't our lives, in some way, written into our blood?

"I meant what I said last week, you know," said Gabriel, setting down his bottle. "You're not like anyone else I've ever met. Not one single person in the world. Where did you come from, Charlie Brown?"

I kicked my heel against the leg of the desk, and my mouth curled into a smile.

"Reading."

Gabriel nudged my shoulder with his.

"That's funny," he said, our bodies pressed together. "You're funny."

On the far side of the room, Melissa was playing beer pong, blindfolded. She was missing all her shots but getting a cheer every time.

"I've been listening to your new song," I said, peering into my lemonade. I could feel Gabriel watching me.

"Do you like it?" he said.

The lyrics from "2 a.m." broke free from their moorings and floated into my memory. *Charlie, I know how your heart beats . . . Quietly, with secrets that you can't keep . . .*

"That first line . . . it's . . ."

I trailed off. Even now, I wasn't sure I could say it.

"I've been trying to finish it for months," said Gabriel, picking up my thread. "I could never find the right words, so we had to scrap it from the album. But then, something happened." His eyes flickered upward. "You happened."

My chest tightened. I tried to sound casual. "You know, there's a rumor going round that you wrote it about Charlotte Stevens . . ."

"Is there?" said Gabriel, innocently. "Nothing to do with me."

We both smiled.

"Did you guys actually date?" I asked.

"Are you kidding? I've never even met her."

I looked down, swinging my legs beneath the desk. I didn't need to ask him why he'd done it, because I already knew.

He'd done it to protect me.

"Listen, Charlie . . ." Gabriel set down his bottle of wine. "I know it was wrong of me to steal Dad's lyrics. He owed me for walking out, but that doesn't excuse it. Thing is, until now, I've never had the confidence to finish a song without him."

He reached out and curled a lock of hair behind my ear.

"This song, it's the first one I've written that's totally my own. It's the first one that really means something."

A heat gathered inside me.

My heart was shaking.

"You changed everything, Charlie Brown."

Gabriel guided my face forward, breath rushing into my lungs, and kissed me. Softly at first, then hard and urgent, his fingers sliding round to interlock with my hair. My shoulders fell, my back arched, and blood powered through my veins.

The room dissolved around us, and I was lost.

"We have a winner"—Yuki's voice—"as Mr. Yuki Harrison Esquire is crowned beer pong champion *once again*, and the crowd goes wild . . . !"

Noisy applause broke out at the other end of the room, and I pulled away, remembering where we were. And who might be watching.

"What's wrong?" said Gabriel.

"It's just . . . all these people."

Across the room, a delighted group of fans were watching Yuki balance a Ping-Pong ball on his nose. Melissa was yapping away at Aiden.

Gabriel smiled.

"Oh yeah. People."

He reached into his pocket and pulled out a pen and a business card.

"I've got something for you."

He scribbled a few words on the plush, cream card, then handed it to me. It was for a hotel called the Rochester. On the back, he'd written "Beaumont Suite. 11th floor xx."

"What's this?"

"It's my room. You can stay tonight, if you want."

"Gabe, I can't."

"We'll order Chinese food, talk, stay up all night. Watch crappy movies."

My shoulders dropped. However much I longed to, I knew I couldn't stay.

"Melissa's here, and besides—"

"She can have a room too," Gabriel said, with a shrug. "I'll book her the penthouse."

"She said no, Gabriel."

We both froze. I could see Olly, standing just beyond Gabriel, watching his every move. At first, no one spoke, and then Gabriel turned, slipped down off the table, and rose to his full height. The bottle of wine was hanging by his side.

"What'd you say, Samson?"

It wasn't a huge room, and it only took seconds for everyone to stop what they were doing and shift their attention to us. Yuki had paused in midthrow.

Silence fell.

"What did you say to me?" demanded Gabriel.

"She said no," repeated Olly. The faintest flicker of doubt crossed his face, but he stood his ground. "So leave her alone."

"How is this any of your business?"

Olly threw a glance at me.

"You're not listening to her. She isn't interested."

I slid off the table.

"Olly, it's fine—"

"It's not, Charlie."

"You're full of it, you know that?" said Gabriel, red wine sloshing in his bottle. Olly squared up to him.

"Look at yourself—you're a mess. You shouldn't have been onstage tonight."

"Sorry, what?"

"You think you can get away with anything because you're Gabriel West, but you can't. You're not invincible."

"I don't have to listen to this," said Gabriel, turning back to me. He was about to take my hand when Olly grabbed him from behind and started dragging him across the floor. Gabriel lashed out, but he'd been caught off guard and Olly had him in a deadlock. They scrambled together for several seconds, wine spilling from the bottle, until Olly eventually let go and Gabriel stumbled away.

Olly spoke calmly, eyes fixed on his bandmate.

"I think you should go."

"What? Are you kidding?"

Nobody said anything.

Gabriel turned to Yuki and Aiden. "Boys . . . ?"

Yuki stared right back at him but said nothing. Aiden went red and looked at the floor. The fans standing behind them kept a wide-eyed silence.

Clenching his jaw, Gabriel straightened his T-shirt, discarded his bottle on a nearby table, and walked to the door. Just before he disappeared, he looked over his shoulder and caught my eye. It was a look that, despite everything, I found hard to resist.

I wanted more than anything in the world to go with him.

"I can't believe you made us leave a Fire&Lights after-party," groaned Melissa as we trudged down the platform at Paddington. "This is the worst day of my life, EVER."

"It's complicated," I replied, buttoning my coat. It was another cold night, and rain was on the way.

"Complicated? There's nothing complicated about hanging out with pop stars, Charlie."

How little she knows, I thought to myself.

"There was so much I still wanted to do," she was saying as we stepped onto the train. "At the very least I wanted to let Aiden touch my boob."

"Melissa!"

We found an empty set of four seats and slumped down opposite each other. The train was full of snoozing drunks and glum-looking commuters eating Burger King.

"Don't judge me," she protested, dumping her handbag on the seat next to her. "There's nothing wrong with that. I'd only've let him touch *one* boob . . . and then I'd never have washed it again."

"That is so gross."

The train crawled out of the station, and the minutes limped by as we passed in and out of the drab, low-lit towns that littered the journey home. Ealing Broadway, Southall, Hayes and Harlington. We sat in silence, pawing at our phones.

During the after-party, I'd received another slew of messages from Fire&Lights fans. My number must have been screen-grabbed and shared to Instagram or published on a forum, because they kept coming through, day and night. The only way to stop them now was to change my number, and since the bill was in his name, that would mean telling Dad.

Which meant I just had to grin and bear it.

Hey slut, wanna hook up

Saw u on that fan blog charlie, LEAVE GABRIEL ALONE

Ur pix suck charlie bloom

It had occurred to me, more than once, that the trolls sending me hate messages could have been the very same people complimenting my anonymous photos at Fan HQ only days earlier. It was unnerving, the way people moved in herds. Especially when you were the prey.

Patiently, I scrolled through the messages in my inbox and, one by one, deleted them.

"Oh my gosh, I've just realized I haven't peed all night!" blurted Melissa, sitting bolt upright. The irony seemed to have escaped her.

"It's just up there," I said, pointing down the carriage. Making her way past a gang of sleeping goths, she reached the cubicle and timidly clicked open the door.

"Eeewww, train toilet . . ." she whimpered, venturing in with her fingers pinching her nose. When the door closed, I noticed she'd left her phone unattended on the seat. She really was dappy sometimes.

I picked up the phone and was dropping it into her handbag when a notification on the home screen caught my eye: "You have one new e-mail."

> *[SUBJECT: Your blog has new followers!]*
> *Congratulations, Melissa, your blog has gained ten new*
> *followers! Click this link to visit the page:*
> *< FIRE&LIGHTS FOREVER >*

My blood went cold.

It couldn't be.

30

I read the e-mail alert again, and again, and again.

It couldn't be true. It simply couldn't.

All this time.

It was *Melissa.*

"Oh my God, those toilets are SOOOOOO disgusting. I swear, if I have to . . ."

Melissa trailed off when she saw me holding her phone.

"Hey, that's my phone."

I didn't answer.

"Say something, Charlie, you're freaking me out," she said, squeezing past the goths and grabbing the phone from my hand. Before slipping it into her bag, she glanced at the home screen, and her face went white.

"Charlie, it's not what you think, honestl—"

"Tell me it wasn't you."

"I didn't mean t—"

"Tell me it wasn't you."

Tears gathered in her eyes, and she dropped to the corner of the seat, both hands to her mouth. Her breathing was ragged.

"I'm sorry—it all got out of control, I wasn't thinking—please don't hate me . . ."

I didn't know what to feel first. Pain, betrayal, anger . . . they were collecting in my stomach, burning me up from inside.

"How could you? *How could you?*"

Melissa wasn't looking at me. Tears were rolling down her cheeks, and she was shaking her head repeatedly.

"It wasn't meant to happen. I just needed . . . I mean, nobody was using the site, apart from those stupid Year Eights, and I thought . . . I thought maybe if everyone started reading my blog, and leaving comments and stuff, then maybe . . . maybe I wouldn't feel like such a geek for the rest of my life."

I stared at her, into the face of my best friend, and saw a stranger. A stranger, crying, on a train.

"You used me."

"I was only going to do it once, I promise. I thought . . . I don't know . . ." She was pushing out the words between sobs. ". . . I thought I would just say one thing, just post the photo, and then—"

"The photo," I repeated, stunned, the events of the past month flashing back to me in broken shards. When Melissa had hacked into my Facebook account to send Olly the fake message, it had all seemed like a joke . . . but now I saw that she'd been checking my inbox ever since.

Acid bubbled in my gut.

"Did you . . . did you steal it from me?"

"I wish I hadn't—it was an awful thing to do . . . but after I replied to Olly for you, my computer stayed logged into your account, and I found your message to Gabriel . . . it was an accident . . . but the photo, I . . . God, I don't know. I put it online and suddenly I was getting all these comments on my posts, and hundreds of followers . . ."

"I'm your *best friend*, Melissa. Don't you understand? Followers don't mean anything if . . . *if this is how you treat your friends.*"

Tears crisscrossed my cheeks as I realized what I'd done. I'd blamed innocent people for this. I'd lashed out at Gabriel, I'd bad-mouthed Carla. I'd gotten it all so horribly wrong.

"Do you know how many sleepless nights I've had because of this?"

"I know, I do . . . but I tried to fix it. You have to believe me. When people started trolling you, I knew it was my fault . . . but I thought if they knew who you were, if they knew that you were this amazing photographer, not just some groupie . . . but it didn't . . ."

"That's not how trolls work, surely you realize that?"

Her eyes were open wide, desperate, her pupils enlarged. Mascara was streaming down her face.

"The things people have said to me . . . the *hate* . . ."

"I didn't know Aimee was going to post your number, honest, and if I'd known that then—"

"But I *expected* that from her, Melissa!" I cried, nearly breaking down. "Don't you see? She's not my . . . She's not supposed to be my friend . . ."

This felt like a lie to me now. *My friend.* The words were ashen in my mouth.

"I . . . please, Charlie . . ." Melissa's face had bruised into horrible red patches, a speckled rash blushing the skin, and she was choking on her words. "I tried to fix it, I tried so hard, but it was too late . . . Charlie . . . oh God . . ."

I stood up, my head light, my vision dizzy. We were pulling into a station, and I didn't know where we were, but I did know that I couldn't stand to be around her anymore.

I had to get off the train.

"Where are you going?"

"I'm getting off."

"What?" She looked very lost all of a sudden. "You can't."

"I don't even want to look at you, Mel."

"Charlie, please don't go. I'm sorry . . . I'm so sorry . . ."

Melissa was in hysterics, and by now all the sleeping passengers in our carriage were awake, and the sad-looking men in crumpled suits were staring at me, and the train was slowing down, and the door lights were flashing, and I pressed the button, took one last look at her, and stepped out into the night.

Standing on the platform, I watched the midnight service to Reading carry Melissa away, and I realized that now, finally, I was truly alone. I couldn't call my father, because I'd broken my punishment, and there was no one else at home to come and find me. I was on my own in a strange town with hardly any money, and no London taxi would take me out to Reading at this time of night. I considered waiting in the station, but the weather was bleak, icy cold, and the next train home didn't leave until four a.m.

I reached into my handbag.

There was only one place left to go.

"The Rochester Hotel, please," I said to the taxi driver. I was praying I had enough cash on me to get there.

West Drayton was a dismal place. I'd walked out of the station straight onto an industrial estate, searching for the main road, the rain slicing down in sharp, freezing sheets. When I eventually found the high street, I stood in the cold for fifteen minutes waiting for a taxi with its orange light on, trying to ignore the dead-eyed stares of passing men.

"You OK, love?" said the driver, clicking on the meter. I nodded silently, noting my appearance in the rearview mirror. My hair was tangled, my face tear-strewn.

"I'm . . . fine. Will forty pounds be enough?" I said, sifting through the last few crumpled notes in my wallet.

"Uh . . ."

I looked up. The driver was watching me in the mirror.

"Staying at the Rochester, are you?"

I paused. Judging from the business card, the kind of people who stayed at the Rochester wouldn't struggle to pay for taxis.

"Oh, God, no. No, I could never afford that. I'm just . . . meeting someone."

He thought for a while, his expression pained.

I didn't have enough money.

"I-if it's not enough," I said, haltingly, "maybe just drop me . . . wherever?"

He blinked at me, and shook his head.

"Nah, come on, nonsense. Can't have a young girl wandering the streets in the middle of the night. Got a teenager of my own, y'know." He shifted the taxi into gear. "Forty's plenty, love."

"Thank you. Thank you so much . . ."

"Rough night this is, eh!" he remarked as we pulled back out into the road. Rain was pelting the windows, and, staring out through the quivering sheet of water, I thought of Melissa on that train on her own, upset and terrified.

This was a real mess.

I remembered the little piano studio at the Clapham Grand, where I'd laid into Gabriel about the fan blog. My accusations, his denials, the theories about Carla. And through it all, it had never once occurred to me that the real culprit was back at home, living next door to me, bent over a laptop in the dark.

Curling up in the corner of the taxi, I closed my eyes, still aching from the tears, and listened to the driver humming to himself as we traveled through the night.

By the time the cab pulled up outside the Rochester, the neon streets of London still bustling around us, my beating heart had slowed, and my hands were almost steady. Gazing up at the floor-upon-floor of luxury hotel suites, I scanned the balconies, wondering which one was Gabriel's. I imagined what he'd say when I arrived, thinking of how he'd lock his tanned hands into my hair, how he'd pull me toward him and call me Charlie Brown.

"Forty quid please, love."

I glanced at the dashboard. It read £59.40.

"Never mind the meter, kid," he said with a wink. "We don't use the meter after one a.m."

I half smiled at him, grateful for the kindness.

"Look after yourself, eh?" he said as I stepped out of the car.

The Rochester was the kind of hotel where men in top hats stood outside the entrance opening car doors for rich people. I didn't belong here, that was obvious, but it didn't matter. Gabriel belonged here, and right now, I belonged with him.

My phone buzzed again, so I pulled it from my bag and found fourteen unread messages from Melissa. Not now, I thought. Another day.

Another time.

I walked toward the steps, where the top-hatted doorman was open-ing a car door for a woman in a sequined ball gown, and paused. Fire&Lights were staying here, and surely the staff would take one look at me—the rain-soaked clothes, the tear-lashed cheeks—and assume I was some deranged stalker.

I would have to sneak in.

While the doorman greeted the lady in the ball gown, I took my chance and headed straight through the revolving doors, emerging into the lobby. It was empty apart from the clerk behind the desk and a drunk man in an expensive-looking suit, his loosened tie pitched at a jaunty angle, one shirt cuff hanging from his sleeve. He was leaning over the counter and berating the clerk in an American accent.

"Listen, pal, in New York I can get a magnum of Cristal any time of the day or night. *Any time.* I'm tryna throw a party here . . ."

The lift was directly ahead of me. Scanning both ways for hotel staff, I strode toward it and pressed the call button.

"I have money," slurred the man in the suit. "You wanna see money?"

He scattered a handful of credit cards across the counter, and the clerk, smiling placidly, stacked them into a pile with his white-gloved hands.

"I'm sure we can arrange something," he purred, nostrils twitch-ing, as the lift dinged in front of me. This caught his attention, but I was already inside with the doors closing behind me. There was a sign on the wall reminding me that the Beaumont Suite was on the elev-enth floor, so I hit the button, leaned against the rail, and waited.

As the lift trundled upward, I turned my face to the mirror and cringed. My eyes were red from crying, my hair was tangled and damp, and I was soaked from head to toe. There couldn't be another girl on earth, surely, who would go to meet Gabriel West looking like this.

When the lift dinged, I stepped out into the corridor, searching for signs. At one end were two ornate doors leading to a large balcony, and at the other, according to the sign on the wall, was the Beaumont Suite. I crept along the thickly carpeted floor, afraid that another guest would appear at any moment and call security on me.

When I reached Gabriel's door, I knocked quietly and listened for movement. At first, nothing happened. Was he asleep? Or maybe they'd all gone out to a club? What would I do then?

Soon, I heard the handle turning, and the door opened.

Standing in the doorway was international movie star Tammie Austin, dressed in pajama shorts and a faded T-shirt.

"Oh God, sorry," I stammered, hand on mouth. "I've got the wrong room."

She was even more stunning in person than on the big screen. I winced. Not only had I knocked on the door of a Hollywood actress in the middle of the night, but I'd done so looking like a drowned rat.

How had I screwed this up? If this was the wrong hotel, I'd be stranded.

"S'all right," she drawled vacantly, but with an odd expression on her face. She was about to close the door when she pointed at me.

"Hey, don't I know you?"

Famous at last, I thought.

"No, you don't," I said, glancing down the way I'd come. Had I walked one door too far?

"Seriously, I've seen your face before."

"You haven't. I'm sorry to disturb you . . . I'll go."

My cheeks burning, I turned to walk back down the corridor when I heard the toilet flushing, an inside door opening, and a second voice floating out from the room.

"Hey yo, babe. Get back in here. Did we finish that wine . . . ?"

It was Gabriel.

31

"There's a girl at the door, Gabe," said Tammie, as every atom in my body froze.

"D'you order room service?" he replied, yawning. "Maybe she can get us a beer or something . . ."

Gabriel appeared behind Tammie, scrolling on his phone. He still hadn't seen me.

"You wanna order takeaway?" he said, leaning an arm against the door frame. I tried to swallow, but my mouth was completely dry. It felt like someone had reached down my throat, taken hold of my lungs, and twisted them like baker's dough.

"I don't think she's room service," said Tammie, squinting at me. She tugged at the collar of her T-shirt, and I realized, with a jolt, that I'd seen it before. Jim Morrison, wearing aviator shades. It was Gabriel's.

"Well, if she's not room service," said Gabriel, lifting his head, "then what's she doing up here in the middle of th—"

And that was when his eyes met mine.

"Charlie?"

Two small, quiet words fell from my mouth.

"Oh, God . . ."

"Charlie, what the—"

My head spinning, I turned and ran down the corridor. When I got to the lift I repeatedly pounded the button, but the light told me it was still in the lobby, eleven floors away. I glanced down to the far end of the hallway and out across the balcony. Maybe there were steps down to a lower level?

All I knew was I couldn't see him, or talk to him, or let him touch me ever again. And so I kept running.

When I reached the balcony doors, I yanked them open and stumbled out into the night. It was bitterly cold, the rain was whipping at my skin, and I couldn't see another exit. Gabriel grabbed my arm from behind and I tugged for freedom, but he was too strong. Spinning round, I found him standing in front of me, bare feet on the concrete, freezing raindrops clinging to his face.

"Whoa, Charlie, slow down."

I wrenched my arm from his grip.

"Don't touch me."

"Will you let me explain?"

My hands were shaking, maybe from the cold, maybe from sheer anger. I balled them into little fists.

"Explain? There's nothing to talk about."

"You've got it wrong . . . this whole thing . . ."

He ran both hands through his wet hair and looked at me intensely. He seemed wired, on edge.

"Is this what you do, Gabriel?" I said, pointing back inside the hotel. Tammie was out of sight. "Is this what happens every time I leave a concert?"

"It's not what it looks like, I promise."

"Oh, you *promise*? And what do you think one of your promises is worth, exactly?"

He didn't have an answer for this. Behind him, one of the balcony doors slammed shut in the wind.

"Tammie's an old friend," he said, finally. "She was in town, she had this massive row with her boyfriend . . . we were just having a drink, watching TV."

I shook my head at him, sickness rising in my chest.

"Anyway—jeez, Charlie, it's two o'clock in the morning. I thought you went home. What are you doing here?"

I didn't want to say it. I didn't want him to hear it, not anymore, but the words still crawled from my mouth.

"I came here because . . . I needed someone, Gabriel. I needed . . . you."

He hung his head, those long black strands of hair looping down over his face, dripping wet.

"But I guess I misread the signs, didn't I? So I'll just go. I mean, shouldn't you be getting back to Tammie anyway?"

Gabriel glanced over his shoulder.

"She's just a friend, nothing more. You have to believe me."

"Oh, but you and I are *meant to be*, right?" I replied, my voice beginning to crack. I turned away from him, walked to the balcony edge, and waited for his reply.

His words were nearly lost beneath the sound of the pounding rain.

"Charlie, I think . . . I think I'm falling in love with you."

There was a tiny, treacherous part of me that wanted to believe him. To turn around and say it back. And as I stood there on the eleventh floor looking down at the city below, at the lights from the cars and the burning streetlamps and the shops and the bars and the neon signs, I remembered that day on the cliffs, how Gabriel took me so close to the edge and we talked about music and memory and the families we'd lost, and it felt like nothing could break us apart.

I could feel him standing right behind me, but I didn't move. Tears were racing down my cheeks.

"Charlie, look at me, plea—"

"You're a liar!" I yelled, spinning round. "You think you can get away with anything because of who you are, but . . . not this time. *Not with me.*"

Gabriel began to speak, but his words were jumbled, broken sounds that evaporated instantly in the wind.

"I let you in, Gabriel. Don't you understand that?" His amber eyes were incandescent, but this time I wasn't going to fall for it. "I told you secrets. I told you things almost no one else knows, and you . . . you do this."

"This isn't over."

"You don't get to decide that."

He reached out to grab me again.

"Leave me alone," I snapped.

"You don't mean that."

"Aren't you listening? *I never want to see you again.*"

I turned away from him again, sobbing, choking on my tears.

"Charlie . . ."

He grabbed me and dragged me back round, pinning me against the railing. In his eyes, there was almost the hint of regret.

Almost.

"Don't you see, Charlie? You and me, we're connected."

"Let go of me."

"We're connected."

I pushed hard, but he wouldn't let go, and I felt myself falling into him.

"You keep saying that, but you're not connected to anyone. You don't care about *anyone* except yourself."

I didn't know what was rain and what were tears anymore, and Gabriel was just a blur in my mind, a shapeless figure in the night.

"Listen to me," he said, pulling me close. "This picture you have of me, in your head . . . *it isn't the person I want to be.*"

"Maybe not," I replied, staring up at him through the rain. And it was then, in that single dark and hopeless moment, that my heart finally broke.

". . . But it is who you are."

"What the hell's going on?"

A new voice, coming from behind us. It was Olly, standing in the doorway, rainfall blotting his clothes.

"Are you all right, Charlie?" he said, walking toward us. Gabriel stepped into his path.

"She's fine, mate. Go to bed. This has nothing to do with you."

Olly glared at Gabriel, and a look of realization spread across his face.

"You slept with Tammie, didn't you?"

"I said leave it."

"You're drunk, Gabriel. You need to leave Charlie alone."

Gabriel straightened up and leaned into Olly's face.

"You've never liked me, have you?"

They were eye to eye now, their breathing oddly synchronized. Down below, a police siren wailed.

"What's that supposed to mean?"

"Come on, don't screw me about. You never wanted me in Fire&-Lights. And now you don't want me with Charlie."

Olly's eyes lingered on mine, and I shivered in the cold.

"She deserves better."

Gabriel seized him by the collar of his T-shirt.

"Don't you think I know that?"

"Then what the hell is wrong with you?" seethed Olly, struggling against Gabriel's grip, rainwater cascading down his face. "Why can't you just let her go?"

"What are you gonna do, Samson, huh? You gonna fire me? You gonna throw me out of the band?"

Gabriel's fists clenched, and his eyes hardened, and with the sky churning and sirens wailing, he pressed his face into Olly's and spoke in a low, ragged voice.

"*I am* the band."

Finally, Olly broke. In one swift movement he drew back his arm, leaned onto his back foot, and threw a punch at Gabriel that sent him spinning like a rag doll into a nearby table and chairs. Furniture toppled over and clattered to the ground, and for a few seconds Gabriel lay still on the shimmering tiles. Then he groaned and rolled over.

"Let's go inside," said Olly, slipping off his jacket and wrapping it round my shoulders. He guided me toward the doors and, as we walked through, I told myself not to look back. But I had to.

Gabriel was spread out on the ground, limbs twisted from the fall, eyes all but lost in shadow.

"How did you know we were up there?" I asked, shivering, as we traveled down in the lift. Olly laughed, softly.

"My room's below the balcony. I think half the hotel heard."

I closed my eyes, and they stung from salty tears.

"I don't know what to do. I can't go home, I haven't got any money, but I've got nowhere to go—"

"Charlie, it's fine. You can stay in my room."

I began to protest.

"Relax, I mean as friends. You take the bed, I'll sleep on the sofa."

I allowed a fragile smile onto my face.

"I just want to make sure you're OK."

"Thanks," I said, and the lift dinged.

In Olly's marble bathroom I dragged myself out of my wet clothes, took a hot shower, and slipped into the baggy T-shirt he had lent me. My reflection in the mirror was worn, tired, almost ghostly, but at least I was warm and dry and had a soft place to sleep.

It was approaching three a.m. I would have to get up again in just a few hours; otherwise my dad would arrive home and find me gone.

"Do you need anything?" said Olly as he lay down on the sofa, his shoulders blue in the moonlight. The sofa was way too short for him, and his feet hung over the edge.

"I'm fine," I said, as he pulled a scratchy-looking blanket over his body. My bed was enormous, big enough for three people, but I was curled up in one corner, coiled into a ball.

We listened to each other breathe for a while.

"Hey," said Olly, after a few minutes, talking to the ceiling. "D'you remember Magic Mickey?"

I rolled over onto my back.

"What?"

"Magic Mickey. He worked at the corner store opposite the school, years back."

I thought about everyone who had worked at that little store across from the school gates. The staff seemed to change every few weeks, but I did have a vague memory of a stooped, bald guy with big eyes who, if I was remembering him right, everyone called Magic Mickey.

"I think so."

"He just . . . he really loved candy, and whenever you went in there to buy some, whatever you picked, you'd put the candy on the counter and he'd say 'Ooh, I *love* those.' With *everything*. And the more stuff you put on the counter, the more excited he'd get. 'Ooh, you're buying those? I LOVE THOSE.'" Olly tried to keep his composure, but a warm, infectious laugh bubbled out of him. "Remember that?"

His laughter tickled me, and I began to giggle too.

"Yeah . . . yeah, I do."

"Magic Mickey," said Olly again, chuckling to himself. *"I love those."*

The clock by the bedside was blinking furiously, and I could hardly believe how late it was. Outside in the street, car engines still grumbled, music blared from nightclubs.

"Night," said Olly, and I heard the swish of the blanket as he rolled over onto his side.

"Night," I said, warm and numb beneath the duvet.

For a little while longer I lay awake, listening to the sound of the rain on the windows, wondering what Gabriel had done next. Had he gone back to Tammie? Had he asked her to leave? Maybe he'd gone out on the streets in search of another drink, or another girl.

The minutes ticked by and, though I fought them with the little strength I had left, flashes of his face, his hands, his eyes dominated my thoughts until I fell, finally, to sleep.

32

When my alarm woke me, the sun was about to rise.

On the other side of the curtains, London was already alive, truck drivers shouting from windows, cabs and buses honking. Yawning, I reached for the glass of water beside the bed and found a white envelope next to it, with something handwritten on the front. Inside was fifty pounds in crisp, new banknotes, and the message read: "For the train. O xx."

I picked up a pen from the nearby desk. "Thanks, Olly," I wrote beneath his note. "For everything. I promise I'll pay you back." But as I slid the cash into my wallet, I paused. Did Olly have this money lying around his hotel room, or had he waited for me to fall asleep and gone out into the rain to fetch it? I looked over at him, laid out on the sofa in last night's T-shirt, his chest gently rising and falling. From a gap in the curtains, a beam of light from the slowly waking sun lay across him, illuminating dancing dust motes.

As if from the tail end of a dream, I heard Gabriel's voice in my head. Something he had said on that TV chat show, underneath his breath, buried in the laughter from the crowd.

I'm the fire, he's the light.

Hearing it now, it felt like a warning. Is this what he meant?

All this time, had I been with the wrong person . . . ?

Banishing the thought, I pulled on my still-damp clothes from the night before and slipped quietly away.

My road was peaceful, mostly silent, when I got back to Reading. It was about twenty to eleven in the morning and, as I walked up the garden path, I prayed that Dad hadn't decided to come home early.

Nudging open the door, I glanced up at Melissa's bedroom window. I could see her Fire&Lights posters on the far wall, and her ant farm on the windowsill. Staring at familiar fragments of my best friend, I felt the memory of her betrayal burning again in my chest and stepped inside the house.

I couldn't imagine ever forgiving her.

Upstairs, I opened the desk drawer to stash away my keys and was confronted with endless reminders of him. A packet of candy from the tour bus, the note he had left in my camera case. My VIP wristbands. After I'd rested, I would get rid of these things. Burn them, throw them out, whatever I needed to do. They were pieces of Gabriel, and they no longer belonged in my life.

I slipped into bed, dragged the duvet right up to my chin, and closed my aching eyes. Within seconds, as Dad's key turned in the lock downstairs, I drifted away into the deepest of sleeps.

33

Nearly two weeks had passed since that night on the balcony.

Christmas was coming up, and Caversham High was unraveling. Teachers were stressed, classrooms were looking shabby and run-down, students were delirious with boredom. My days were filled with mock exams, essays, and equations; it was mundane, but after the chaos of November, it made me feel numb, disconnected, and oddly calm. Aimee's friends liked to remind me, now and again, that it was my fault she'd been expelled, but for the most part, they left me well alone. And with their ringleader gone, I could walk the school halls without looking constantly over my shoulder.

I tried to ignore Fire&Lights—on the web, on the television, in the conversations of my classmates. But avoiding Fire&Lights was like trying to avoid oxygen, and every day, without fail, they'd find a way into my life.

GABRIEL WEST HOOKS UP
WITH TAMMIE AUSTIN
< ALL THE LATEST GOSS!! >

"SONGS ABOUT A GIRL" SET TO BREAK ALL
THE RECORDS . . . Gabriel & Co. gear up for
massive world tour

EXCLUSIVE INTERVIEW WITH GORGEOUS
GABRIEL—we quiz him about dating Tammie
Austin, being a teen icon, and more!

I didn't hate Tammie. I didn't really feel anything toward her. I just wanted her to go away. But she wouldn't, and neither would Gabriel. The band were only getting bigger, and the New Year would see them embarking on a world tour that, from what everyone was saying, would complete their transformation into the one of the biggest boy bands in pop history.

At least he would be out of the country.

As for me and my fifteen minutes of fame, it was over; I was old news. A footnote in the gossip archive. The Internet had moved on.

Unfortunately, Caversham High had not.

"I heard Gabriel dumped her for Tammie Austin."

"Tammie Austin is so hot."

"I heard she made the whole thing up."

"Yeah, apparently she Photoshopped that picture."

"That is so desperate."

"You guys wanna finish my fries . . . ?"

Sometimes I could rise above it, block it out, like white noise on a television. At other times, though, I would reach instinctively for my phone and start writing to Melissa.

Seeing her name, I'd suddenly remember, and my heart would start to ache.

We hadn't spoken since I stepped off the train.

I thought about Olly a lot, too. The day after the Rochester, he'd sent me a Facebook message: If you ever need to talk, i'm here. I considered messaging him from time to time, or even calling him, but always backed out. He might have been my friend, but he was still a member of Fire&Lights. He was still a part of that world.

Finally, there was Gabriel. As the days went by, the time I'd spent with him was beginning to feel like a distant dream. All those connections between us—Mum's notebook, his lyrics, the memories we seemed to share—I began to see them for what they were: coincidences. And as time passed, I hoped I would find a way to forget it all forever.

That is, until one frosty evening, when I received an unexpected e-mail.

For Charlie re: Fire&Lights

Goose bumps blossomed on my neck. If it was him, I would just delete it. Straightaway, without a moment's thought.

Charlie, my name's Patricia Davis, and I work for Satellite Publishing. We're releasing the next Fire&Lights fan book and are currently collecting together all the images and footage from the last tour. I hope you don't mind me contacting you like this, but Barry King said we should drop you a line . . .

Barry King? I frowned at the screen. We'd only met that one time, outside Gabriel's hotel room. Had he actually liked my work after all?

. . . Basically, we've seen your photos on the F&L fan page, and we think they're fabulous. When it comes to capturing

*the boys' spirit, it seems you have a magic touch! And with
that in mind, we'd like to use a few of your photos in the
book. There are some wonderful shots: Gabriel dancing with
a fan, Aiden strumming his guitar backstage, Yuki juggling
bananas! Various other ones, too—details in the attached
document . . .*

I thought back to late October, and the way I'd felt when I first replied to Olly. How I didn't think I was good enough, how I was just a
kid, how I couldn't understand why they'd want me instead of a professional. But now, reading this e-mail, it was obvious why the band
needed my pictures. The shots Patricia had mentioned, those fleeting
moments between the boys . . . *no one else saw them happen.* Not the way
I did. A professional photographer might have had better equipment
than me, and more experience, but they wouldn't have *seen* the band
like I did, for who they really were.

Four ordinary teenage boys, who happened to be living extraordinary lives.

*. . . There'll be a small fee in it for you, and your name will
appear in the credits. We'll just need a parental signature
etc., so do drop me a line and we'll take things from there.
Thanks! PD.*

I listened for my father, downstairs, typing in his study. I'd need to
fake his signature, but it wouldn't exactly be the first time. So I wrote a
speedy reply, accepting Patricia's offer. Then, as I was about to sign off,
I hesitated above the keys, questions creeping into my mind. Was this a
bad idea? Should I just ignore the e-mail, pretend I'd never seen it?
Wasn't I trying to forget this whole thing and move on with my life?

No. I had earned this. I had given everything to it. Above all else, my time with Fire&Lights wasn't really about Gabriel West.

It was about me.

Breathing deeply, I signed my name at the end of the message and hit Send.

A **week later**, I **was** walking back from school alone, a light snow gathering on my coat sleeves. It had been snowing all day, the kind that dusts the road and the trees like icing sugar, and the air had a crystalline quality, like it might shatter if you touched it.

"Charlie."

A voice I hadn't heard for weeks scuttled up my spine. I kept walking.

"Hey, Charlie. *Slow down.*"

Aimee emerged from an alleyway and fell into step with me. My heart began to thud as I tried to outpace her, fractured memories from the schoolyard shooting through my mind. The girls' hands all over me; Aimee's hair falling loose as she swung my camera into the brickwork.

"Leave me alone. Please."

"Just wait."

"I've got nothing to say to y—"

"*Listen,*" she snapped, seizing my arm. I looked down, eyes wide, and she let go straightaway. "I'm not . . . I mean . . . ah, man."

We had stopped underneath a deserted bus shelter. Aimee wasn't wearing a coat, just an old T-shirt, and she looked cold.

I hugged my arms to my chest.

"What do you want?"

She reached into her back pocket. I stepped away, but my back met the plastic wall of the bus stop.

"Aimee, pl—"

Her arm was outstretched.

She was holding my hat.

"This is yours," she said, looking right at me. I stared at her, astonished, the hat hanging from her fingers.

She waved it at me.

"Don't you want it back?"

"Yes . . . yes, I do."

I took it from her, and sank my fingers into the wool. It felt soft and familiar against my skin.

She lit a cigarette, shivering, and I eyed her, silently, as she took a long, deep draw and blew the smoke above her head. It hit the roof, billowing out into a flat cloud.

"Why are you doing this?" I asked, gripping tightly to my hat, but Aimee just shrugged. We stared at each other for a while, and I wondered if I should tell her. Tell her what it had been like to be me this past month or so. Take her through every sickening moment: the whispers in the hall, the vicious, anonymous hatred. The threats and insults on my phone.

Maybe, though, she already knew. And that was why she was here.

"So . . . being expelled sucks," she said, sucking hard on her cigarette, as if trying to draw warmth from it. Tiny, transparent snowflakes eddied around her head.

"Oh. Right."

"Yeah. I just sit at home with Dad all day, in front of the telly." She sniffed. "He doesn't like it."

She tapped ash onto the ground, and I watched the hot, gray specks sink into the gathering snow.

"He's an angry bastard," she continued, wiping her nose with the back of her hand. "And I don't want . . . I mean . . . that's not me, y'know?" Her voice shrank, until it almost disappeared. "That's not me."

Strangely, I found myself thinking of my conversation with Gabriel, weeks earlier at the after-party. *Our parents don't get to decide what kind of people we are. That's up to us.*

A car crackled by on the icy road.

"I should probably go," I said, slipping my hat on. "But thanks for bringing my hat back."

Aimee looked at me, and I realized that she wasn't wearing any makeup. It was the first time I'd really seen her face, and her features were softer, her skin paler, than I'd ever imagined at school. Wet snow was settling in her hair.

Tightening my scarf, I walked back out onto the street and carried on my way. As I turned the corner on to Tower Close, I looked back over my shoulder one last time. Aimee was sitting on the bus stop's metal bench, watching me leave, her eyes drained of color. She rubbed her bare arms to keep out the cold.

All around us, snow fell.

There was a lump in my throat as I approached the house.

Aimee had seemed smaller, somehow, outside school. The way she had looked at me from that bus stop, it made everything that had happened—the fights, the accusations—seem phony and ridiculous.

I wondered what would happen when she got home.

I wondered what her father would do.

"Charlie . . . ! Charlie."

Rosie was hurrying down the garden path toward me, waving. I hadn't been round to Melissa's house since that night on the train.

"Charlie, sweetheart."

"Hi, Rosie."

She reached the end of the path, and I stopped on the other side of the locked gate. She crossed her arms against the cold, and a snowflake landed on her nose.

"Everything OK?"

I nodded.

"It's freezing out here," she said, and my gaze flickered upward to Melissa's bedroom window.

"Don't worry, love. She's not home."

I nodded again.

"Will you come in for a cup of tea . . . ?"

Rosie clinked away at the sink, snow whipping at the windows, while I sat at the kitchen table, hands wrapped around a mug of tea. Megabyte hopped onto my lap.

"Melissa feels horrible, you know," Rosie was saying, as she arranged snacks on a plate. "I don't think she's slept properly since you two fell out."

Rosie slid the plate onto the table between us and sat down in front of her tea. She nudged the food toward me.

"Here you go: Brian's chocolate flapjack. It's about a billion calories per slice, but absolutely guaranteed to cheer you up."

I took a piece silently, and Megabyte craned her neck to sniff it.

"You don't want to talk to *me* about all this, I know that," Rosie continued with a smile, "and, really, it's none of my business."

"It's OK."

"But whatever happened, it can't be worth throwing away ten years of friendship over, can it?"

Rosie let the question hang in the air between us, and I thought of Melissa, standing at the school gates, dressed in a duffle coat and her favorite gloves. The purple ones, chewed at the fingers.

"Hey, Charlie."

"Hi, Mel."

We'd bumped into each other a few days earlier on the way out of school, among a seething crowd of people. Students were pushing past us, shouting, backpacks swinging from their shoulders.

"So . . . you good?" she asked, glancing at her feet. They were turned inward, as if in conversation.

"All right. You?"

Her face looked pained, and she wrinkled her mouth.

"I know you probably don't want to talk to me, but—"

"It's fine."

I felt strangely calm, but Melissa was fidgeting and chewing on her glove. Finally, she blurted out: "I'm really, really sorry."

At first, most of what I'd felt toward Melissa had been anger. Anger, and bitterness. But looking at her now, standing in front of me in the spitty rain, I mainly felt sad.

"You know you can't do that sort of thing to a friend, don't you?" I said.

"I know."

"What you did, Mel, it was . . . just horrible."

"I know."

She bit back tears.

"I'm so sorry, Charlie, I feel awful. I barely sleep anymore; I just keep thinking about . . ."

She stopped, the end of her sentence written all over her face. *About what I did to you.* I pictured her in bed at night, staring at the ceiling, duvet pulled up to her chin. Across the garden, behind my curtains, I'd have been lying awake too.

"I see you've taken the blog off-line."

Her face brightened a little.

"I shut it down . . . for you. I know it's too late, but . . ."

It wasn't as if there was nothing for Melissa to write about. Between the album release, Gabriel's fling with Tammie, and the upcoming tour, the Internet was alive with Fire&Lights gossip. She could have kept it going and ridden the wave of popularity. But she hadn't.

"I noticed. Thanks."

For several long seconds, we stood there in silence. People pushed past us on their way out of the gate.

"Can I walk home with you?" asked Melissa, a tremble on her lip. I looked back on the face I'd known for very nearly my entire life, and doubt clenched my stomach.

"Maybe some other time," I said, passing through the gate without her. "Nice to talk to you, Mel."

I joined the chattering crowd, kids laughing and swearing and playing music on their phones, and it swept me back out into the world, Melissa watching me as I went.

As the memory faded, I found myself back in Rosie's kitchen, staring at a photograph on the fridge. Melissa and I were standing side by side in the garden, aged around six, dressed as pirates. She was wearing a giant fake mustache, and we were both laughing our heads off.

"You OK?" said Rosie, laying her hand on mine. I looked at her, suddenly aware I hadn't said anything for over a minute.

"Um, yeah . . . I think so."

Megabyte wriggled on my lap and mewed.

"I don't want to preach to you, Charlie, because that's boring, but . . ." She squeezed my hand gently. "There are two things that matter in this world, above all others. Family . . . and friends. Once you know where you are with those, everything else falls into place."

I slid my key into the front door, and the automatic light clicked on above me. All around, the weather was closing in, covering everything in a clean, white blanket of snow.

Rosie's words had settled in my mind.

Family . . . and friends.

When I opened the front door, Dad was pottering in the kitchen, chatting to himself. I hung my coat next to his, on the rack.

"Oh, Charlie," he said, looking up from the sink. "You're home."

"Hi, Dad."

I wandered down the hall and stopped in the kitchen doorway.

"School all right?" he asked.

"Not too bad. How was work?"

"Erm . . . the usual. Jen's still doing my head in, but . . ." He was eyeing me curiously while he filled the kettle. "Everything all right?"

My heart skipped, and the words I'd been rehearsing fell helter-skelter from my mouth.

"I'm so sorry, Dad."

He put the kettle down.

"What for?"

I stumbled momentarily. Words jostled for attention inside my head.

"What for, Charlie?"

"For . . . all the lies. For going off with the band, and keeping secrets from you." I dropped my bag by my side. "I didn't mean to upset you. Honestly."

Dad's eyes widened at me.

"Oh . . . Charlie," he said, padding toward me in his socks. "That's OK."

I shook my head.

"It's not OK. I know I haven't been easy to live with these past two months."

He thought about this.

"No. But I don't suppose I have either."

I thought of the papers I had found in Dad's study all those weeks ago. His awards, his PhD, the life he'd left behind to look after me when Mum was gone.

"I know it's been difficult since Mum died," I said. "I just . . . I wish we could be a proper family."

He touched a tentative hand to my shoulder.

"We *are* a proper family," he said, with a catch in his voice. Our eyes met, fleetingly, and I went back to staring at the floor.

"Anyway," I said to my feet, "I was thinking. About Birthday Cinema Club."

"Oh?"

"I know my birthday was last month, but . . . maybe it's not too late. Maybe we could do it, like, one day next week."

"I thought you were too old for that, kiddo."

I shrugged.

"You're never too old for *Toy Story*."

Though I couldn't see Dad's face, I could hear him smiling above me.

"Yes. Yes, of course. I think we can find the time for Birthday Cinema Club." Then he added, in a funny voice: "I shall consult my diary."

I sat down awkwardly on the bottom stair, and blood rushed to my cheeks.

Dad cleared his throat.

"Um . . . now. There's something in your bedroom I think you'll want to see."

I looked up.

"What do you mean?"

"You'll see. In your bedroom."

Dad gestured to the top of the house with a nod and a strange little smile. Dubiously, I walked up the stairs to my room, hand trailing along the banister. Had he . . . bought me something else for my birthday? Or an early Christmas present?

When I opened the door, I found Melissa sitting cross-legged on the bed, her hands curled in a ball in her lap.

And the room was filled with marshmallows.

34

"Hi," said Melissa.

I stared back at her, dumbfounded. A single marshmallow tumbled off the bookshelf.

"Oh my God . . ."

They were *everywhere*. Lining the windowsill, strewn across my pillow, piled in miniature pyramids on the desk. She'd even marked out my initials on the bed: *C* in pink, *B* in white.

If you were ever really sad, d'you know what I'd do? I'd fill your bedroom with marshmallows.

"I . . . can't believe you did this," I whispered, noticing a marshmallow in one of my slippers. "I can't believe . . . you did this." It was like walking into a dream. "You're crazy."

Melissa looked crestfallen.

"What . . . you don't like it?"

I could tell she was holding back tears.

"No," I said, breaking into a smile. "No. I love it. I . . ."

Melissa's knees were jiggling, and she bit her lip.

"I love it, you big stupid idiot."

She sat up on the bed, and the words spilled out of her.

"I know this doesn't change what I did," she gabbled, knocking marshmallows onto the carpet. "I know I can never take that back, ever. But I can be your best friend again, Charlie. I know I can."

She looked at me, eyes huge, tears beginning to form.

"If you'll have me."

I stared back at Melissa, her face filled with hope and heartache. Without her, my life was black and white. I knew that. Nothing was fun anymore. It was like a piece of me was gone.

No one else in the world would do something like this for me.

"I've missed you," I said, stepping forward, accidentally squishing a marshmallow. Melissa nodded, her chest swelling.

"*So much.*"

We were quiet for a few seconds, cocooned in our marshmallow dream world.

"Charlie?"

"Uh-huh?"

Melissa's lip wobbled.

"Is it OK if I cry now?"

Before I could say anything, little sobs started falling out of her, and I hurried across the room, sending marshmallow piles flying. I sat down next to her on the bed and hugged her tight against me.

She gazed up at me, face sticky with tears, and sniffed.

"I spent all my allowance."

She sobbed into my jumper for a little while and then reemerged, wiping her face with the back of her hand.

"It's impossible to be sad when you're eating marshmallows. That's a scientific fact."

I scanned the room, struggling to count Melissa's haul. There were hundreds and hundreds of them.

"If we eat all this, we are so going to puke," I said, and Melissa squeaked.

"I CAN'T WAIT."

For a while, we just sat next to each other in silence, a sugary scent in the air, and I realized I suddenly had everything I could ever need, sitting right here in my bedroom.

I had my best friend back.

"I've got SO much to tell you," said Melissa with a sniff and a bounce, as we settled back into our established places, cross-legged at either end of the bed. "They made me president of Computer Club last week, which is a bit weird, because what does a computer club need a president for?" As she talked, an unstoppable smile was spreading across my face. "But then again, it *is* kinda cool, 'cause I get my own certificate and a wicked badge. And like a bajillion PC World vouchers."

I tossed a marshmallow at her. She caught it and popped it in her mouth.

"Hey," she said, pointing at my head, chewing. "Your hat's back!"

"You'll never believe who I saw this afternoon . . ."

I told her all about my encounter with Aimee at the bus stop, about how she'd waited for me on the way home and returned my hat. About how I'd expected her to lay into me . . . but she didn't.

"This is unbelievable!" exclaimed Melissa, knocking marshmallows off the bed. "This means you win, Charlie. *You win.* It's a Christmas MIRACLE." She raised her hand. "Don't leave me hanging, sister." I high-fived her, shaking my head. "But enough about her. Talk to me about GABRIEL WEST . . ."

Melissa listened, wide-eyed, as I recounted the story of my night at the Rochester. It was strange, hearing myself tell it out loud, and as I spoke, memories I'd tried hard to bury came rushing back to me. I could feel the midnight chill on the back of my hands. I could hear the rumble of traffic on the streets below. I could see the rain rushing down in columns toward the pavement as I leaned over the balcony.

Reliving it all over again, I realized I'd almost forgotten how wretched Gabriel had made me feel. How much I'd hated him for treating me that way.

"So, hang on," said Melissa, when I'd finished. "You're not talking to Gabriel anymore . . . *at all?*"

"Of course not."

"But . . . Charlie . . ."

Melissa was gawping at me.

"What?" I said. "Why are you looking at me like that?"

She clicked her fingers.

"I need your laptop."

I passed Melissa my computer and, flipping the lid, she typed frantically for a few seconds, then spun the laptop round and presented me with a YouTube video.

"What's this?"

"Just watch," she said, sitting back against the headboard. The video, which turned out to be a *Pop Gossip* news report, began to play.

A man and a woman were sitting next to each other behind a fake news desk. Above their heads, a composite photo of Gabriel and Tammie hovered in one corner, a little spinning globe in the other.

". . . Now, Sandy," said the man, in a syrupy American accent, "*talk to me* about Gabriel West. What. Is. Going. On. There."

The woman pointed a manicured finger in the air.

"Well, listen up, 'cause there's been *serious* speculation about

Gabriel and the actress Tammie Austin, who was seen arriving at his hotel last month in, like, the middle of the night. This sparked a *huuuuge* debate about whether they were an item, but we think we've got to the bottom of it."

"Oh, I bet they are," said the man, nodding at the screen. "They would be so *cute* together, no?"

"Maybe, maybe not, but here's what happened when our reporter on the ground caught up with both Tammie *and* Gabriel at this year's USA Music Awards . . ."

The video cut to a red carpet, lights flashing, music playing, journalists calling out for attention. Celebrities posed in ball gowns and crisp black tuxedos.

Tammie Austin was looking into the camera.

"So . . . Tammie," asked the reporter. "Tell me about you and Gabriel West. There's something going on there, right?"

Tammie laughed, and then frowned. "Are you kidding me? Gabe?"

The reporter wiggled her microphone. "Now come *on*, Tammie, we know you've been chilling at his hotel, and you've been close ever since the band formed, so . . . what's the goss?"

Tammie flicked her hair back over her shoulder.

"Sure, we've been close for, like, a year now . . . but he's just a friend, always has been."

In the distance, another reporter shouted Tammie's name. She ignored him.

"Plus, I have a boyfriend, and Gabriel is *so* not my type. He's a pretty boy. Way too skinny. I like guys with big arms, you know?"

I peered over the laptop at Melissa.

"Why are we watching this?"

"Quiet!" said Melissa, pointing at the screen. "It's not finished."

The report cut back to the studio. The composite image in the top corner had been replaced with a photo of Gabriel and Tammie stepping out of a nightclub together.

"Do we trust Tammie Austin, though?" said the man, his hands upturned. "If she cheated on her boy, she ain't gonna 'fess up on TV, is she?"

"Well, just wait," replied his cohost, "because *here* . . . is Gabriel's side of the story."

Gabriel appeared on-screen, walking the same red carpet, looking irritable. He ran a hand through his hair, which was unkempt and wild.

"Gabriel, hey, Gabe!"

He stopped in front of the camera. His eyes had a sunken look to them, as if he hadn't been sleeping.

"Hey," he said, forcing a smile.

"Talk to us about Tammie Austin. You guys . . . you're an item, right?"

Gabriel took a deep breath.

"She's just a friend. I've told you people a hundred times. Don't ask me that again."

Gabriel started to walk away, but the reporter kept yapping at him.

"Now come *on*, Gabe. Everyone's talking about it." He thrust the microphone forward. "You wouldn't lie to us, would ya?"

Exasperated, Gabriel turned on his heel and looked straight into the camera.

"No," he said, firmly. "I wouldn't. But I guess it's too late now, right?"

Gabriel set off toward the venue, ignoring the reporter, who was still spouting something about the Rochester and Tammie's argument with her boyfriend.

But I wasn't thinking about that.

I was thinking about the look I'd seen in Gabriel's eyes, just before he turned away. Just after he said "I guess it's too late." It was a look I'd seen before, on the cliff side, when he'd opened up to me about his father's suicide. It was the closest I'd ever felt to him, that moment, and I realized, for the first time, I was seeing the real Gabriel. Exposed, insecure, like any other eighteen-year-old.

It cut me right to the core, and I knew straightaway.

I knew he was telling the truth.

"Oh my God . . ."

I pushed the laptop across the bed. Blood was rushing to my face.

"You see, *this* is why you need me," said Melissa, biting into a marshmallow. "Because of all my knowledge."

Things Gabriel had said on the balcony were crashing back to me, things I'd assumed were lies, things that had made me hate him even more. *You've got it wrong . . . this whole thing . . . You have to believe me, Charlie. She's a friend. Nothing more.*

"What do I do, Mel?" I said, my heart racing. "I don't . . . What do I do?"

A knock at my door.

"Girls?"

"*Hellooo?*" said Melissa, perkily.

"Can I come in?"

"Enter, stranger," said Melissa, and the door opened. I closed my computer.

"I meant to tell you," said Dad, stretching out his hand, "you got some post this morning."

He set a padded envelope down on my desk.

"Ooh, interesting," said Melissa, craning her neck to see. Dad threw me a look.

"Everything OK, Charlie?"

"Um . . . yeah," I said, distractedly. "Fine."

"We're all good," added Melissa with an enthusiastic nod. "We're just hanging out on YouTube, watching some vids."

"Right," said Dad. He glanced around at the forest of marshmallows and gave Melissa a little wink. "I'll leave you to it, then."

Dad backed out of the door, closing it behind him, and I peered at the package on my desk. I barely ever received post, except bank statements and school letters, and this didn't look like either of those.

Slipping off the bed, I walked to my desk and picked it up. The minute I saw the handwriting, my stomach flipped.

It was Gabriel's.

35

"Whatcha got there?"

I ran my hands around the package. There was something square-shaped inside.

"Hey . . . *Charlie.*"

I looked up.

"Who's sending you post?" asked Melissa. I stared, again, at the handwriting on the front.

"Gabriel."

Her mouth fell open.

"No . . . *way.*"

"Why would he . . ."

Melissa drummed her hands on the bed.

"Open it, then."

My hand was on my mouth.

"What?"

"Open it, dinkus."

I'd been wrong about Gabriel, again. I'd accused him of lying, cheating, and only caring about himself. I'd made the exact mistake he warned me against, on that empty stage in Brighton. *Don't believe everything you read on the Internet.*

"Charlie, you're killing me here."

"Sorry, Melissa, I . . ."

I'd gone too far this time, surely. How could he forgive me after the things I'd said?

I crossed over to the bed, sat down opposite Melissa, and tore the seal on the envelope. Reaching inside, I pulled out the square-shaped object.

It was a CD, in a plastic case.

The case was battered and scratched and had a long crack along the front panel. The album cover, which looked amateurish, maybe even homemade, was a deep shade of red, with three words printed across it in a spidery white font.

Little Boy Blue.

"Oh my God . . ."

"What?"

I opened the case, revealing the CD. Light from my bedside lamp glinted off the shiny surface in a rainbow of colors.

"What is it?"

"It's the band Gabriel told me about. His dad's band."

"Wait . . . that's where the lyrics in your mum's notebook come from, right?"

I nodded.

"Man, I came round at the right time. This is *awesome* . . ."

I slid the album sleeve out from behind its plastic teeth. Exactly as Gabriel had said, there was very little information inside, only a list of the guys in the band, the sentence "All songs by Harry West," and a date. February 1998.

Melissa waved for my attention.

"Aren't you going to play it?"

"Huh?"

She clicked open my laptop and gestured for the CD.

"We're not just going to sit here and look at it, are we?"

"No, I . . . guess not."

I plucked the CD from its molded tray and handed it to Melissa. She slid it into my computer, and the ancient drive whirred and sputtered to life.

Seconds later, the first song began to play.

"This sounds cool," said Melissa, bobbing her head. A driving piano hammered out chords beneath the distant wail of an electric guitar. "Totally nineties, though."

Soon, Harry's vocal struck up over the chords. His voice was, in a way I couldn't quite place, familiar. Like when you catch someone's scent on the air, and it evaporates a second later.

> *I met a girl in winter*
> *She played piano in a local bar*
> *She sang Aretha over whiskey and soda*
>
> *I took a drink and sat down beside her*
> *I said, "D'you know how to play 'Piano Man'?"*
> *She said, "I don't take requests from strangers . . ."*

The song went on like that for a verse or two. The story of a guy meeting a confusing, mysterious girl and falling for her. Then, after a guitar solo, the music dropped and the voice came back, and something happened that made my chest tight.

She lives her life in pictures
She keeps secrets in her heart
The whole world could burn around her

Realization bloomed on Melissa's face.

"Those lines . . . they're *Fire&Lights lyrics.*"

"Yeah," I said breathily, as I thought back to my conversation with Gabriel on the cliff side. This must have been Gabriel's only copy of his father's album. Why was he sending it to me?

"That's so weird . . ."

We both stared at the open envelope.

"Is there anything else in there?" asked Melissa, and I reached back inside. My fingers brushed against a sheet of paper, and I pulled it out.

A handwritten letter.

Charlie

You probably weren't expecting to hear from me. Maybe you'll tear this up before you even read it.

But if you've got this far, please hear me out.

Talking to you about my father changed everything. You opened my eyes. I'd always thought of him as just this coward who deserted me, but you changed that. You made me see him as a person.

So I went back to my foster home and asked them for everything, anything they had, that belonged to my parents. They made some calls, followed up some old leads, and a week later, they sent me a box full of stuff. Stuff that when I left last year, I'd told them I didn't want. Photos, letters, keepsakes. More of my dad's lyrics.

*When you told me about your mother, and her notebook, we figured
she was just some random fan. But I think we were wrong. I think,
somehow . . . our parents knew each other.*

*I can't explain in a letter. I can only hope you read this, and call me.
You have my number. I'll meet you anywhere.*

This is bigger than us, Charlie.

G. x

I was gripping the letter tight. It quivered between my fingers.

What did he mean, our parents *knew* each other . . . ? *What did he
mean?*

"Oh, wait. There's something else in here."

Melissa was peering into the envelope.

"What is it?"

She turned the bag upside down, and one final item dropped out.

"It's a photograph."

Melissa passed the photo to me, and I held it under my bedside lamp.
I could tell instantly that it was an old picture, at least ten years old,
maybe more. A boy of around five was kneeling on the carpet, amid a
scattered pile of half-opened presents, at what looked like a birthday
party. He had tanned skin and dark hair and was looking right into the
lens through a pair of keen, amber eyes.

It was Gabriel.

He wasn't alone. Several other children of varying ages were gathered around him, picking at food on paper plates and tearing up strips
of wrapping paper. Then, on the edge of the photo, I noticed a lone toddler, sitting a meter or so away from the rest of the group with its back
to the camera. It was difficult to say without seeing its face, but from
the way it was dressed, it looked like a girl.

And that was when I saw it. The unusual white patch on the back of her neck. A distinctive blemish on the skin, just beneath the hairline, around the size of an avocado stone. A birthmark in the shape of a flame.

The little girl was me.

"Dance with You"

Take me home
'Cause I've been dreaming of a girl I know
The night draws in, and with a shiver on my skin
I still remember everything

I took her hand
I held her close and felt the beating of her heart
And then we danced

I wanna dance with you, girl, till the sun goes down
I wanna feel every rush that you feel
I wanna hear every sound when your heart cries out
So sing it with me tonight

I call her name
I keep her picture in a silver frame
So she will know, that if I ever come home
She will never be alone

We took a ride
We stood on the edge and said we'd never be apart
It's in your eyes

I wanna dance with you, girl, till the sun goes down
I wanna feel every rush that you feel
I wanna hear every sound when your heart cries out
So sing it with me tonight

Chris Russell has written and recorded some of the songs that feature in this novel, including "Dance with You."

To listen, visit:

www.songsaboutagirl.com
www.chrisrussellwrites.com

Acknowledgments

Thanks go to Pip, for being the jam in my sandwich. My agent, Ed Wilson, for his tenacity, razor-sharp wit, and magnificent trousers. My American agents, Ginger Clark and Noah Ballard, at Curtis Brown, for very much the same reasons (though I can't comment on their trousers) and for affording me the opportunity to legitimately say "my people in New York are on the case." My wonderful editor, Sarah Barley, along with the whole team at Flatiron, for not only taking a chance on a debut novel about a quirky British pop band but for making me a better writer in the process.

To Mum, Dad, and my army of brothers, you are spectacular human beings, and I owe everything to you. Gran and Grandpa, you told me when I was little to follow my passion—thank you, endlessly, for that— and you always call me Christopher, which never fails to make me smile.

George, when we started a band, I had no idea it would lead to this, but I'm rather pleased it has. Along with the rest of The Lightyears, you've taught me that being in a band is a bit like being married to three grown men, which is a lot more fun than it sounds.

John Howlett, you were the first "proper" writer to read my work, and you may never know what a difference your words of encouragement made. It is a debt I hope to pay forward one day. And to Jerry Owens, Jane Watret, Maureen Lenehan, and Professor David Punter, you were unforgettable teachers, and I thank every one of you for inspiring me.

Finally, I would like to thank all the boy bands, and their fans, around the world. You are the beating heart behind the pages of this book.